HOSEA

HOSEA

A Novel

by Larry Christenson

Printed in the United States of America by Bethany Press, 6820 West 115th Street, Bloomington Minnesota 55438.

ISBN: 978-0-578-12374-5

Dedication

With fond remembrance, this book is dedicated to the memory of BERT MITCHELL ANDERSON.

I can only describe Bert as an eccentric genius. He was a private literary consultant, alike to aspiring writers and published authors. I was privileged to consult with him, one on one, when this book was in its early stages.

Sunday afternoons Bert held five hour lectures on writing. His "textbook" for whatever kind of writing we were studying was any well written published work — an article in *Reader's Digest*, a personal story from *Time*, a best-selling novel. He took the work apart and showed how it was put together. He understood the craft of writing like no person I have ever known.

Teaching on the novel, Bert spent several months presenting *The Female* by Paul Wellman. He invited Wellman to visit our class on the last Sunday he would be lecturing from the author's best-selling novel. Wellman, along with the rest of us, sat and listened to Bert lecture for five hours, demonstrating from Wellman's book basic principles of novel writing. At the end of five hours he invited Wellman to say a few words to the class.

Wellman stood up and said he was astonished that another person could climb inside his mind and recreate his writing process as accurately as Bert had done for five hours that afternoon.

My hope is that some of Bert's amazing insight into the craft of writing has found itself into my portrayal of a great love story.

List of Characters

Hosea	— son of the priest Beeri, a prophet
Beeri	— father of Hosea, a countryside priest in Israel
Rachel	— wife of Beeri, mother of Hosea
Gomer	— daughter of Diblaim, wife of Hosea
Diblaim	— father of Gomer
Anna	— wife of Diblaim, mother of Gomer
Jezebel	— great grandmother of Gomer
Amos	— a shepherd from Tekoa in Judah, a prophet
Odenjah	— faithful disciple of Amos and of Hosea
Obed	— Hosea's best boyhood friend, husband of Shania
Shania	— sister of Hosea, wife of Obed
Anakah	— High priest of the temple in Samaria
Amaziah	— High priest of the temple in Bethel
Remaliah	— Captain in the army of Israel; father of Pekah, the 18th king of Israel
Donath	— a paramour of Gomer
Midemi	— Egyptian envoy to the court of Israel, paramour of Gomer.
Tania	— consort of Midemi
Tongo	— giant Nubian slave of Tania
Judas ben Ishbaal	— wealthy merchant in Israel; paramour of Gomer
Tiglath-Pileser	— King of Assyria, also called Pul

Shalmanezer   — King of Assyria following Tiglath-Pileser

KINGS OF ISRAEL

Jeroboam II   — 13th King of Israel, reigned during the prophecy of Amos.

Zechariah   — Son of Jeroboam; 14th King of Israel

Shallum   — 15th King of Israel, following Zechariah; paramour of Gomer

Menahem   — 16th King of Israel, following Shallum

Pekahiah   — son of Menahem; 17th King of Israel, following Menahem

Pekah   — son of Remaliah, 18th King of Israel, following Pekahiah

Hoshea   — captain in the army of Israel, boyhood friend of Hosea; 19th and last king of Israel.

Table of Contents

Part One: **The Word of the LORD** 1

Chapter 1:   *Hosea ben Beeri* 3

Chapter 2:   *A Hero in Israel* 13

Chapter 3:   *A Voice of Thunder* 19

Chapter 4:   *The First Meeting* 33

Chapter 5:   *Gomer bath Diblaim* 37

Chapter 6:   *Hosea and the Prophet* 45

Chapter 7:   *Hard Words For Israel* 55

Chapter 8:   *The Plot Against Amos* 61

Chapter 9:   *Amos and the High Priest* 75

Chapter 10:   *A Happy Homecoming* 81

Chapter 11:   *A Prophecy Completed* 89

Part Two: **Take to Yourself A Wife** 105

Chapter 12:   *The Betrothal* 107

Chapter 13:   *The Plot of Shallum ben Jabesh* 137

Chapter 14:   *Gathering Clouds* 143

Chapter 15:   *Gomer the Wife* 149

Chapter 16:   *Gomer Goes Aside* 155

Chapter 17:   *Gomer Discovered* 165

Chapter 18:   *Shallum, King of Israel* 177

Chapter 19:   *A Brief Reign* 191

Chapter 20:   *Uneasy Days* 205

Chapter 21:   *A Troubled Home* 213

Chapter 22:   *A Birth, a Death* 229

Chapter 23:   *Envoys From Egypt* 245

Chapter 24: *The Golden Calf* 261
Chapter 25: *The Scheme of Tania* 275
Chapter 26: *The Plot Against Pekahiah* 289
Chapter 27: *A Contest of Strength* 301
Chapter 28: *A Fateful Tryst* 315
Chapter 29: *Tania and Pekah* 331
Chapter 30: *The Twins* 337
Chapter 31: *Begone From This House!* 363

Part Three: Famine in the Land............................... **369**
Chapter 32: *The Silence of God* 371
Chapter 33: *Judas ben Ishbaal* 387
Chapter 34: *An Uneasy Truce* 399
Chapter 35: *O Gomer! O Gomer!* 415
Chapter 36: *Israel's Dark Hour* 435
Chapter 37: *Uncertain Days* 443
Chapter 38: *Shalmanezer Strikes* 449
Chapter 39: *The Fall of Samaria* 461

Part Four: Captivity **473**
Chapter 40: *Deported* 475
Chapter 41: *Life in the New Land* 487
Chapter 42: *Hosea's Prayer* 499
Chapter 43: *The Search for Gomer* 505
Chapter 44: *You Must Dwell as Mine* 523

Epilogue **529**

Foreword

The background for this historical novel is found in the book of Hosea, in the Bible. It weaves together two stories.

The *epic story* recounts the tumultuous years when Israel is caught between the dwindling power of once mighty Egypt and the brash power of Assyria looming in the East.

The *personal story* of Hosea's marriage to Gomer, though recounted briefly in Scripture, is one of the most profound and moving portrayals of marriage in the entire Bible.

Some years ago I contributed an article on family relationships to a Study Bible published by Thomas Nelson. The heart of the article fell on verses from the book of Hosea:

Through the tragic story of Hosea and Gomer, God reveals the depth and power of His love for Israel, and the depth and power of the marriage bond.

God suffers the pain and humiliation of Israel's unfaithfulness; in obedience to God, Hosea suffers the pain and humiliation of his own wife's unfaithfulness. But God shows him how the marriage can be saved: through suffering and forgiveness.

This is one of the most profound revelations about marriage found anywhere in Scripture. Successful marriage is not a business of perfect people living perfectly by perfect principles. Rather, marriage is a place in which very imperfect people often hurt and humiliate one another, yet find the grace to extend forgiveness to one another, and so allow the redemptive power of God to transform their marriage.[1]

[1] Jack Hayford, General Editor, Litt.D., *Spirit Filled Life Bible*, New King James Version (Nashville: Thomas Nelson Publishers, 1991) p. 1260.

Part One

The Word of the Lᴏʀᴅ

When Israel was a child, I loved him,
and out of Egypt I called my son.
The more I called them,
the more they went from me;
they kept sacrificing to the Baals,
and burning incense to idols.
My people are bent on turning away from me;
so they are appointed to the yoke,
and none shall remove it.

Chapter 1

Hosea ben Beeri

Ten years ago, when I was nine years old, I heard the notable Voice of the LORD for the first time.

My mother traveled to visit her father and mother in Parah by the Jordan River. She took my two sisters with her. They traveled in the safety of a small caravan going to Judah on the way to Egypt. I was closer to my mother than either of my sisters. I wanted to make the trip to Parah and see my beloved grandparents. Their little home in the hills overlooking the Jordan River was like a safe, tiny kingdom. Mother decided I should stay with my father and brothers and help in the barley harvest.

When my mother and sisters left, I walked with them to the hill outside our village of Dothan. Mother kissed me and said they would return "as quick as you can say 'faithful' and 'steadfast.'" I cried as I watched the caravan descend into the valley without me and wind out of sight, circling the base of the opposite hill.

Then I heard a voice speak the words: *When Israel was a child, I loved him, and out of Egypt I called my son. The more I called them, the more they went from me; they kept sacrificing to the Baals, and burning incense to idols. My people are bent on turning away from me; so they are appointed to the yoke, and none shall remove it.*

I stood for a time. The strange speaking puzzled me. I looked around to see whether someone nearby had spoken but I stood alone on the hillside. It was different than any speaking I had ever heard.

The meaning of the words was not strange. No week went by that Father did not lament the decline of true worship in Israel. But the words were more than stirrings in my own thoughts or words remembered from my father, the priest. The words had come from outside me, yet they were for my ears only.

As I trudged back to our house I thought about the story Mother had told me many times, the story of the boy Samuel whom the LORD once called by name in the middle of the night. "Maybe it was like that," I thought, but immediately I thought otherwise: "The voice was already speaking to others. I but overheard it."

I did not at first tell Father what had happened. I waited until Mother returned home, some weeks later. When we were alone I told her, "The day you left, I heard a voice."

Mother stopped short at the bread dough she was kneading. She took me by the shoulders and looked into my eyes. After some moments she said, "Tell me."

I told her the words I heard and described the voice: "The speaking was not loud but each word was clear. And the voice — it was like no voice I ever heard. It spoke with great authority. It was not a voice you would quarrel with."

Mother embraced me and kissed me. "The LORD has bound your life to His word," she said.

Since that time in childhood I have heard the notable Voice at various times in my life. Sometimes words have been directed to me, though often the words seem to be spoken beyond me, or away from me, and I simply overhear them.

While Mother lived I told her whenever I heard the notable Voice. She encouraged me to study the scrolls with my father. "The hand of the LORD is upon you, my son. Pay heed to His words, even if they are dark of understanding or mysterious. Hold them in your heart. The LORD does not speak idly."

I live in Dothan, a half day's journey north of Samaria. My eyes are sky blue, uncommon in Israel. Mother's younger brother, who died in childhood, had blue eyes, so Mother remembered.

My younger sister, Shania, lives with us in Dothan. An older sister and two older brothers have already married. Our older sister lives in Judah. She married into our mother's tribe of Benjamin. My brothers live in Bethshan, east of Dothan. They have taken up the weaving trade. The father-in-law of the eldest is a noted weaver, but elderly, with no sons. He drew first my older brother and then the second into his trade.

At eighteen years I became a priest and began to minister alongside my father, Beeri. I stood four cubits and a span, a head taller than most other men. I was always the biggest and quickest of my age. By fourteen years no one could stand up to me, not even my brothers, five and seven years older. I never thought much on it. It was the way things were.

My closest friend in Dothan is Obed. He is short — three cubits, less a span.

People sometimes point at us and laugh when the two of us walk together, because of the difference in our size. When elders laugh, we pass by in silence. But young men who laugh, or even throw stones, sometimes need a lesson.

I once strode up to a loud band of seven young men, come into Dothan from outlying villages. They mocked Obed's short stature. I picked up the biggest of the group, lifted him over my head, and threw him to the ground. Two others from the group made a move toward me. I sprang behind them and knocked their heads together. They slumped to the ground. The remaining ones backed away, muttering apologies.

I never thought much about my strength or quickness. I had no need to prove or avenge myself; no one in Dothan threatened me. If things gave way to mindless taunting of a friend or an attack on someone helpless, I made a fight.

The word of Father was scripture to me: "What a person looks like is not what counts, but how he acts." Obed stood tall in my judgment because he was a loyal friend; he never broke a promise. His word, once given, was like iron. He once promised to bring me some clusters of fresh grapes from a visit to his uncle near Bethshan, more than half a day's journey. Obed was nearly back home when he remembered the grapes, and his promise. He turned around at once and walked all the way back to his uncle's vineyard, returning the following day with the grapes.

"Friendship is strong when promises are kept," I said as Obed and I parted that evening.

"You would have done the same," Obed returned.

I clapped Obed on the shoulder. The bond of friendship stood higher between us than well-spoken excuses.

* * *

I grew up hearing my father read from the scrolls and hearing my mother pray to the LORD as directly as she spoke to her husband or children. Sitting at Mother's feet I learned the stories and songs and laws of our people. She taught me to recite how God delivered His people from slavery in Egypt, how He guided His people when they wandered in the wilderness forty years, and how He made them a glorious kingdom under David and Solomon. Her voice hushed to a whisper when she told me, "Now we stand a shamefully divided kingdom, Israel in the north and Judah in the south."

* * *

I once overheard the LORD speak a word that drew me close to my younger sister, Shania. Late one afternoon, when I was fifteen years old, I came upon her in the embrace of a young man of the village, two years older than me and of bad reputation. Shania was thirteen, the one in the family closest to me in age and affection. We grew up playing together. I drew back, at first in sheer surprise. I had never thought of my sister other than as a child, was all but blind to her budding womanhood. My surprise turned quickly to anger, finding her in the arms of this worthless fellow. The young man stuttered a greeting that was half apology. I silenced him with a toss of my head and the fellow ran off.

Half pleading, half in anger, I spoke to Shania. "Why would you suffer such a fellow to touch you?"

"He has been kind to me," she protested. "He likes me."

"He likes you? Surely he does! As he would like anyone he could lay his hands on."

"It is not like that!"

"What do you know? You are a girl. Every boy in Dothan knows about him. You keep clean away from him!"

"You cannot tell me that!" she said, stubbornly setting herself against me.

"I do tell you," I said, raising my voice. "And I will tell our father as well, if I must."

"Do not do that, Hosea," she cried, suddenly pleading.

"Keep away from him."

"I will, if I must. Do not tell our father." Then she added, "or our mother." She knew the closeness between our mother and me, a closeness neither she nor her sister enjoyed.

My face, I believe, hardened. I turned and strode back toward the house.

In the days that followed I barely spoke to my sister until Mother noticed it and spoke to me.

"What is amiss between you and Shania?"

"Nothing is amiss," I said.

"When you avoid my eyes, I know you are not speaking the truth," Mother said.

"It is nothing."

"I came on her lying abed last evening, weeping," Mother said.

"She has nothing to weep for in me," I returned, my voice edged with rudeness. I could not give her my eyes.

Mother stared straight at me for a moment, then shrugged and went back to sewing a robe for Shania.

The thought of my sister in the arms of that low-grade fellow tortured me for more than three weeks. I could not bring myself to speak to her, yet my heart was uneasy since Mother told me of her weeping.

One morning she followed me out into the field where I was going to reset boundary stones that had washed loose in a heavy rain. She overtook me. There were tears in her eyes.

"Hosea, why have you turned against me?"

"I have not . . ." I started to speak, but when I saw the despair in her face I could not go on.

"Don't you love me any longer? We have always loved each other, my brother."

"That fellow —"

"That fellow is gone. He means nothing to me."

Suddenly I overheard the notable Voice: *Come, let us return to the LORD; for He has torn, that He may heal us. He has stricken, and He will bind us up.*

I looked at Shania and nodded. I knew she spoke the truth. I reached out and took her in my arms. "Little sister, I could never do anything but love you."

Shania hugged her arms around my waist. We stood for some moments. Then we walked together toward the boundary stones I had to reset. Neither of us spoke, but Shania held my hand as we walked.

"How badly I have acted toward her," I thought. "Given her only anger and scolding."

* * *

Our mother died in the month of Abib, nine months before I turned nineteen. She lay abed two months, growing weaker each day. Her last words were spoken to me while I sat beside her on the day of her death. "Seek the LORD with all your heart. Find your life in Him. Follow Him, even with tears."

Our father could no longer look at familiar things without sorrow. Everything was bound up with memories of his wife. Our uncle, the brother of our father, told Father that he grieved over much.

"Other men lose wives," he said. "They marry again, and the sorrow is forgotten." Father vowed he would not marry again. He had no heart for another woman. "Ours was a marriage like Jacob and Rachel," he told Shania and me one evening. "We loved each other from the day of our first meeting and only loved each other more in marriage. I have had one good wife. I desire no other."

* * *

Seven months after Mother's death something happened that would change my life. Father had gone to visit a cousin who was a priest at a countryside altar west of Samaria. The family of Jorbach ben Issachar asked me to prepare a sacrifice for the naming of their newborn child. I had made such sacrifices with Father many times; it would be the first time I had ministered at the altar by myself.

When I had completed the ritual, and laid the meat of sacrifice on the altar fire, four Ammonites suddenly appeared on the brow of the hill overlooking our altar. Ammonites lived to the east, on the far side of the Jordan River. Sometimes small bands came marauding into Israel, stealing what they could before scampering back to safety across the Jordan.

They gave a whoop when they saw only me and Jorbach, together with his wife, babe, and daughter of seven years. They came running down the hill. With loud yells they scooped the meat off the altar, seized Jorbach's older daughter, and started up the hill again, shouting and laughing.

I streaked up the hill ahead of them, then turned to block their way. "Oh ho! An Israelite wants to make a fight of it!" shouted their leader.

I ran at him and felled him with a blow to his throat. He fell gasping to the ground. Jorbach's daughter wrenched free and ran to her mother. The two closest to me — one tall, one shorter — came at me, their clubs raised. I dove at them like a rolling log, knocking their feet out from under them. I sprang instantly to my feet, knowing I must move more quickly than they. They were face down, starting to rise. I leaped high and came down, crashing the full weight of my boots into their backs. The tall man let out a shriek, cut short when his head smashed into the large rock at the corner of the altar. The two fallen men lay at the foot of the fourth man, halting him for a moment. He swung his club, catching me with a blow on my left arm. I snatched the club from his hand and swung it in an arc. It smashed into his head. He collapsed to the ground. The other three struggled to their feet and backed away. Then they turned and ran up the hill and disappeared over the top.

Jorbach stooped over the fallen Ammonite. "I think he is dead," he said.

News of my fight with the Ammonites spread from village to village and soon was the talk of all Israel it seemed. Word came that Anakah, the high priest of the Temple in Samaria, would speak with the young man who slew the Ammonite, and with his father, the priest, Beeri. Rumor had it that he would offer me a priesthood in the Temple of Samaria.

* * *

One afternoon, before Father and I were to travel to Samaria to meet with the high priest, we prepared a sacrifice for seven families of Dothan, all brothers, for the weaning of a child. My father had seen each of the seven brothers grow to manhood, marry, and raise children; he was like a second father to all of them. I stood to one side after laying wood on the altar. "These are his people, and precious," I thought. "He is a priest here in Dothan, and I a priest beside him. They could become my people as well."

Why go to Samaria? One should not easily uproot from a home where the people and way of life are settled and understood by all.

Then I overheard the notable Voice, as though the LORD stood and spoke in the midst of a council of elders. *If there be no witness in Samaria, how shall the righteous endure?*

The words sounded a familiar ring. They were like words Father so often spoke: "Hope for Israel lies with a remnant that remains faithful to the LORD."

"This invitation of the high priest, summoning us to Samaria — why do I not like it?" I asked myself. Now it troubled me in a new way: "Dare I put my reluctance above a word from the LORD?" I wondered.

Chapter 2

A Hero in Israel

A long day's journey north from the border of Israel and Judah, a day's walk inland from the Great Sea, stood the walled city of Samaria. On a high mountain she was set, her wall half concealing the summit, like the ornament on a harlot's breast. When King Solomon died nearly two hundred years before, the Hebrew nation broke apart, north and south. Samaria became the chief city of the northern kingdom, called Israel.

Near the east gate of Samaria, in the wide street opposite the Temple, Beeri and Hosea stood talking with one another. It was early morning, yet they were dressed in fine ceremonial vestments — turban, coat, breeches of fine linen, outer robes the deep blue of summer sky, bells and pomegranates filigreed around the skirt, a girdle of fine twined linen drawing in the robe, delicately embroidered with blue, purple, and scarlet needlework.

They stood for some time in the street, speaking with one another, some uneasiness evident between them. Beeri spoke most, his face alive with excitement, giving Hosea the same careful advice over and over again. This could be the most important day in his son's life. Anakah, the high priest in Samaria, had summoned them from their village of Dothan. It was rumored Hosea might be offered a priesthood in Samaria, an honor coveted by every country priest in the land.

Hosea listened respectfully to his father, but the sidewise glancing of his eyes told that he did not altogether share his father's excitement.

Beeri stepped back, looked his son up and down one last time, straightened his coat, and then, apparently satisfied, led the way across the street and up the steps of the Temple.

A quarter hour later father and son stood in the tapestried chamber of Anakah, high priest of Samaria. They had exchanged formal words of greeting, and now Anakah stroked his trimmed beard and looked the young man up and down, as one might appraise an animal for sale. The father stood by, his hands rubbing one against the other, waiting anxiously for a word from the high priest. Hosea returned Anakah's bold stare without embarrassment, almost without concern.

"Yes, yes," Anakah said, at length, "a fine looking son you have, Beeri."

Beeri bowed his head, hiding a pleased smile. Anakah went on, speaking to Hosea: "And you are the young man who killed seven Ammonites with your bare hands?"

"Sir, there were four, and I killed only one, with a club."

Anakah laughed. "You see how stories spread? Already they would make a Samson out of him." In the past three weeks Anakah had heard of nothing, it seemed, but the young priest in Dothan who had slain the Ammonites. "How did it come about?" he asked.

"Four of them came over the hill and rushed down on our altar. They took the meat of the sacrifice and tried to carry off a daughter of the family I was serving. One of the men hit me with a club. I seized the club from him and swung it back at him. He took a blow on the head and died."

"You were alone against the four?"

"Yes."

Anakah spoke with amused understanding: "From the stories I have heard, I thought you would be Goliath size, though you do stand a shoulder high."

"It is not only size, but strength," Beeri said proudly. "He has the strength of two, and the quickness of a lion."

Hosea glanced sidewise at his father, frowning.

Anakah gazed toward the ceiling of the chamber. "How old are you, my son?"

"Nineteen years."

"He will be twenty before the latter rains," Beeri added quickly.

"And your name is Hosea?" Anakah asked, purposely ignoring the father's eager remarks.

"Yes."

"Would you like to become a priest in Samaria, Hosea?"

Hosea did not answer at once. He had lived all his life close to his father's reverence for the God of Israel. No sacrifice or festival of other gods found welcome at Beeri's altar. In the Temple in Samaria, the worship of Baal and Ashtarte mixed easily with the worship of Israel's God. Beeri knew this as all Israel knew it. For years Beeri had seen the true worship of God wither away in the land. He held quietly to his beliefs; he sought to shape his life and priesthood according to Israel's holy writings, as did some few priests in the countryside. He longed for Israel to be cleansed of any worship except worship of the LORD God of Israel.

Beeri did not believe redemption would come in one grand sweep, but through a remnant. "If here one priest, and there another, quietly stands true to the God of Israel, Israel can be redeemed. Redeemed by a remnant." Beeri counted himself part of the remnant. He hoped the same for Hosea, that he might become a righteous presence in the Temple of Samaria.

Hosea's hesitant response irked Anakah. "Perhaps you are content where you are, becoming a priest alongside your father in the worthless village of Dothan." It pleased him little that a young man from the countryside, even one who had become a hero, should demure at the chance to become a priest in Samaria.

Beeri looked sharply at Hosea and indicated with a covered gesture that he should speak out.

"I would like to be a priest in Samaria," Hosea said carefully.

"You seem not overly excited by the thought."

"It is the honor — the honor," Beeri said nervously. "He cannot find words."

"Perhaps that is so," Anakah said. "Let us say no more of it for now."

"Sir, he would be honored, much honored —" Beeri would himself have pled the cause of his son, but Anakah stood abruptly, indicating the audience was at an end.

"Let us speak together again in four days, after tomorrow's dedication of the new high priestess."

"In four days," Beeri repeated. "We shall be here; we shall be here, most surely!"

"Perhaps you would be my guests at the Festival of Dedication?"

Beeri's eyes widened in disbelief. He had thought all was lost, and now — "We would be honored — honored!"

Anakah smiled and nodded them dismissal. Beeri and Hosea bowed and backed from the room.

* * *

Anakah remained standing after they had left, his hands on his hips. This Hosea was a strange young man. He was no mere brute, as Anakah had supposed he might be, though he was certainly a man of some strength and skill in fighting, daring to match himself against four Ammonites.

The news of Hosea's barehanded fight with the Ammonites had made him a popular hero in Israel. Anakah thought to turn the popularity to his own advantage by bringing the young priest to the Temple in Samaria before Amaziah, the high priest of Bethel, might think to do likewise. The high priest of Samaria missed no chance to better his stand against the high priest of Bethel, his chief rival for religious leadership in Israel.

* * *

In the outer court of the Temple, Beeri spoke angry words to Hosea: "Why did you hold your tongue when he asked you? Have you come so far, now to lose it all with your thick tongue?"

"I said what was expected."

"Ah, but the way you said it. You spoke it like a funeral dirge."

"Then let it be a funeral dirge," Hosea said, suddenly angry. "It could well be my own funeral to become a priest in Samaria."

"Hosea, Hosea, what do you say? Samaria — it is the seat of the kingdom, chief temple in Israel."

"What have we seen here in our three days?" Hosea said in challenge. "What have we seen in this Temple but drunkenness, reveling, and loose lying with Temple harlots? This is no calling for a priest, but a whoremonger!"

"Sh, sh!" Beeri cautioned. His voice turned soft and wheedling, rehearsing the rule of his priesthood that Hosea could have repeated word for word: "You know my belief: *the LORD God of Israel, Him only shall you worship.* We live in fallen times. Neither screams nor separation will change the times, only the quiet example that we live out in the midst of our people." He laid a hand on Hosea's shoulder. "When you are a priest you can order worship as you desire, bring the people back to true worship. They cannot force Baal worship on you or your priesthood. Son, ponder these things when some time has passed, when you have had more experience. Give it time. The LORD has a remnant, as in the days of Elijah. A little yeast can change a whole loaf. We are a remnant.

"Ah, I know, you are still bitter that your young Johanna went a harlot to the temple in Joppa. You are young. You will find another."

"Another Johanna or another harlot?" Hosea asked, with bitter irony.

"Would you throw your whole life in the wind for a child-hood love?"

"It is behind me," Hosea said.

"Then look to what stands before you. Think, my son, you are not yet twenty years old. Twenty years, and a priest in Samaria! Think what that means. You could one day be high priest, high priest of all Israel! Think what change that could bring in the land."

Hosea looked away and did not speak.

"You want that, my son. Is it not so? You want that."

"Does not every true priest of the LORD want that?"

"Then mend your words with Anakah when we sit with him at the Festival tomorrow. Tell him you lost your tongue—that such an honor should come to you. Tell him —"

"Yes, the words, the words. I know," Hosea said curtly.

"And you will use them?" Beeri waited a moment, then asked again, more sternly, "You will use them?"

"I know not," Hosea said, looking back toward the inner court, where already the temple harlots were moving gracefully along the columned walks.

Chapter 3

A Voice of Thunder

1

The next day great crowds thronged toward Samaria's Temple to witness the dedication of the new high priestess. Once each year, before the late planting, a high priestess, a virgin, was singled out for each of the great temples of Israel to portray before the people the drama of Baal and Ashtarte. No religious festival in all Israel was fraught with such meaning and consequence.

Baal was the LORD and owner of the ground. When the latter rains came after the sleep of winter, and earth and water mingled, the mysterious powers of growth stirred in the ground once again. This rebirth in nature, so it was believed, came about because of the mating of Baal with his partner, Ashtarte.

Yet, men did not believe that this rebirth would come each year of itself. The marriage of Baal and Ashtarte must be assisted and encouraged by ritual enactments of the sacred union. Each year the union of Baal and Ashtarte was acted out before the people in rich pageantry and drama, in the belief that this ritual would bring Baal and Ashtarte together in a fertile union, assuring another season of growth and plenty.

When the children of Israel came into the land of Canaan more than five hundred years before, they brought with them the worship of Israel's God, called the LORD, the One whose mighty acts had rescued them out of slavery in Egypt, and the One who had been their God during forty years of nomad wandering. When the men of Israel turned from the nomad life to become men of the land, they began to turn to the gods of the land, the Baals. After the kingdom divided upon the death of King Solomon, the worship of Israel's God in the northern kingdom of Israel mingled with the worship of Baal and Ashtarte throughout the land. Only at the altars of some countryside priests was the worship of Baal turned aside.

The crowds that milled about the Temple courts were brightly dressed and in gay mood. The Festival of Dedication was a time for easy laughing and jesting. The Festival began the eighth hour of the day, four hours before sunset. It did not end until long past sunset. After the drama of Baal and Ashtarte had been enacted by the high priestess and her partner, the ritual extended to the people.

All semblance of worship gave way to rash reveling and lust. Harlots of the Temple turned aside with any man who touched a hand to them. Husbands and wives left each other for friends or strangers. Virgins went aside with male prostitutes of the Temple. Boys lay with older women. Old men found budding nubile girls. During the Festival of Dedication, no passion was held base or unnatural. The troubles and hardships of life gave way to a spirit of forgetfulness and abandon, while crowds of people looked on.

* * *

Hardly anyone noticed the slim young man in shepherd's garb thread his way through the crowds toward the steps of the Temple. The shepherd worked himself up to the top step, which commanded a view both of the outer and inner courts. He paused with his eyes closed and seemed to pray.

A man close by made a jesting remark about the blind shepherd who was looking for a lost flock in the Temple, and a few others close by joined in the laughter.

Then suddenly a voice of thunder broke over Samaria: "The LORD roars from Zion and utters his voice from Jerusalem! The pastures of the shepherds mourn, and the top of Carmel withers!"

A sudden hush fell on the crowd. A thousand faces turned toward the gaunt shepherd figure. No image in all Israel forebode such evil as the withering of Mount Carmel — the rains do not come, the grain never breaks the soil, wells run dry, dying sheep dot the hillsides, desolation reigns in all the land.

The voice of the shepherd rose again, now like the rising of a great wind. "Thus says the LORD: For the three transgressions of Damascus, and now a fourth, I will lay my hand of punishment upon them . . ."

He spoke in a common idiom — three transgressions can be borne, a fourth is unbearable. The upturned faces relaxed and even turned to a neighbor to nod and agree that Damascus could well be punished.

"Thus says the LORD: For the three transgressions of the Ammonites, and now a fourth, I will lay my hand of punishment . . ." He painted a picture of the punishment — fire devouring their cities, kings and princes led into exile.

The rhythm and pattern of his speech cast a spell on the crowd: the phrase repeated, the punishment described. Some began to half chant his refrain.

"Thus says the LORD: for the three transgressions of Gaza, *and now a fourth* . . ." More heads nodded. The shepherd quickened his speech, telling the doom of Israel's neighbors — Tyre, Edom, Gilead, Moab, and Judah — the ring of nations that surrounded Israel. Hated, feared, mistrusted — the LORD would punish them! This man spoke smooth words. Shouts of agreement went up. Hands waved in the air. The shepherd swept his eyes over the crowd. He held them in his hand as a potter holds clay.

"Thus says the LORD!"

The crowd tensed. The color of the shepherd's voice changed, darkened. "For the three transgressions of Israel, and now a fourth, I will lay my hand of punishment upon them!"

A sudden hush fell upon the people. No voice rose to echo his chant. The transgressions of *Israel*!

"Because they sell the righteous for silver and the needy for a pair of shoes! They trample the heads of the poor into the dust of the earth and turn aside the way of the afflicted!"

He gave them no breath to speak against him, to raise a tumult of shouting. His voice thundered over them like no voice they had ever heard.

"Hear this word that the LORD has spoken against you, O people of Israel, against the whole family I brought up out of the land of Egypt: You only have I known of all the peoples of the earth. Therefore I will punish you for all your evil.

"An enemy shall surround your land. Your defenses shall collapse over your head, and your strongholds be plundered. Flight shall perish from the swift, and the strong shall lose his strength. He who handles the bow shall lose his life and he who rides the horse. The swift of foot shall falter in his path, and the great and mighty shall flee away naked in that day!

"The LORD has said this, O Israel! He who makes the morning darkness and treads on the heights of the earth, the LORD God of hosts is His name!"

The voice lowered. He warned of the power of Assyria rising in the east. Since the death of Assyria's king, Adadnirari, some forty years before, no single man had been able to bend the proud Assyrian chieftains to a single rule. But in recent years one tribal chief had begun to rise above the others — Tiglath Pileser. Even now, neighboring tribes and walled cities quailed at the mention of his name.

His soldiers sacked small villages on the western border of Assyria. They tossed young babes into the air and caught them on the up thrust points of their steel swords.

They dragged pregnant women into the street and ripped them open from belly to throat. They tied young Syrian warriors with their hands to the rear of one chariot, their feet to another, and ripped them apart as the chariots churned off in opposite directions.

It was not sheer ferocity in battle that gave success to the armies of Tiglath Pileser. Other tribes were also fierce in battle. It was what Pileser did when the battle was over — what he did to hold his victories fast — that raised him so quickly to power. When a tribe or a city was conquered, Pileser at once deported its leaders to a distant part of his growing domain. All those who might lead revolt were separated from those who would support them in rebellion; then the soldiers of Pileser were free for new conquest. It was this, even more than his ways of warfare, which filled the enemies of Pileser with dread. To fall in battle was a part of life. One came to accept it, as one accepts birth and marriage and death itself. But to be uprooted from the ancestral home, to be separated forever from the tribe, and even from one's own family, was more frightful than death.

Slowly, tribe by tribe, chieftain by chieftain, man by man, Pileser was drawing power into his fist. For more than five hundred years Assyria had dreamed of conquest — an Assyrian empire stretching eastward to the Great Sea and south to the cataracts of the Nile. It was now known in Assyria, whispered even in the courts of rival chieftains, that Pileser was the man who one day would sit on the Assyrian throne and send forth warriors to bring the dream of empire to pass.

He might be hailed king by a rally of chieftains, or he might take the throne by sheer force, when the time was ripe. No one yet knew. However he might come to power, the land of Israel would number her days from the hour Tiglath Pileser ascended the throne of Assyria.

The word *prophet* began to be whispered through the crowd as the shepherd-clad man called on the people to return to the God they had forsaken. No heads smiled and nodded now, nor did an eye dare move from the leather-girthed figure who seemed to tower above them. A man almost feared to breathe. This was no prophet of the guilds. He spoke words of authority. Not a man stood in the sound of the thundering voice that did not feel it. The LORD had raised up a prophet in Israel.

From the inner court, six Temple guards pushed through the crowd toward the shepherd figure. At their head was Hosea, the son of the priest of Dothan. Anakah and Beeri watched from within.

A murmuring went through the crowd. This was the young priest of Dothan who slew the Ammonites. Anakah smiled.

The shepherd saw the guards approaching, and for a moment quavered. Then he said to himself, "LORD, if I must be thrown down, then let it be so, but may your name be glorified."

His voice broke out again, harsh and mocking: "Behold, they come with strong men to stop my mouth. Do they think to force silence on the LORD?"

Hosea stopped several cubits away and spoke: "The Festival of Dedication is about to begin. The high priest has said, 'Go to the gate with your preaching.'"

The shepherd answered, his voice echoing to the farthest corner of the Temple: "Thus has the LORD said: 'I hate, I despise your feasts. I take no delight in your festival assemblies. Bring me your burnt offerings and your cereal offerings. I will not accept them. The peace offerings of your fatted beasts, I will not look on them. Take away from me the noise of your songs. To the melody of your harps I will not listen! But let justice roll down like waters, and righteousness like an everflowing stream!'" For a moment there was no sound in the Temple except the shepherd's heavy breathing. Hosea's eyes were cast down, as though in thought.

One of the guards made a move to take the shepherd, as Anakah had ordered. Hosea shook his head and barred the way with an outstretched arm. The guard, puzzled, moved to step around Hosea. Hosea pushed him back.

"We are to take him," the guard muttered, as though Hosea had forgotten.

Again Hosea shook his head. The guard glanced at his companions. He barely knew this young priest of Dothan, whom Anakah had asked to accompany them. But he knew the high priest well, and it was from him that the orders were given. He jerked his head for the others to follow and took a step past Hosea. Hosea whirled and threw the guard back against his comrades.

"Leave the man alone."

"The high priest has said ——"

"Leave him alone," Hosea said, his voice low and hard.

The guards looked at one another. They had heard stories of the young priest from Dothan and the Ammonites. They backed off slowly until the crowd closed around them, then turned and moved into the inner court, talking low among themselves.

For a moment Hosea met the shepherd's eyes. Then he turned and moved down the steps of the Temple, through the crowd that parted before him. The next moment the shepherd was gone from his place, moving through the crowds. The mood of jesting and gay laughter was gone from the Temple.

2

Near sunset the following day I returned to the inn where Father, Shania, and I had taken lodging in Samaria. I rang the bell at the outer gate. The innkeeper called out to his daughter, who stood in the doorway, "Is it someone seeking lodging? We have no room."

The girl called back into the inn, "No, it is one of our guests, the young priest of Dothan."

The girl ran across to the gate. Her gown swirled behind her as she ran, pressing the youthful curves of her body into outline. At the gate she put her hand to the latch but did not at once open it.

"Your latch is drawn early this evening," I said.

She met my eyes through the gate and spoke in a low voice, "To you the latch is never drawn."

She lifted the latch and pushed the gate ajar, holding it with one hand so that I had to pass close to her as I entered. "You were missed last night," she said, close to my ear.

I thought she would have renewed our friendly talk from the day before. We were standing close to one another. I looked down into her face, and though my thoughts were heavy, I could not hold back a smile that answered hers. She was an innkeeper's daughter, with smiles for many men, yet I felt warmly drawn to her the first time we met. She had a way, with a word or a glance of the eye, of seeming to reach out and enfold you with the warmth of her woman's body.

"Your father has asked after you the whole day," she was saying. "He waits for you in your room — he and a handsome young soldier."

"Oh, that will be Hoshea. He was to visit us here."

"Yes, Hoshea ben Elah is the name he gave — like your own name, except the speaking of it. He is a friend?" Her smile was frank, almost teasing.

"Our families have been long acquainted."

I touched my hand to her shoulder and turned toward the inn. The warmth, which came for a moment, was gone. The heaviness had returned.

"Hosea, where have you been?" Father cried out as I opened the door of our room.

"Out in the countryside," I answered with forced calmness. "Hoshea, it is good to see you again."

I joined hands with the soldier who stood beside Father, a thickset young man, rugged and handsome, half a head shorter and two years older than me. We had grown up together in Dothan. Hoshea was now a captain in the king's army, quartered in Samaria. He had come to take Father and me to a festivity where we would meet some of his friends and some of the notable people of Samaria.

"Where have you been this night and day?" Father demanded.

"I was in the countryside of Samaria."

"Oh, oh — in the countryside. There do all madmen repair. What took possession of you in the Temple? Do you know what you have done? Do you know how it stands now between us and the high priest?"

"Not well, I suppose."

"Not well! Hoshea, my son has gone mad! He comes to Samaria to receive a priesthood. He insults the high priest on their first meeting, flaunts his command on their second, falls out of sight for a night and a day while all Samaria is talking about him, and then wanders back mildly, supposing that all might not be well!"

Hoshea laughed. "The same Hosea, going your own way despite all." He patted me on the shoulder.

"Hoshea, if you could have heard the man speak — nay, not only speak, *prophesy*!" I said with some heat. "A voice of thunder — power and authority. A prophet, a true prophet!"

"I heard from others what he said about Assyria. In that he spoke no idle words."

"He is a madman," Father said with disgust.

"Madman, Father? Then was Abraham our father mad, and Isaac, and Moses, and Joshua, and every man of God among our people."

The voice of the shepherd had sounded deep into my breast and stirred a storm within me. His words rang with truth, yet they were like a sword-thrust in my heart. Not since Mother died, now eight months gone, had the thought of God touched so closely to my heart. I could almost see her fair round face and the glow in her eyes when she set me down before her, in the manner of Hebrew mothers, to teach me of God and sing me the psalms and hymns of our people:

The LORD, the LORD, a God merciful and gracious, slow to anger and abounding in steadfast love and faithfulness, keeping steadfast love for thousands, forgiving iniquity and transgression and sin.

These were the words Mother loved, words of God's love and faithfulness, words of forgiveness and new life spoken by the LORD to Moses, handed down from generation to generation since the days of our nomad wandering, words treasured in the Psalms of King David: *Sing praises to the LORD, O you His saints, and give thanks to His holy name. For His anger is but for a moment, and his favor is for a lifetime.*

Mother felt God's love for Israel deeply. Something of that love became a part of herself. No woman in all Dothan, it was said, lived closer to the LORD, was more loving of heart and open of hand, than Rachel, the wife of Beeri. Women of the village, carrying a child in the last month, would come to her and beg her prayers for an easy birth. Her ear was ever ready to listen, her hand to help. No stranger went hungry from her door. If Father chided her for giving too freely of our food, she would share her own meal with those who came to beg. When sorrow came to a neighbor, Mother was first to share the tears. Her heart seemed bred to understand sorrow and need, to feel it as her own, and to share its burden.

When the voice of thunder broke forth in the Temple, I felt something like a deep and sudden hurt, as Mother would have felt. The shepherd foretold the doom of Israel — the Israel I had learned from Mother to love, the Israel that was my own people, the Israel whom God Himself had loved and made His own possession.

Yet the words that thundered over the Temple rang out a bitter truth. From both Father and Mother I had learned of the evil in Israel, the idolatry and injustice, for they had spoken bitterly against it. But the shepherd did what I had not done: he prophesied that this evil would bring Israel to destruction. This it was that cut to my heart. When destruction is visited on something beloved, heartache must follow.

For a long night and day I wandered the countryside of Samaria, perplexed and heavy-spirited. The words of this man — surely a prophet — spoke to my heart, but I could not see what shape it might take in my own life.

Father broke in on my thoughts: "Who are you to judge, and call this man a prophet, when the high priest —"

"His word is from the LORD," I maintained firmly. I looked into Father's eyes and spoke quietly. "Father, you know it is true. His word is from the LORD. It is no different than what you have said from your own altar in Dothan. No man can speak as he speaks, except it be from the LORD."

Father turned his eyes away. "My son, the high priest —"

"The high priest or no, I could not have ordered him thrown down. No more than I could throw you down, Father. Or the LORD."

"Hosea! What am I to do with such a son!" Father paced across the room, shaking his head. Yet the lightened tone of his voice told me I had touched his heart.

Hoshea spoke: "Are you fully set against coming to the Temple in Samaria as priest?"

"Oh, I do not know," I said with despair.

That question plagued me the night and day I wandered the countryside of Samaria. The words of the prophet confounded me. The words decried the idolatry of Israel's worship, yet the words gave me no freedom to turn away from becoming a priest in Samaria. Say what I would, I am the son of my father, a priest in Israel. Might not even the prophet say that I could serve God

29

as a righteous priest in Samaria? Might not Father be right, that I would outgrow my distaste for some of the practices and customs that went on in the city, and especially bitterness toward temple harlotry, after the losing of Johanna?

Johanna was the daughter of a potter in Dothan. We had grown up and played together like brother and sister. One afternoon, when I had passed my seventeenth year, I met Johanna out in the country, walking along a stream. We waded together in the water, threw pebbles at an old stump, and lay cooling ourselves beneath an oak. Johanna reached up and touched her hand to my cheek. I looked down at her but held myself still — hesitant, uncertain.

"Hosea, you are more than a brother to me," she said softly. She drew my head to her breast and held me with timid, trembling hands.

I raised my head. "Then you are more than a sister to me," I said.

We looked into each other's eyes, then smiled and laughed in our old way. I sprang to my feet and pulled Johanna up by her arm.

"This is our secret place," Johanna said. "The place where we first spoke love to each other." We swore to love each other forever.

I ran home, my heart bursting. I wanted to tell Mother that I loved Johanna, but I knew I could not. I must first speak to Father about arranging a marriage when the time was right. I could not sleep that night for thinking of her. The next day I ran back to the stream, hoping she would be there.

She did not come. She never came again. When I met her in the village, she said we must not speak again of love because her father had promised her to the Temple in Joppa. It was no uncommon thing in Israel for the poor, who could afford no dowry for their daughters, to sell them into the service of the temple, which was held an honorable station for a woman. I protested that we had promised our love to one another. Johanna, speaking a phrase she had heard from older people, said we would forget.

Johanna forgot. Two months ago she went to the Temple in Joppa. I forgot more slowly. I think there was in me some of Mother's determined constancy. She could take no affection lightly.

Father spoke to Hoshea, "What good even to speak of the priesthood, now? I have little doubt what Anakah will say when we meet him tomorrow."

"You have too little craftiness," Hoshea said, his eye a-twinkle.

"What then?" Father asked.

"It is clear what purpose the high priest had in calling Hosea to Samaria. He wanted to capture this young hero for his own temple before Bethel or Joppa could do so."

"Oh, that we have heard," Father said wearily. "Yet it is of small avail now."

"Not if the right ears hear the right stories."

"You mean what I did in the Temple yesterday?" I asked.

"Yes, that. But some quiet rumor alongside, that news of it has reached Amaziah, and he is on the verge of calling you to be a priest in Bethel. That will rouse a jealousy in Anakah and make him think more lightly of this business between you and the shepherd prophet."

"It is a fair plan," Father agreed, "and not far from possible."

"How do you think on it, Hosea?"

We looked at one another, and for a moment our eyes sparkled in that way of our youth, when with a silent glance we agreed upon some mischief together. We both laughed aloud, remembering, and I felt some lightening of my spirit. Hoshea always had a way of lifting me out of a dark mood.

"It is all but done," Hoshea said gaily. "Tonight's festivity serves a double purpose. A word spoken in the house of Diblaim the leather merchant will be as good as spoken in the high priest's chamber. Hosea will prevail!"

Chapter 4

The First Meeting

Atop one of the many little hills within Samaria's wall, half hidden from the Temple, which lay straight away from it three hundred and twenty cubits, rose the house of Diblaim the leather merchant. It was screened on all sides by a double row of evergreen oak, carefully planted and nurtured by Diblaim, and so held itself aloof from the stone mansions of the rich, the Temple, the palace, and the mud huts of the poor — indeed, from the entire city.

Diblaim was a man who asked only to be left alone, to live his life in his own way. He cared little for custom. While other merchants haggled and bargained in the marketplace according to ancient practice, Diblaim arranged most of his business in his own house, over a meal table or a friendly glass of wine. A festive meal for Diblaim was most often a matter of business.

As an officer in the king's army, Hoshea had occasion to buy leather supplies: saddles, harnesses, shields, belts, lacings. Like many others in Samaria, he found himself buying from Diblaim; he made buying pleasant. Hoshea suspected Diblaim's prices ran high, but not so high he would take his buying elsewhere.

Diblaim's hospitality, like his way of doing business, was relaxed and careless of custom. Men and women mixed freely in his house and ate together at the same table. A man might come to a party alone, or he could bring his wife, or a woman friend, or a harlot of the Temple — each man felt free to follow his own way in the house of Diblaim, as long as he remained pleasant and friendly with other guests.

Hosea found himself liking Diblaim almost at once. He had come to the festivity somewhat uneasy, thinking he would be asked this question and that question about the slaying of the Ammonite or his defense of the shepherd-prophet in the Temple. Since he was a boy, it seemed, people chiefly remembered Hosea because of his unusual strength and the sudden temper that sometimes accompanied it. This embarrassed Hosea. He disliked violence, even, and perhaps especially, in himself. Diblaim asked no embarrassing questions. He met and accepted Hosea and Beeri as he did everyone, simply for what they were — a priest and his son visiting in Samaria, friends of Hoshea.

After they had talked together a little, Diblaim excused himself. Hoshea took Hosea and Beeri around to meet other guests. At the back of the house, near an archway leading out onto a porch, stood a young woman. As they approached, she turned to greet them.

Hosea thought he had never seen someone so utterly a woman. She stood barely to Hosea's shoulder, her hair black as ebony, her skin astonishingly fair. Her beauty struck him as strangely imperfect, yet perfect still. Her nose was too sharp for her rounded cheeks, but it pointed to the sensuous curve of her lips. Her eyes seemed overlarge in the oval of her face, but they flashed with challenging fire and aliveness. Generous breasts and flaring hips gave her a plump bearing, but her waist was slim and girlish. All added to a stunning womanliness.

Hoshea presented his guests. "This is Beeri, a priest from Dothan, and his son Hosea." Then he turned back to Hosea and said, "This is Gomer, the daughter of our host."

Hosea stared at her for an embarrassing moment before he responded. "Samaria is full of surprises," he said huskily.

"Pleasant surprises?"

"Just now, very pleasant."

Gomer smiled, showing clean white teeth, straight and perfect. "You are a strange mixture," she said.

"How is that?"

"A Samson and one who flatters women seldom find company in the same person."

Hoshea laughed aloud, and Hosea gave way to an embarrassed smile.

"Have you seen the gardens or the rest of the house?" she asked, looking only at Hosea.

"No."

Gomer looked to Hoshea and Beeri. "Will you excuse me, if I show him around?"

"Could we say no if we wanted?" Hoshea answered, glancing sidewise at Beeri.

The porch outside the house looked toward a garden. In the center was a small square of flowers that Diblaim kept blooming year around by bringing in water.

Gomer and Hosea sat on a low bench at the edge of the porch, facing toward the garden. On their other side, through the archway half screened by a curtain of linen strips, the shadows and figures of other guests moved back and forth.

Hosea lingered in a kind of spell from the moment his eyes first rested on Gomer. A strange thought hovered around him that if he could reach out at just the right moment, he might touch all the loveliness that was ever created in a woman.

"I have heard much about you," she said.

"What have you heard?"

"Oh, how you protected our Israelite women from the Ammonites, and how you stood against the Temple guards in the Temple yesterday —"

Hosea glanced away. She laughed, shaking the hair loose from her shoulders with a tipping motion of her head.

"Why did you do it?"

"What matter?" Hosea would have turned their talk to other things.

"You think him a prophet?"

"You would think that strange, for a priest?"

"Perhaps." She looked up at him with sober eyes. "But I am only a woman." She laughed again, tipping her head to one side and looking at him sidewise.

They sat thus for some time, talking, laughing now and then. Yet something in Gomer's manner disturbed Hosea. She answered his questions, spoke when he was silent, but never quit a kind of half restless glancing about them, as though she were anxious to leave or looked for someone else. But when Hosea moved to go, she touched his arm and asked to remain.

Chapter 5

Gomer bath Diblaim

Those close to Gomer knew how quickly and boldly she could venture something new or untried. Already when she was a child it was said, "Where a new adventure is afoot, look for Gomer in the middle of it." If something captured her interest or concern, she was wont to plunge in headlong.

The very thing Diblaim loved in his daughter — her bold spontaneity — gave him cause for concern. He once cautioned her: "You are bold, my pigeon. You dive in when others dither on the bank. But you must also be clever. The voice of the moment speaks pleasant words, but the words are not always wise. Be cautious before you plunge in. Take time to bethink yourself."

Three generations earlier, Ahab, the king of Israel, took to wife Jezebel, the daughter of Ethbaal, king of the Sidonians. She wore the queen's crown in Israel with pride and with iron purpose. She championed the worship of Baal and Ashtarte, the gods of her people. She plotted and schemed to advance the fortunes of her husband. Anyone who stood in the way of her plans felt the sting of her wrath and her constant scheming.

Dorea, the third daughter of Ahab and Jezebel, bore a striking resemblance to her mother. As a small girl she wormed her way into becoming the helper of her mother's personal attendant, so she spent more time at the side of her mother than was common for a royal child. By the child's seventh year she had become a small copy of the queen, not only in looks, but in manner, speech, and thought. The legacy of Jezebel passed on, mother to daughter: esteem for the Baal gods that assured good harvest and prosperity, and canny scheming to get her way or to advance the welfare of her house.

At thirteen, somewhat younger than usual in the royal house, Dorea was married to Joseph ben Achar, a merchant in Samaria, an Israelite from the tribe of Manasseh. That early marriage saved her life, for it secluded her in the household of her husband when, two years later, Jehu seized the throne of Israel and put the royal house to the sword.

As Jezebel had done in the kingdom, her daughter Dorea undertook to do in the life and trade of Samaria. Wherever she saw a chance to advance her husband's profit, she conspired and plotted, and with notable success. Her schemes brought remarkable wealth into her husband's house.

A daughter, Anna, was born to Dorea late in life — her only child. The legacy of Jezebel passed on a second time, mother to daughter. When Anna set her mind to some purpose, like her mother she seldom turned aside. She participated with her mother in the rituals and festivals of Baal. From her father, Joseph, she absorbed something of the faith of Israel. The two beliefs stood side by side in her life, as they did for many in Israel in that day.

When Dorea died with no male heir, the family wealth stayed in the house with Anna, her late-born daughter, who became the wife of Diblaim.

When Anna went into labor with her first child, before it was known whether the babe would be a boy or a girl, she cried out, "Call her name Gomer!" The portent proved true. A daughter was born. Gomer grew up with her mother's words and plans never far from her hearing. The legacy of Jezebel passed on a third time, mother to daughter.

Two more children were born to Diblaim and Anna, both boys. The first lived but one month. The second, named Aram, was born a year later. Gomer, now six, loved and cared for him like a small mother. He came down with a high fever in his third year. Anna grieved mostly in private. Life she could twist to her purpose; sickness and death struck her helpless.

Diblaim paced back and forth by his son's bed, shaking his head, wiping tears from his eyes, moaning wordless sounds. Never had Gomer seen her father so distraught. She said she would not eat until her little brother was well again. The boy lingered for two weeks. Gomer never left his side. When he died, her piteous mourns keened through the house for ten days, and still she would not eat. Two weeks passed. Only when both her mother and father set a bowl of lentils before her and commanded her to eat did Gomer begin to mend from her sorrow. The shared sorrow strengthened the bond between Gomer and her father.

Gomer's father endowed her with a peaceful agreeableness that contrasted with her mother's intense spirit. Diblaim was an Israelite from the tribe of Ephraim. He grew up enjoying a natural contentment with himself and his own way of life, belonging, as he did, to the proudest of the northern tribes. Unlike many Israelites, his sense of contentment and pride in who he was and where he came from did not particularly bond him to other Israelites, nor did it create discord with those who were different.

In a time when life was governed in settled ways by family, tribe, and nation, one's heritage and way of life remained for Diblaim a private matter. By declining to lay demands on others, he cordoned off his own life from trespass. He left other people free to live their lives the way they wanted to, asking only that they accord him the same liberty. He seldom felt the need to justify his own life or actions, for he almost never required it of others.

He married Anna with no regard for old notions that judged it base for a man of Ephraim to marry into Sidonian blood or into the fervent worship of Baal. He liked the easy way they talked and laughed together. He found her desirable. She was a comely woman and ardent in love.

As they lived together, Diblaim frequently gave in to Anna's manipulating ways. He could be taken for a man easily managed by his wife, but the truth was that he simply allowed her the freedom he allowed everyone else and that he desired for himself.

A moil of inbred willfulness and a heart-felt love for her husband battled within Anna. The more Diblaim gave in to her demands — the more freedom he allowed her — the more Anna secretly wanted him to overwhelm her, subdue her, and draw her into the fortress of his own guarded life.

As a child, Gomer noticed that her father treated her mother differently than other men treated their wives. Other husbands would speak sharply to their wives, or silence them with a glance, or even beat them with a rod when they overstepped themselves. Diblaim never did such things. Gomer sometimes wished that he would. "It would do Mother good not always to have her own way!" she muttered when she was by herself.

Once, on the way to Samaria's well, Gomer overheard two women talking about her father and mother, saying that a man who would not stand up to his wife was not worthy of respect. Gomer stepped quickly into a side street because she was close on their heels and afraid they might turn and see her. She smashed her fist against a wall until it bled, angry against her mother because she had dishonored her father in the eyes of these women.

Yet Gomer loved her mother, almost fiercely. Even when Gomer was a child, Anna spoke to her as though she were a grown woman. They talked together constantly, and about everything. When she sought to do something new or understand something unfamiliar, it was to her mother Gomer turned.

As a child Gomer accompanied her mother to Baal festivals in the countryside. It was a festive time. The children ran free, playing games with one another. Once, when Gomer was five years old, she became separated from the other children. She came on her mother in a poplar grove, lying astride a strange man, kissing him on the mouth, naked to the waist. She told Gomer to go behind the trees and wait for her. She was red-cheeked when she and the strange man came to Gomer.

The strange man laid his hand on Anna's shoulder and said, "Perhaps we will meet again. It would gladden me."

"Would gladden me as well," Anna replied, looking down. The man walked away by himself.

"Who is he?" Gomer asked.

"He was a stranger, come for the festival. I do not know him." Gomer looked up at her mother. "Was he nice?"

"Yes, he was nice," her mother said quietly, as much to herself as in answer to Gomer. "He was truly nice."

"You were kissing him."

"Yes."

"Is it like when you kiss Father?"

"Somewhat. It happens during festival, to satisfy the Baal."

Anna deemed it a pleasant task to lie with another worshiper during a festival. It brought blessing and prosperity to their house in the coming year.

Gomer scarcely understood what had passed between her mother and the strange man. That evening she watched her mother catch her father in a warm embrace. "It is different with Father," she thought.

Gomer grew up seeing her mother enter intensely into different situations and relationships, always driving to shape the outcome to her own purpose. She came to know her mother's manipulating ways, and they became Gomer's ways as well. Outside the narrows of the family, Gomer loved to see her mother triumph when she set herself to some accomplishment. But when tensions arose within the family, Gomer silently sided with her father.

Gomer could wheedle her father when she wanted something, as she had seen her mother do. But with her father Gomer also learned to stand by, to exercise a measure of patience that did not come naturally to her.

When it came to Gomer, Diblaim seemed to set aside notions of freedom, which established a certain reserve or distance in a relationship. For Gomer he would more likely let slip a warm show of affection, for she was the darling of his heart. Gomer lived for such moments.

Sometimes, if Gomer found him alone in the early morning, she would go to him, wind her arms around his waist, and squeeze until he gasped, "I am dying. Three kisses if you release me."

With her mother, Gomer often found herself locked in a battle of wills. She knew her mother would sacrifice anything, even life itself, for Gomer's good, yet she was too much the daughter of her mother to easily set aside her own will.

It was more in resistance to her mother than out of religious agreement that Gomer became, as a young girl, a worshiper of the God of Israel. Her mother followed Baal worship in agreement with her own mother, and the chronicle of her grandmother, Jezebel.

Diblaim had no great interest in religious practices, yet he found Baal worship unsuited to his Israelite heritage. For a time he tried to dissuade his wife from taking part in Baal rites. In the end he gave up. Baal worship had become too widespread in Israel. Her attachment to it was stronger than Diblaim's indifference.

When Gomer was ten years old her mother made brightly colored matching robes for herself and Gomer, which they would wear at a Baal planting festival. Gomer was entranced with the gown. Her mother was skilled with loom and cloth and needle. But Gomer sensed the time was ripe for something more valuable than a brightly colored robe. She saw a chance to stand up to her mother. Carefully choosing her time, following a midday meal, she quietly let it be known that she did not want to go to the Baal planting festival.

"Of course you will go," her mother said, dismissing Gomer's protest with a smile, as she often did.

Gomer flushed and said, "I want to be a worshiper of the LORD, the God of Israel, not of Baal."

Diblaim raised an eyebrow but did not speak. Her mother eyed her coldly, for she saw in Gomer a hint of determination that would not be lightly set aside.

"We are all worshipers of the LORD," she said crisply. "We serve Baal also. He brings us prosperity and good fortune."

"I do not want to serve Baal," Gomer said. Her voice remained soft and calm, but within she trembled. "The Law says we shall have no other gods beside the LORD."

"Yes, that is the Law, true enough," Diblaim reflected amiably, seemingly unaware of the contest of wills going on between his wife and daughter.

Then Gomer did what she had never done before. She turned to her father and appealed to him against her mother. "Father, do not make me go to the Baal festival. I want to be a worshiper of the LORD."

"*Make* you go? I — I — what can you mean?" Diblaim sputtered. He had suffered his wife to take part in Baal worship and had raised no question when she began to take Gomer with her, but that it should suddenly be put to him that *he* was forcing this on his daughter — that he was responsible — so caught him by surprise that he had no ready words.

"Please, Father," Gomer insisted.

"Other children go to the festival and make no complaint," her mother said in a more determined tone.

"But others do not," Gomer said, still looking straight at her father.

This was a challenge Diblaim had not faced before, the necessity to judge between the two women he loved, and who could otherwise, either one of them individually, usually gain their way with him. Gomer's tactic won. She touched his sympathies as an Israelite. She shamed him that he would force her into idolatry that he himself found vaguely distasteful.

"The festival is thronged with people," he said easily. "Our little Gomer will scarcely be missed."

"I have prepared our robes," his wife said.

"They can be worn still, on other occasions," Diblaim said with some finality.

Gomer looked fearfully from her mother to her father, scarcely breathing. Had she gone too far? Would she lose her father? Her mother?

Her mother glared at Diblaim but spoke no further. She could perhaps overturn her husband's word if she pressed it, but she saw in her young daughter something unknown and still fragile — something she must consider more carefully.

Thus it was that Gomer became what some in Israel scornfully called "Yahweh tether" — tied to one god only, the God of Israel. She was no longer like children who went along with their families to traditional rituals and sacrifices. She had aligned herself with the God of Israel by her own choice. Whether it was a choice against her mother or for the God of Israel was another question, for another day.

Chapter 6

Hosea and the Prophet

1

Hosea and Gomer, seated in Diblaim's garden, had talked for some time, and Hosea still gazed on her as though his eyes must each moment recapture her beauty. "It is time for the meal," she said, smiling with pleasure at the look of desire in his eyes. "Father is motioning the guests into the dinner hall."

"I would rather stay here and talk with you."

"But I am hungry," she said.

With that she turned and slipped into the house without a backward glance to see whether Hosea followed her.

In the dinner hall, Hosea was seated next to Hoshea and Beeri, across the hall from Gomer.

"You disappeared nicely with the daughter of the house," Hoshea said.

Hosea smiled and shook his head, as a man does when suddenly wakened in the morning.

"She is a beautiful woman," Hoshea said.

Hosea nodded without speaking. His eyes could not move from watching Gomer.

Gomer purposely avoided Hosea's intent gaze. The man who sat beside her was a young innkeeper who had already sent a go-between to Diblaim, proposing marriage to Gomer. Anna had spoken to Diblaim against the proposal. Gomer could command a better dowry and marriage, she insisted.

Gomer played with the man openly, curling her arm under his, laughing at his poor jokes, listening intently to every word he spoke, and whispering him little secrets, her lips close to his ear. Donath was the man's name. He responded happily to Gomer's attentions. He never noticed how her eyes glanced so quickly, and so often, across the dining hall to where the young priest from Dothan sat. He had no inkling that her every move was meant only for Hosea.

Hosea gulped his food, hardly chewing it. Already he felt possessive of this woman. He liked it little that she spoke so intimately with the man at her side. There ran through Hosea a streak of jealousy as strong as his temper. He had lain three nights without sleeping when Johanna at last went to the Temple in Joppa, though he had long known she would go. Hoshea spoke to him, simply making conversation, and Hosea snapped back like a dog interrupted at his meal.

Gomer continued her play-acting with Donath, but she could not see how deeply it disturbed Hosea. He seemed hardly to notice her, she thought, and this roused her anger, as well as her curiosity. She played with Donath more boldly, until the other guests began to notice it, and her father frowned from the head of the table.

Hosea finished eating before anyone in the hall. He sat in his place, grinding his teeth together, pretending to chew on a piece of meat. He quaffed two goblets of wine, and as he finished each goblet, he glowered over the rim at Gomer.

No hint of wisdom threaded into his thoughts to say, "This is foolish. I have known her less than an hour. What difference to me if she carries on? She is just another woman."

No such thought. From the moment he set his eyes on Gomer, she became more to him than just another woman. In years to come he would wonder and despair over what bound him to this one woman. Every word she spoke to Donath, every smile she gave him, every laugh and toss of her head, filled Hosea with fires of jealousy.

Down the table two places from Hosea a man named Boammi leaned forward and spoke, "I hear you will soon be leaving our city for the Temple in Bethel."

"Oh, I know not," Hosea answered abruptly, in honest surprise. He could not believe Hoshea's rumor would return to him so quickly.

His reply left Boammi little chance to continue, and for a moment no one nearby spoke. Then the man sitting next to Boammi spoke up. "It is said your prophet was at the gate this morning, preaching the same woes." His voice was faintly mocking.

"Why say you 'my prophet?'" Hosea asked.

"Why, is he not a friend? From your stand in the Temple, I thought."

The false sweetness of the man's voice roused Hosea's anger. He turned from looking across at Gomer and spoke sharply. "Before yesterday I never saw the man. I gave thought to the words he spoke."

Beeri spoke up with smoothing words, "It was said the crowds were much moved by the man and might have raised a shouting if the guards had seized him."

"That I have not heard," said the man sitting by Boammi. "The only shouting I heard was that of the madman."

Hosea broke in hotly. "Madman, you say?"

"Yes, madman. Who but a madman would stand up at the Festival of Dedication and sing out the woes of the land?"

"Who but a madman would close his ears to the words of a prophet?"

"You think the man a prophet?"

Hosea stopped short. Then he said slowly, "Yes, I think him a prophet. Not of the guilds, but a prophet."

Boammi snorted with disgust. "Then are we all prophets, for we could all dream up woes as dire and fantastic as his — 'Assyria has assembled on the mountain of Samaria!' What is Assyria? A village, a tent-camp, a nothing."

Hosea leaped to his feet, shaking off Beeri's restraining hand. "You would not know prophecy if it struck you in the face. Ask Hoshea, here, how the army of Israel would stand against the armies of Assyria!" Hosea's voice had risen to a loud pitch, and other guests stopped their talk to hear what the argument was about.

"Soldiers always shout alarm," said the man next to Boammi. "It is their business. But small cause for us to walk in dread of a tribe of barbarians on the far side of Damascus."

Hosea spoke evenly, "This prophet you make light of speaks truth. Close your eyes and your ears to his truth and you will wake up one day with a sword of steel at your throat!" Hosea broke off abruptly. For a moment there was tense silence.

A man across the room spoke up. "I believe you must be a disciple of the madman."

Another joined in. "It is said he will preach at the east gate tonight. Are you not staying over long at dinner?"

A ripple of laughter spread through the room. Donath joined in heartily. He did not notice that Gomer, sitting beside him, laughed not at all. Her eyes were fixed on Hosea, standing boldly against the other guests.

Hoshea leaped to his feet. His voice sounded with sharp authority. "If Israel herself were disciple to this man and paid him heed, there might be some man here tonight who would live to see a birthright passed on to a son of his flesh. If your eyes and ears are so closed to truth when it is thrust before you that you take it for madness, then you yourselves will see your wives and children dragged through the streets of Samaria by Assyrian hooks."

Diblaim struggled to his feet, his face flushed, his head bobbing from side to side.

"Please, please," he cried, "this is a dinner, not a war council. Let us forget this affair and continue with our food and agreeable talk."

"I am sorry for the disturbance of your dinner," Hosea said evenly. "There is a time to let pass in silence and a time to speak. I thank you for your generous hospitality."

For an instant he turned his eyes to Gomer. She was looking directly back at him, and she had turned aside from the man who sat next to her. Hosea stepped back from the table and strode out of the dinner hall.

2

The man in shepherd dress who stood in the east gate of the city spoke quietly, no hint of anger or rebuke in his voice. A small fire of dogwood sticks flickered at his feet, dancing long shadows over his thin, angular face. Gathered around him was a group of men and women, their clothing patched many times over, their faces drawn by years of toil and need: the poor of the city and countryside.

His words had thundered judgment over all Israel, rich and poor alike, for mixing worship of the LORD with worship of Baal. Yet they had come to him, begging to hear his words, for he had also taken up their plight against the oppression of the rich. What could he say to them? He had no word but the word of judgment and destruction. Would it crash down on the poor and helpless as well as the rich and comfortable?

A hunched old woman, sitting cross-legged at his feet, began to weep. He halted his speaking. After a moment he stepped uncertainly toward the woman and laid his hand on her head. She seized his hand and pressed it to her lips.

"May the LORD have mercy on us for your sake," she cried.

He slowly withdrew his hand. He looked uneasily over the crowd. Worn and tired faces turned toward him, still waiting.

"Return to the LORD, worship Him only," he said quietly. "He may yet show mercy to a remnant of Israel."

He turned from them, a yawning emptiness in his heart. Judgment and condemnation came easily to his lips. For these poor of the land he had no words.

To look at him, one would never think the shepherd to be a man of rude or ill-tempered words. His face wore an open innocent look, like that of a child. Back home he seldom spoke. He would sit whole evenings by the shepherds' fire and say not a word, as though he were not yet of age and must content himself to listen to the wisdom of his elders. His slight build and the shock of unruly hair that fell across his brow gave him a sweet favored, boyish look. One might have taken him for a youth of sixteen rather than a grown man now past his twenty-fourth year.

When he spoke, all seemed to change. His voice broke silence like a clap of thunder, brilliant and loud. His eyes opened wide and seemed fired by intense passion. Even in quiet speech with a friend, his voice seemed to rumble up from the earth itself, and his eyes held the other in such a gaze that strangers nearby would stop their talking and turn to stare at the man with the loud voice and the entrancing eyes. When he was silent, one could see the boy in him; when words came to his tongue, only the man could be seen. He passed the last person seated and turned up the street that led back toward the Temple.

In his path stood Hosea. They looked at each other without speaking for some moments.

"You are the one who stood against the guards in the Temple," the man said.

"Yes. I heard you would be at the east gate tonight. I came because I must speak with you."

"Of what would you speak?"

"Who are you?" Hosea burst out passionately.

"I am Amos of Tekoa, a shepherd," Amos answered simply, straightening his shoulders and looking more closely at the young man who stood before him.

"You are from Judah?"

"Yes."

"Are you a prophet?"

"I am no prophet of the guilds. Why do you question me?"

"I must know whether you speak truth or falsehood."

"If I said I speak truth it would mean nothing," Amos replied. "A false man would say the same. If God and my words grasp hands within your heart, then you know that what I say is from God."

"I have known no peace since I heard your voice."

"Who are you?" Amos asked.

"My name is Hosea. I am the son of Beeri, a priest in Dothan."

"And you, also, are a priest?"

"It is said I may soon be given a priesthood in Samaria."

"But you are young."

"Nineteen years, soon twenty."

Amos looked about them and lowered his voice. "I stay at the house of Odenjah the stone mason, toward the west wall of the city. You can find it by inquiring of the neighbors. Come tomorrow, in the early morning, and we can talk together."

"I shall," Hosea said quickly.

Amos turned and was gone into the darkness.

3

As I stood watching after him, I felt a strange crawling on my neck — the feeling that someone was near me. I turned. A figure wrapped in a close-fitting gown stood at my side, a hood drawn over the head. From beneath the hood burned the intense eyes of Gomer.

"What are you doing here?" I asked, startled.

"So you are a friend of this man."

"I do not know him. I came to speak with him. Why are you here?"

"I came to see what sort of man could command such loyalty."

I glanced about us in the darkened street. The crowd had moved off. The dying embers of the fire cast a dim light out from the city wall.

"You should not be out like this, after dark. The streets are not safe for a woman."

Gomer glanced downward shyly.

"Come, I will see you to your house," I said.

She followed without a word. For some distance we walked thus, not speaking, picking our way through the darkened streets.

"You do not care what people think, do you?" Gomer said suddenly.

"Why do you ask such a question?"

"Because of the way you spoke out in my father's house tonight."

"I care for what this man thinks."

"More than for what my father's guests think." She stated it, not as a question. Her manner was subdued, respectful.

I stopped and turned toward her. I could see her fair skin dimly in the light of a clouded moon. "Gomer —" It was the first time I had called her by name. "Is there anything between you and the man who sat with you at dinner?"

Her jaw seemed to tighten. "I know not what you mean."

"When we sat together on the porch, I thought something came to life between us. Yet in the dinner hall —"

She spoke quickly. "There is naught between the man and me. He sent a go-between to my father, proposing marriage. My father did not receive it."

"I would like to believe it."

"It is true."

She ran her arm through mine and we continued toward her house. "After you spoke in the dinner hall, I wanted to know more about you," she said.

"I supposed my speaking out would be an end between you and me."

She shook her head. "It was brave of you."

We had come to the row of evergreen oak that bordered her father's property. I found nothing to say, but her womanly beauty held my eyes captive. She seemed to take my silence for disapproval.

"I fear I speak too freely on short acquaintance," she said.

She turned to go. I reached out and held her shoulders.

"'The tear of my beloved is as dew on my heart, and her weeping as the latter rains.'" A word I knew from the High Song of Solomon.

"Hosea —" Her voice trembled.

"Will your father allow me in your house after this evening?" I asked, half in jest.

"If I want you, he shall want you."

"I go in the morning to speak with the prophet. In the evening, I shall come and present myself to your father."

"I will wait for you."

She turned and walked slowly to the house. At the door she stopped and looked back.

Suddenly I heard the notable Voice, *What shall I do with you, O Ephraim? Your love is like a morning cloud, like the dew that goes early away.* A strange word.

Somehow I knew that my life, for having met this woman, was changed.

Chapter 7

Hard Words for Israel

1

Hoshea's rumor reached Anakah as Hoshea had expected, but with it came the report of Hosea's bold defense of the prophet in the house of Diblaim. Anakah weighed the issues carefully and decided to let Amaziah of Bethel have the young priest, if he wanted him. A young man so outspoken could be a source of trouble in the Temple.

Anakah came to regret his decision. In days to come, Hosea was much seen in the company of the prophet; Amos seldom spoke that Hosea was not standing nearby, lending the weight of his name to what Amos said. Anakah found it difficult to openly oppose the thunderings of the prophet. He wished he had taken Hosea into the Temple after all, where he would have some authority over him.

2

Hosea and Gomer walked in the countryside west of Samaria.

In families that held to old ways, a father would not allow an unmarried daughter to be alone with a man. Diblaim was careless of such customs or the gossip of neighbors. Gomer had let him know that she looked on Hosea with favor. Hosea's speaking out at the dinner Diblaim accepted as the man's way. When Hosea asked permission to visit his daughter, Diblaim judged him a trustworthy man, despite his outspokenness at the meal. Diblaim wanted only assurance that Gomer would be honored and safe. When Gomer told him she and Hosea wanted to walk together in the countryside, she cajoled Diblaim that the man who slew twenty Ammonites would be protector enough.

Protector. Yes, Hosea was surely that; one to trust, one to share secrets with, one to talk with! They had known each other only seven days, spoken with one another only four times, but how they could talk! About everything and anything. "I know more about you than friends I have known all my life," Gomer said. "And I want to know more."

Hosea told her it had always been understood that he would become a priest like his father. He did not expect this to interest her, but she brightened at once. She told him she had become a worshiper of the LORD when she was a child, but she wanted to know more about the LORD.

Hosea told her things he had learned from his mother and father and things he was learning from Amos. She asked questions. As soon as he answered, she came up with another question or gave voice to a thought of her own. It startled Hosea how quickly and exactly she grasped the heart of whatever they talked about. They talked on. The afternoon passed as if only moments had gone by.

She had twice heard Amos speak. She listened carefully to his words because she knew the words were important to Hosea. Mostly, her eyes were on Hosea. Justice and righteousness were the affairs of men, she told herself. It was sufficient for a woman to listen to the word of her husband in such things.

"Husband!" she thought. Hosea had not spoken of marriage either to her or to her father. For Gomer, the word stood like a sentinel over her every thought of Hosea.

When they came back to Samaria's east gate they found themselves alone outside the city wall. Hosea touched her shoulder and turned her to face him.

"I have no fitting words of my own, I only borrow words from Solomon's High Song: 'How graceful are your feet in sandals, O queenly maiden!'" he said.

"'Queenly maiden'— how fine. But, *feet*? Only my feet?"

"'Your neck is like an ivory tower, your eyes are pools in Heshbon.'"

"I like his words. I must learn more of them. I only have words of my own: you stand over four cubits and have heaven blue eyes. You are the most handsome man in all Israel!" Gomer said happily.

3

Amos stood boldly in the midst of Samaria's marketplace. He directed his words to the rich women of the city: "Hear this word, you cows of Bashan! You who lie about in the mountain of Samaria, oppressing the poor, crushing the needy, saying to your husbands, 'Bring wine, that we may drink!' You will be dragged by fishhooks through these streets, so the LORD has sworn!"

A woman standing close by had her mouth wide open to receive a tasty fig delicacy, while a train of six servants stood dutifully by. Her face flooded red, and with a toss of her fat neck she stomped out of the market place, muttering that it was time someone put to silence the madman from Judah.

In three months' time the voice of Amos had become a familiar sound in Samaria. His name passed in conversation from the palace of the king to the gates of the city. Some dismissed him as a madman. Some held a quiet admiration for a man brave enough to stand up and denounce every power and authority. Some believed the king should silence him, for he was a threat to peace and order. Some thought him a prophet of God.

Back home, Amos lived a simple life. "I am not a prophet or a prophet's son," he told himself again and again. "I am a shepherd and a dresser of sycamore trees." In the hot months of summer, after the sheep were shorn, he and some of his fellow shepherds traveled across Judah to work in the sycamore groves along the Great Sea. They first bruised the figs, else they would not ripen; then, when they ripened, they harvested the figs, a staple food for the poor. This was his life; he yearned after nothing greater.

Amos knew the standing of a prophet in Israel. In the chronicles of nations, no other people preserved a tradition to compare with Israel's peculiar office of the prophet. A prophet, if he were a true prophet, could speak a word against even the king, as did the prophet Nathan when he judged great King David blameworthy of adultery and murder.

Yet prophets lived an uncertain life in Israel. A prophet might be killed or imprisoned or shunned or shouted to silence when he spoke dread words of judgment. Years afterward, when he had passed from the scene, his words might be held in regard, even awe, but in the hour he spoke a prophet could stir up fear and great wrath against himself.

Amos stopped little to consider how people thought of him, whether he was hated or loved or feared. When a man once behaved rudely at the altar of the temple in Bethel some months earlier, the image of a basket of summer fruit rose up within Amos, and with it the words, *The end has come upon My people Israel.* A peculiar urgency to speak gripped him. He scarcely took thought for what he would say. He lifted up his voice; the flow of words came to his lips almost of themselves. His piercing eyes searched out evil that set his soul afire. His tongue broke loose with fierce and terrible condemnation. Every moment he saw the rottenness in Israel bring the sword of Assyria — God's judgment — closer and closer. He threatened, demanded, denounced, pled, and warned. He came to know the awful burden of aloneness that is the lot of those who speak unwanted words, the feeling that he only, alone and unaided, must awaken the spirit of Israel to repentance.

What answered to his prophecy was a mounting spirit of anger. The stone houses in the east of Samaria rumbled with displeasure. Voices that first laughed turned to low mutterings. Indulgent smiles gave way to thin-lipped demands that the madman from Judah must be silenced.

Chapter 8

The Plot Against Amos

1

In the walled palace of Jeroboam II, close to the center of Samaria, the thirteenth king of Israel paced back and forth in his marble-floored chamber. Near a window that looked east toward the markets and bazaars of the city stood the heir to the throne, Jeroboam's only son, Zechariah, wincing under the red-faced storm of his father's wrath.

"How am I to maintain a kingdom when the son of the throne takes up with every wild cult that springs out of this god-spawning soil?"

Zechariah, hands behind his back, eyes looking to the floor, did not answer. "From three different sources today come reports that in the very forefront of the crowd that gathered to hear this man from Judah, was the prince of Israel, my own son — you!"

"What harm in hearing what he has to say?" Zechariah ventured meekly.

"Great harm," Jeroboam roared, "when the man speaks against the kingdom!"

In thirty-nine years of rule, Jeroboam had weathered many storms. He knew the symptoms of crisis, he knew the cure, and, more importantly, he knew the dangers that could upset a cure.

Israel was overrun with guild-prophets who made their living by telling people what they wanted to hear. They had little effect on the people or on the smooth running of the

61

kingdom. But this man Amos was no prophet of the guilds. From the moment he entered Samaria, he had stirred up division among the people. The rich merchants at first laughed, then their humors cooled, and when Amos bore in on them without let, their soberness turned to anger. The pressure of this opposition found its way into the palace.

From other wings came opposite and growing pressures. The poor and the rabble hailed Amos as a prophet of God, and in their sheer mass, these people wielded power and influence. Soldiers in the army of the king spoke openly in support of Amos. His words struck a chord of truth. Certain captains within the army saw the mounting threat of Assyria and rumbled the need for reform, the very reform Amos cried for. In an emergency, the great bulk of an army must come from the poor classes. If these people were crushed and cheated and abused, their support might defect and crumble in the press of war.

Jeroboam sensed these pressures and cross currents as a bird feels the gust and swell of the winds. He knew Israel's character and how she must be governed. He knew when he must bend, when he must give way, when he must stand firm, and when he must lash out in rage and fury. He was no ruthless monarch who made his every utterance law. In Israel that kind of monarch fell too easily victim to the assassin's blade.

Jeroboam carefully balanced the forces and factions within the kingdom, playing one off against the other so no power could assault the throne without summoning another faction, out of its own interest, to the throne's defense. As king he had played this delicate balancing game, yielding where he must, asserting his power skillfully and at the right moment, giving the land of Israel, withal, thirty-nine years of stable rule.

When word came to him that Zechariah had stood among the people, listening raptly while Amos denounced the wealthy landowners of Samaria, he knew at once that the delicate scales of power might be jolted out of balance. Where he had wanted to ignore the man from Judah and keep his hands clear of the controversy, Jeroboam might now be forced to take action. The wealthy merchants would take Zechariah's attendance as a sign of Jeroboam's approval. Their grumbling might break out in demands that the king halt the prophet's activity. If the pressure grew strong enough, Jeroboam would have to bow to it at the risk of displeasing the army, ever ready to bend an ear to whispers of rebellion.

"A king and his family must live above and away from the squabbles of the market!" Jeroboam said, speaking into his son's face.

Zechariah did not respond.

"Do you understand that you will never again follow after this madman?" Jeroboam demanded, through a sudden, choking cough.

Zechariah spoke softly, looking almost fearfully at his father's red-splotched face. Though subdued, his voice carried a hint of Jeroboam's fire and determination.. "Is it mad to say the things that any man with eyes can see? A farmer goes off to fight invading tribes on the border of Gilead, and when he returns his landmarks are moved, and he must indenture himself for half his crops to pay for the land that is rightfully his own. Or a poor crop forces a man to borrow grain so he and his family may eat, and his crop for seven years is pledged — is it madness to call this evil?"

Jeroboam fingered the lacing of his waist-length purple cape. He breathed deeply before he spoke, as a man does who is accustomed to tiring easily.

"I have let you talk on at this length," he said evenly, "that you might get it out of you once and for all. This dreamy concern you have for justice is well enough in the privacy of my chamber, but let it begin and end here. The day is not far distant when you will take the throne of this kingdom. I have ruled long enough, and this red-faced choking will be my end before long." Now, as he spoke, his face drained of color, and his voice was empty of feeling. "When that day arrives, you must know that one who would rule long and well cannot tie himself to a rigid book of laws and judgments. You must follow the shifting tides of pressure and power. These people are not Philistines or Egyptians or Assyrians that bow meekly before any man who assembles a thrust of power to put himself on a throne. They are a proud and stiff-necked people. He who rules over them does so at their behest, not his own. Only so long as you please the people — the people who wield power and wealth and influence — will they allow you to sit on your throne over them."

"What honor to be king to such a people?"

"The honor of preventing their own headstrong passions from destroying them," Jeroboam answered. "Before I mounted this throne, the sun did not set on the streets of Samaria except they ran wet with royal blood. A whole generation has now passed that has known peace and well being."

"For the few," Zechariah said sullenly.

"Better wealth for the few than war and destruction for all. Do not contend with me over the way of ruling this nation, my son. I know these people, and I know how to rule them."

Zechariah turned from his father, suddenly, and walked quickly toward the door of the chamber. "Zechariah!" Jeroboam called out. The scarlet flush returned to his cheeks.

Zechariah stopped, and turned. "This business turns sour in my stomach," he said bitterly.

"Take care of your stomach as you will," Jeroboam said sternly. "But show no open leaning toward this prophet, or you will live in this palace under guard. Is that understood?"

Zechariah closed his eyes.

"Is that understood?"

Zechariah nodded grudgingly as he always had, and always must, in the face of his father's authority. He too much feared the rages that had plagued Jeroboam in his later years, that brought him to his knees, gasping for breath, his face gone purple and black.

Disobedience was the only pressure Zechariah could lean against his father, and out of fear he dared not wield it. He remembered with dread the whispered conversation he overheard between two women who nursed him as a child; according to ancient prophecy, the house of Jehu would fall in the fourth generation. Jehu was Zechariah's great grandfather.

* * *

Again, Jeroboam had rightly sensed the mood of his subjects. A landowner who held pledges on land as far north as Galilee had seen Zechariah standing in the front of the crowd gathered to hear Amos speak. That evening he called seventeen of the richest men in Samaria together and found agreement that they could not allow the king to lend approval to the prophet from Judah.

Twelve hours later a delegation of wealthy men presented their demands to Jeroboam.

An hour before dusk a trusted captain of the palace guard received a message to take the prophet from Judah prisoner secretly, and without public commotion.

2

"If you plan to stay on in Samaria, you can have the use of my rooms," Hoshea was saying. "I would as soon have them in use. The rats took over the last time I took my tour on the frontier."

"Thank you," Hosea said vaguely.

His father and sister had returned to Dothan, but Hosea had stayed in Samaria, living with Hoshea. His plans for the future were unsure. He had joined himself openly with Amos, and of this he had no regret. Yet how long the unspoken agreement between himself and Amos might continue, Hosea could not tell. The next year or the next day Amos might end his prophecy, and what then? Would he remain in Samaria or return to Dothan? Would that be an end to it all?

What of himself and Gomer? He had been seeing her, now, for three months. A man more bound to custom than Diblaim would have taken such conduct as an affront. It was past time when a man should send a go-between to propose betrothal agreements. Yet Hosea had not spoken of marriage because his lot with Amos was uncertain. This had caused some hard words between him and Gomer.

"Who truly has your heart?" she had asked with cool voice. "Me, or the prophet from Judah?"

A knock on the door broke in on his thoughts. Hoshea opened it, and Gomer stood quite breathless on the threshold. She wore the same gown and cloak she had worn that first night when she followed Hosea to the east gate. She appealed to Hoshea with her eyes, and he stepped outside, leaving them alone.

On their last meeting Hosea had told her that he and Amos would be gone from Samaria for a week, visiting nearby villages. She had turned away from him in anger. He had not seen her since his return.

"I come to warn you," she said, raising her eyes to him. The hood fell back from her face, loosing her hair so it fell gently over her temples, softening the sharp line of her cheeks.

"To warn me?"

She took his hands impulsively. "Do not look on me so coldly. I came because you and your friend are in danger and because I said things I did not mean —"

"We are in danger?"

"My mother learned that the king will take Amos prisoner."

"The king? Amos?" Hosea asked, startled.

"Yes. He has sent palace guards to capture him tonight, quietly and without disturbance."

"This we have feared."

"They know within a few houses where he stays."

"You are sure of this?"

"My mother learned it on first hand."

"Hoshea!" Hosea called through the door.

"He is a soldier of the king," Gomer said under her breath.

"No. He will help."

Hoshea opened the door and came inside.

"The king is going to seize Amos," Hosea said.

Hoshea glanced quickly from Hosea to Gomer. "How do you know?"

"My mother learned it through a trusted servant," Gomer said firmly. "Amos must leave the city. The king's order will not follow him beyond the gates."

"The gates will be locked to him," Hoshea said.

"But open to you," said Hosea.

"I cannot go against an order of the king."

"The order has not come . . . to you," Gomer suggested.

"I am a captain in the army of the king."

"Are you not first a servant of Israel?" Hosea asked with sudden urgency. "Would you stand by and watch the vultures pick Amos to pieces?"

"The time slips by too quickly," Gomer warned.

"Hoshea!" Hosea pleaded. "He speaks your own thoughts. You have said so yourself."

Gomer softened the edge of the argument. "If a man slips past the gate while you speak with the guards of some military matter, can the blame fall on you?"

Hoshea mused, taking hold on the excuse, "So far as I know, this is all your imagining . . ."

"Quickly, then," Hosea said, leading the way into the darkened streets.

* * *

In the home of Odenjah, the stone mason who had become Amos' first follower, Amos paced back and forth near the fire pit, while Hosea told him of the king's order. Before Hosea could finish, a sharp knock sounded at the door. They stiffened and looked warily at one another. Odenjah opened the door a crack.

"What do you want?" he asked, brushing a wisp of white hair back from his eyes. "We want to speak with the man Amos, who is called a prophet." The voice on the outside had a strange, hollow sound to it.

"What do you want with him?"

"That is no concern of yours. Open your door so we may come in," said another voice.

"That is not necessary," Odenjah said suddenly. "I am the one you seek."

Amos opened his mouth to speak, but Hoshea grasped his arm and whispered tensely, "When they see their mistake, they will let Odenjah go."

"Come along with us," said the hollow-sounding voice, "by order of the king."

"Do we go now to Bethel?" Odenjah whispered quickly.

Amos looked at Hosea and Hoshea and nodded.

"I will meet you at the east gate or in Bethel," Odenjah whispered. He threw a cloak over his shoulders. Pulling the hood far down over his face, he stepped out.

"It is chilly tonight," he said in a light voice as he headed toward the palace enclosure between the two soldiers.

A captain with long hair knotted at the back met Odenjah and the two soldiers at the palace gate. When he set eyes on Odenjah, he cursed himself for having sent two men newly arrived in Samaria to take the prophet into custody. In the fashion of routine military men, he let the soldiers believe the fault was theirs.

"I send you for the man called Amos, and you bring me this?"

The two men looked sheepishly at one another and then at Odenjah. "He — he said he was the one called Amos."

"Amos, you say?" Odenjah broke in. "No, I thought you said it was a *mason* you wanted, and that I am."

The captain stepped forward and thrust his face close to Odenjah's. "Is this some kind of a trick? Come out with it now, who are you? Are you some friend or disciple of this man?"

"I do not know what man you speak of. I am Odenjah the stone mason, as I have said."

The captain cursed himself again because he had taken the king's order too lightly and had not ordered the gates of the city guarded against Amos' passage. News had a way of traveling in Samaria. The prophet likely knew of the king's order an hour after it was given.

"Did you order the gates barred against the man's passage?" the captain asked the two soldiers.

"You said nothing of ordering the gates."

"Must I tell you to breathe, also?"

Before either soldier could stammer a reply, the captain ordered them to run to each of the city's four gates and order them barred against the prophet of Judah. When this was happening, Odenjah backed away from the captain and the soldiers, and when he was six or eight cubits away, he whirled and dashed off into the shadows of the city. The soldiers started after him.

"Forget the old man!" the captain shouted. "Run to the gates of the city. The man may have already escaped through your witless conduct. Start at the east gate. The man is from Judah and will likely take the road to Bethel if he heads toward his home."

In a shadow of buildings near the east gate of Samaria, Hoshea, Amos, Gomer, and Hosea waited anxiously for Odenjah.

"They may hold him the rest of the night," Hoshea whispered, "if they suspect that he tricked them on purpose. It may be better to leave without him."

"I like it not," Amos said, shaking his head.

Gomer was the first to see Odenjah, flitting toward them from building to building, keeping well in the shadows. "Odenjah, we are over here," Hosea called in a loud whisper.

"Hurry!" Odenjah said, coming up to them. "They have not yet ordered the gates barred."

"The gates are not barred?" Hoshea asked. Then, soldier-like, he asked, "Who was the captain in charge?"

"I know not," Odenjah replied in low, rapid speech. "A thin man. He had long hair, tied in a kind of knot at the back. Come, we are losing time. The soldiers are dispatched to warn the gates."

"Remaliah!" Hoshea muttered. A worse captain Hoshea could not imagine. For once, Remaliah's stupidity served some good cause. Odenjah took Amos by the arm. "This is of no matter. Hurry!"

Amos stepped from the shadows after Odenjah. The gate stood less than fifteen cubits away. The guard leaned against the wall, half dozing. Suddenly Odenjah pulled Amos back into the building's shadow. The hollow-voiced soldier trotted up to the gatekeeper, delivered his message, and ran along the wall toward the northeast edge of the city.

"We are too late," Odenjah breathed.

"Get back behind the building," Hoshea whispered. "When I draw the guard away from the gate entrance, slip out."

He straightened his shoulders and walked briskly toward the gate. That Remaliah was part of the scheme to take Amos into custody did away with Hoshea's last reluctance to go against his king by helping the prophet escape.

Odenjah slid around the building. Amos started after him, then stopped. "You are coming?" he asked Hosea, looking directly into his eyes.

Until that moment Hosea had thought neither of leaving nor remaining. All had happened so quickly. He looked at Gomer, standing by his side, the hood drawn over her head, hiding her face.

"In a moment," he said to Amos.

"You are leaving again?" Gomer asked, a harshness edging her voice.

"I will come back."

"Yes, and when? In a week? A year?"

"In days."

"And then you will be off somewhere else again."

Hosea put his hands to her shoulders, gently. She pushed him away. "Go — go to your prophet."

"Gomer —"

"Go! You are bound to your prophet, not to me!" She turned away from him.

"Yes, it is true, I am bound to him. I know not why myself, but I am. Yet not so much, nor in the ways, that I am bound to you."

"Hosea!" Hoshea's voice came from the shadow of the wall in a loud whisper. He motioned that the others had made their way through the gate.

"I will come back to you," Hosea said.

"It is no matter to me," Gomer said coldly. "Two days ago another man made betrothal representations to my father. I may be wed when you come again."

"Must we leave in such temper?"

She would not answer. Hosea waited a moment, then walked swiftly past Hoshea without speaking. The guard at the gate held a lantern up to his face and passed him through the gate of the city.

"Hosea, Hosea." Gomer held her hands to her lips and whispered his name like a kiss.

Why, why must he leave her? What had this man from Judah to offer Hosea that she could not give him? Why must men forever launch themselves into rough uncertain seas? The authorities could seize him. He could be killed.

Hosea! His one finger touching hers could stir her to more passion than hot caressing she could imagine from another man.

What kind of life could she have with such a man? Never would she know at night if he would return, or if she would receive word that he had been seized by authorities or stoned by the crowd! No woman could live with such uncertainty hanging over every day of her life.

* * *

"Gomer?" Hoshea came up to her. "I will see you to your house."

"Very well."

"No word of this, now, to anyone."

Gomer nodded. They walked on for some time in silence. In a narrow street they were hid from the moonlight, and in the darkness Gomer took Hoshea's arm. It was the arm of a soldier, a strong arm. Gomer clung more closely. She bit her lower lip, a childhood habit when a lure of adventure gripped her; playmates knew Gomer could not easily resist a dare.

"Hoshea?"

"Yes."

"How do you think toward me?"

"How ought I to think?"

"As your heart leads you."

They turned into a broader street, and Hoshea looked down on her. The hood had fallen back from her face.

"It would lead me too far, I fear."

"How can you know if you do not follow?"

Hoshea laid his hand on her arm. They stopped in the street, facing one another. "How is it between you and Hosea?" he asked.

She shook her head, not speaking. Her eyes glistened with a strange excitement. She stepped close and turned her lips up to him.

"Gomer, why —"

She stopped his words, kissing his mouth. Gomer knew well how to flirt and tease men on when they were attracted to her, but she had never kissed a man before, not even Hosea when they were alone. She felt a sudden thrill, pressing her mouth to his. For a moment Hoshea held her. Then he pushed back.

"This is all too sudden."

"Is it?" Her voice was soft and faint.

He took her arm, and they continued on their way. She leaned her head on his shoulder and ran her fingers up and down his arm. He brushed her hand away.

"Why did you do that?" she asked.

"Gomer, I leave for the northern border in a matter of days. What can there be between us?"

"You shall be gone long?"

"A year, perhaps."

"Oh."

She straightened and let loose his arm. They walked on in silence. When they had come to Diblaim's gate, Hoshea said, "There is something amiss between you and Hosea, is there not?"

"It is no concern of yours," Gomer answered sullenly.

"Yes, but when you do as you did back there, you make it my concern."

She turned her eyes away. Hoshea pursed his lips thoughtfully and looked back toward the east gate of the city.

"I think between you two there is something uncommon and wonderful," he said quietly. "Let nothing spoil it, Gomer."

He kissed her forehead, as a brother. Gomer watched after him for a moment as he walked away. A hint of resentment smoldered in her eyes. Then she brushed the thought of Hoshea aside. "He is nothing," she said to herself.

She turned toward the house. In the footpath she half stumbled; the moon had passed under a cloud. She pushed open the door to the house and entered. The old house servant, Abraham, stood to his feet in welcome. Gomer motioned him to sit again.

"Leaving unfriends with Hosea — what was I thinking?" she muttered angrily to herself. "How can I undo what I have done?"

Chapter 9

Amos and the High Priest

1

Judas ben Ishbaal, son of the Canaanite Ishbaal ben Eben and the Israelite Esther bath Jacob, husband to twenty wives, LORD of a hundred and six concubines, master of six hundred and sixty servants, owner of four hundred flocks, nine hundred and four yoke of oxen, a thousand and two hundred cattle, eight hundred and seventy camels, and four thousand two hundred and seventy debtors pledged for indenture, strode into the vaulted chamber of Amaziah, high priest of Bethel.

"Now has this prophet over-reached himself!"

Amaziah rose from his couch, startled by Judas' sudden entrance. "Judas ben Ishbaal, honored friend, peace —"

"Peace, peace," Judas returned abruptly. "We can measure our speech another time. We have solemn business to see to."

"You speak of the prophet called Amos?" Amaziah asked with pretended indifference. He hoped Judas had not heard how Amos had silenced him in the Temple, before all the people, with a stinging rebuke. But if Judas had heard, Amaziah did not want him to suspect how deeply the affair had disturbed him.

"Yes, the prophet from Judah. Today in the gate he roused the people to render judgment against me."

"In what matter?"

"The land of Esdras ben Joad," Judas replied with bitterness.

"I know the land," Amaziah said.

He pinched the jowls of his cheek between his thumb and forefinger, as he always did when something secretly amused him. This took some of the sting out of his own encounter with the prophet. Judas had long schemed to get that wretched plot of land. He had gained the land on either side, and it rankled him that his lands must remain divided because little Esdras was too proud to sell and too crafty to let himself fall into a debt he could not repay.

"How is it the judgment went against you?"

"He borrowed seed for spring planting. He brought forward two men who witnessed that payment was not due until after the Feast of Booths."

"What of your own witnesses?"

"They were shouted down by the people. This prophet climbed atop the city wall, stood mocking their testimony, and turned the people against them."

Amaziah smiled. "You have always been able to persuade the people . . ."

"Leave off the pinching of your fat cheeks," Judas said, his voice level and belittling. "Your gloating can wait. We have business to settle with this prophet from Judah."

"I have heard of him," Amaziah said coldly, half turning away.

Judas ignored Amaziah's shallow play at dignity. He had long since grown used to the high priest's absurd posturing.

Judas and Amaziah had little liking for one another. Amaziah envied Judas's cleverness and his wealth. Judas despised Amaziah's weakness and servility. Yet their lots fell together by common need. Judas, in his dealings, needed the quiet approval of the priesthood, and Amaziah coveted the gifts Judas offered to obtain this approval.

Judas spoke in quiet, even tones, "Amaziah, this man must be killed."

"Killed?"

"Yes, killed. There is no other way to silence him, and silenced he must be." Amaziah's pretenses fell away. Ever since Amos had humiliated him in the Temple, he had thought on ways of revenge. But killing he had not dared think on. Even when another gave it utterance, he drew back with a fear he could not name.

"Judas, the man arrived in Bethel only three days ago. These prophets come one day and are forgotten the next."

"Not this man, and well you know it. I heard how he frightened you to silence in the Temple with his prophecies. That will not soon be forgotten."

Amaziah flushed at the memory. Judas went on: "He molds the crowd into a single person. Such a man can upset every house and authority in Israel — mine, yours, even the king, perhaps."

"Yes, yes, he must be dealt with. But not by killing. It goes too far."

"He must be stopped before he gains a following. There is no other sure way. Killing it must be."

"No, I cannot — I will not allow —"

"The choice is not yours, Amaziah."

Amaziah stared at Judas, then looked away and sank down on his couch.

"He must be taken by soldiers of the king," Judas said, "so the blame will not fall on us here in Bethel."

"How — how can it be done?"

"You must send a letter to Jeroboam. Tell him this prophet is preaching blasphemy and rebellion in the land. Secure from him an order for his captain here in Bethel to seize the man and bring him to you for judgment. Your judgment will be death by stoning — the penalty for blasphemy."

Amaziah stared down at the floor of his chamber, inlaid with intricate mosaics brought in from Egypt at great cost. For a moment something within him had rebelled against joining his hand in the death of the prophet — the memory, perhaps, of what it had once meant to be a priest in Israel, the memory of something holy. But this memory was nurtured only by story and legend. It was not so dear and near as the oil and grain and silver and costly robes and summerhouses that now adorned his life. Not so near as the voice of Judas ben Ishbaal. Not so near as his own thirsting for revenge on the man who had humbled him before the people.

Amaziah pushed his misgivings down into the cellar of forgotten ideals and thought ahead to the words he must write to Jeroboam, king of Israel.

* * *

The next day, Amaziah sent to Jeroboam a letter, saying, "Amos has conspired against you in the midst of the house of Israel. The land is not able to bear all his words. For thus Amos has said: 'Jeroboam shall die by the sword, and Israel must go into exile away from his land.'"

To the messenger who was to deliver the letter, Amaziah gave instructions: "Seek the king's leave for us to use his soldiers in bringing the prophet to judgment."

2

Harsh rebuke and fearless condemnation readily gathers a crowd of people. When the rebuke is coupled with fervor and conviction, a curious crowd can become an impassioned following. Such was the appeal of Amos. If he chose, he could have set the whole land of Israel into rebellion.

"Lead! We will follow!" The mood of the crowds was not far from it.

Amos would not do this. Though he spoke against the rich, he was not the champion of the poor. For Amos, the struggle was not between rich and poor, between blasphemous and devout, but between a holy God and idolatrous men. Not the misery of the poor, but the injured holiness of God put fury on the lips of Amos. He had no thought to set one group in Israel against another. Punishment would not come from the hand of Israelite rising against Israelite but from the hand of God, and his instrument, the sword of Assyria. Only in turning again to the ways of the LORD could Israel stay the hand of destruction.

Amos saw no hint of such a turning. His prophecy rolled out over Israel, heedless of the cries that rose up to meet it — cries of praise or cries of hatred — heedless of aught but the call of the LORD that still burned in his breast.

Amos had been in Bethel less than a week, yet already in the streets one heard whispers of a plot against the prophet.

"Perhaps it would be well to leave Bethel for a time," Odenjah suggested, "until tempers have cooled. It is said Judas ben Ishbaal is stirring up some mischief against you."

Amos stood in the doorway of the small mud house where they had taken lodging with a cousin of Odenjah. He was looking north toward the Temple.

"In two days the Feast of Booths will begin, with great celebrations in the Temple. The LORD's name will be chanted and sung aloud as they go out into the fields to begin the harvest, but it is the Baal that will be worshipped before the week is out." Amos turned to Odenjah. "No, I cannot leave. It is to this very feast I was called, I now think."

"You will speak in the Temple that night?"

"It seems right."

"I fear it. All has happened too quickly here in Bethel."

"Destruction comes on more quickly."

"Yes, for you, my teacher." Odenjah came up to Amos in the doorway, speaking low and earnest. "You are young and I am old, yet I call you 'my teacher,' for I know you to be a prophet of the LORD. This you have not told me, but God Himself told me when your words fell on my ear that day in the Temple at

Samaria. As the LORD called you to speak His word, in that day He called me to serve you how I might, and so I have.

"Now let my years serve you with simple wisdom. The words of men are quickly heard and soon forgotten. You have been in Israel but one summer season. If some mischance befalls you now, all the words you have spoken will be washed away with the early rains. But if you stay and speak your words again next year, and the year following, and more, then those words will take root and bear some fruit. A prophecy, if it comes to bloom quickly like the desert flower, will as quickly wilt.

"Take care for your safety now, Amos. If there be some truth in this rumor of a plot against you, let your tongue rest in silence for a time."

Amos looked still toward the Temple, deep in thought. After a time he spoke: "Your words are much loved, Odenjah, for they come from your heart. Yet I find no room for them in my own. A man's words are soon forgotten, as you say. But the words I speak are not my own. They are the LORD's. It is He who must bring them to harvest, not my voice or my length of years or my way with a crowd, but His power. If He leads me to speak His word in the Temple, then He will take care that the word does not die, whatever may come to me."

"Yes, if *He* leads you. Many a man has made folly his god, and followed its leading."

Amos touched a finger to his lips, and a frown darkened his brow. "Many another has made a faint heart his god and followed its leading."

After some moments Odenjah said quietly: "If it be the will of God, then I am content."

Amos touched the older man's arm. "Yes, if it be the will of God." His voice as he spoke was somehow less sure.

Chapter 10

A Happy Homecoming

The third day after our arrival in Bethel I went to visit my father in Dothan, a two-day journey north of Bethel. The journey was pleasant this time of year. Hillsides were purple with grapes awaiting the harvest; a cooling breeze blew in from the Sea, bringing an end to the heat of summer; the sound of laughter and singing rang out in the countryside as the people lashed together the simple booths of poles and branches in which they would live during the Feast of Booths, the week-long harvest festival when all Israel came out into the country-side to share in the work and ritual of harvest.

I stopped and talked with people along the way, as one did traveling through the countryside. It pleased me to hear again the familiar slur of their speech and the friendliness of their words after the weeks in Samaria and days of tumult in Bethel, where the harsh shriek of the market and the voice of haggling and bargaining continually crowded into one's ears. I had almost forgotten how slowly and peacefully life moved in the countryside.

In the few days since I came to Bethel with Amos a strange thing had happened. So much was Gomer in my thoughts that the prophecy of Amos was like an intruder. When I heard Amos preach in Samaria, knowing that in the evening or the day following I would see Gomer, the words of the prophet rang with truth. With Gomer absent from my life, I found company with Amos a growing burden.

I had thought of leaving Amos and returning to Samaria. Yet neither did this thought bring me comfort. Something still bound me to the prophet. If I stood again in the gate of Samaria, as I did the night of our leaving, I knew that I would make the same choice again. Amos' words had laid a burden upon my heart that I could not put aside.

In Dothan I was received with gladness and feasting. Everyone greeted me with warmth. It was as though I had never left and would never leave again.

To my surprise, my friend Obed met me stiffly. We exchanged but a few words, then Obed begged to leave. He was distant and speechless. It disturbed me, but I let it pass.

Father had been on the point of traveling to Samaria to see me, not having heard that I was now in Bethel. A distant cousin of Father, a priest who ministered at a hilltop altar west of Samaria, had come to Dothan to speak with Father. He was past seventy years and feeble. He wanted a young priest to come and live with him, to minister with him at the altar, and to bury him when he died, for he had no family still living. He had come to ask for me.

Father thought ahead. His cousin owned a house in Samaria; the altar was a short walk from the city walls. The house would fall to me at his death, and was something to be considered. It would be a long time before I would have a house to call my own, were I to return to Dothan. But something more lay in Father's plans. Living in Samaria and ministering at an altar nearby, I would be in sight of the Temple. In time, moods and tempers could change. If I drew many people to my altar, the high priest might think again to call me into the Temple. I would be older, more settled. Perhaps I would not act so brashly a second time. Father still held to his dream that I should one day be high priest.

When the evening meal was over, Father took me to the edge of the village where his altar was set. He wanted to speak with me alone. He seemed to choose his words with great care. He knew me so well. He knew I did not make choices only by the weighing of arguments but by testimony of the heart. Something of this, I suppose, lay beneath my sudden temper, my strong affections, my brooding silences. The thoughts of a man can be told in words, but the language of the heart is gentle caresses, quiet anguish, angry blows, and tears. When I did not at once speak, Father took it for a good sign. I suppose he thought the affair with the prophet had run its course.

"It is a fair sounding proposal," I said after silence.

"After the Feast of Booths, we could travel together to Samaria and speak with our cousin directly," Father suggested.

I did not answer. Father waited a moment, then spoke again. "What think you?"

"I know not."

"What argues against it?"

I looked at Father. "My tie to the prophet."

"Is that still with you?"

"Yes."

"How much longer will it continue?"

I shook my head and looked off into the approaching darkness. Yes, how much longer? How much longer to be torn between the call to serve a prophet of God and being drawn to the love of a woman? Here was a chance for the two to be joined — an altar outside Samaria, a house in the city where a man might live with his wife. Why could it not be mine?

"Samaria is much in my thoughts," I said abruptly, turning to face Father.

"How is it so?"

"I found there a woman."

"A woman? Ah! Is she of good family?"

"She is the daughter of Diblaim the leather merchant."

"Our host, the friend of Hoshea? Yes, I remember her. She seemed taken with you when we first met. Beautiful she was, too."

"I think I have never known such a woman."

"How old is she?"

"Seventeen years."

"Well ready to wed. Such a one will not go long unbetrothed, if you are long away from Samaria."

I nodded. Such a thought had troubled me, especially when I thought on our unfriendly leave-taking. I knew she was given to harsh words and moods that came on suddenly and vanished as quickly. Yet, how long her love would burn with me not there to feed its fire, I dared not think.

"My path is not clear. I am drawn back to Samaria, but I am held by the prophet."

"My son, the prophet is a thing of a season. In Samaria is your whole life."

"It is so, and yet I am bound. He has wakened in my heart a hunger for the LORD that is like a gnawing inside me. While he continues in Israel, I must be at his side, at his feet."

"Even if you lose the daughter of Diblaim in the passing?"

"No!" The word burst from my lips. Tears welled in my eyes. "Oh, I know not, I know not," I moaned.

"Your love for this woman is strong."

"Yes, perhaps too strong."

"Go to her, Hosea. Make her your wife."

I could not speak. I went to the altar, laid my hands on it and lifted my eyes upward. I had thought to pray, then I overheard the notable Voice I knew so well: *Go, take to yourself a wife of harlotry and children of harlotry; for the land commits great harlotry by forsaking the LORD.*

I did not always understand the words of the LORD that I overheard. From the first time it happened, back in childhood, I sensed I was listening in on words being spoken in divine council. Sometimes the meaning was clear, but the words could also be mysterious or poetic. The words I now heard were terribly strange. Gomer would be a wife of good family, not of harlotry.

Was the LORD speaking of someone else? Johanna? Redeem her from the Temple in Joppa and make her my wife?

No, the word settled with no doubt on Gomer. It was more than permission to marry; *it was a command.*

For a moment a dark cloud rose within me, thunder and lightning and a beckoning hand. It was a vision or dream from childhood. It seemed at greater distance, and lasted but moments, but I shrank before the dread hand, as I always did.

When I returned Father asked, "What were you doing?"

"I was praying."

"But you laid no offering upon the altar."

"I laid there my heart."

We walked back into the village in silence. After a time Father asked, "Can there be sacrifice with no sweet smell of burning going up into heaven?"

"It is knowledge of Him the LORD requires, not burnt offerings."

"You learned these words from the prophet?"

"I have learned from the prophet to know the LORD. The words were not his." Father looked into my eyes. "What will you do now?"

"Return to Bethel."

"Do you then turn your back on Samaria?"

"No. I must speak with the prophet of what lies on my heart."

* * *

When we returned to the house, my sister, Shania, sprang to her feet to greet us. "Father! Hosea! Do you remain longer in Dothan, my brother?"

"No. I must return to Bethel."

"I feared as much. But then I must speak sooner than I had planned."

"What is it?" I asked uneasily. I read something of uncertainty, even of fear, in her eyes.

"Father already knows," she answered quickly, glancing aside at Father, then returning her look directly to me. "It is not — it is not sudden, but I — I have been asked for in marriage!" she blurted out.

I leaned back and looked my sister up and down. "Shania, my little sister, ready to be a bride?" I answered warmly. "I suppose you will always be my 'little sister,' but you have become a woman, a beautiful woman!"

"Father has given his consent." Her voice trembled. "It is special. I need your consent as well."

"He is a good man? A good family?"

Shania nodded.

"You want to marry him?"

"I do, with all my heart."

"Who is it, then?"

She looked into my face. "Please think carefully, Hosea. It is Obed . . ."

"Obed?" I echoed, little above a whisper. "My friend, Obed?"

Shania stood unmoving, her face an open picture of waiting despair. "I know, I know . . ." she said.

"Know what?"

"He is small. I am nearly a cubit taller."

I stood silent a moment, then broke into a hearty laugh. "You and Obed? My best friend and my dear sister?" I reached out and took Shania in my arms.

"You — you will consent?" she asked.

I held her at arm's length by both shoulders. Then I took her by the waist and lifted her high above me. "Consent? I rejoice! Could you ever doubt it?"

Shania threw her arms around me as I lowered her to the ground. "Oh, I am happy!" she cried. "So happy." She clung to me and buried her face in my robe.

"What were you thinking?" I asked. "Your face was like granite."

"I was afraid you would not give your consent."

"Not give my consent?"

"He is small."

"As everyone in Dothan knows."

"Some have already laughed and made jokes about us."

"Ah, that. Now I understand why Obed was loath to talk with me — the laughter and jokes. We two lived with that forever and gave back as good as we got. The betrothal was on his mind. He thought — I don't know, but I will assure him. Pay those fools no heed, Shania. They are blind. Your husband will stand among the elders in the gate a giant, a giant of honor and courage."

Shania's face lightened like morning sun. "Oh Hosea! You are happy then, happy with Obed? Happy with me?"

"Only one thing could make me happier."

Shania and Father looked at me with surprise, uncertain what I meant.

I smiled and added quietly, "I could only wish to make so good a match for myself."

* * *

I stopped by the house of Obed on my way out of Dothan. When Obed came to the door, I affected a solemn bearing.

"My old friend," I said. "I have heard something of solemn moment concerning you."

Obed nodded and looked down without speaking.

"I heard that you have proposed betrothal for the most beautiful girl in Dothan." Obed nodded without looking up.

"I did not want to leave Dothan without paying respect to your excellent judgment!"

Obed looked up, barely comprehending, then slowly gave way to a ten cubit smile. "You — you approve?"

I clapped my hands to his shoulders. "My best friend and my dear sister? *Approve* is too small a word. I agree with all my heart, I dance, I shout my joy to the heavens!"

"Hosea! My friend, ever my friend!" Obed cried.

We gripped each other's hands and spun around in the street, laughing and shouting. The void between us vanished. No words were needed.

Chapter 11

A Prophecy Completed

1

The day that the Feast of Booths was to begin, Amaziah received a letter from Jeroboam. It spoke of him not as the high priest of Bethel but as priest of all Israel and praised his wisdom and loyalty — giving him authority to use the soldiers of the king in bringing the prophet to judgment.

The high approval of the king soothed the conscience of Amaziah. Had not the king addressed him as priest of all Israel and deemed him wise and loyal? And was he not so indeed — ridding the land of this troublesome man?

The real cause of the king's approval Amaziah did not know. It was not the loyalty and wisdom of Bethel's high priest that struck Jeroboam. It was rather the chance this offered to have affairs with the prophet settled somewhere else than in Samaria.

In the weeks since he had come from Tekoa, Amos had lost his boyish look. Now, as he sat cross-legged in the shade of the house, his back leaning against the north wall, his face was tired and lined, like a man well on in years. He had slept little the past two nights.

Hosea had returned to Bethel at noontime, and after their usual meal of coarse barley loaves and date wine, he spoke with Amos of the proposal from his father's cousin, and of Gomer. As Hosea spoke, Amos' thoughts went back to that day in the Temple of Samaria, when Hosea had stood against the guards of the high priest and defended him. Ever since that day, Hosea had been a quiet strength to Amos, and Amos indeed wondered how long he might have continued except for Hosea's presence with him. Now Hosea spoke of leaving. Amos' countenance darkened.

All his prophecy, it seemed, had led to this one night, when all Israel would gather in Bethel. City dwellers and country dwellers, travelers and visitors would stream into the countryside to begin the Feast of Booths. In that gathering Amos could raise his voice and all Israel would hear. Yet as the day was upon him, he stood suddenly alone. Odenjah discouraged him, Hosea stood on the point of leaving him. "It is no easy life you have come to with me," Amos said with little warmth.

"I have no regret in it, only this, that I am — what else can I say? — I love a woman, and want to make her my wife."

"And this other, the altar near Samaria?"

"Yes, that too. I am the son of a priest. Is not this altar a place where I might serve the LORD?"

"Better than by following a mad prophet?"

"Be not harsh with me," Hosea pleaded. "This is no easy thing."

"To follow the LORD is never an easy thing."

"Might I not follow the LORD as a priest at his altar?"

"That you must answer yourself."

Hosea went on more eagerly: "A priest who would lead the people in right worship, and counsel them in righteousness and justice — could he not stay the destruction you prophesy?"

"From one hilltop altar you would lead Israel to repentance?"

"No, no, not I — not I, alone — but a remnant faithful to the LORD —"

Hosea stopped. Amos waited, not speaking. After a time, Hosea raised his eyes and looked out over the walls of the city. "I know so little of the will of God, and you are his prophet. Yet one thing has come to me over and over, and more these days in Bethel. There must be some help — some word of comfort —"

"Comfort! A people turns wantonly from their God, and you would comfort them in their sin?"

"Not in their sin, but in their — in their helplessness —"

"Are they so helpless they cannot repent? Let them return to the LORD, for He will pardon and look on their sin no more. There is comfort, Hosea."

"Yes, and yet —"

"What more?"

Hosea's lips trembled. Something stirred within him but he could find no words.

Amos was a man of few affections, and his ties were not in Israel but in Judah. He stood apart from Israel. He could foresee her destroyed by the righteous anger of God.

Hosea's heart wrenched at words of judgment. He knew well Israel's fall into idolatry and saw the withering of righteousness within her borders — this was a staple of knowledge and wisdom, growing up in the house of Beeri — but he could not give up hope for Israel. In her wickedness he saw wretchedness as well as evil. The wretchedness became his own. It streaked his anger with compassion.

Amos asked again, "Is there any word but judgment and destruction for those who will not return to the LORD?"

"I know not," Hosea said at last.

"Can you serve the LORD as priest at this hilltop altar outside Samaria? Throughout Israel these have become altars of sinning, with the lust and reveling of Baal."

"It need not be so. Is not so with my father."

"Yes, but this altar near Samaria? Does the memory of lust still cling to its stones? Will you gain the ear of the people if you speak a word from the LORD? Will your tongue be free to speak?"

"If the LORD gives me words, I will speak."

"Well said." Amos paused, then spoke again, softly. "Yes, well said."

For a time neither man spoke. Again, Amos thought on the night that lay before him — and the uncertainty that lay beyond. Hosea's words stirred a memory. He went back to the night Hosea found him by the east wall in Samaria. He remembered the upturned faces of the poor, the wretched poor of Samaria. He felt again the yawning emptiness beneath his heart, because he had no words to speak to them. No words of . . . comfort. That was the word Hosea had spoken. Words of condemnation — they were given him. They were true. Yet something lay beyond.

Amos pondered his thoughts in silence. Was this indeed God's way of leading him — first Odenjah, then Hosea? Was his prophecy now at an end, and should this night be passed in silence?

* * *

Shortly past sunset a loud knocking came at the door of the house where Amos had finished his evening meal. The wife of Odenjah's cousin set her bread dough back from the fire pit and stepped to the door. A soldier, thick through the chest and short in height, stood on the outer side of the door.

"Does the man from Judah called Amos lodge with you?" he asked.

"My — my husband is not yet returned from the country," the woman said. She threw an anxious look back at Amos. Odenjah and Hosea had gone into the country to help her husband build the shelter-booth they would live in during harvest week. Amos went to the door and motioned the woman aside.

"You are Amos of Judah?" the soldier asked.

"Yes. Who are you?" Amos kept the door partly closed.

"I am Menahem ben Gadi, captain of the king's garrison in Bethel. May I come inside?"

"You are alone?"

"Yes."

Amos opened the door cautiously, and Menahem entered. "What do you want?" Amos asked.

"I will speak bluntly. I have come to give you a warning and an opportunity to leave Bethel while you may."

"What kind of warning is this, coming from a soldier in the king's army?"

"There is an order from the king to take you prisoner. Amaziah, the High Priest, arranged for it. The duty is mine to carry out."

"I see . . ."

"I am afraid you do not see. I have not come here to take you prisoner, but to warn you, as I said. I have no part in this business, and no stomach for it. I have heard you speak here in Bethel. What you say is well said. The high priest and his doings are none of mine."

"What, then, are you here to tell me?"

"That you must leave Bethel at once, and for good. If you go now, I will say that you left before I could take you prisoner."

"Why are you doing this for me? What am I to you?"

"You are a man with courage. I respect courage. You are a man who speaks his mind, and that also I respect. I would like you to escape this trap Amaziah has set for you."

"What would your king say if he knew of this?"

"He has no way of knowing, unless you tell him — or this woman tells him."

"I have heard nothing," the woman said without looking up from her baking.

Menahem looked directly at Amos. "A king so witless that he would join in a plot with these greedy landowners and priests must be overruled."

"Men have lost their heads for such words."

"Kingdoms have fallen for lack of them. That is why I came. You have done Israel a service and ill deserve to die for it. Is it well understood? You must leave Bethel at once."

"The Feast of Booths begins this night. I have planned to speak to those who gather," Amos said slowly.

Menahem shook his head. "If you are seen in public from this moment, I will be forced to take you prisoner. Your speaking is at an end here in Bethel."

"I must think on this. There is much at issue."

"I can not be responsible for your safety if you are delivered to Amaziah."

"Thank you for your visit, captain. Even if I cannot do as you say, I thank you."

Menahem walked through the door and into the street. "I hope I shall not see you again," he said, turning back to Amos.

"Are the fires lit in front of the Temple?" Amos asked.

"Not yet."

"Then I have a little time. Thank you, captain."

Now it had come. No whispered plot, but a spoken threat. He might stir the crowds to his cause, but this captain was not one to be easily turned aside from his duty once he launched into it. Even Hosea could not stand off armed soldiers.

He thought on the hills of Tekoa, the lonesome nights of star watching, the peace, and he wondered if his prophecy had run its course. "O LORD God," he breathed, "have I finished? Is it now done?"

From the Temple came the rumble of drums, calling the people to worship. The streets sprang alive with people moving toward the Temple. All Israel gathered this night to sway to the chanting of the high priest.

If Amos stood up to speak this night, he called out for his own destruction. And yet it was this night that called him from the hills of Tekoa, and this gathering that waited always at the end of his path. He had no way of knowing what turn of events lay in wait for him this night, but a quiet, unmoving certainty took shape within his thoughts: a time comes when all one has fought and strived and lived for can only be kept if one risks it utterly, even unto death.

The fire in his breast had not gone out. Blown and scattered it had been, but still it burned. The hand of the LORD God of Israel was upon him. The drums from the Temple were a call.

2

At the head of the Street of Tanners, in the shadow of a low building, stood two soldiers. Twenty paces away, at the head of the Street of Shoemakers, stood two more soldiers. On their other side, at the head of a street that bore no name, two more soldiers stood waiting. Twelve streets opened unto the Temple grounds, and at the head of each stood two soldiers of Menahem ben Gadi.

A sergeant walked up to the two men who stood in the Street of Tanners. "Any sign of the man yet?" he asked sharply.

"No sign," the shorter one answered wearily.

"Keep alert. If he slips past, it will be the worse for you. Give the call the moment you see him." The sergeant moved on toward the Street of Shoemakers.

"'It will be the worse for you,'" said the short soldier, mocking the sergeant's high, clipped way of speaking. Turning to his partner, a lean pole of a man, he said, "How does a man like that come to be a sergeant?"

"I think he is not a man but a woman in disguise, and he pleasures our captain."

"I could well believe it. That lily-white face. Oh! For one great fistful of mud, and him outside the city wall on a dark night."

"Pity Israel if ever he becomes a captain."

"Captain!" The short man cried, clutching his breast and sinking to his knees. "Save me! The thought alone has half slain me."

The lean man stood straight up and clicked his boots together. "On your feet, man, or it will be the worse for you."

"Yes, Sergeant, on my feet. Indeed, Sergeant. What more, Sergeant? May I polish your sword, Sergeant? Is the food done to your taste, Sergeant? Could I mash it somewhat, Sergeant? You are not long from your mother's breast —"

"Sh! Someone comes."

The two soldiers faced into the darkened street, tense and ready. Three men approached.

"It is him — the one in the middle," the lean soldier whispered. "Yes. Give the call."

"On the run — the Street of Tanners! On the run — the Street of Tanners!" The two soldiers drew their swords and blocked the street as Hosea, Odenjah, and Amos came up.

"What is this?" Hosea asked.

"The man from Judah must come with us," said the lean soldier.

"By whose order?"

"By order of Menahem ben Gadi, captain in the army of the king."

"What have I done?" Amos asked hotly. "I have not yet even spoken."

"No matter. The order is to take you on sight."

Hosea broke in angrily: "Who is this Menahem, to take a man prisoner at his pleasure? What has been done? What is the offense?"

He made a move toward the soldiers but stopped short when two more soldiers ran up behind them, swords drawn. In the next moments all twenty-four of Menahem's guards trotted up to the Street of Tanners, and presently Menahem himself and the sergeant joined them. Menahem came close to Amos and spoke in a whisper: "Why did you come?"

"I must speak in the Temple."

Menahem shook his head. "You cannot. I warned you not to show yourself. Now you leave me no choice."

"What is to be done?" Odenjah asked, puzzled at Amos' seeming acquaintance with the captain.

"He is to be delivered to Amaziah for judgment."

"By whose order?"

"By order of the king."

"He has not spoken," Hosea said. "He has done nothing."

"Why did you not let me speak before you took me?" Amos asked intensely.

"I could not risk your way with the crowds. Some of my soldiers might have been hurt."

"Can you let him go if we leave now?" Odenjah asked.

Menahem shook his head and nodded toward his soldiers. "Too many eyes have seen. I have no choice."

"No!" Hosea said suddenly. "You cannot —" He pushed Amos behind him and stood facing Menahem, his eyes narrow and threatening.

"I want no trouble in this," Menahem said, touching Hosea's chest. "I know who you are, but my soldiers are not unarmed Ammonites. I will tell them to kill you if you make any trouble." Menahem leaned closer to Hosea and spoke low. "I like this no more than you. I gave him warning. Now I have no choice."

"You gave him warning?" Hosea said.

"Yes," Amos said, speaking to Hosea. "We have naught against him. He did warn me. Yet I thought I would first be able to speak."

"Come along," Menahem said, taking Amos by the arm and turning toward the Temple.

"What will become of him?" Hosea asked.

"The word of Amaziah will decide that," said Menahem.

* * *

Amaziah's sandaled foot beat a rhythm on the tiled floor of his chamber — an uneven rhythm, matching the ceaseless shifting of his eyes. He glanced at Judas ben Ishbaal, seated an arm's length away from him, rubbing the tips of his fingers together, cracking one fingernail against another. The closer came his moment of revenge, the more Amaziah's eagerness slackened.

He remembered again the burning eyes of the prophet, and he held a dread of meeting them again. In a corner of his thoughts, Amaziah held a fearful respect for this man from Judah.

In his earliest memory, Amaziah stood by while his father, a priest like himself, laughingly put off a prophet who condemned his misuse of the Temple gifts. Three days later his father died of a stomach distress, doubled up in pain, shrieking out for the prophet's forgiveness.

He followed in his father's calling, and gradually he took up his father's way of living. Yet he never quite found peace in his way of living — never quite escaped a shuddering of conscience when he took an offering from the people to buy jewelry for his beautiful Canaanite wife or emptied the coffers of the Temple to add to his private land holdings.

To soothe his conscience, Amaziah fasted thrice weekly and observed the laws of ceremony with great care. And never did Amaziah utter the name of the LORD, but he did it with head bowed, in seemly awe and reverence.

When the door of the chamber opened and Amos bristled into the room between two of Menahem's soldiers, Amaziah felt as if a weight pressed him to his seat. It took the greatest effort for him to rise. Amos was ignorant of the customs regarding the high priest, or he chose purposely to ignore them. The two soldiers came alongside and indicated that he was to prostrate himself before the high priest.

"Before God I bow, and before no one else," Amos said.

"In Israel you bow before the high priest," said one of the soldiers, directly and without anger.

They put hands to his shoulders and would have forced him to his knees, but Amos spun from their grasp. "Let him be," Amaziah said.

The soldiers shrugged and backed off a pace.

"You know why you are brought here?" Amaziah asked Amos, averting the prophet's gaze.

"I am brought here because I speak the word of the LORD!" Amos said in a loud voice, as though he stood before a multitude of people.

"You disturb the peace and tranquility of the kingdom."

"Peace and tranquility? There is no peace where the knowledge of God has fallen away, nor tranquility in the worship of Baal."

Judas rose from his chair. "You are no longer preaching to ignorant crowds. Guard your tongue, or you will find yourself without it."

"Judas ben Ishbaal, you are one to guard, and guard well," Amos replied darkly, "You have built houses in the city and summer houses in the country, from the labor of indentures and false bargaining. Now hear — you shall spend your last days in a hutch of mud and die with a thousand sores on your body in a foreign land. So has God sworn by his righteousness."

"Can you think of nothing more?"

"Be silent, Judas," Amaziah said.

"Be silent? In the face of a madman? Has he set a spell on you also, Amaziah?"

"This is my chamber. Be silent or leave."

"Yes," said Judas with contempt, "I bow before the word of the high priest." In low voice he said to Amaziah, "Who is it stands in judgment — you or the prophet?" Amaziah gave no answer but turned with anger on Amos: "You stand in judgment for the words you have spoken against the Temple and against the king."

"The words I have spoken are the words of Him who made the Pleiades and Orion, who turns deep darkness into morning and darkens the day into night, who calls for the waters of the sea and pours them out on the face of the earth. The LORD is His name. The words I have spoken, they are the LORD's. The destruction I have foreseen, it lies in His hand."

"Who are you to know the word and will of Him who dwells in the heavens and prophesy destruction in His name? You are but a man."

"Three visions the LORD showed me," Amos said. His voice lowered, and a strange fire came into his eyes, as though he knew that the words now spoken would be his last. "Behold, He was forming locusts in the time of the king's mowing. When they had finished eating the grass, I said, 'O LORD God, forgive, I beseech Thee! How can Israel stand? He is so small!' The LORD repented concerning this. 'It shall not be,' He said.

"A second vision the LORD showed me: Behold, the LORD God was calling for a judgment by fire, and it devoured the great deep and was eating up the land. Then I said, 'LORD God, cease, I beseech Thee! How can Israel stand? He is so small!' The LORD repented concerning this. 'This also shall not be,' said the LORD God.

"A third vision He showed me: Behold, the LORD was standing beside a wall holding a plumb line in His hand. And the LORD said to me, 'Amos, what do you see?' And I said, 'A plumb line.' Then the LORD said, 'Behold, I am setting a plumb line in the midst of my people, Israel. I will never again pass them by. The hilltop altars shall be made desolate, and the sanctuaries of Israel shall be laid waste, and I will rise against the house of Jeroboam with the sword.'"

Judas began to speak. "Soldiers, take this man —"

"No!" Amaziah shrilled. "Be silent, Judas ben Ishbaal. You are a man of Canaan. This is none of your affair."

"This is much my affair," Judas replied coldly. "I have told you what must be done with this madman, and now it seems I must show you how." He moved a step closer to Amos. "Soldiers, take this man outside the city wall. You know the penalty for blasphemy."

"Hold your place!" Amaziah cried out to the soldiers. "You are sent to me, not to Judas." He turned to Amos. "If I spare your life, as it lies now in my hand to do, will you speak truly and say your prophecy is spoken from your own lips only?"

"What I have spoken cannot be unspoken."

Judas spoke through clenched teeth: "Will you listen to this madman endlessly?"

"You throw yourself to your death," Amaziah said to Amos, barely above a whisper. "Israel cannot bear your words."

"Light has gone out of Israel. The hand of the LORD is on the sword of Assyria."

"Say it will change, prophet. Say it, or you shall die. I swear it."

Amos lowered his head and did not speak. A weight lifted from his spirit. The tumult in his breast subsided into a wistful calm.

"Can you not speak?"

Amos looked up at Amaziah. The fire was gone from his eyes.

"Take him away!" Amaziah screamed.

"At last you come to your senses," Judas declared.

The soldiers led Amos toward the door. Amaziah sank to his seat.

"No, no!" Amaziah cried out before Amos reached the doorway. "To the border of Judah, take him. To the border of Judah. Return him to his own land."

"Are you now gone mad?" Judas demanded. "He will return, and with him a wild people, rebellion full scale."

"I will not have his blood on my hands! O seer, go, flee away to the land of Judah, and eat your bread there, and prophesy there. But never again prophesy in Bethel, for it is the king's sanctuary, and a Temple of the kingdom."

Then Amos answered Amaziah, "I am no prophet, nor a prophet's son. I am a herdsman, and a dresser of sycamore trees. The LORD took me from following my flock and said to me, 'Go, prophesy to my people Israel.' Now you say, 'Do not prophesy against Israel, and do not preach against the people of Isaac.' Yet the word of the LORD remains: 'Your wife shall be made a harlot in the city, and your sons and daughters shall fall by the sword, and your lands shall be parceled out by line, and you yourself shall die in an unclean land, and all Israel shall go into exile away from its land.'"

"Go to Judah. Never more return," Amaziah moaned.

Amos turned and walked from the chamber.

"Now is your folly complete," said Judas.

Amaziah answered nothing. He walked toward the archway that led into the Temple, wrapping his velvet cloak about him tightly against the chill night air.

* * *

In the courtyard outside the high priest's chamber, Hosea and Odenjah waited. Apart from them stood Menahem and seven of his soldiers.

Amos came into the courtyard between the two soldiers who had taken him before the high priest. The soldiers spoke briefly with Menahem and then led Amos toward the Street of Weavers, which took one to the gate of the city. Hosea and Odenjah started after them. Menahem stepped into their path.

"No harm will come to him. He is to be returned to Judah."

"Only that?" Odenjah asked anxiously.

Menahem nodded.

"Praise the LORD!" Odenjah cried.

"We must speak with him," Hosea said, pushing past Menahem.

They overtook Amos and the soldiers at the edge of the Temple grounds. "Amos, we have heard —" Odenjah said.

Amos turned, smiling, and there was something boyish in the way he shrugged his shoulders. "So — I return to my flocks."

"Can you?" Hosea asked hesitantly.

"Yes, it is over." He touched a finger to his breast. "The fire is gone. I am again a shepherd."

"What was said between you and the high priest?" Odenjah asked.

"No more than was said to all Israel these months. Only that."

"We thought you would be killed. Such was the rumor."

"Yes, such were my own thoughts. It is strange. I thought tonight I would preach to all Israel and then go to my death, my words cut off. But the will of the LORD was that I preach before a single man and go back to my flocks, my prophecy completed. The LORD gives me peace again."

"What will we do?" Hosea asked.

Amos looked keenly at Hosea. The basket of summer fruit rose quietly within him. The fruit lay spoiled; ants crawled over the basket. One sycamore fig lay apart, unable to ripen unless first bruised. Amos spoke quietly: "Follow after the LORD, Hosea. Dark days lie ahead for Israel. Judgment, but not unto death. You He will bruise, but unto healing."

"How can I know these things?"

"The LORD will seek you out. He drew me close to His mouth. You, I think, He will draw close to His heart."

"Finish with your words," said one of the soldiers. "It is time to be on the way."

"Be friends to one another," Amos said, "as you have been friends to me. Dark days lie ahead for Israel."

The two men nodded and watched Amos disappear down the darkened street between the two soldiers.

"I could die, now," Odenjah said quietly. "My life is full."

"Yes," said Hosea, in a whisper. For a time neither man spoke. The noise of reveling began to drift out from the Temple, the shouts of men, the high laughter of women. Odenjah spoke: "Will you remain in Bethel for the Feast of Booths?"

"No."

"Myself neither. I am back to Samaria."

"We can travel together."

"You return to Samaria also? For what purpose?"

"To make betrothal agreements with Diblaim, if I can."

Part Two

Take to Yourself A Wife

Go, take to yourself a wife of harlotry
and children of harlotry;
for the land commits great harlotry
by forsaking the LORD.

Chapter 12

The Betrothal

1

When he returned to Samaria, Hosea went to the house of Hoshea ben Elah, who was keeping his few belongings. Hoshea had his own clothing, weapons, and camping supplies sorted in piles.

"You just caught me," he said in greeting to Hosea. "I leave for the northern border tomorrow morning."

Hosea briefly told Hoshea what had befallen Amos in Bethel and what he himself would now do. "I also take leave of your house," he said. "My father's cousin has invited me to join myself to his priesthood. He has an altar in the countryside west of Samaria and a house in the city."

"So you will be living in Samaria and be a priest in nearby countryside."

"Yes."

Hoshea touched a hand to his ear, a longtime habit when he was uncertain what to say. He walked slowly to a bench across the room and took a flask of wine. He poured a cup for himself, then took a second cup and held it toward Hosea, with a tip of his head. Hosea nodded and walked over to him. Hoshea filled the cup with wine and handed it to Hosea. He slid down to a blanket spread out on the floor.

"No good place to sit, I fear." He motioned to another blanket lying opposite and Hosea sat down across from him.

"How stands it with you and the daughter of Diblaim?" Hoshea asked.

"I hope it will stand well," Hosea answered, smiling in the shy way that had become his habit when he spoke of Gomer. Half his purpose in coming had been to tell Hoshea what was afoot. "Odenjah is my go-between. He goes to Diblaim tomorrow to propose betrothal."

"I had expected it some weeks ago. You had eyes only for one another. But what of your parting the night you left Samaria? What was that? She seemed unfriendly."

"That troubled me. Troubles me still," Hosea said quickly. He took hold of the chance to talk with his boyhood friend. Growing up together in Dothan, they had always shared thoughts and plans with one another. "I hope it was only a passing thing. Gomer can change quickly."

"You are quite certain she is the wife for you?"

Hosea looked at Hoshea without speaking, as though expecting him to say something further. When he did not speak, Hosea said, "You think of Johanna? That I still cling to Johanna?"

"No. Not Johanna," Hoshea answered, shaking his head. "No other woman. Only Gomer."

"You yourself speak for me: 'No other woman. Only Gomer.' I cannot think of myself with any other woman."

Hoshea sipped his wine and slowly nodded. What good to tell Hosea of the embarrassing kiss between himself and Gomer the night Hosea left Samaria? It was a passing thing. Nothing came of it. She would be the wife of Hosea. She is the love of his heart. He raised his wine cup and smiled at his tall boyhood friend, whom he yielded to the priesthood unwillingly: he would have made a splendid soldier. "I only regret I will not be present for the wedding celebration," he declared.

* * *

The next day Odenjah presented himself at the house of Diblaim as go-between for Hosea and proposed betrothal agreements for Gomer. Diblaim said he would consider the proposal with "solemn regard." Himself, he liked the man, but he did not know what Gomer's mother might think; nor indeed, what Gomer herself might say. Each of six previous proposals Gomer had declined, four immediately, two after a day's consideration. Between himself and Gomer stood an unspoken but clear understanding that he would not force her into a marriage against her will. With his wife the matter stood open. Diblaim knew Anna had set a high standard for the marriage of their daughter. He had told her about each of the six previous proposals. She rejected each of them. Since Gomer had done the same, that had been the end of it. He and Anna had not discussed the matter further. Diblaim contented himself that this proposal, like the others, would be considered. In due time, Gomer would marry, if not with this man, then another. Yet she could not delay forever. She was no longer a child.

Anna's response to the proposal was immediate and strong: "He is a man of no wealth and no prospects. Do you want your daughter out in the streets begging bread?"

Diblaim demurred. "It is said he could one day be high priest."

"Not likely. Everyone knows he is a follower of the mad prophet from Judah."

"Perhaps we must wait a season and see how things stand."

"Betrothal proposals are best answered speedily. Else other and better ones weary of standing by and walk away."

Diblaim caught her about the waist and took her into a loose embrace. It was not a matter they would settle by argument. "You think wisely, my pigeon. We must inquire with Gomer also."

"Think you her wisdom at seventeen years matches yours at forty . . . or mine at thirty-five?" She kissed his neck and bit his ear, her promise of good things to come.

* * *

That evening, following the evening meal, Diblaim took Gomer by the hand. "Come, let us walk in the garden," he said.

This was his way when he wanted to talk with her about something important or personal. Gomer had not seen Hosea since he returned from Bethel, but she surmised what was happening. She had seen Odenjah when he came to the house, though she did not speak with him. Twice during the day she came upon her father and mother in earnest conversation, then suddenly saw them go silent when she drew near.

Hosea's ten-day absence from Samaria had been an eternity for Gomer. She kept to herself, torn between what she knew was love and . . . and *what*? Uncertainty? Fear? Disdain? No! Not that. Never.

Never had she so wanted and so rejected the very same thing, this man Hosea. When they were together her life was closed in, complete. But then he was gone and she could do nothing about it. It annoyed her that she could not wheedle Hosea, could not gain her way with him when she wanted to. Yet the same thing — his will, his determination — drew her to him.

"What a beautiful woman you have become," Diblaim said.

"You brought me to the garden to tell me that?" Gomer said, pinching his arm and bending her head to lie on his shoulder.

Diblaim laughed. "I must declare the truth to myself, else think of you as I always have — my little daughter, my child."

"So, suddenly I am a woman."

"Yes, for the seventh time now."

Gomer tingled with excitement. She knew what was coming but spoke in measured tones: "The *seventh* time? Then it is another marriage proposal."

"Yes."

Neither spoke for some moments. Each waited on the other. Gomer could not endure a long silence. "Who is it, then?" she asked, though she well knew.

"The stone mason Odenjah came on behalf of Hosea, the young priest from Dothan."

"He has visited in our house these past months. You gave us leave to walk together in the countryside."

"Yes."

Gomer laughed, as though taking it lightly: "They say he is the strongest man in all Israel!"

"I had not thought on that, but it is true. He has such a reputation."

"What are your thoughts on him?" Gomer asked, suddenly serious.

"The very thing I would ask you," Diblaim replied. "It is you, not I, who must make a life with a husband."

"Give me some days to think on it," she said pensively, "and invite him to visit."

Diblaim nodded without speaking. Gomer spoke again: "What says Mother?"

"She wants you to be well wed."

"So she has told me the past fifteen or sixteen years!"

When it came to the betrothal of Gomer, the ways of Baal counted for nothing with Anna. The Israelite side of her heritage held sway. Their daughter must be a virgin, betrothed to a good family, able to command a good dowry.

"A country priest lives with — well, with no great measure of wealth."

"That is Mother's concern? What properties he has?"

"It is no idle concern."

"So it is not," Gomer responded. Then she gave her father a quick kiss on the cheek and her voice took on a sharper edge: "But do send word for him to visit again. Marriage is more than property and wealth."

Diblaim's wealth had shielded Gomer from concern about practical necessities. Such thoughts had scarcely occurred to her when she thought of Hosea. She was absorbed in the task of arguing with her own wonderings — convincing her misgivings that she could marry this man whom she loved with all her heart, yet who sorely troubled her; he did not readily bend to her ways.

Suddenly she realized that her mother could pose a greater hindrance to marriage with Hosea than her own wonderings. Immediately she shut her wonderings down to silence and commenced a plan to win her father's agreement, and her mother's as well.

* * *

Hosea visited Gomer at her house with greater formality than before. All was now ordered toward awaiting Diblaim's answer to the betrothal appeal. He visited not more than twice in a week. Each time he first presented himself to her father and mother, ready to speak or answer any question at their behest. He and Gomer met together always in plain view, though out of earshot.

Gomer knew that the decision regarding Hosea's betrothal proposal would hang on three conversations she must have in the coming days. The first was between Hosea and herself, on his first visit. They sat in the garden, on the same bench as the first night they had met. It began with awkward silence between them, though Gomer felt at peace. He had made his decision. He had chosen her. She had no thought but to tell him her love. She waited for Hosea to speak first.

"I have thought of nothing but you these two weeks, and now my tongue is a leaden oaf," he said with a hapless shrug.

Gomer smiled. Head and shoulders taller than other men, yet so like a boy when he spoke from his heart. "We have seldom been at loss for words, we two. You told me beautiful poetry when we walked together in the countryside. You told me good things about the LORD. You even told me you thought me beautiful. We talked well together."

Hosea told her what had happened to Amos in Bethel and about his own plans to live now in Samaria. He did not dwell on it. The betrothal stood at the front of his thoughts.

"I hope you think it not rude or thoughtless, my sending Odenjah to your father before speaking with you. Betrothal has been my only thought." He laughed nervously. "I did not want to risk finding another ahead of me."

"There is no other, Hosea."

"When we parted, you said —"

"That was my bad temper speaking."

"No other?"

"For me, no other. You are the love of my heart."

"You of mine." He spoke the words back to her with a warmth more tender than she had ever heard him speak. "You make me a wealthy man."

"If love be wealth, then I have untold riches to bestow upon you," she laughed.

"Your father is a wealthy man — in money," he said, more darkly.

"It is so, though I seldom think of him in that way. He is — my father, only that. He loves me, though he does not always show it."

"Perhaps in his marriage he is also rich in love. I do not know your mother. I have spoken to her only twice."

"He is rich there also."

"It was so with my father and mother. After our mother died, Father told my sister and me that theirs was a Jacob and Rachel love."

"That is grand. Let it be ours as well." Gomer did not move beside him but quietly took his hand.

"Yes, if your father will welcome me. He is wealthy and I am but a priest at an altar in the countryside. Will he accept me?"

"He is a good and righteous man. When I tell him I want you, he will give his permission . . . and his blessing."

Hosea looked down on the midnight black of Gomer's hair as she sat beside him, quiet and content. He had approached this evening with some qualm after their parting two weeks earlier. Her generous words breathed back into him life and hope, and an overwhelming flow of love. Still, he could not wholly banish the fear that the practical and wealthy leather merchant in Diblaim would overrule the loving father.

* * *

Two weeks later, Gomer rose early on the Sabbath, the seventh day of the week and a day of rest for worshippers of the LORD. Diblaim still observed the day, though many in Israel no longer did. Gomer found him by the small square of flowers that bloomed the year around, his favorite place in the garden.

She stood by his side, waiting to see his mood as she often did. "Is it a happy day for you, Father?" she asked.

Diblaim nodded but did not speak. He and Anna had argued late into the night about the betrothal proposal from the priest Hosea. He liked the man well enough, but he was beginning to hope Gomer would decline the proposal, else it could lead to bitter warfare between her and her mother.

Gomer knelt at his feet. "Father, may I speak with you?" she asked.

Diblaim looked down at the little daughter who would squeeze him in her arms, laughing and playing and loving him — now become a woman. "Well, it is the Sabbath. I cannot say I must work. What would you speak?" He knew well what she would speak.

"Hosea has visited me now four times, and then the weeks before as well." Diblaim nodded but did not speak.

"May I tell you what I am thinking?" He nodded again.

"Father, I will say it plainly: I love him, with all my heart."

He nodded, closed his eyes and opened them again. "It is no surprise. Your eyes have told it to me from the first day."

"Will you receive him?"

"Your mother has great misgivings. He is a man without means, and likely to remain so."

"Father, can you look on him and say he is 'without means'?" Gomer knew that men looked with some awe on Hosea's strength and manliness. "He smote the Ammonites. All Samaria knows him — all Israel. Already it is said they will stream to his countryside altar for their festivals and sacrifices."

"His father is a known Yahweh tether — no festival or rich sacrifice to Baal at his altar."

Gomer ventured to take his hand in hers. "Have you forgotten, Father, that I too am Yahweh tether?" Diblaim remained silent, though he well remembered her childhood choice, and how he stood with her against her mother. "True worshippers of the LORD bring tithes to a faithful priest. It has always been so with his father, Beeri, and they have lived well."

Diblaim nodded his head slowly, spoke nothing.

"Father, think of this handsome blue-eyed man. There is not one like him in all Israel. For you, Father, it holds a promise, a great hidden promise."

"A promise? How a promise?"

"Think, Father, what sons and daughters I shall have by this man. This is my promise, Father. The first blue-eyed son shall be named for my sweet brother, shall be your grandson Aram."

As carefully as she had prepared her words, Gomer could not have imagined what next happened. Diblaim shrieked aloud and buried his face in his lap where Gomer held his hand. Never had she beheld such an outpouring in her father, not even when his infant son Aram lay dying. She laid her other hand on his head, slowly moving her fingers in comfort.

Some moments passed. When Diblaim raised his head, his cheeks were wet with tears, but he spoke with a steady voice: "Your heart is firmly set on this one man?"

"On him only. We are meant for each other."

Diblaim nodded, one sharp movement. "Then you shall have my blessing. You shall marry him."

He stood to his feet and drew Gomer up. She fell against his chest and clasped her arms around him. Through her own tears she cried out: "Now I will squeeze you until you give me three kisses!"

* * *

Two days later, Anna accosted Gomer in the kitchen where she was beating a mutton shank. Diblaim seldom participated in religious festivals where the meat of sacrifice was eaten, but he liked good meat so it was eaten in his home. Gomer beat the mutton vigorously with an iron maul. She knew her father liked the meat tender.

"What is between you and your father?" her mother asked brusquely.

Gomer knew by the tone of her mother's voice that serious speech was forthcoming. "What is between Father and me? Honor, I should hope. And love. Much love for such a father."

"He avoids me. Will not talk with me. Last night he avoided me in bed. For certain it concerns this priest and his betrothal appeal. Is there something between you?"

"Between Hosea and me? The betrothal appeal, only that."

"Between you and your father, I mean. Has he spoken to you, made any decision?"

Gomer laid down the iron maul and looked into her mother's eyes. As joyful as she was over her father's approval of the betrothal, she knew her joy would be blemished if it came at the cost of her mother's disapproval. "Mama, this man I love. He is for me, and I am for him."

Anna swept her hand, as though to brush away an unwanted scrap. Gomer took her mother's hands in her own and fell to her knees before her.

"Mama, Father has given his blessing. Only one thing remains, your kiss and approval."

Anna sucked in a breath. The Gomer who could argue and fight with her over little things and big things, that Gomer she knew well. But this beseeching daughter kneeling before her —

"I need you, Mama. How can I become a wife and a mother if you are not there to teach me, as you have always taught me? It is all new to me."

"I . . . teach you?"

"O yes, Mama! You make Father happy. How does a wife do that? I watch you with Father and I learn something. But there must be secrets, also — secrets you can teach me."

Anna looked down at her daughter, her eyes misted in wonderment. Her only thought had been for Gomer's safety and security — the security of money and position. Teach her? Teach her about marriage? Teach her about a man?

"You do love this man," she said low, not as a question but as a truth discovered.

"Yes, Mama."

"And you want to make *him* happy? Tell me this, will he make *you* happy?"

"In choosing me, he has already made me happy. Look on him, Mama. In all Israel what man is his equal? Except Father!" she added with a gentle laugh.

Anna stood silent for some moments. Then she pulled Gomer to her feet. "He is a man for certain," she said with a knowing smile. "And he is the one for you? You are certain of that?"

"Most certain."

"Then we must welcome him!" Anna said, throwing her head back with a flourish, shaking her hair loose. She stood shorter than Gomer. She went up on her tiptoes, took Gomer in her arms and kissed her cheek.

"Mama, you pour more happiness over me than I have ever known!"

"We must look to the happiness ahead of you!" Anna could not remember when she had felt such lightness of heart.

* * *

Later in the day Anna sought Diblaim out in the room where he conducted his business, found him surrounded by scrolls and tablets.

"You are buried in business," she said cheerfully. "I beg time only to tell you an important business you must undertake."

Diblaim was accustomed to Anna's business schemes. More often than not they increased his profits. He looked up and waited for her to speak.

Anna drew close to him and laid a hand on his shoulder. "You have been avoiding my advice on this business, but now I will tell you. In the matter of the betrothal appeal: you have given Gomer your blessing." She felt his shoulders tense. She continued in her best business voice, "Well done! He is a considerable figure of a man. And she loves him." Diblaim looked up at her in astonishment. She smiled and put her other hand on him. "Now, it is for us to discover ways that will help him prosper. You yourself should be giving greater attention to helping his priesthood. You are a true Israelite, of Ephraim tribe. You can discover ways, many ways, to help a priest prosper. And gifts. All the money you make from trading in leather — more than you and I need only for ourselves. So there must be gifts when necessary, especially to begin with. And most especially when children come!"

Diblaim stood up and faced Anna, his face lit in speechless marvel at this wife who forever found ways to surprise him. "Your business schemes have often been sound, have made me good profit. But in this you outdo yourself."

"Are we agreed?"

"In every regard."

"And gifts. After they are married. Gifts, when needed?"

"Gifts on every occasion."

"You can afford it," she said with a decisive nod. She put her arms around his neck and kissed him on the mouth. "You also are no little figure of a man."

2

The wheat stood at the knee on the hillsides of Samaria. Spring was fast giving way to summer. In another month the wedding feast would be celebrated. Hosea and Gomer would be wed.

Hosea lived alone, now, in the house he had inherited from his father's cousin. The old priest had died four months after the Feast of Booths. The house, near the south wall of Samaria, was an hour's walk from Hosea's hilltop altar in the country-side west of Samaria.

A priest held a place of unique honor and distinction in Israel. Almost any occasion in the life of an Israelite was cause for religious celebration — marriage, birth, betrothal, the spring planting, the harvest, the weaning of a child, preparation for battle, a successful business dealing, death, a judgment won in the city gate. Every good and every evil of life was visited on a man by the will of the LORD, or by other gods and spirits, so the man of Israel believed. Sacrifice and offerings were the way to win the favor of the gods and provide for the weal of one's household. The priest who ministered at an altar received gifts of food, oil, precious metal, and even live animals from those who came to make sacrifice and offering. The priest whose altar was much frequented gained honor and wealth in the community.

People came to Hosea's altar at first out of curiosity. His name had become known as the one who had slain the Ammonites at Dothan, and who had been a follower of the prophet from Judah. Some came but once, to satisfy their curiosity, and returned no more. Some returned and began to build a small community that worshipped only the God of Israel. The poor soon found that they could offer sacrifice at Hosea's altar and leave only a token gift, if they could spare no more. Devout Israelites, who had grown weary of elaborate rituals by priests who cared more for gifts than for worship, found a fresh simplicity in worship at Hosea's altar.

Though his days were spent to good purpose, it was the evenings that Hosea lived for, when his words were not for people in the city gate or at his countryside altar but for Gomer alone.

By custom, a man saw little of his betrothed in the months before the wedding feast, and was never alone with her. Diblaim made light of such customs. He spoke openly with Hosea after the betrothal agreement and contented himself that Hosea would bring his daughter a virgin to her wedding bed. It was not uncommon in Baal worship for a girl to give up her maidenhood as early as her thirteenth year to a priest or male prostitute as a religious observance, or to couple with a worshipper during a religious festival. Anna believed the Baals bestowed prosperity and good fortune and must be worshipped, but for her unmarried daughter she held to the ways of Israel. When families of quality sought a bride for their son, they sought a virgin bride as a matter of course. When Hosea came to the house, Diblaim often found something to do elsewhere so the two could be together, though never out of sight.

When Diblaim, making conversation, would ask Gomer what the two of them had done, he soon came to anticipate what she would say: "We talked. Talked, talked, talked. We talk about anything and everything." Day by day the report was the same, varying only in details she would add.

"How we do talk together. If it continues after we are wed, I shall become the most learned woman in all Israel!

Today we talked about the bronze serpent Moses lifted up in the wilderness. Did you know about that, Father? Poisonous snakes came into the camp and bit people. If they looked on the bronze serpent, they did not die." Another day she reported, "We talked about children. Hosea wants daughters as much as he wants sons! What do you think of that?"

* * *

Shortly past dusk of an evening two weeks before Hosea and Gomer were to wed, Odenjah came to Hosea at his house. In the months since they returned from Bethel, Hosea and Odenjah were much together. The parting word of Amos, that they be friends to one another, had become more than a remembrance. In some unspoken way they sensed that they must continue the prophecy of Amos.

A neighbor of Odenjah, Beniah, was this night taking his family and leading a procession of friends and onlookers to a hilltop altar west of the city. Beniah owned vineyards near Samaria, and in the past three years hailstorms had destroyed much of his crop. A daughter was new born into the family. She was to be taken to the hilltop altar and sacrificed to appease the anger of the Baals.

"This is no sacrifice to the LORD," Odenjah said. "Did not our father Abraham teach us no more to sacrifice our children when the LORD spared his son Isaac?"

"Did Beniah come to speak with you, asking counsel?"

"Not he, but the grandmother of the child. She believes it is evil, but her words avail nothing against her daughter and son-in-law. Both of them are set on it. The priest has promised God's blessing on such a sacrifice."

Hosea seemed for a moment to be lost in his thoughts. His words came quietly, as though in search of a meaning not yet fully known: "Where is this to be?"

"At the altar of Askew, westward."

"If they came to my altar, I could turn them away, or show them a better way. But the altar of another priest? Another priest would never intrude at my altar."

"A child sacrifice? In all Israel where is it done?"

"An abomination." Hosea ground the words out like the meshing of millstones.

"So I told the grandmother. Yet Beniah is bent on it."

"Come —" Hosea said abruptly. He wheeled toward the door, his face set, resolute.

Hosea and Odenjah walked westward from Samaria at a swift pace. Two hours from the city wall they came on a hilltop altar surrounded by seventy or eighty people. At the altar itself stood the priest.

"Is this how you worship the LORD?" Hosea said as he reached the inner edge of the crowd.

"What are you doing here?" the priest asked.

"I am a priest of the LORD."

"You cannot share in the ritual. This is my altar."

"I have not come to steal away your gifts," Hosea said with contempt. "Is a child to be sacrificed here this night?"

"These people have come to a rightful festival," the priest replied in strained tones.

"Is it rightful to take life which the LORD has given and sacrifice it to Baal? An abomination!" Hosea's eyes were strangely lit. Odenjah looked at him somewhat in wonder. He knew Hosea allowed only worship of the LORD at his altar, but he had never heard Hosea speak openly in such tones against Baal worship.

The man called Beniah stepped forward, challenging Hosea. "Hold your peace. The priest speaks truly, Hosea ben Beeri. This is a rightful festival. We know you to be a man of the LORD, but we must do what must be done. Three years our crop has been lost to hail. We can not again risk the anger of the Baal."

"There is your answer," said the priest.

"Is it now that you put your first trust in Baal, and not in the God of Israel?"

"Get on with it," Beniah said, looking away from Hosea.

"This altar lies under the curse of the LORD," Hosea cried out, sweeping his arm over the crowd. "Cursed be the man or woman who worships at this altar, cursed be his land, his flock, and his harvest. So the LORD has spoken!"

The crowd for a moment fell deathly silent, and then a low buzzing whispered through their midst.

"This man blasphemes!" the priest called out. "Bring forth the child."

Hosea and Odenjah faced the priest and the crowd of people.

"Bring it forth!" the priest repeated. "Will this man take away from you your just due from the Baal of his land?"

The woman who stood by Beniah stepped toward the fire, urged on by those who stood about her. In her arms she carried a babe.

"Hold your place," Hosea said sternly, moving toward the woman.

"Let her be," Beniah warned. "Your words we will not stop. But do not hinder us in our worship. The Baals must be satisfied. We know what must be done."

"Do you believe this child, thrown on the fire, will bring you the harvest?"

"Yes," Beniah answered.

"Nay, my son," said a woman of middle years, who stood close by, "the wine will turn sour in your mouth on the thought of the babe."

"Be silent, woman."

"The mother of your wife speaks truth," Hosea said.

Beniah looked from Hosea to his wife's mother, then to his wife, who only shook her head.

"Step back," he said stiffly.

"Give ear, Israel!" Hosea called out, raising his voice over the crowd. "As this child withers in the fire, so will the grape wither on the vine. No more is this an altar of the LORD, but an altar of sinning, so the LORD has spoken!"

A whispering went through the crowd of people. Beniah and his wife looked to the ground. This young priest spoke as one who knew the very thoughts of the LORD. Yet mixed with awe was honest doubt. "In three years," Beniah thought, "I have harvested a meager crop. Surely, in some way, I have displeased the Baal of my vineyard. If the LORD God of Israel has not protected me before, how can I expect His help now? The Baal rules in the vineyard. The Baal must be satisfied."

"The child must be sacrificed," he said.

"Come with me," Hosea challenged, his voice turning soft. "Come with me and worship the LORD God of Israel. He brings the harvest."

"These people are come to my altar. Go to your own," the priest hissed.

Hosea ignored the priest. Turning to the woman who held the babe, he said, "What of you? Is this the child of your flesh?"

"Yes," she whispered in fright.

"You would commit him to the fire?"

"It is a girl."

"The mother of sturdy children."

"We — we dare not displease the Baal."

"The LORD takes displeasure in your delay," the priest warned.

"If you commit your child to the fire, then you will bring on yourself the wrath of the LORD God," Hosea said sternly. "Come, bring the child and follow me."

"Your vines shall rot!" the priest said darkly.

"Come, all of you, down from this mountain. Evil dwells here, not God."

"Baal is the god of harvest," a man called out from the crowd. "We honor the LORD of the harvest."

"The LORD of hosts is LORD also of the harvest! Come," Hosea said to the woman who held the babe, "the LORD did not give you this child that you should commit murder against it."

"No, no," the woman cried. "It is not so!"

"If you go to the altar it will be so. Murder, knowing and willful, a sin against the LORD."

"Ben Appel, it is not so," the woman said desperately, turning to the priest.

"It is not so," the priest answered solemnly. He stepped past Hosea, taking courage in the woman's fright.

"Bring the child to the altar."

For a moment Hosea would have thrust the priest aside, but he held back. This struggle would not be settled with the arm of flesh.

"Bring the child," the priest repeated.

"Already I have seven children," the woman said to Hosea. "What shall we do if this year again we have a poor crop? Better this one should die, who does not know what it is to live, than all of us starve."

The crowd murmured agreement with the woman. "We must have crops or die!" shouted a high voice.

"Pray to the LORD. He will guard your crops."

"Baal is our lord!"

"Bring forth the child," the priest shouted, joining his voice to the rising agreement of the crowd.

The woman looked once more at Hosea, fearfully, and then stepped toward the stone altar on which burned the sacrificial fire.

"Israel has forgotten his Maker!" Hosea shouted. "Destruction is in the hand of the LORD!"

The crowd ignored his shouting, surged past him, and crowded around the fire. "To the lord of seed and harvest . . ." the priest began to chant.

Hosea cried out against the crowd, but his voice was lost in the voices of the people. They joined in the chanting of the priest. Then there was a sudden hush, a screaming, and the hiss of burning flesh.

"The days of punishment have come! The days of recompense are at hand!" Hosea shouted.

The crowd turned aside from the altar. For a moment there was silence, and then the sudden swish of wine from wine skins and the beginning of the festival dance.

Hosea had spoken more than he had thought to speak. The urge had come on him suddenly — to walk quickly into the countryside and intervene at another priest's altar. From childhood, abhorrence of child sacrifice stood like an armed sentinel over his thoughts; he believed as his father believed. Beeri would have counseled the way of quiet example, not harsh rebuke at the altar of another priest. Yet the urge to intrude at the altar of another priest had come on Hosea like a command of the LORD. He did not overhear the LORD speak words, as on other occasions. He felt a surge of anger. Words came almost unbidden to his lips, in the way Amos had told him. When the priest and his worshippers turned a deaf ear and went ahead with the sacrifice, the words left Hosea. He felt an aching emptiness within, and puzzlement, as though life had quickened for a moment within him and then died, leaving a painful trace of sorrow.

"Let us be gone," he said to Odenjah.

He strode from the fire with Odenjah at his side.

3

The guests who crowded into Diblaim's house for the wedding celebration proved a hardy lot. On the seventh day of the weeklong festivity, they showed little sign of wearying of Diblaim's hospitality.

The house was fested with palm branches and clusters of mountain berries. Servants moved among the guests with never ending trays of wine, yeast cakes, fish delicacies, olives, fruits, and assortments of meat. The dinner hall echoed to the soft plucking of harps. In and out of the house, and out into the garden, wedding guests milled about in brightly colored robes and gay headdresses, talked noisily, ate and drank their fill, and agreed together that Diblaim indeed hosted a festive wedding.

During the first two days, Gomer moved gaily among the guests, greeting all with eagerness and dignity. But as the celebration wore on, she began to weary of it. The customary tributes to the grace and beauty of the bride at first pleased her but soon became empty sound, only words.

She wanted now for it to be over. Three days would be celebration enough, she thought, as she stood listening to a woman who regaled her with stories of the eating habits of her second husband. Another woman joined them. Raising the sleeve of her gown to shield her words, she whispered advice on how to prepare a sauce that would slow Hosea's passion.

"You cannot imagine what animals they can be," the woman said. The other woman nodded agreement. Gomer lowered her eyes but paid them no heed. Her mother had instructed her at length, rehearsing ways to share pleasure with her husband. She longed now to go to her husband's house.

Across the room she caught Hosea's eye. He was surrounded by several older men, who laughed and slapped their thighs as they told him stories young husbands have always been told. Hosea looked longingly at Gomer, and her heart leaped to know that he, too, wished to be with her as she wished to be with him.

Hosea broke away from the circle of men and threaded through the crowd of guests toward the garden entrance. He motioned to Gomer, and she came toward him. They met by the entrance and touched hands. Gomer squeezed his fingers. Hosea glanced about then whirled Gomer through the archway and out onto the porch. For the moment, it was deserted. He caught her up in his arms and kissed her for the third time.

"Oh, my love," she sighed. "I am so weary of this."

"Tonight it ends."

"Yes, tonight. Oh, Hosea!"

She reached up about his neck until her feet left the ground and kissed him fiercely.

"I hate them," she said.

"They wish you well."

"But they keep me from you, and so I hate them. Whatever keeps me from you, I hate," she said with a toss of her head that swirled the hair about her neck.

All at once the voices within the house fell into a sudden hush. Hosea and Gomer looked at one another and moved to the archway. Just inside the main entrance of the house, attired in a robe of Tyrian purple and wearing a headdress set with seven great rubies, stood Zechariah, prince of Israel, the only son of King Jeroboam. Two soldiers stood behind him. At his side, wearing a red robe with a broad white girth about the middle, stood Shallum ben Jabesh, chief minister of the king.

By custom, the royal house was invited to every wedding in Israel, though their presence was rarely expected. Diblaim was ill prepared for the prince's arrival. He stumbled toward the door, bowing at every step and tripping over the feet of the astonished guests who had not the wit to clear a path for him.

"Prince Zechariah," he stammered, "I — I did not expect —"

"This is the house that celebrates the wedding of Hosea ben Beeri?" Zechariah asked, himself embarrassed by Diblaim's discomfort.

"It is, it is," Diblaim said. "He is wed to my daughter, Gomer." Diblaim turned around and looked wildly about the hall. "Gomer, Gomer!"

Gomer and Hosea stepped quickly in from the porch and made their way to the place where Diblaim stood.

"Yes, yes. This is she — my daughter, Gomer." Gomer bowed her head and lowered her eyes.

"You are indeed lovely," Zechariah said with little feeling.

"This is the bridegroom," Diblaim said, grasping Hosea's robe and half pulling him forward.

"Yes, I know," the prince replied. "Peace, Hosea ben Beeri. I wish you great happiness."

He walked to where Hosea stood and began to speak with him in a more personal way, indicating to the other guests that they might continue their festivities. A whisper went through the crowd. It was known that the prince was given to much talk and inquiry in religious matters. That he should attend this wedding feast spoke well of his feeling toward the young priest, who was known to be a follower of the prophet Amos.

Gomer stood by as Zechariah spoke with Hosea. It piqued her that the prince spoke only of religious matters and directed no words to her. By custom, a wedding guest paid greater attention to the bride than to the bridegroom.

When she turned away for a moment, she found the eyes of Shallum ben Jabesh resting on her. He had caught the resentment in her eyes and smiled at her attempt to hide it with a careless shrug. He moved closer and spoke low: "The prince does you little justice, calling you no more than 'lovely.'"

Gomer looked up at him. He is handsome, she thought. "Thank you," she said coolly, but she smiled as she spoke.

"I am the king's minister, Shallum ben Jabesh."

Gomer nodded and smiled once again.

"Do you find it warm?" he asked.

"Sir?"

Shallum nodded toward the porch. Gomer glanced at Hosea and Zechariah, still speaking intently with one another.

With a toss of her head she turned away and walked toward the archway with Shallum.

A few guests noticed them leave and leaned to whisper to one another. It was not uncommon at a wedding celebration for a bride to be free with male guests, or even to lie with them, during the seven days and nights of drinking and feasting.

On the porch Gomer and Shallum found themselves alone. The other guests had crowded inside at the arrival of the prince. The shadows of dusk were settling upon the city.

"Zechariah may keep your husband talking for hours," Shallum said carelessly. "He is that way in matters of religion."

"Oh?" Gomer spoke as though it mattered little to her.

"You wear a lovely gown."

Gomer turned her head and looked at him askance. It was her way to set a little distance between herself and a man, when the man intrigued her. He moved a step closer and put his hands on her shoulders.

"Yet the gown is not so lovely as the wearer."

He leaned down and touched his lips to her shoulder, then her neck. "Not so lovely by far," he whispered.

Gomer realized suddenly that he was going to kiss her. She knew that such things were done at wedding feasts, but she had spoken alone to no man in the seven days. She drew back, but he held her. He did not hurry. He lifted her head. His eyes were cool and self possessed. He took her lips in a quiet kiss.

"Sir —"

"Is it not the custom for the bride to give some pleasure to her guests?" Shallum asked, still holding her and looking down on her with a boldness that both flattered and frightened Gomer.

Gomer looked away. She dared not speak for fear she would betray herself. There had been a sudden thrill in his kiss.

He seemed to read her thoughts. His voice was low and smooth: "Our lips touch well together."

"You are free with another man's virgin bride," Gomer said weakly.

"No more than you yourself want."

He smiled and let his hands drop from her shoulders. There was something almost of scorn in his eyes, yet still he looked on her with that same boldness.

"Do not look on me so," Gomer said.

"If you would lead me to a darker place, our looking might give way to better things."

"Better that we go back to the house."

Gomer started away. Shallum held her by the arm. "Are you afraid?"

"I am not pleased."

"Many a bride would be pleased to lie with the king's minister."

"Not I."

"No?" Shallum shrugged indifferently. "I would teach you pleasures you will not learn from your husband."

Gomer pulled away and walked quickly into the house. Shallum's soft laugh trailed after her. Gomer returned to Hosea's side. He looked aside at her, frowning. When Shallum came back into the house, she could not look at him, though he continued to look on her.

Presently, the prince took his leave of Hosea. He thanked Diblaim for his hospitality and again paid respect to the beauty of the bride.

Gomer stole a glance at Shallum as he was leaving. She thought his back would be turned. He was looking directly back at her, waiting for her to look up. A smile touched his lips, then he followed Zechariah out of the house.

"Why did you go out with him?" Hosea asked, turning to Gomer. There was sharpness in his voice.

"He wanted to see the gardens."

"I liked not the way he looked on you, in leaving."

"It was nothing."

Hosea paused a moment, then nodded. "Strange —" he said, thinking on the prince once more, "he has many fears, for one so young — Zechariah."

"Hosea," Gomer said, suddenly gripping his arm, "Can we not leave?"

"Leave?" Hosea looked down into her strangely troubled eyes.

"The sun set some moments ago. It is the eighth day."

"I had forgotten," Hosea said, half laughing.

"Please —"

Suddenly Gomer wanted only to be away from this crowd of people, to be alone in the shelter of Hosea's embrace. The boldness of Shallum ben Jabesh frightened her more than she dared think. It was not his words, or the kiss, but the thought that part of her had wanted it. There had been a moment of desire.

Gomer had thought, as any young bride would think, that she must keep her husband from straying into the arms of another woman. But how much more evil if she should stray — if she should be unfaithful to Hosea. She clung to Hosea's arm, in sudden dread of her inconstant heart.

"Let us say goodbye to our fathers," Hosea whispered, "and then we shall leave." He took her trembling hand in his and led her through the crowd of people to where Diblaim and Beeri stood talking with one another. Hosea and Gomer spoke their farewells and began to make their way toward the gate leading into the city.

Anna saw them and raised a hand. She left the circle of women she was talking with and hurried over to them.

She embraced Gomer and said, "My daughter!" She looked Hosea full in the face. "My little girl is now a woman," she said. "May you find pleasure together." She stretched up and kissed Hosea on the cheek. "Be good to her, my son."

* * *

An hour later Gomer and Hosea sat across from one another in Hosea's small house. The door was closed. A lone lamp lit their table. They each held a small glass of wine. They sipped the wine slowly.

"We are alone," Gomer said, looking into her glass.

"Yes."

"I thought the seven days would never end."

"The longest week of my life."

Hosea moved his hand slowly across the table until it touched Gomer's fingers. She looked up, a shy smile on her lips.

"I love you, my husband."

"We have been long in coming to this day."

"Yes, long."

"Are you frightened?"

They did not speak for some moments. Then Gomer leaned forward and blew out the lamp.

"'Even if I walk in the valley of death, I fear no evil,'" Gomer said low and half laughing, playing on the words of King David's shepherd psalm, "if you are with me."

Hosea's hands trembled as Gomer rose to her feet. The fading light of dusk slanted through the window. Gomer was barely visible. Hosea stood up. She stepped toward him. She knew, now, what she must do. *You must both lead and follow,* her mother told her.

"My husband. Will you unclothe me?" She took his hand and led it underneath the fold of her robe. "The tie of my robe is here."

Hosea pulled the tie free. Gomer stepped back, shrugged free of her gown. It whispered over her skin and slid to the floor. She came to Hosea, just touching him with her nakedness.

"My husband, no man has ever known me. All that I have is for you, only for you."

She stepped away and went to the bed in the corner of the house. She drew a white cloth out of her bridal pack and spread it on the bed. "I lay me down on the blanket of my virginity."

Hosea came to the bed. In the last light of day he could no longer see her, only her form lying on the bed. She spoke up to him: "Come to me, my husband."

Hosea knelt beside her, reached out his hand. He touched her arm, ran his hand down and clasped her hand in his.

"My husband . . ."

"You like calling me 'my husband.'"

"I do like it! It is new and it is precious."

"My wife."

"My husband, make me your wife indeed."

Hosea leaned down and found her mouth in a lingering kiss.

Gomer rose to a half sitting position. *Come slowly to him. Speak but little. Explore him with your hands and your mouth. Find what gives him pleasure.* "I want to know you . . ." she whispered, her lips against his ear, "want to know what pleases you."

Hosea would have clasped her more closely, but she held him a little away. *Guide his touch, his kisses. Show him what gives you pleasure. His greatest pleasure comes in knowing he gives you pleasure.*

Slowly she guided and followed.

When they came together, Gomer gave a little cry and clutched herself to him. "Show me no pity, my husband, until you obtain the tokens of my virginity."

Some time later, Hosea bunched up the white cloth from their bed, with a small bloodstain on it, and threw it out the door, as was the custom. He returned to the bed. Gomer spoke in the darkness. "You give me great pleasure, my husband."

He sank beside her, taking her face between his hands. "*I* give *you* pleasure? 'Your lips distil nectar, my bride; honey and milk are under your tongue.'"

Gomer laughed low in her throat and answered with another word from Solomon's High Song, "'Your love is better than wine. O that you would kiss me with the kisses of your mouth!'"

* * *

At the beginning of the former rains, a dark-eyed child was born. According to custom, the child would be named on its eighth day, at the countryside altar. On the child's second day, as Hosea was stacking odd pieces of wood in the shed at the side of their house, he heard the notable Voice: *Call his name Jezreel; for yet a little while, and I will punish the house of Jehu for the blood of Jezreel, and I will put an end to the kingdom of the house of Israel. And on that day, I will break the bow of Israel in the valley of Jezreel.* The voice was familiar, the same he had overheard from childhood. But Hosea realized that the speaking was different. He was not overhearing the LORD speak in divine councils. The LORD was speaking to him directly and the words were a plain command, not poetic or mysterious.

Jezreel, the great valley to the north, in the tribe of Issachar, looking down toward the Jordan River — a name well known in Israel, but not for the naming of a child. In the valley of Jezreel Jehu spilled a river of blood when he overthrew the throne of Ahab more than a hundred years before.

The word was not veiled in picture or poetry. His son should be named according to a word of prophecy. The parting counsel of Amos came back to him: "Dark days lie ahead for Israel. Judgment, but not unto death . . . you He will bruise, but unto healing." Hosea's prophecy in Israel would be told not only in words. His life — and now the life of his family — would speak a message from the LORD.

When Diblaim and Anna came by a third time to see their grandson, Gomer and Anna were soon in a corner talking furiously with one another, Anna holding the baby. Anna was Gomer's mother, well enough, but also her confidante and best friend.

Gomer told her Hosea had received a word from the LORD, to name the child Jezreel. Gomer little liked the name. The general meaning was good enough — *God sows*. God had sown indeed, bringing them a son in their first year. Yet in the valley itself, the word had a second meaning, 'God scatters.' Hosea laughed that sowing and scattering were all one.

Gomer repeated the word Hosea had received from the LORD, word for word, as he had told it to her. To Gomer's surprise, Anna gave a sudden nod and said, "It is a good name, and a good omen: the blood shed by Jehu shall be avenged."

Gomer spoke, a question hanging in her voice, "Our grandmother . . ."

"Our grandmother, Jezebel. Jehu spilled her blood in Jezreel."

On the child's eighth day a small group gathered at Hosea's countryside altar. Hosea whispered into the child's ear, then raised him high and called out, "His name shall be Jezreel!"

chapter 13

The Plot of Shallum ben Jabesh

In the month following the olive harvest, Jeroboam died. His son, Zechariah, became the fourteenth king of Israel. He was the great-grandson of Jehu, who came to the throne of Israel a hundred years before with great shedding of blood on the plain of Jezreel. According to an ancient prophecy, the house of Jehu would fall in the fourth generation.

Shallum ben Jabesh had thought to gain influence in the palace at the death of Jeroboam. Seven years he had served as the king's first minister. He knew well the ways of governance. He planned that his counsel would direct the young Zechariah, who cared little for the day-by-day burden of ruling.

Yet, in the five months of his rule, Zechariah had steadfastly resisted Shallum's counsel. Shallum was in league with a party of wealthy merchants and landowners. They believed a treaty with Egypt would gain them rich trade opportunities and would offer protection against Assyria. While Jeroboam lived, Shallum said no word of such a treaty, nor let it be known that he was on close terms with those who sought it. He knew that Jeroboam little trusted the power of Egypt, and that he feared a rebellion within his army where such a course followed. When Jeroboam died, Shallum pressed Zechariah to enter into treaty with Egypt. Zechariah listened each day to the same demands, the same wheedling arguments, and each day he retired from Shallum's presence with an indifferent shrug and a promise to think on the matter.

Those who came to Zechariah with other demands received similar treatment. The constant play of pressure and cross-pressure within the palace wearied the young king. He soon learned that any choice he made brought opposition from another quarter. His answer was to make as few decisions as possible, for he disliked argument and strife.

It was this, perhaps, that led to his concern in religious matters. He seemed ever to be in search of a magic word that would wash away the struggle and ugliness of life.

Shallum chafed under Zechariah's indecision until at last he struck on a plan by which he might take matters into his own hands. The merchants and landowners of Samaria had paid him well for his influence with the king, and they were growing impatient.

"Shallum ben Jabesh, your seven years with Jeroboam left their mark." Shallum inclined his head, for he knew the high priest intended this as a tribute.

Anakah and Jeroboam had gotten on well together. Yet Shallum's proposal carried some weight of uncertainty. Shallum had come to the decision that only by seizing the throne for himself would he be able to carry out his plans for an alliance between Egypt and Israel. But if such a seizure were to stand, he would need the sanction of the high priest. He must be anointed in the Temple, amidst great pomp and ceremony. He had come to the high priest's chamber and with smooth words had drawn out Anakah's discontent with Zechariah. Nine times in the five months of Zechariah's rule Anakah had gone to him on matters of importance. Nine times Zechariah had done nothing. With well-chosen speech Shallum set his proposal before the high priest. Now he waited. Discontent with one's king might lead to grumbling. It would take something closer to hate for a man like Anakah to join in rebellion.

"How will you set Zechariah aside?" Anakah asked.

"There is but one way." Shallum made the motion of drawing a sword from its sheath.

"And what of the king's soldiers?"

"After the Feast of Dedication Zechariah travels to his summer house at Ibleam. Less than twenty soldiers will attend him. I will have a band of more than forty."

"So you would have me join hands with you in the murder of our king and pour the anointing oil on your head when the business is done?" He looked hard at Shallum, testing him.

"It is known that Zechariah cares more for any soothsayer or prophet who happens along than for the Temple and the established priesthood."

"That I know too well."

"Anoint me king, and the place that was yours under Jeroboam shall be yours again."

"What assurance do I have that you will not forget me, once you are king?"

Shallum shifted in his seat. He had known this question would come. His plan hinged on how Anakah would take to the answer he now proposed.

"Two weeks ago you came to the king in the matter of this young priest, Hosea."

"Yes," Anakah said with bitterness.

"What satisfaction did he give you?"

"Satisfaction! What satisfaction does he ever give? Nothing, nothing!"

"This Hosea took away from your Temple the young girl who was to be high priestess."

"Yes, and no one raised a hand to stop him. This legend of him and the Ammonites has made him a god. No one dares cross his path. He came here with a young man who comes from the same village as our high priestess. It seems the two were lovers, or there had been some talk of betrothal between them. He pled his cause with Hosea to have her released so they could wed. Hosea forced his way into the chamber where she is kept in seclusion until the Dedication and carried her off. We had to dedicate a second woman, who is no match in beauty. And now this mad priest preaches that the Feast of Dedication is an abomination before the LORD."

"So I have heard."

"I laid it before the king. This challenges the very life of the Temple — of the kingdom. And what did he answer? 'I see no cause for alarm.' A sixth of our Temple offerings come in at the Feast of Dedication, and he sees no cause for alarm!"

"If I told you I would silence Hosea, would you join your hand with mine in putting Zechariah aside?"

"How am I to know you would keep your word? The man is gaining a following. People listen to his words. You may choose to throw your lot in with him once I have served your purpose."

Shallum stood up from his seat and walked slowly across the room. He stopped and fingered a tapestry of Egypt, showing the daughters of Pharaoh bathing in the Nile.

"Tell me, Anakah," he said slowly, "what do you think would happen if this young priest were killed?"

"Again, how do I know you would keep your word?"

"But if I did?"

"Then it would be well."

Shallum whirled and faced Anakah squarely. "No, Anakah, it would not be well! Two years ago Amos of Judah came to Samaria and set all Israel in commotion. We hounded him out of Samaria, and he went to Bethel. Amaziah sent him from Bethel, and we thought Israel was well rid of him. Now what has happened? This Hosea, who was his follower, has risen up in his place. Already they are calling him a prophet, for his condemnation of Baal worship and the harlots in the Temple. His following is said to be as great as Amos. You say kill him. Do you know what would happen? Another would rise up in his place, more dangerous still. Prophets have a way of coming to life again in their followers. Kings can be killed. Prophets must be silenced."

"How silence him, except by killing? He listens to no man."

Shallum spoke each word slowly: "I will silence him with laughter."

"Laughter?"

"Yes, laughter and ridicule. Tell me, Anakah, how long will the people listen to a man preach against Temple harlots if his own wife plays the harlot?"

"The wife of Hosea?"

"Yes."

"You would have her play the harlot to sully his words?"

"That is my plan."

Anakah twirled his beard between his fingers. "Can it be done?"

"We two met at their wedding feast less than two years past. She was much taken with me."

"You yourself would have her?"

"I know of no other she would have so willingly."

Anakah laughed aloud. "Now I think you are something more than Jeroboam. The plan has wit about it."

"Are we agreed, then?"

"Yet still I ask, how do I know you will keep your word?"

"The Festival of Dedication comes in two weeks time. I will have the matter done before that day — before I follow Zechariah to Ibleam — before you anoint me king. It is I who should ask proof of you."

"You make a good bargain, Shallum ben Jabesh."

"Is it agreed?"

"By the LORD of the earth, it is agreed."

Chapter 14

Gathering Clouds

Hosea's father and sister, Beeri and Shania, and childhood friend, Obed, betrothed to Shania, had come from Dothan to Hosea and Gomer's wedding festival. Twice Shania and Beeri had visited Hosea and Gomer in Samaria, but Gomer had not yet visited in Dothan. In three weeks time Shania and Obed were to wed. Hosea and Gomer planned to go to Dothan for one or two days of the celebration.

Two days before Sabbath, shortly before noonday, when she was about to lie down for a rest with Jezreel, Gomer answered a knock at the door. Obed stood outside. Gomer received him into the house warmly.

"I bear a peculiar request from Shania," he said.

"What is it?" Gomer asked, immediately interested.

Obed explained that Shania's mother was no longer alive, and her older sister lived far away in Judah. Shania had no woman to help her get ready for the wedding. Would Hosea allow Gomer to travel back to Dothan with Obed and be like an older sister to Shania these three weeks?

"How beautiful!" Gomer said. She remembered how tirelessly her mother had managed all the preparations for her wedding with Hosea. "I will go with you," she said at once.

"It will be well with Hosea?"

"For his favorite sister? I should think so!" Gomer returned gaily. "I will go next door and leave word for Hosea with Deborah. We can start at once."

Gomer bound Jezreel in a sling across her bosom and walked beside Obed at a brisk pace. She thought it a splendid adventure, going to help Shania like an older sister. After two hours Obed suggested they stop and rest, but Gomer insisted she was not in the least weary. They arrived in Dothan before sunset.

Shania embraced Gomer warmly. "What a dear sister, to come so quickly," she exclaimed. An hour later, when Beeri returned to the house, he found them talking and planning at high tempo.

In the days that followed, Shania and Beeri waited each morning for Gomer to order the events of the day. Neither of them knew Gomer's mother well, but in Gomer they were watching Anna at work. Beeri sprang into service for the smallest task, happy that someone in the house knew what needed to be done. Gomer arranged times for private talk with Shania.

"Dear sister," Gomer said on the third day, when the two of them were alone in Beeri's olive orchard, "have you ever known a man?"

"Known a man?" Shania whispered back, in shock. "In the body, you mean?"

"Yes."

"Oh Gomer, never."

"I thought as much, but these are disorderly days. So you come a virgin to Obed's bed, as I came a virgin to your brother's bed."

"Oh yes!" Shania cried, suddenly embracing Gomer. She drew back, still holding Gomer. "But I know so little. Mother died — she never spoke to me . . ."

Gomer sat down on the ground by the trunk of an olive tree and motioned Shania to join her. She remembered what her mother had told to her, and told the same to Shania, changing hardly a word. *You must both lead and follow.*

"Oh Gomer, will it go well with us?"

"Why should it not go well?"

"We are so different — I am taller by a cubit."

Gomer laughed and kissed Shania on the cheek. "Have no fear. You will come together well. He will lie between your breasts."

Gomer planned the wedding festival to last three days.

"Seven days is too long," she explained to Shania and Beeri, and to Hosea when he arrived a day before the celebration. "Too long for the Bride and Bridegroom to wait," she added with a laugh, "and too long to overfeed and overdrink all of Dothan. Let them go home and break open their own wineskins."

Hosea and Gomer returned to Samaria two days after the wedding festival. Hosea smiled at Shania and Gomer whispering together before they left and thought it a glad happening that each had found a sister in the other.

* * *

The evening meal was finished. Hosea lay on a mat on the housetop, watching the sun sink slowly beneath the wall of the city. The breeze from the north was warm and spring-laden. A new season would soon be born.

Three years, Hosea was thinking. Three years since the voice of Amos first thundered over Samaria.

In the past weeks, Hosea had thought much about worship in Israel — festivals and new moons, rituals of offering and sacrifice, rites of fertility. He had come to think that more evil lay rooted here than even Amos had said.

As ever it was with Hosea, understanding began not in hard thought but in events that stirred his heart. Some months before, Jacob, a young man from Tirzah, had come to his altar and told him that his betrothed had been chosen to become high priestess of the Temple in Samaria.

Such an honor could not lightly be refused. The prosperity of all Israel hung on the rituals of the planting season, so it was believed. If a family refused their daughter to the Temple, and a crop were lost, the name of the family would become a curse in the land.

Jacob had proposed a betrothal agreement for the girl before she was chosen to become high priestess. He sought out Hosea in despair, declaring that it was well agreed by both families that the two would wed. Then came the call from the Temple in Samaria. It stirred memories of Johanna and the heartbreak Hosea felt when she went to the Temple at Joppa. When he learned the girl had gone to the Temple against her will, Hosea suddenly put on a cloak and said he would see the girl released.

Together with Jacob he went to the Temple. It was rumored afterward that he had knocked two guards against the wall until they could no longer stand, in order to force entrance into the chamber where the girl was kept. In truth, the two guards stepped aside and made no protest when they saw who he was.

Hosea took the lovers to his own house. Gomer harbored some misgivings about Hosea's clash with the Temple in Samaria. Would it threaten their life and livelihood? When Gomer saw how the frightened girl clung to her young man, she bit her lower lip, a childhood habit when she set herself to do something new or unexpected. She reached out to embrace and comfort the girl.

"Let them find another girl for the Temple!" Gomer announced boldly. "Have no fear. My husband will protect you."

The girl, Rachel, was tiny, almost childlike, and stunningly beautiful. When evening came, Gomer drew Rachel to her own bed. "Rachel can sleep with me, with Jezreel between us. She will be a mother in Israel. Let her have a taste." Gomer drew a coverlet over them. Rachel reached out and drew Jezreel close to herself.

"Thank you," she whispered to Gomer. "You know what is good better than I."

The following day Hosea walked with them to their home in Tirzah, a morning's walk east of Samaria. He asked to speak privately with Rachel's father: "I took your daughter from the Temple," he said bluntly. "Jacob said there was a betrothal agreement between your two families, that he and Rachel have pledged themselves to one another."

The father nodded. He stood in some awe of this priest who slew the Ammonites. "They have grown up together, like brother and sister."

"It pains me none to take her from the Temple. It is ugly worship there. You are her father. I ask only that you bethink yourself, as a son of Israel, concerning your daughter and the young man, Jacob."

"The word from the Temple was strong."

"I well believe it. They think to drown out the truth of the LORD with their loud cries and warnings."

"It is no small thing to refuse her to the Temple."

"It is more holy unto the LORD for Rachel to become a mother in Israel than a priestess in Samaria."

It surprised Hosea himself that he could speak with such certainty concerning the LORD's will in the matter, yet such was his feeling. He and Rachel's father spoke on for some time. In the end, the father allowed that the two should wed if the two of them, and Rachel's mother, agreed on it.

* * *

In the days that followed, the feeling grew that more lay at issue in this event than a young man and a young woman. Something corrupt lay in the very rite of worship when the act of love was taken from the marriage bed and made into a spectacle — lust and reveling and adultery turned into acts of worship. How could such worship take place in Israel? It was the worship of Baal, not worship of the LORD. This he knew from childhood, growing up in the house of Beeri, but now it was no longer only for himself and his altar.

In the days of King Ahab, the prophet Elijah had called Israel to choose between the LORD and Baal: *"How long will you go limping with two different opinions? If the LORD is God, follow Him; but if Baal, then follow him."*

This melting together of Baal-worship and LORD-worship was the root evil. His father believed so. At his own countryside altar, Beeri turned away all worship of Baal as a quiet example of righteousness. For Hosea, the boundary between his own altar and all Israel was crumbling away. He knew the task he faced. More and more openly he set himself against the worship of Baal. He might as easily tell Israel that sleeping and eating were an abomination before the LORD, so deeply did the fear and worship of Baal grip the people.

Yet, like Amos before him, Hosea felt the impulse of a divine call, too strong to be denied. It was not yet laid straight away before him, as with Amos. Yet it was strong. As it took hold on him, Hosea began more and more to raise his voice, not only at his own countryside altar, but in the gate and market place of Samaria, calling the people to turn from Baal and worship the LORD God of Israel alone.

Chapter 15

Gomer the Wife

"What are you thinking about, lying up here so quietly?"

Gomer appeared suddenly above the parapet of the house-top, standing on the ladder that led up from the ground.

"I am thinking about this land of ours."

Gomer jumped onto the housetop and walked over to where Hosea lay. "What land of ours? Have you bought some land?"

"No, no — our land of Israel."

"Oh, that. Well, it is not all ours, though we would be rich if it were." She laughed and sank to her knees beside her husband.

"Were you hiding from me?" she asked.

"No."

"I could not find you at once. I thought you had gone to a neighbor's."

"I came here after our meal."

"I would be angry if you had gone to a neighbor."

"Why?"

"I want you all alone. Kiss me."

She leaned down and touched her mouth to his. He held her by the shoulders, lightly.

"Do you still desire me, my husband — after many nights together, these two years?"

"If you stay with me until the day's light no longer betrays us to our neighbors, I will show you —"

Gomer lay down close beside him in the curl of his arm. She ran her hand inside his robe, against his chest, and with her teeth she bit lightly his ear and then his neck.

"Always you must bite," he said.

"They are love-bites."

Suddenly a loud voice called out from a neighboring housetop. It was Deborah, the wife of Ebarth the carpenter, who lived in the next house.

"Hello across the way! It is a nice evening to be up. How have you been? What are you doing?"

"What are we doing?" Gomer muttered. "What does she think? I would like to give her a bite, and not a love-bite."

"She has a good heart."

"Yes, and double-good eyes, for seeing what goes on in every house but her own."

"Hello!" Deborah said again. "I see you there. Are you sleeping?"

Hosea sat up. "We are up enjoying the warm breeze."

"It is pleasant indeed."

"What are you up enjoying?" Gomer asked pointedly.

"Well, I am getting too old to enjoy what you enjoy," Deborah said with a laugh. She had a blunt and cheerful way that most often made her dear to Gomer. In their two years as neighbors, she had become something like a second mother; she cheerfully looked after Jezreel when Gomer had an errand or went to the market. Yet Deborah did have an irksome way of keeping watch on their lovemaking, always seeming to know when Hosea had come to Gomer's bed or Gomer to his. If Hosea and Gomer would be apart for more than a few days, Deborah would begin to ask questions and offer advice.

"How is little Jonathan?" Gomer asked, more friendly.

Hosea had come home two weeks before and found the house empty. He had walked across Samaria, thinking Gomer had gone to her father's house. He found her at last next door, in the house of Ebarth and Deborah, whose youngest son, Jonathan, had fallen ill with a fever. Gomer sat beside his bed, wiping his face with a wet cloth. She had been at his side the daylong. She told Hosea she would stay through the night so Deborah and Ebarth could rest.

"I thought Jonathan was up here," Deborah said. "He should stay close to the fire until the fever has been gone a week. I came up to get him. He must have gone across to Zebulun's." Deborah had five sons still at home — the oldest just past fifteen, the youngest, little Jonathan, now in his sixth year.

"Peace to Ebarth," Hosea said.

"Oh peace, peace," Deborah said. "I am leaving you alone."

She threw her leg over the parapet and disappeared down the ladder on the far side of her house.

"I will set the ladder down," she called out, "so the boys will not be up and down, making a bother."

Hosea laughed a little. "She is ever concerned for our bedding together."

"Yes, and most time I like it little. It is no fair concern of hers."

They lay down together once again.

"Are you cold, my Gomer? Your hand is chill."

"Let me warm it in you."

She put her hand again within his robe, and her other about his neck. "Make me warm," she said. "Tell me again you love me."

He pulled her close against him, and kissed her. They lay for some time thus. "Oh, my dearest heart," Gomer whispered, "I must be so sure, so very sure of your love. I forget if you do not tell me of it each moment." She held his head on her breast as a mother holds a child. Never in her life had Gomer known such moments of contentment as she had found in the arms of this strong man. In one moment he could rouse her to passion with his kisses, and in the next he would quiet her to such an ecstasy of peacefulness, as at this moment, that tears of happiness welled in her eyes.

151

"The sun is well down," she said after a while.

"Yes."

"You are lost in your thoughts again. What do you think?"

"I think how little this land of Israel cares for her LORD."

"That is much in your thoughts since you took the girl Rachel from the Temple."

"It is not the one girl only. Why must any in Israel worship thus with feasting and reveling as we do? We did none of it in the wilderness."

"Neither did we raise grain and grape and olive in the wilderness."

"Yet the LORD provided."

"The Baals have provided us well. Our fields give good yield and our vines hang full. When has Israel known better days?"

"Ah, that is ever the cry," Hosea said with some feeling, half rising up. "'Baal has given us the grain and grape and olive' — yet who can say that it is not the LORD?"

"Sh —" Gomer pulled him back toward her. "It is time for other things than preaching."

"This is what the priests of the Temple say against me — the same words."

"I was only making talk. I know nothing of such matters."

"Yes, but it is rooted so in our hearts, deep rooted."

"Nay, I have but one thing deep rooted in my heart." Gomer drew him back to the sleeping mat and kissed him lingeringly on the mouth. "There is my answer to such questions," she said.

Hosea half smiled, and tousled her hair with his fingers. "That is your answer for all questions."

Gomer laughed low in her throat. "Give me reply, my husband."

"Think you we —"

"Sh — not words — here and here and here." She led his hand to touch her. "Give me no words but those whispered down on my ear."

Darkness settled on the city. Gomer and Hosea still lay on the housetop when a knocking came at the door, below.

"Is that on our house?" Gomer whispered.

"Yes."

"Who would come at such an hour?"

The knock came again, louder.

"He will wake Jezreel," Gomer said. "He has been fitful with me all day."

Hosea rose up and went to the edge of the housetop.

"Who is there?"

"Is this the house of Hosea ben Beeri?" a man's voice called up.

"Yes, I am Hosea ben Beeri."

"May I speak with you?"

"The hour is late. Who are you?"

"I am Menahem ben Gadi. We met one time in Bethel."

"Menahem, the captain?"

"Yes."

"Wait there a moment." Hosea went back to Gomer. "It is a captain in the king's army, the one who took Amos to Amaziah in Bethel."

"Is he come for you?" Gomer asked, suddenly anxious.

"I think not. He is alone, and he was friendly toward Amos. I will go down and speak with him."

"Come back to me on the housetop. I want to stay all night with you here."

"It will be cold before morning."

"Bring us blankets."

"Will you be warm while I am gone?"

"Memories warm not for long," Gomer laughed. "Hurry back to me."

Chapter 16

Gomer Goes Aside

1

I climbed down the ladder and met Menahem at the door. We exchanged greetings in half whispers. Inside, I struck a flint to tinder and lit a lamp. We sat down on the far side of the room from where Jezreel lay sleeping.

"What brings you to see me at this hour?" I asked.

"My visit is better kept secret. My presence in Samaria is not known. I came to ask something of you."

"What is that?"

"There is trouble afoot in Israel. Since the death of Jeroboam, a group favoring alliance with Egypt has been gaining influence with the king. The first minister is in league with them, Shallum ben Jabesh."

"What is this to me?"

"Alliance with Egypt is folly. Those who favor it, landowners and merchants, think only of trade advantages and the smaller army they think they will have to support, with Egypt on our side. Egypt is a hollow reed. Her armies are nothing. Assyria is our danger, and Israel must prepare to meet the danger alone."

"You think my words would be more listened to than those of Amos? He said the same."

"I think not on your words with the people, rather the word you could say to the king. It is known that he hangs on your words."

"The king hangs on many words but he does none of them."

155

"If you go to him and warn him against the Egyptian party, he would listen. He does not listen to the army."

I shook my head. "I will tell you something. Zechariah has come twice to my house, dressed in common clothing for disguise, and asked me for some word from the LORD. Yet he shook his head at every word I spoke — this word would stumble against one party, that word would be an offense to another faction. He seeks one word that all Israel will take well to, and there is no such word."

Menahem hit his fist against his thigh. "If he does not gird the army for Assyria, there will be one word in all Israel — exile."

"So did Amos prophesy, and so it will be, if Israel does not return to her LORD."

"We need army!"

"Yes, but army alone will not save Israel. Israel is no match for Assyria on the battlefield unless the LORD be with her, as He was in the day of Joshua."

Menahem stood up and paced across the room, hands clenched behind his back. "What you say, I know too well. Assyria is strong and grows stronger. If I myself were king, I know not how Israel would fare."

"There is a rottenness in the land," I said. "I myself am only beginning to see how deep it goes, yet I know it lies close to the heart of Israel's sickness — a worship corrupt and unclean —"

Menahem broke in suddenly, his voice tense: "Can you say nothing to the king that will avail?"

"He would listen and do nothing. Yet even if he would give ear, I could not say to him what you would say. It is Israel herself that must be girded, not only her army. The army cannot be strong if worship is corrupt."

"I am too long a soldier to put my trust in sacrifice and ritual."

"Nay, but in the LORD."

Menahem shook his head. He walked slowly to the door and set his hand to the latch. "I had hoped we might avail something with the king. Now I know not. These are dark days for Israel."

When Menahem had left, I sat for a time in the flickering light of the lamp, thinking on the things we had spoken.

"Our understanding is darkened," I mused. "There is no knowledge of God to lighten the land."

I laid a blanket over Jezreel, tucking it close about his little head. I thought on the child's name, 'God sows.' Yet how dark a prophecy lay hidden in the name. An enemy from the east would be met by Israel's army in the valley of Jezreel, and there Israel's blood would flow.

When I returned to the housetop, Gomer had fallen asleep. I covered her and lay down at her side, but for a long time I did not fall asleep.

2

"Hello. You are the wife of Hosea, the priest, are you not?"

Gomer was on the circular steps that led down to the well of Samaria. She set her water jar down and looked back over her shoulder. At the top of the steps stood Shallum ben Jabesh. He had waited in the shadow of a nearby building for three hours; he had learned that she came to draw in late afternoon.

"Yes."

"Now I see your face, I would have no need to ask." Shallum walked down to where Gomer stood. "I am Shallum ben Jabesh."

"Yes, I know who you are."

"You remember me?"

"Yes." Gomer blushed and looked down. Her heart was beating fast, and there was a trembling in her limbs.

"I was on my way to your house. May I carry your jar for you?"

"It is not yet filled."

"I shall fill it for you."

He picked up the jar, and they went down to the well, Gomer leading.

"I know not if my husband is yet home," Gomer said, hoping to hide her unease by turning to the purpose of his trip, which must be to speak with her husband, so she thought.

"I can wait. I found myself free of duties this afternoon. That is why I came myself, rather than send a messenger."

"How came you by the well? It is out of the way from the palace."

"Yes, and so it is. Yet I came on you, so my journey is well rewarded."

Again Gomer flushed. She took the jar from Shallum and lowered it into the well. When she pulled it up, he took it from her. For a moment their hands touched on the jar.

"You tremble," he said quickly.

Gomer drew her hand back slowly. When she looked up at him from lowered eyes, he was smiling. She smiled in return.

He is indeed handsome, Gomer thought.

They walked back up to the street and headed across the city toward Hosea's house. On the way, Shallum told her the purpose of his visit. The king, he said, had bought a new vineyard outside Samaria. Two evenings hence was to be a ceremony of dedication, to assure the first crop. Certain high-ranking families were given special invitation to attend the ceremony, and the king had made mention of Hosea.

In actual truth, the king had owned the vineyard more than nine months. The thought of a dedication ceremony had never come to him, until Shallum suggested it. Yet it was the kind of thought Zechariah would take to, as Shallum knew. Shallum told the young king he would make all arrangements, and he and Shallum parted on better terms than for some time.

To all other guests Shallum sent a messenger. To the one guest for whom the celebration was in truth planned, Shallum had come himself.

As they walked along, no word was spoken of their meeting at the wedding feast two years before. Yet it hung between them, unspoken, a quiet uneasiness, but also excitement.

Hosea stood in the doorway of the house when they returned. Gomer was laughing at something Shallum had said and touched his arm in her impulsive way. When she saw Hosea, she at once turned sober, and her eyes shifted away from his. Hosea frowned. It was not the custom for a man and woman to walk abreast of one another in the street.

Shallum explained his visit to Hosea and took his leave.

"I like him not," Hosea said.

"Why?"

"There is something too honeyed about him."

"You are jealous," Gomer said, laughing.

"Jealous?"

"Yes, because he carried my water jar."

"Jealous I am not — not while I alone carry *you.*"

He swung her up in his arms and carried her laughing and protesting into the house.

Deborah called across from her doorway: "You forgot your water jar in the street."

Gomer ran outside and picked it up, made a wry face at Deborah, and ran back into the house.

All evening and the day following a strange excitement possessed Gomer. She flitted about the house, never finishing one task before she began another. She sang and hummed to herself, which was not her way. When Deborah came across, she talked on so that Deborah could scarce get in a word. When Hosea came near her, she would slip teasingly away from him. In the evening she talked and laughed when he tried to caress her, so he did not come to her bed. She kept herself from any quiet moment when she might bethink herself.

* * *

The king's vineyard lay west and south of Samaria. One must go out the east gate and circle the city to arrive at it. A stone altar had been raised in the center of the vineyard. Fires were set in a circle around it. At sundown, on the night of dedication, the fires were lit.

Shallum had seen that word of the ceremony was spread through the city. More than seven hundred people, besides those invited by name, wound their way around the city wall to the king's vineyard. Sixty standing jars of wine stood in rows, a short way from the altar. The king's musicians were at hand with timbrel, harp, and sistrum. Harlots from the Temple mingled among the people. The dedication of the king's vineyard was to be a festive occasion. Anakah himself was to minister at the altar.

Anakah began the ceremony with a wailing chant, calling upon the LORD of the ground to receive their worship. The people swayed to his chanting and sang back the mournful refrain. When the chant was done, a young bull was slain and burned on the altar. The meat of the sacrifice was passed among the people and eaten, and the drinking of wine began.

Gomer and Hosea sat together not far from the altar. The high priest came up to them, bowed, and exchanged indifferent words with Hosea. Gomer listened and smiled when the high priest looked at her, but her eyes kept glancing away, scanning the crowds of people that milled around them, moving in and out among the grape arbors.

"Why is he so sweet mouthed with me this night?" Hosea asked when the high priest had left.

"He wants to be friends with you."

"He knows I took the girl from the Temple and spoke out against the Festival of Dedication — he should have little friendliness toward me."

"Hosea, you are glum as a mourner!" Gomer said. "This is a festive celebration. Here, drink with me."

Hosea took the wine without speaking and drank it slowly. Something in this night disturbed him, but he knew not what.

Some time later Gomer and Hosea were standing by one of the wine jars, talking with another priest and his wife. Shallum came up at their side. He touched Gomer's arm ever so lightly, and they exchanged a glance before he spoke to the others. "Peace, and I hope you are well," he said. "Is the wine to your taste?"

"Peace. All is well," Hosea answered shortly.

Shallum looked aside at the other priest, lifted his eyebrows, and said nothing. The priest caught his meaning. He coughed uneasily and took his leave with some mumbled words to Gomer and Hosea.

"This wine is not our best," Shallum said. "Would you come and have something better with me?"

For a moment Hosea did not answer. He looked at Shallum, as though waiting for him to speak something further. Then he said, "We have had enough."

"It is the finest in the kingdom."

"We want none," Hosea said, looking to the ground.

"Hosea." Gomer's voice sounded low at his side, reproving his rudeness.

"I would think myself selfish drinking it alone — you are sure?"

Hosea glanced up, but said nothing.

"You?" Shallum inclined his head to Gomer.

She bit her lower lip. "Yes. I will have some," she said with sudden determination. "I am thirsty."

Shallum showed no expression but merely nodded and motioned with his hand: "The king set it in the west arbor for his personal guests."

Gomer started to go. Hosea took her arm, firmly. "I want to go," she said.

"We are soon leaving."

"I want some wine." She glared at Hosea, hot and defiant.

Hosea turned to Shallum. "Another time."

Shallum shrugged his shoulders and departed.

"You made me low before him!" Gomer burst out.

"Yes, and you so far forgot yourself to go openly against your husband."

"What would be amiss in a drink of wine? This is a festal celebration."

"I do not like the man."

"Oh, you do not like the man! You like nothing tonight." Gomer tossed her head and turned away from Hosea.

Presently the harps and timbrels and sistrums struck out the slow rhythm of the ritual dance, which portrayed the love of Ashtarte for Baal. Twelve harlots of the Temple began the dance before the people, a slow languid swaying of the body, the feet scarcely moving at all.

As the tempo quickened, the dancers moved out among the people. Crowds formed around each one, clapping to the music. The dancers grew more impassioned, called for faster rhythms. Women began to join in the dancing and were urged on by the clapping and shouting of the men. Here and there a woman would single out one man and dance around him in a circle, until at last she let herself come close enough for him to grasp her.

In one circle a Temple harlot danced challengingly up to Hosea. He was the only person who stood silent in the group that surrounded her, neither clapping nor shouting. The harlot began to dance around him, slowly. The people caught her purpose and clapped louder. Gomer laughed and clapped with the others.

The harlot had a proud tilt to her head. She well knew the allure of her body. Her movements were sure and skillful. Not without cause, a sought-after woman in the Temple.

Hosea shifted uncomfortably.

"Let us be gone from here," he said, reaching for Gomer's arm.

Gomer stepped back from him, laughing. Clapping her hands over her head, she began to dance before him, together with the harlot. The crowd shouted and clapped their hands and called for the music to play faster.

Around and around him they danced, faster and faster. Hosea's face had gone sober, and his eyes flashed anger. He reached out to take hold on Gomer, but the harlot slid in front, and took hold on his arms. They fell back against the crowd together.

Gomer laughed and danced on alone in the middle of the circle. She pretended a haughty look at Hosea, standing by the harlot, and made to find some man she would dance with. Two other women stepped into the circle and began to dance, then three more. An excitement took hold on the crowd. The music played faster; more joined in the dance. Gomer found herself caught up in a swirl of clapping hands and dancing feet. Hosea was lost from sight. The music played so fast she could scarce keep her feet. Near the edge of the crowd she whirled around and came suddenly face to face with Shallum ben Jabesh.

He took her by the waist, lifted her up, and whirled her around and around until she fell breathless and laughing against his chest.

"Oh stop, stop," she pleaded. "I can not dance another step."

For a moment they stood together. She could feel his heart beating against her.

She looked up at him, and there was fire and desire in his eyes. He held her arms in a hard grip. Then suddenly she broke away from him, and she was running through the vineyard, laughing, and he was following her.

At a terebinth tree near the north edge of the vineyard he caught her. She leaned against the tree, breathless and exhausted. They were laughing together. He leaned his hands against the tree, holding her between them. Then there was a moment of terrible quiet. He took her in his arms. His face was close to hers, but he did not move closer. Her arms went around his neck. She drew his head down and pressed her mouth to his mouth.

"Come," he whispered.

She made no protest. She followed him toward the edge of the vineyard. Off to one side they heard a woman's soft laughing and something spoken low by a man, and then silence. Coming around a tree they nearly stumbled over two people, lying together in close embrace.

"Everyone has the same thought," Gomer whispered to herself.

At the edge of the vineyard was a thick hedge, nearly the height of a man. Shallum showed her through a narrow opening, and they found themselves in a small garden. Shallum stood behind her. His hands rested on her arms.

"Gomer."

It was the first time he had spoken her name. She could not answer. Her knees trembled beneath her. From the first word she spoke with him at the well, she had known this time would come — had wanted it to come, though she dared not think it.

His hands slid around her and held against her bosom. She put her own hands over his, pressing them closer. His lips were on her neck and shoulder, burning. Slowly he turned her in his arms. His fingers, steady and calm, loosed her robe.

She bit her lower lip, her longtime habit when she braved a new adventure. She knew: with a man, you must both lead and follow.

Chapter 17

Gomer Discovered

1

Two hours before sunset on the day of the Festival of Dedication, Shallum stood before a band of men in the cellar of an inn, near the east wall of Samaria. Posted at the doorway to the cellar were four men of the king's army, trusted cohorts of Shallum. Forty men squatted in front of him, recruited in the back streets of the city. "A quick earning for a day's work, a shade beyond the law," they had been told.

Such men were easy to come by in Samaria.

Shallum flung a pouch of silver into their midst. "Two shekels of silver for each man, and double that when the business is done."

"What is the duty, friend?"

"Murder," Shallum said evenly.

"He must be a high-born creature to have his life weigh in at two hundred forty shekels of silver. Who is the man?"

"The king of Israel," Shallum answered.

"Oh!"

"You said nothing of the king," a slight-built man exclaimed.

"What is the king to you? What are any of you but dung on his feet? When tomorrow's work is done Israel will have a new king, and I do not forget my friends."

"You take the throne yourself?" another asked.

"Yes."

"This is more than I bargained for," the slight man said.

He made for the door of the cellar. The soldiers stepped together and blocked his way.

"Hold him," Shallum said sharply.

Shallum drew his sword. Two of the soldiers held the man fast between them. With no word spoken, Shallum plunged his sword low into the man's belly and cut violently up.

A gasp burst from the group, as from a single man. Shallum turned on them. "You knew the bargain when you came — 'a shade beyond the law.' Your lot is thrown in with me, however you choose to regard it."

"What of the king's bodyguard?" a man ventured.

"The king leaves in the morning for Ibleam. He is attended by less than twenty soldiers. You thirty-nine and I will be at Ibleam to greet him when he arrives."

Shallum roved his eyes over the men squatting on the floor before him. Every eye was fastened on him. He smiled and thought to himself that the slight built man had served a good purpose. No man would challenge his commands.

"We have no weapons. The king's soldiers will be armed," a man said in respectful voice.

"You will be armed when the time comes. Meantime, you will not leave this cellar until we depart the city. Our acquaintance is yet short. I would not have word of our plans leak out. My soldiers will keep you company."

He stepped over the body of the man who was killed and spoke low with his soldiers. "We leave three hours past sunset, in scattered groups of four or five, so our going will not arouse suspicion."

"You will return, or do we meet you outside the city?"

"Nay, I will return as soon as our business is complete."

"What remains to be done?"

"I have yet a bargain to keep with the high priest."

* * *

Toward sunset a wind blew in from the west. The sky lowered and grew dark. Torches were lit in the Temple. Great crowds had gathered for the Festival of Dedication. The ritual was soon to begin.

Down the steps of the Temple hurried the figure of Odenjah. He crossed the street to where Hosea stood waiting beside the cart of a fruit vendor.

"I think the time is right," he said, a little out of breath. "The high priest has come to his seat."

Hosea nodded, and they walked toward the Temple. Ever since he had taken the vowed high priestess from the Temple and raised his voice in condemnation of the Festival of Dedication, Hosea knew this day would come. Yet only in this moment did the full weight of it come to rest on him. Only now did he sense the terrifying power that had driven Amos to prophesy. Only now did he sense how deeply he had fallen into the grip of that power. He was the chosen spokesman of the LORD.

It was not outright fear Hosea felt. The guards of the Temple would not likely challenge him, nor would the king do anything against him. Yet, he felt something of unease as he walked up the steps of the Temple, as from an unknown danger.

People stepped back from his path as he came to the top of the steps. A whispering spread through the crowd of people within the Temple, for it was rumored that Hosea would speak out at the Festival of Dedication. Then a sudden hush of expectancy fell over the Temple, and Hosea's voice called out, "Are you gathered for a festival? What will you do on the day of appointed festival and on the feast day of the LORD? For behold, you are going to Assyria!"

A murmuring rose up, but Hosea's voice spoke above it: "In the house of the LORD I see a horrible thing, the harlotry of Israel!

"Like grapes in the wilderness I found Israel. Like the first fruit on the fig tree in its first season, I saw your fathers. But they turned to the gods of Moab and gave themselves to Baal. Yet I, I am the LORD your God, from the land of Egypt, and beside me there is none to save you."

Within the Temple, Anakah turned to Shallum, sitting beside him. "Now put him to silence, as you swore."

"Let him speak a little yet, until his own words ensnare him."

"The LORD finds no pleasure in your worship," Hosea called out. "You have forsaken your God. By altar and wine-vat and threshing floor you pour out wine and offer up sacrifice and play the harlot — and Israel is defiled. You have loved a harlot's hire and not the worship of your God. Corrupt is your worship, an abomination before the LORD!"

Suddenly, Shallum stood up from his seat beside Anakah and called out in a loud, mocking voice, "How is the fruit of the ground brought forth but by the loins of our women, given to Baal? Has it not been so from days of old?"

Hosea peered into the inner court. The seat of the high priest was raised above the Temple floor. A torch hanging on the wall lit Shallum's face.

"The earth is the LORD's, Shallum ben Jabesh," Hosea answered. "Harlotry is none of His worship. Never has it been from days of old."

"Our women who give themselves at Feast of Booths and festal celebrations — are they an abomination before the LORD? Is this the charge you bring against them?" Shallum asked.

"Harlotry is an abomination before the LORD."

"Then is your own wife an abomination before the LORD," Shallum said with a laugh.

The crowd in the Temple broke into wordless murmurs and uneasy laughter. A sudden trembling came over Hosea. Shallum called out across the crowd, "If harlotry be sin, then see to the sin of your wife and let Israel alone!"

The people grew silent, waiting for Hosea to speak. His voice came low and strained: "What do you know of my wife?"

"That she has been known."

"You lie."

"Learn it from her own lips. They are lips of sweetest honey."

The crowd laughed again, and shouting went up against Hosea from the inner court, near the seat of the high priest. Hosea turned to Odenjah, and in his eyes there was anger and hurt and confusion.

"This is some trick against you," Odenjah said, taking Hosea's arm.

Hosea shook his head. He pulled loose his arm and walked alone down the steps of the Temple.

2

How could I not have known? In the king's vineyard she had disappeared during the ritual dance. I searched through the vineyard for her, and when I returned to the altar she was there and asked laughingly where I had gone with the Temple harlot. Yet as we walked home she was strangely silent, and in the days following a tenseness grew between us. Whenever I spoke the name of Shallum ben Jabesh she looked away.

Gomer had Jezreel on her breast when I came into the house.

"You are home soon," she said.

A lone lamp lit the room. In the dark she could not see my face. Yet when I spoke, her voice went suddenly tense.

"What does Shallum ben Jabesh know of you?" I asked.

"What should he know?"

I dropped to my knee beside her and looked into her face. "Has he known you?"

"Why do you ask such a thing?"

"Tell me."

She buried her face against Jezreel. "I cannot say."

"He has known you. What he said was true."

She looked up. "He said?"

"Yes, in the hearing of all Samaria."

"What?"

"That I should little condemn the shame of Israel when my own wife plays the harlot."

Gomer held a hand to her mouth. Fearfully she asked, "What more did he say?"

"What more need he say?" I cried, standing to my feet. "That he himself had you?"

The child whimpered at Gomer's breast; she took him to her shoulder, hiding her face against his neck. Almost in a whisper she spoke, "My husband, it was the festal celebration. Everyone entered into it."

"Yes, you first of all. I should have known when he spoke with us — the way he looked at you. And then the dancing —"

"It is the way of a festival. It is part of the celebration."

Gomer looked up at me, tears in her eyes. "What will you do with me?"

"What is done with a harlot?"

"Would you call all the women of Samaria harlot? The queen herself went into the trees with a soldier of the guard."

"I do not care about other wives! I care about you."

My own words caught me. I looked down on her, crouched at my feet, this woman I had taken to wife, this wife who filled my heart. Tears came to my own eyes. I turned away from her.

"Will you turn me out?" she asked.

"I know not what I will do."

The child began to cry. Gomer took him again to her breast, but he turned from it and would not be comforted.

"Be still, be still," she hushed.

More and more he cried, until I turned and said sharply, "See you not the child is tired? Set him to his bed."

"Yes," Gomer said meekly.

She crept to the corner of the room and laid the child on his mat. After some moments he left off crying and shortly fell asleep. Gomer kissed his cheek and said low, "Ah Jezreel, I can never do right for you. We are ever at odds, you and I."

I sat across the room, my head in my hands. Gomer stayed on her knees next to the child, waiting. Neither of us spoke. The anger I felt subsided, and in its place came a hurt and bewilderment. I thought on the love we had given each other — the touch and kiss and secret word with meaning only for the other, a giving and receiving that was ours alone, that none could share. How could it now be carelessly given to another?

How it had come back on me — my words against Baal worship. My own wife —

"Hosea," Gomer said cautiously, "I would never do such a thing again, if you stand against it."

"If I stand against it! Have you learned nothing? Have we talked together of the LORD all these months and nothing of His ways taken root? Whole scrolls you can speak from memory — to what purpose? To forsake our bed and play the harlot at the first opportunity?"

"It was festival, only festival. My mother embraced other worshippers at festival yet loved my father only more, was no harlot. It is the way in all Israel."

"It was not the way of Israel in the wilderness — no god but the LORD, the LORD alone. The ways of the LORD and the ways of Baal side by side! It is the ruin of all Israel."

"My husband," Gomer said impulsively, rising and crossing over to me.

I continued to speak, but low, mostly to myself. "Nighttime and morning, on every hilltop — harlots, virgins, brides, all one. O LORD God, it is an abomination!"

"I will do no such thing again," Gomer said impulsively. "I did not bethink myself."

I looked at her, kneeling by my side. I took her face between my hands and felt her soft hair fall about my fingers.

"Yet do I love you," I said.

"I love you, my husband, only you."

Then, as though she would be certain, she said, "You will not turn me out?"

I shook my head. My hands dropped away from her face. She smiled, invitingly. But I only shook my head and stared into the lamp's flickering light.

3

The next day Gomer bundled up Jezreel and walked to her father's house. Diblaim greeted her with a muttered, "Peace," and went to the room where he kept the scrolls and tablets of his leather business.

His brusque greeting proved what Gomer feared: her father and mother already knew of Shallum's open boast in the Temple, and they were shamed.

It had become common practice in Israel to go aside with other mates during Baal festivals. Diblaim's own wife believed it helped secure their prosperity. It might have passed without incident for Gomer, except that Hosea had thundered against Baal worship, calling it harlotry against the LORD. When Shallum stood up and challenged Hosea, saying the prophet's own wife must be a harlot for he himself had her, Hosea was shamed to silence. No matter that it happened during a Baal festival, the name *harlot* fastened nakedly on Gomer. In the streets she was so named and judged.

She found her mother in the garden. Anna embraced her. "My child." She at once took Jezreel in her arms. "My little darling."

"Father barely spoke to me. He is angry."

"As well he might be," Anna returned, cheerless but without anger. "We are shamed before all Samaria."

"Oh, Mama," Gomer cried. "What have I done?"

"You must tell me," Anna replied sternly.

"It was festival. I went into a garden with Shallum ben Jabesh."

"Did you know him before that?"

"He was present at our wedding celebration with Zechariah, then prince."

Anna spoke sharply, "You knew him then?"

"No, Mama! He tried to take me aside, but I refused. I came a virgin to Hosea's bed."

They sat together on the bench where first Gomer sat with Hosea. The evening before, when a servant brought the news, Diblaim was stricken. He went to his workroom and did not come out until the early hours of the morning. Anna said nothing but at once set herself on Gomer's side. Her daughter might need rebuke, but Anna gave small thought to that. Something was afoot. She knew the odors of intrigue that swirled in the air of Samaria. She suspected a scheme on Shallum's side and began to consider how it could be turned aside. She spoke slowly, "At the festival, then. That was the first time this man knew you."

Gomer nodded.

"And the last?" Anna asked. Gomer sat silent.

"He has come to you again?" Anna asked. When Gomer did not answer Anna spoke solemnly, not as a question, "You have gone to him."

Gomer nodded. "He summoned me to the palace." They sat silent for a time.

"Does your husband know?" Anna asked.

"I do not think so."

"How many times?"

"Twice." Silence. "Oh, Mama, what am I to do? When you embraced worshippers at festival, did they never come back to you?"

Anna lifted Jezreel to her shoulder and patted him. Her eyes looked far away. "At festival one might think of it, even speak of it. It happened only once."

"Someone from a festival came back to you?"

"Yes."

"What did Father do?"

"He was on a journey to Egypt."

"He never knew?"

Anna shook her head. "Nor you, either. We were very secret."

"You liked him?"

"At the time I thought it pleasant."

"But it stopped?"

"I cut it off weeks before your father returned. Your father is the best man in Samaria. This man was little above a stranger. I made a foolish mistake."

"Oh, Mama! You taught me so well for my husband. But this — this having pleasure with another man — what is it?"

"At festival, it can be a pleasant adventure. You entreat the Baal, you seek blessing for the coming year."

"Baal means nothing to me," Gomer returned bitterly. "I pled with Hosea that it was only festival, but it rang false even in my own ears. I knew before I said it that it would find no hearing with Hosea."

"You became Yahweh tether as a child. I remember it well. You chose to worship the God of Israel alone. Have you gone away from it? Do you now worship neither Baal nor the LORD of Israel?"

"I am one with Hosea. We talk endlessly of the LORD and I learn from the scrolls. I am a daughter of Israel, but —"

"But not in this," Anna said pointedly. "The Seventh Word stands against you."

Gomer nodded and looked to the ground. "I can recite whole scrolls from memory. The words are bright in my thoughts. But when Shallum ben Jabesh sent for me the words were only in my thoughts, not in my heart."

"You cannot provoke the gods, whether the Baal or the LORD," Anna said curtly, raising her voice as she did when Gomer fought with her as a child. "You yourself chose to be Yahweh tether. You must live so! What were you thinking?"

"I was drawn to him. When he sought me, I — I wanted to go to him."

"And no thought beyond that moment," Anna said flatly.

Gomer nodded. "Also in the garden. I was swept up in the festival. He wanted me."

Anna's voice turned suddenly soft. "That has ever been your way. When something grips you, you take hold of it, no thought for the consequences, no thought even for yourself. You sat by your brother's bed from the moment he took ill — not eating, hardly sleeping — and remained there until long after he died." Anna cuddled Jezreel closer to herself. "Precious," she whispered, whether to Jezreel or in the memory of tiny Aram, the tone was uncertain.

Gomer bit her lip and sat straight up. Suddenly she shook her head and spoke against herself, almost as against another person: "I know the scroll, the Seventh Word. Adultery. It is not precious."

"That is the other side. Living in the moment can be pleasant. But it can also be *dangerous*."

"Father always warned me to *bethink* myself." She shook her head helplessly. "The man summoned me. I did not bethink myself. Now my husband mistrusts me. Could put me away. Could have me stoned."

"You desire this other man above your husband?"

Gomer drew back, her face a picture of astonishment. "More than Hosea? Hosea is — he is my *husband*. It is with me as it is with you, even as you have said: no worshipper at festival was the equal of Father. No man in Israel is the equal of Hosea."

Anna laid her free hand on Gomer's shoulder. "You pled these very words to me when Hosea sought betrothal. No man in all Israel was his equal." Her voice turned commanding: "Bethink yourself! None in all Israel is the equal of your husband, and none worth losing him. You must order your every whisper, word, and touch to winning back your husband's love and trust."

Gomer embraced her mother and little Jezreel.

"It will not be easy, my child," Anna said, settling Jezreel back in Gomer's arms.

"Forgive me, Mama, for bringing shame on you. Plead with Father to forgive me."

Gomer left quickly. She feared meeting with her father.

Anna watched her until she turned down a street, out of sight. Anna knew so well the world of intrigue that swirled in the air of Samaria. "This man Shallum is up to something," she thought. "He is using Gomer to silence Hosea. Menahem should be alerted. He is a man of sense."

Chapter 18

Shallum, King of Israel

1

The midday sun filtered through the cedars of Ibleam, casting a pattern of gently dancing yellow light on the housetops of Zechariah's forest community. The cedars had been brought as saplings from the foothills of Lebanon by Jehu. They screened the little community from the oak and terebinth and scrub that dotted the east end of the valley of Jezreel, in which Ibleam lay.

South and west a half-day's journey lay the walls of Samaria. Northeast a day's journey were the borderlands of Galilee and Kazor. Ibleam nestled comfortably between the intrigue of Samaria and the threat of Assyria, caring little for either, content with the cool shade and peaceful rustling of the great cedars. Zechariah was alone on the housetop of the main house. He paced back and forth, muttering over and over the verses of a poem he had begun to write. On the ride to Ibleam, the thought came to him that he should enrich his people with poetry, pour out the questing of his spirit in high language. He had worked on it from the moment he arrived, but the words came out clumsily, and he was growing discouraged.

Perhaps he would be better to stay at his harp. Music was peaceful, soothing. How peaceful to be away from the city!

Here no one hungered or thirsted. Merchant did not contend with merchant, nor farmer with tradesman. The army could not press him for defenses against Assyria, nor the landowners for a treaty with Egypt. They all cursed his quiet ways, his indecision. But slowly his wisdom was winning out. Shallum had begun to see it. Others would follow. Even the bothersome priest Hosea must come to see that struggle breeds only struggle. One must bear patiently. They whispered in the corridors of the palace that he was weak and cowardly. He knew. But they were wrong. His way would prevail.

A footfall sounded on the steps leading up to the housetop. Zechariah did not look up, supposing it to be the physician with his bowl of bitter herbs.

"Set it down," he said.

"Turn and see to whom you speak."

"Shallum?" The king turned around in great surprise. "What brings you to Ibleam?"

"Good fortune," Shallum said darkly, unsheathing his sword.

"If you have come to plead again for an Egyptian treaty, your journey is in vain."

"I plead no longer, Zechariah ben Jeroboam," Shallum said, calling the king by his name for the first time. "Today, I take what is mine by every right of gift and calling."

"What do you mean?" Zechariah giggled uneasily at Shallum's expression.

"I am come to take your throne and your life."

"Are you mad? My soldiers are within sound of my voice."

"Your soldiers are at my sword-point."

Shallum took a quick step toward Zechariah. "Stop! Guards, guards!"

"You have lived too long with your dreams, O king. You have put me off, scorned my advice, and turned away my counsel. Now, I ask no longer. In everything save birth I am your better, more fit to rule. I have courage where you have none; decision, and you know not the word. One cannot rule with dreams, Zechariah, but with this —"

Shallum drew back and thrust his sword into the middle of the king's chest. Zechariah screamed in pain and rolled backward under the impact of Shallum's thrust. He toppled to the stone flooring of the housetop, wrenching the sword from Shallum's hand. His mouth fell open, and blood trickled over his lips. Shallum reached out, grasped the sword, withdrew it, and stood by, motionless.

For a moment Zechariah looked up at Shallum, confused, unbelieving. Then his tortured eyes rolled up. The house of Jehu ended as it began, in blood, in the fourth generation, according to ancient prophecy.

* * *

The day following, with great pomp and ceremony, Shallum ben Jabesh knelt at the altar in the Temple of Samaria. The high priest Anakah anointed him the fifteenth king to rule Israel.

2

The fourth day of Shallum's rule, Tiglath Pileser took the throne of Assyria. From Babylon to Damascus, like brush fire, spread the fear that fifty years of peace were at an end. Three days later Hoshea ben Elah rode into Bethel from Israel's eastern border. He met briefly with Menahem ben Gadi. Together they rode north to Samaria. A day later Hoshea and Menahem stood in the palace of Samaria before Shallum ben Jabesh, eight days king of Israel.

For three years Hoshea had been stationed on Israel's eastern border. He had traveled four times to Assyria to learn what he could of their war plans. At his last trip, the tribes of Assyria still fought among themselves, and no sure plan of conquest was afoot. Yet one thing Hoshea knew: the day Assyria's chieftains united under a single hand, no land from Nineveh to the Great Sea and the cataracts of the Nile would breathe free of danger.

Together with Menahem he had come now to lay the danger before Shallum — warn him against a fruitless alliance with Egypt and make preparations to strengthen the armies of Israel.

"We will be blunt," Hoshea said. "What you have done, you have done, and cannot be mended. In another day we would have come against you with arms to right the murder of the son of Jeroboam."

"Guard your tongue," Shallum warned. "You speak now to your king."

"King by whose word?" Menahem asked coldly. In a brief encounter with the wife of Diblaim near the east gate of Samaria, he had learned how Shallum gained some standing with the people when he brought the prophet Hosea to silence. The wife of Diblaim assured Menahem that Hosea was an honorable man, as surely as Shallum was dishonorable, which Menahem readily believed, though now too late.

Hoshea motioned Menahem silent and spoke on: "A king of eight days, who mounted the throne with bloodstained sword, holds little loyalty, you will find. Yet you know well the ways of governance. In that Israel has need of you. With Tiglath Pileser on the throne of Assyria, we can little afford useless bloodletting in Israel."

"What now do you propose?" Shallum asked coldly.

"Three things: That you make no treaty or alliance with Egypt, the sworn enemy of Assyria; that you send messengers to Pileser, to do him worship, and to make alliance with him if possible; and then you double the size of Israel's army, and when that army is trained, double it again. How long Pileser will honor an alliance and hold back his armies we do not know. Our only safety lies in strength."

"You seem to sense well the needs of the kingdom," Shallum said, his voice flat with sarcasm.

"I will not play at words with you. But this I say — do as we advise, and we will swear you the loyalty of the king's army."

"And if I do not?"

"You have no choice," Menahem said.

Shallum touched a finger to his lips. Then he said, "You please me, both of you. You have vision and courage. I had thought you might weaken if I pressed you. You did not. I like that."

"Save flattering for your landowners," Menahem said without humor.

"What you propose is already accomplished," Shallum said.

Menahem made ready to reply, but Shallum held up his hand. One lesson he had learned well from Jeroboam: *when wisdom counsels false words, then let the lie be told with flourish and confidence.*

"I am not such a dreamer as was the son of Jeroboam. I have known of this danger. Many are the times I tried to persuade the king to do the very thing you now propose."

Hoshea and Menahem looked at one another uncertainly. This they had not expected. Shallum was said to be in league with those who favored an alliance with Egypt.

"When at last I despaired of gaining the king's agreement, I took the only step left open to me, if Israel was to be saved. Within an hour of Zechariah's end, my messengers were on their way to Pileser."

"Pileser was not then king," Hoshea said.

Shallum looked down on Hoshea with a haughty smile.

"Those with wisdom to see have long known that Pileser would come to the throne before barley harvest. It was this that led me to act when I did. My messengers did Pileser worship before he took the throne, and so our treaty with him is the more sure."

"A treaty with Pileser is sealed?"

"From the fourth day of my rule. My messengers rode day and night to Nineveh, stopping only to water and feed their mounts."

Menahem and Hoshea looked again at one another, each hoping the other would find some word to speak.

"Oh, have no fear," Shallum said, gaining courage as he measured the effect of his words on the two men. "I will not take it ill that you have spoken thus boldly to your king. A king has need of men with courage."

"What of the other — the building up of Israel's army?" Menahem asked.

Shallum stroked his beard thoughtfully. The fear that had gripped him moments before gave way to quiet self-assurance. His hurried ruse had worked better than he dared hope. Looking at Menahem he said, "Already my plans for the army are being shaped. It is a fair chance that brings you to Samaria this day, for I was on the point of calling you from Bethel."

"How so?"

"You are to take over our garrison at Tirzah."

"Tirzah! It is nothing but a dung heap — twelve soldiers."

"Yes, so it is now. It is to become a chief garrison of the kingdom. I want there a captain experienced in training soldiers. Soldiers are better trained for battle in the countryside, away from distractions of the city — women and wine —"

"You speak well," Hoshea said cautiously. "Yet we know not how long Pileser will honor your treaty. It may be months, even years. We can not bring soldiers to battle readiness and then hold them in the country with nothing to do, if Pileser should not attack."

"That is the concern of one who knows better than you the plans of Tiglath Pileser," Shallum said coldly. "Menahem, you will go tomorrow to the garrison at Tirzah and await my orders."

"What of me?" Hoshea asked.

"You will remain at the garrison here in Samaria. You are yet young, Hoshea ben Elah, but I see worth in you. I want to observe you more closely."

"If all is as you say, it may be well for Israel," Menahem said. "If not — Tirzah is but a half day's journey away."

Shallum ignored the warning in Menahem's words. He knew that Menahem could well menace his throne; he commanded great loyalty in the army. Yet Shallum knew also that a captain was no more powerful than the men he commanded. Set off in Tirzah, with only twelve men to command, Menahem would be forgotten. Shallum could set captains of his own choosing in the chief garrisons of the kingdom. In two months time, Menahem's power in the army would be broken.

Hoshea he would keep in Samaria. He, too, commanded respect in the army. But he seemed more open to argument and suggestion than Menahem. His loyalty might be won over; it would be a loyalty worth having.

Shallum indicated with a nod that he had finished speaking. Hoshea and Menahem bowed stiffly and backed out of the king's chamber. When they had gone, Shallum smiled and then broke into a laugh. Jeroboam himself could not have done better. Treaty with Pileser — indeed!

* * *

In the courtyard outside, Menahem spoke low to Hoshea: "I like it not. He is too smooth with his words."

"Yes, but a treaty with Pileser. That is more than we ourselves had thought to gain."

"We must see about this treaty to our own satisfaction."

"How? You are ordered to Tirzah. I remain in Samaria. Whom could we trust?" Hoshea asked.

"I will take my son with me from the garrison in Bethel."

"Pekahiah?"

"Yes. It is only right that a man have his own son under his command."

"What do you intend?"

"I will send Pekahiah to Assyria. He can make the trip and return before twenty days are out. Then we shall know in truth how it stands between Israel and Pileser."

"And if it stands not well?"

"Then the rule of Shallum ben Jabesh will be short indeed."

* * *

In the eleventh day of his rule, Shallum set his seal on more than five years of scheming. Secretly met in his chamber were two envoys of the Pharaoh of Egypt who lived in residence west of the palace, and twenty of the richest landowners and merchants of Samaria. With pledges of everlasting friendship, a solemn treaty was sealed between Israel and Egypt.

Shallum swore all present to secrecy until he himself should speak the word. Until his stand with the army was more secure, he wanted no whisper of a treaty with Egypt to reach the ears of Menahem, or those who would support him.

3

"I want to speak with you," Shallum said.

"No, you cannot come in. My husband is not home."

"I know he is not home. I waited until he left." Gomer held the door against him, but Shallum pushed her back and forced his way into the house. They stood facing one another. Shallum spoke, anger edging his voice: "Why did you not come to the palace at my bidding?"

"I am no harlot of the street to be summoned at your pleasure," Gomer answered proudly.

"You were not loath to come to me before I was king."

"Yes, and before you shamed me to all Samaria."

"I shamed you not —"

"Shame me you did — telling my husband in the hearing of all the Temple that you had lain with me."

"I spoke of the festal celebration only. No shame for us in that, or all Israel is shameful."

Gomer drew back and looked at him curiously. She had expected him to try smooth words with her and make artful

184

denial. But he straightway admitted his words. And more, he set himself together with her: no shame is there *for us*, he had said.

"The shame is his," Shallum said coolly, "that he sets himself against righteous festival worship."

He seemed to speak her own words, words she had tried to tell herself since the day Hosea found her out. Yet, still she must hold something against Shallum for her humiliation.

"When I go to the well all talk goes to whispers, and fingers point."

"Let them whisper and point. Not a one of them has turned a lover away at festival."

"Yes, but the lover does not make a boast of it from the high altar of Samaria."

Shallum took hold her shoulders. "They are jealous. They themselves would have the king of Israel."

Gomer took his arms, and pushed them slowly away. "My husband's name is laughter in the streets."

"What is that to you?"

"A wife bears the name of her husband, for good or for ill. His shame falls also on me."

"I will make you forget your husband."

Gomer still held him off. Two weeks had passed since the night Hosea returned from the Temple, when he learned of her encounter with Shallum. Three times since then Hosea had come to her bed, but it was no longer the same between them. They spoke no further word of the affair, yet it stood a silent barrier between them.

"I want you, Gomer," Shallum said low. He spoke the words straight, almost in coldness. To begin with, she had been only a peg in his scheme, a necessary conquest. Now he wanted her for herself, as a woman — a woman who had met him with a passion he could not forget.

"You are king, now," she said. "You have no need of me."

"The scepter has destroyed none of my passion."

"You can have any woman in the kingdom."

He shook her roughly by the shoulders. "I want you, and I will have you!"

"My husband will turn me out, have me stoned even."

"He will never know."

"It is an evil thing."

"What do we know of evil? We know each other."

He drew her into his arms and kissed her cruelly on the mouth.

She had held him away. Suddenly she let go his shoulder and looked up at him, unafraid. She knew her command of him. She touched her fingers to his lips. "You are too hard with your kisses. One who loves must be gentle."

"Tell me you want done with it," he snapped. "Tell me!"

Gomer looked aside but took no step away. "My child."

Shallum looked to the corner where Jezreel lay sleeping. "He sleeps."

Gomer let go the hand that still held him away.

Later they lay side by side on the sleeping mat. Gomer had drawn a coverlet over herself. She gazed up at the low ceiling of the house, blackened many times over from the soot of the fire pit. One window and two narrow slits, high up on the south wall, let in the only light. Gomer was thinking how pleasant it would be to live again in a house like her father's, more than one room — a room only for sleeping, another only for eating, broad windows — like the palace.

How strange, she thought, that she could lie here, next to a man not her husband, and think such things. Her thoughts should be hot with remorse, yet they were not. Shallum excited in her a reckless passion that knew only the moment. She clung to the memory of it.

The word of the LORD stood against her. She knew the scrolls. She could speak many rolls from memory, but they were words, only words. They were like links of a chain, each one standing separate, no connection between them. No strength. No comfort.

Hosea — ah, she loved him not the less. This she truly believed. It seemed she almost loved Hosea the more, as though what she had stolen with another must now be given back to her husband in double.

When they were first wed, Hosea spent much time together with her. Now he was ever out on the city, preaching in the market place or in the gate or meeting at his countryside altar with those who had become his followers. Must the fire in her bosom wait only on him? What were amiss in taking some pleasure with another? It was no more than many another wife in Samaria did.

Gomer looked over toward the corner where Jezreel lay. His eyes were wide open, and he looked on her. She gasped.

"What is it?" Shallum asked, rising up.

"Jezreel. He saw us."

"The child? How old is he?"

"Soon six months."

Shallum laughed. "Our secret is safe enough."

"Yes, but he *saw*."

"It is not the first time, I trow."

"It is indeed."

"With your husband, I mean." Shallum rose up on his elbow and looked down on her, smiling. "Or have there been others?"

"You speak wickedly."

"Nay, I but look on life as it is." He pulled the coverlet down from her bosom. "I should be surprised if no other man has tried to have his way with you before me."

Gomer covered herself again and turned from him. She liked it not, such speaking. It was as though she were only a piece for his pleasure. Shallum laughed low, in the way he did when he was pleased with himself. She grew hot with anger. "You shame me."

He turned her toward him and looked on her with cold assurance, his voice gently mocking: "Nay, I desire you. I would be a poor mark of a man if I desired a woman no other man would desire. You are a woman — I shame you none by saying it."

She lowered her eyes, so as not to look on him. He had a way of softening her with his words. She found it pleasant but also lacking. It was thus from the first time they embraced — beneath the words and the pleasure something of emptiness, half known and unnamed.

"What think you," he said, "that you have lain in the arms of the king of Israel?"

Gomer made him a face and half smiled. "I think the king of Israel stays over long in the house of his subject."

"Yes."

He leaned down and kissed her lightly. He pulled his robe about him and stood up from the mat.

"You will come to the palace when I send for you?" he asked.

She looked at him but did not answer.

"Yes, you will come," he laughed.

She set her lips hard and looked away. It vexed her when he spoke so and looked on her with arrogance. Yet she knew that when the message came she would go. In the bedchamber, the voice of pleading would be his, not hers.

"Go quietly," she said.

The latch clicked open, and he was gone. Gomer lay still on the sleeping mat. A sudden loneliness welled up inside her. She looked across to Jezreel. He looked on her as before. She rose to her feet. The coverlet fell away, and she was naked. She hurried across to him and picked him up in her arms. She would have cuddled him to her breast, which he always liked, but he struggled in her arms and turned from her and cried. She walked with him, cooing softly, but he only cried the more until, at last, she could only lay him back on his bed. She took up her robe and put it on slowly.

Oh, she was alone, so alone. What was happening with her life? Her husband, a man like none in all Israel. What darkness lay between them?

When she looked back at Jezreel, he was looking on her again, his eyes wide and sober. Gomer bit her lip and closed her eyes to hold back the tears.

Chapter 19

A Brief Reign

1

In the twenty-sixth day of Shallum's rule, Pekahiah returned from Nineveh. He reported to Menahem that Israel held no treaty with Assyria. Menahem took his twelve soldiers from Tirzah and swung south as far as Bethel, gathering an army to overthrow the rule of Shallum ben Jabesh.

When word of Menahem's advance reached Samaria, Shallum hurriedly summoned Hoshea to his presence. He promised him the rank of chief captain in the army of the king if he would rally the army and stop Menahem's advance. Shallum knew that no one but Hoshea could set himself against the authority of Menahem.

Hoshea told Shallum coldly that if he had done as he boasted, Israel would be spared blood. Shallum brushed away the words and appealed to the soldier pride that he knew ran deep in Hoshea. "Israel needs a Joshua in her hour of trial. You are the man. Rally the army, Hoshea ben Elah. Save Israel from the one who would destroy her, and no request you make shall go unheeded."

Even as he silently cursed the man who sat on Israel's throne, Hoshea knew that he must serve him. The land could little afford an upheaval within in these desperate times.

"I will serve you," Hoshea said grimly. "In peaceful times, I would move heaven and earth to upset your rule. But because I love this people and this land more than I hate you, I will serve you."

With sunset less than an hour away, Hoshea and five other captains in the army of the king rode out the gate of Samaria and headed south to meet the advancing army of Menahem ben Gadi.

* * *

The village of Tappuah lay a four hour ride south of Samaria. From mid-afternoon till sunset the soldiers of Menahem had stood by while their captain argued with the elders of the village. Menahem expected of them what he had received from other villages: young men to join his army, food and drink for his men. But the elders of Tappuah refused him entrance. They barred their gate and said they wanted no part in his rebellion.

At sunset, Menahem laid siege to the walls, gained entrance, and put the village to sack. The elders were killed without mercy, young maidens raped, women with child ripped open. Grimly, Menahem said as he went out through the gates, "If they are not with us, they are against us."

He made camp outside the village and waited the dawn that would bring him to the gates of Samaria.

An hour past midnight, Hoshea and the other captains came past the gates of Tappuah and into the camp of Menahem. Menahem met with them in his tent. Eight men, in all, were gathered, each a captain in the army of the king. Two lamps lit their council.

"Why will you trust a man whose whole history is one of deceit?" Menahem asked hotly, when Hoshea had said they must abide under Shallum's rule.

"It is not that I trust him," Hoshea said slowly, "but that I like less the spilling of Israel's own blood, as you have done this day in Tappuah."

"Better some few should fall, than all Israel be led into exile."

"Better yet that we find some way to stand — all of us together. Shallum is crafty, true, but he is wise in the ways of governance."

"Is it wisdom that makes treaty with Egypt, to the scorn of Assyria?"

"What treaty with Egypt?" Hoshea asked.

"It is known," Menahem said.

"Yes, by marketplace rumor anything can be known."

"He is in league with the Egyptian party."

"It is not known."

"Nor was it known that he lied concerning the treaty with Assyria. Ask Pekahiah, here, how it stands with Israel and Pileser."

"The Assyrian knows nothing of a treaty with Israel," said the son of Menahem. He spoke low and nodded to Hoshea that he meant no disrespect. Hoshea was only four years older than Pekahiah, but in the army Hoshea commanded a respect and authority greater than men twice his age — equal, even, to Menahem. No soldier in all Israel could wield sword or spear with the skill of Hoshea ben Elah.

"It may be, Menahem, that your move was hasty," ventured an older man sitting beside Hoshea. He had long hair, tied in a knot at the back — Remaliah, disliked both by Menahem and Hoshea, but a man of some weight in the army.

Remaliah noted Pekahiah's reluctance to speak out strongly for his own father. He determined that his own greater advantage would come from siding with Hoshea. Yet he spoke cautiously, so he might shift loyalty, should the others turn to support Menahem.

"At the least you must give Hoshea time to use his influence upon the king," Remaliah said smoothly.

"You are in the midst of my camp," Menahem said, waving his arm at Remaliah. "Who are you to tell me what I must do and what I must not do?"

The man opposite Remaliah, Jazer ben Issachar, held up his hand. "Let there be no threats among us, Menahem. You know full well that those under our command would rise against you as a man if you did us violence. We are met to find common agreement, not to set ourselves against each other."

Menahem nodded. When Jazer spoke, he left little room for argument.

Pekahiah glanced at his father and asked quietly, "Might Hoshea speak with the king face to face and lay the danger of Assyria before him clearly?"

"That we have done already," Menahem said curtly.

"Yes, it is not as though he were unwarned of the danger. It is of long standing." This was spoken by the one sitting next to Pekahiah — Pekah, twenty years old and the only son of Remaliah.

Pekah and Pekahiah were equal in age, born within an hour of one another. Their appearance, too, was similar. Both stood four cubits high, and both had the same light beards and sharply pointed noses. In the army they were known as the Twins, inseparable comrades.

Yet between them lay a family rivalry. Left-handed, like his father, Remaliah, Pekah boasted his left hand could out-throw Pekahiah's right hand by a third in any contest. Remaliah had long nursed envy of the honor accorded Menahem, right-handed and respected. Beneath their comradeship, right-handed Pekahiah and left-handed Pekah echoed the rivalry between their fathers, right-handed Menahem and left-handed Remaliah.

When Pekah saw Pekahiah's quiet respect for Hoshea, even seeming to side with him against his own father, Pekah from impulse spoke out oppositely, on the side of Menahem. He glanced sidewise at Pekahiah, as though to shame him for not standing firmly with his own father.

Hoshea looked about the circle of men. He had hoped that it would not come to a contest of authority between himself and Menahem, and yet it seemed that such it would be.

Eight men. Together they commanded the power of the king's army, each of some faction or company: Menahem, Hoshea, Remaliah, Pekahiah the son of Menahem, Pekah the son of Remaliah, Jothan who had sold his loyalty to Shallum, Nabaal and Jazer whose loyalties were unknown though they were thought to lean toward Hoshea.

Hoshea spoke directly to Menahem: "If we spill the blood of Israel, we bring only judgment on ourselves."

"Better some blood be spilt than the whole body torn asunder."

"We are soldiers, not rulers, Menahem. The times are unripe. We must stand with the king."

"He is no king to me," Menahem said coldly.

Hoshea stood up for he knew, now, that argument was at an end. "Menahem ben Gadi, I stand against you. You are more dear to me than my own father, but no other way lies open."

Menahem glowered up at Hoshea. Slowly he looked from man to man. If he stood against Hoshea now, and did not gain support, his command in the army would be lost. In the test he would have failed, and he had not the youth nor skill in arms to regain his stand, as would Hoshea. Yet, if he bowed to Hoshea's authority, Israel herself would be lost. This Menahem steadfastly believed.

"I will not see Israel's army ripped up by Assyria, while a two tongued deceiver parleys with Egypt," Menahem said, rising to his feet. "I stand against you, Hoshea ben Elah."

Pekahiah looked to Hoshea, then Menahem. He rose slowly and spoke in a quiet voice: "I stand at the right hand of my father."

Jothan took his stand beside Hoshea. "I stand with Hoshea and with the king."

Pekah glanced at his father, sitting rigidly in his place, drumming the fingers of his left hand against his knee, darting his eyes first to Hoshea, then to Menahem. Pekah spoke out, for he knew his father's jealousy of Menahem, and he did not want to be bound by his choice. "I cannot trust the man Shallum. I stand at Menahem's right hand."

The Twins stood side by side.

Remaliah looked fearfully at the two camps growing up around him, trying to determine which way the choice would tilt. Nabaal and Jazer sat across from him. They had ridden with Hoshea from Samaria and seemed to fall in with his arguments.

Menahem looked imploringly at Remaliah. With Remaliah he could at least strike a balance and not lose out altogether. Remaliah returned the look with a grimace, full of bitterness grown up over half a lifetime.

"I stand with Hoshea," Remaliah said.

Hoshea sighed aloud. Menahem tensed and looked to Nabaal and Jazer. Jazer spoke: "The man Shallum has murdered and deceived. He merits no trust. We stand at the right hand of Menahem."

Remaliah gasped. Five captains stood with Menahem, three with Hoshea. Hoshea swore beneath his breath.

"We must act as one," Menahem said quickly, seizing command. "However we stood till this moment, now we stand together. Is it agreed?" Hoshea nodded weakly and sat down. The others sat one by one, all except Menahem, who stood over them and laid out the plan that would make him king of Israel before another setting of the sun.

2

The day following Sabbath, shortly past midday, Hosea came running through the gate of Samaria and west through the city to his own house. The shops and market stands in the city were closed down, the streets mostly deserted, except for soldiers of Menahem here and there.

Hosea burst into the house with a shout. "Gomer!"

Neither she nor Jezreel were in the house. Hosea set the ladder and climbed to the housetop. It was empty. He looked through the streets surrounding, then next door to the house of Ebarth.

Odenjah had sent his young nephew west of Samaria, to Hosea's altar, to tell Hosea the army of Menahem had entered Samaria and laid siege to the palace. There had been raping and looting in Tappuah, and already some in Samaria. The people had taken to their houses and barred their doors. Hosea ran all the way back to the city to see that no harm would come to Gomer and Jezreel. Now he feared he was too late.

He jumped from the ladder, ran across to the house of Ebarth and pounded on the door.

"Open your door," he called out. "Who is there?"

"Hosea."

The door opened a crack. Ebarth peeked out. "Is Gomer with you?"

"No."

"What has happened to her?"

"We — we do not know."

A muffled sound came from behind the door. "Jezreel?" Hosea asked.

Ebarth looked down. Hosea pushed into the house. Deborah stood behind Ebarth. In her arm she held Jezreel. He let out a cry when he saw his father and reached out for him. Hosea took the child, hesitantly.

"Gomer? She is not here?"

Deborah shook her head.

"Where?" he asked in a whisper. Deborah looked away.

"Where is she?" Hosea demanded.

"She — she is gone —"

"Gone? Where gone? Did the soldiers come —"

"No, no."

"Where then?"

"I know not. She left the child with me —"

"Why? Where did she go?"

"I know nothing," Deborah pleaded.

"Yes, you know well enough," Ebarth said, turning and walking to the far wall, where his own children sat huddled together.

"Where?" Hosea asked.

Deborah shook her head and looked to the floor. Hosea seized her arm in a crushing grip. She cried out in pain.

"You know!" Hosea said. "Tell me!"

To the palace — she went to the palace!"

"The palace?"

"Yes."

"When?"

"In the morning."

"The king — Shallum?"

"I know not, I know not."

Hosea dropped her arm and spoke low, "Yes, you know." Then, "How long has it gone on?"

Deborah shook her head. Hosea spoke nothing more. He put Jezreel back in Deborah's arm. The child cried and reached out to him again.

"No, I must go for a little," Hosea said, trying to speak in a soft voice. Jezreel raised up in Deborah's arm and was quiet.

"Keep him here until I come back," Hosea said.

Hosea nodded to Ebarth and stepped out into the street. The door latch sounded behind him. For a moment he leaned back against the door, eyes closed.

For some men, a wife was no more than a cow or a goat or a piece of property to be bought and used. It was never like that with Gomer and Hosea. Often the thought came to Hosea when they were first married, when Hosea ministered at his altar, that the wife he had taken was not his by choice, was too wonderful, was a gift from the LORD.

At sunset, when he turned back toward the city, always there was a lightness in his step and in his heart, thinking how Gomer might greet him, whether with a word or shy glancing or a fleeting kiss or tender embrace, for she was ever changeable, and no two days were alike. One day she would be full of kisses and tender words, and the next day shy and withdrawn so Hosea must pursue her like an unripe virgin, and some days there was only quiet between them, and peacefulness, and a knowing that they were for each other. She was more dear than all the world to Hosea, more dear even than the merry son she had given him.

And then the man Shallum came between them.

Hosea pressed a hand over his eyes, and it seemed blackness would come in and choke out life. He raged within himself. What matter to him that other men cared nothing when their wives light-footed away from the bed? It was done, everywhere it was done, they said. Yes, and the men light-footed it themselves with cult harlots and any they chose. But Gomer! Hosea wanted none other to know her, nor himself wanted to know another —

Now this. No festal celebration but plain adultery, open and shameless. Her sweet body open to another's kisses, caressing, words —

The dark cloud rose up within him, the fearsome thunder and lightning. At first only that, then out of the cloud rose the terrible beckoning hand. It had not come since the day Hosea stood at his father's altar and overheard the word, *Take to yourself a wife of harlotry*, a prophecy for Israel he had thought, but now fraught with darker meaning. Hosea shrank from the dread hand, as he always did, until the vision left him.

"How many times?" he asked himself. "Where? Why, why, why? LORD God!"

Hosea opened his eyes and looked out across the city. Jealousy and pain and anger burned his eyes. Half at a run, he set out toward the palace.

3

At the command of Hoshea, the gates of Samaria had been opened to Menahem's army without struggle. Only the palace guards, still loyal to Shallum, stood between Menahem and the throne of Israel.

For three hours the fighting raged around the palace. Some of the palace guards swung over and joined friend and kin on the side of Menahem, but mostly they clung stubbornly to their posts, cutting away at the invaders with the unyielding valor of those caught up in forces and decisions beyond their own choosing, who know so well how to fight, yet so little of why they fight.

In the throne room of the palace, behind barred doors, guarded by twenty of his sturdiest men, Shallum waited. He had thought the forces of Menahem would be cut down at the gate of the city. So sure was he of Hoshea's authority and command.

He had sent for Gomer, for he wanted her to witness his triumph. He wanted to parade his triumph before her; she seemed to give too little account to his royal majesty.

But now all had gone against him. Hoshea had traitored his cause. The palace guards were falling to the soldiers of Menahem. All his plans and ambitions were crumbling away beneath his very eyes. And Gomer — this woman who dared make light of his position, and even speak jestingly of his rule — who drew him close or held him off as she pleased — she was witness now not to his triumph but his humiliation.

In the bedchamber of the king, which opened onto the throne room from the west, Gomer waited alone.

Sin brings its own punishment.

Often she had heard such words. She had not thought on them much. Now they were cause for dreadful pondering. The fate of Shallum might well be her own.

Oh, if she could but live again this one month! Never, never would she have come to Shallum ben Jabesh. His smooth words and his embraces — what were they to her now? Hosea — if only she could be with Hosea this moment, safe in his arms.

She tried to close her ears against the sounds of battle in the courtyard below, moving now into the palace itself. If only she had not come to the palace this day, she thought wildly. If Hosea had been at home — if the child had been ill — if anything, anything had kept her from the palace.

It was Shallum who brought this on her. Yes, he knew the army of Menahem was moving against him. Yet he brought her into the thick of it, caring nothing for her safety.

If she could only slip unseen from the palace, if she could hide from the soldiers — she was only a woman. She had no part in the conspiracies of the palace — no one knew of her and Shallum.

The sound of a battering ram hit on the doors of the throne room. Moments later, the soldiers of Menahem broke through and poured into the room, overpowering Shallum's guards. Menahem strode in with Pekahiah at his right hand, followed by Hoshea.

"When last we met, I warned you of this day, Shallum ben Jabesh," Menahem said.

"What do you intend?" Shallum croaked. His fears melted into careless despair.

"You must die," Menahem said without bitterness.

"When you have taken the purpose of my life, it is small matter that you take my life as well."

"Yes, as you took the life of Zechariah."

"Draw your sword, Menahem ben Gadi."

Menahem unsheathed his weapon. Shallum's face drained of color. His lips trembled. "You think to rid yourself of a burden by cutting down the only one in Israel who knows the ways of the throne?" At the brink of death, Shallum's despair rallied on one last desperate hope.

"One who has lived as king can look only to death, natural or by the sword," Menahem said. "A land cannot live with two kings, except in fear of upheaval."

"And will you say this when some day you stand in this room, surrounded by the splendor that has marked your days as king, and some harsh-faced usurper stands before you with drawn sword. Will you say then that you must die, that Israel can no longer abide your presence, and this glory you have known for a day leads only to death?"

"In that day, if it comes, the choice will not be mine, as the choice was not Zechariah's. As it is not yours."

Shallum gasped and drew back from the flashing point of Menahem's sword. For a moment there was the cutting and the pain, then a gushing of blood that stopped the breath in his throat, a searing heat in the pit of the stomach, and then strange release from pain, from struggle. Shallum ben Jabesh, king of Israel for twenty-eight days, toppled from the dais of his throne, dead.

The scream of a woman sounded behind him. Menahem whirled. Gomer stood in the doorway of the king's bedchamber, her eyes wide with horror.

With a movement too sudden to be checked, Gomer fled past the soldiers who stood at the doors of the throne room. Blindly she raced into the corridor, half stumbling down the steps leading to the courtyard. Two soldiers turned to follow her.

"Let her go," Menahem commanded. "It is only a serving maid."

Hoshea started to speak but stopped himself. What was the daughter of Diblaim doing in the king's bedchamber at this time? He had thought she and Hosea were wed, though he had no word of them in his three-year absence from Samaria. He had planned several times to call on Diblaim to inquire, but the time had not been convenient. Was she instead wife to the king? Or his concubine?

"Is the king wed?" Hoshea asked Menahem. "Nay. He leaves no heir. We are secure."

Hoshea nodded and followed Menahem from the throne room, walking beside Pekahiah.

* * *

Outside, Gomer raced across the courtyard toward the gate of the palace. Three soldiers made to stop her, but she eluded them and reached the gate. She ran headlong into Hosea as he entered the courtyard.

She let out a muffled cry and pushed back. Then she recognized him and threw herself into his arms.

"Hosea, Hosea they have killed him," she gasped.

"Who?"

"Shallum. Menahem killed him."

"Shallum is killed?"

She nodded, sucking in her breath. She clutched herself to Hosea, unthinking, wanting only the safety of his arms.

He held her back from him, gripping her shoulders. "You were with him — with Shallum?"

Her face went white at the look in his eyes. Her mouth opened, but she could not speak.

"Were you?" he demanded, squeezing her with his powerful hands.

"Oh, Hosea —"

"Whore!"

He struck her a ringing blow with the flat of his hand. She stumbled backward and fell to the ground.

"Hosea, never — never again, I swear to you —"

"Yes, Menahem has seen to that," Hosea said with bitter irony.

She buried her face in her hands and wept and moaned aloud. Hosea held a fist against his mouth and so bit on the forefinger that it drew blood. He trembled through his body in savage rage. She stole her eyes upward to look on him.

"Are you going to kill me?" she asked piteously.

Hosea closed his eyes and covered his face with his hand.

"Spare me," she wept.

"Gomer —" He sank to his knees beside her. "Why? Why?"

"Oh, I know not, I know not. He was king and he summoned me. What was I to do?"

He looked away. She leaned closer to him, pleading: "Take me back to you, I beg. I will be faithful to you, and I will love you —" She bit her lip. "I do love you, my husband."

He looked into her eyes. They were clear, tear laden and sorrowful, with no hiddenness, no deceit. How could she so change in a moment?

"Can it ever be as it was with us?" Hosea moaned.

"It will, it will. I know it. I promise it."

He wiped the blood on his hand against his cloak and rose slowly to his feet. He took her hand and lifted her up.

"You — you will not —"

"I know not," he said.

They walked slowly from the palace across the city toward their house, she a step behind. Neither spoke a word more.

Chapter 20

Uneasy Days

1

People in Israel saw time not as a measuring of months and years, but as a memory of happenings that touched life deeply, as a hope of what tomorrow would bring of joy or sorrow, fortune or mischance. It was not how many days had passed, but what had filled those days, that gave time its meaning. If time was good, people sought to hold all things as they were, that the good might continue. If time was evil, they sought some power — some action or decision or event — that could redeem the time and bring the evil to an end.

When that dark afternoon in the palace courtyard came back to Hosea, it was like yesterday. Days and weeks of forgetfulness would suddenly disappear and that evil afternoon would burst upon him again; that moment when he stood above Gomer, torn within himself, driven to madness by her unfaithfulness, yet in the very moment wanting her and pitying her and loving her. Nothing could banish the hurt and bewilderment of that afternoon.

Hosea took Gomer to his house again. For a time things went better between them. Hard moments there were, but also good times, even some lightness between them. Things went on in this manner for more than two months.

One evening, Hosea was writing something to a scroll by lamplight. Gomer came up beside him in her shift and asked if he was soon to bed. He slipped his arm about her waist, and his fingers came to rest in front. For a moment he was still. Then he rubbed his hand over her belly, slowly, and looked up. She spoke low, eyes downcast: "Yes, it is another child I bear beneath my heart."

"How long have you known?"

"A month — two . . ."

He dropped his arm from around her. She came to her knees beside him. "Look not so, my husband."

"Why have you been long in telling me?"

"For no reason. I wished only to be sure."

"Yes, sure whose child it is you bear beneath your heart!"

At this Gomer covered her face and wept, and there began months with long silences. When things went badly between them, Hosea would take refuge in the shed beside the house. His neighbor, Ebarth, offered to teach him something of the carpenter trade. Hosea proved a ready learner, and the shed was soon filled with carpenter projects.

The child was born in midwinter: a blue-eyed girl.

Gomer sought Hosea's face when he first looked on the child. "She has your blue eyes, my love. And the high cheeks of my mother. A match of us two."

Hosea only shook his head and went to the shed to work on a bench that stood half-finished against the far wall. The child was his by chance, only by chance.

On the child's third day, standing in the shed in the early morning, he overheard the LORD speaking the name the child should bear. As with Jezreel, the name was prophetic of the LORD's mind toward Israel: *Call her name Loruhamah, Not Pitied, for I will no more have pity on the house of Israel, to forgive them at all.*

When the child cried, Hosea made no move to hold or comfort it, as he did with Jezreel. Gomer drew the babe closer to herself, huddling it protectively in her arms. When the eighth day had come, and the child should be taken to the countryside altar for naming, Hosea said they would name her under their own roof.

Gomer cried much at the naming, but she made no protest to Hosea. She was yet fearful he would put her and the child out, to hide away her shame, no matter that he was the child's father. After a month had passed, Hosea came to bear more calmly toward the child, though he still showed it no mark of affection. The name stood like a wall between him and the child, as surely as estrangement stood between the LORD and Israel.

2

The rule of Menahem, the sixteenth king of Israel, brought little change in the worship of the people. Twice Hosea had gone to the palace and pled that the worship of Baal be banished from the Temple. Menahem allowed that Hosea could prophesy as he chose, but the worship of the Temple was in the hands of Anakah. Beyond the offerings the palace received from the Temple treasury, Menahem had no concern for Israel's worship.

The burden of returning Israel to the LORD fell back on Hosea and those who followed him.

The people no longer called Hosea another Amos. Words of rebuke and condemnation were there, more even than with Amos, but alongside words of judgment came words from Hosea's tortured heart, calling Israel back to the LORD. The call to prophesy was intertwined with his life. As long as he clung to Gomer, he must cling also to Israel; while Gomer remained in his house, he dared not despair of Israel after all returning to the house of the LORD.

He stood in the street opposite the Temple. A sacrifice of seven bulls was to be made and great crowds were gathering. "O Israel, Israel — what shall I do with you? Your love is like a morning cloud, like the dew that goes early away. I have hewn you down with my prophets — slain you with the words of my mouth yet you do not understand: I desire steadfast love and not sacrifice, the knowledge of God, rather than burnt offerings."

The course of Hosea's preaching reflected the course of his life with Gomer. When warmth grew between them, his words became soft and pleading: "Can I give you up, O Israel? Nay, my heart turns within me, my compassion grows warm and tender. I will not wreak judgment, I will not destroy. For I am God and not man, the Holy One in your midst, and I will not come to destroy."

Sometimes Hosea and Gomer could almost return to their old ways with one another. When they spoke of the past, Gomer wheedled Hosea into seeing her affair with Shallum as a senseless attraction. He summoned her as king, and she went. "It is over," she averred, a small matter in the past; no harm was done. The warmth and loveliness he had always known in Gomer overshadowed the past.

In the sunlight of midday, when he looked on the Gomer he lived with day by day, Hosea found some comfort in the portrayal of her relationship with Shallum as a small trouble from the past, best forgotten. The woman he loved and trusted stood a reality before him; he could see her, touch her, talk with her as he had done from the day they wed. Let the tale of her attraction to Shallum huddle in a corner of their life, a mum ghost from the past.

But on nights when Hosea lay abed in the dark and Gomer slept, his thoughts would turn distant and angry. It was not a little thing, best ignored and forgotten. She had given the man her heart — taken what had belonged to Hosea only and given it to another man, as Israel takes her love for the LORD and squanders it on Baal.

When Hosea dwelt on such thoughts, things grew cold between them. In the city gate he cried out words of judgment and condemnation.

"Woe to you, O Israel, for you have strayed from me! Destruction, for you have rebelled against me! I would redeem you, but you speak lies!"

Hosea's followers came to know how it stood between the prophet and his wife from the manner of his preaching. Israel was Gomer, and Gomer Israel. How long would their life together or his prophecy continue, under the shadow of such uncertainty?

3

From time to time my father, Beeri, came to visit us in Samaria. He would come by our house unannounced to see his grandchildren, to their delight. One time he came late to the house. I persuaded him to stay the night and return home the next morning. We sat long over a sparse evening meal. Gomer put the children to bed and lay down with them in the far corner, leaving us to talk by ourselves.

"I saw you in the crowd today," I said.

"Yes, I know. I caught your eye. I should have hid myself as I usually do, but there was no tradesman's hut or cart nearby."

"You hide yourself in the crowd when you come to visit us?"

"I have been in the crowd when you have raised your voice — well, let me say, many times."

"More than when you stop to see the children?"

"Many more times."

"Why?" I asked, puzzled.

"To hear what you speak."

"But you know me. I follow in your footsteps."

"Some things you speak sound familiar, like words we spoke around our table. But when you lift up your voice in the street you often speak with — not like we spoke at home — your words are well-spoken, commanding."

I sat quietly for a time. Father nodded but did not speak.

"Whence come the words you speak, my son? They are your own words, but they are more."

"I am not sure," I answered slowly. "As you know, since childhood I sometimes overhear the LORD speak certain words, but when I speak out to the people it is different. I feel the LORD's presence. He is closer than the people. I lift up my voice and the words are in my mouth, sometimes so many words they tumble over one another. Afterward I remember the thought, but not always the exact words. Odenjah has three young men who stand next to him. They make record of the words."

"You walk in other footsteps than mine."

"Not so, Father. I am a countryside priest, proud to be your son."

"The footsteps you follow may be mine in a measure. You have a further calling. Pay heed when you stand in the LORD's presence, my son. The LORD declares Israel's future through your words."

Father rose before the sun and made his way back home. It was the last time we saw him. Three more times he came to Samaria. He stood hidden in the crowd. Odenjah saw him. Seven weeks later he died.

4

Menahem had warned Israel of Assyria before and after he became king, and the Assyrian did not come. The rich in Israel grew weary of Menahem's warnings, more weary yet of the levies that supported his growing army. These rich made common cause with a faction in the army that stood secretly at Remaliah's left hand, a grave threat to Menahem's rule.

Then, suddenly, the Assyrian came. By a strange twisting of circumstance, the enemy Menahem most feared became the very power that secured him on the throne of Israel.

Tiglath Pileser had gathered all Assyria in his fist. In the north, Armenia and the ancient empire of the Hittites had fallen to his resistless armies. Eastern Syria was ruled by his governor in Arpad. When Pileser turned his eyes westward, only Damascus and Israel lay between him and the Great Sea.

In the month of olive harvest, Menahem received word that the armies of Assyria had passed by Damascus and were marching on Israel. His instinct as a soldier, and his pride as an Israelite, counseled him to call his armies and fight. But pride would be little match for the chariots and horsemen of Tiglath Pileser. In the last years, Menahem had come to all but despair of Israel ever standing against Assyria on the battlefield. And so he struck on a desperate plan to avert war — a war he now realized Israel could not hope to win. Alone he traveled northeastward. In Bashan he met Tiglath Pileser and, red with shame, bowed low before the Assyrian conqueror. After three days time, the two men struck a bargain. In return for a tribute of one thousand talents of silver, Pileser would draw back his armies and would recognize Menahem as his vassal king in Israel.

It galled Menahem that his armies in the end had proved of no avail, that he could realize none of his proud hopes for Israel, that he had gone at last to his knees before the Assyrian and that now he must live out his days as a vassal king — if indeed Pileser would continue to allow him that. Yet, Menahem gained grim satisfaction in laying the burden of tribute on those very ones in Israel who had sought to overthrow him.

Menahem set a levy on the wealthy in Israel — fifty shekels of silver to the man. Hoshea ben Elah was put in charge of collecting the levies. When they were gathered, he headed the train of seventy chariots that bore the tribute to Assyria, and then himself remained at Pileser's court to husband Israel's uncertain peace. There was much grumbling and complaint of Menahem's levy but no open threat against the throne. Every man in Israel knew that the armies of Assyria stood behind Menahem. For the time, they could see no course but to submit to his rule.

From the day of his bargain with Tiglath Pileser, Menahem ruled Israel with a heavy hand. No house in the land escaped his levies of grain and wine and oil and forced labor. He exacted more than was needed — more even than he wanted — and used it wastefully. It seemed he would punish all Israel for the shame he suffered when he bent his proud neck and paid homage to Tiglath Pileser.

Chapter 21

A Troubled Home

1

In the months following Loruhamah's birth, Hosea made much with Jezreel, held and cuddled him often; the boy was soon a year and a half. His dark color favored neither Hosea nor Gomer.

If Jezreel was rough with Loruhamah, hitting and pushing, it was Gomer who must set them apart. Hosea would say no word against Jezreel.

Between Gomer and Hosea a measure of warmth came back slowly, though mostly at night when the children had fallen asleep and Hosea would come to her bed in the darkness. A kind of forgetfulness stole over them, and they would embrace, though not like the first days of their marriage, and always over too quickly.

In the daytime, and in everyday affairs, the memory of Shallum ben Jabesh continued to cast a shadow between them, despite Gomer's avowal that it was a small thing, best forgotten.

They fell to picking fault with one another. Gomer's dislike of authority raised its head; she bristled at every rule or instruction from Hosea. They seldom laughed together.

Week by week Gomer took the children across Samaria to the house of her parents, Loruhamah in her arms, Jezreel toddling by her side. She found some comfort visiting with her mother when her life with Hosea turned drear. Anna and Diblaim seemed never to tire of holding and making much of the children.

Mostly Gomer talked with her mother, but one day, while Anna built a hut with the children, Diblaim caught Gomer by the hand and took her into his workroom.

"How goes it between you and your husband?" he asked abruptly. "Sometimes good. But not always," she answered, not meeting his eyes.

Gomer remembered well the ways of her father. When something came between them, she could always devise a way to wheedle herself back into his favor. But she was no longer a child, and this was no childish matter. She saw no way to draw close and coax out of him some show of favor or love, the game she loved to play as a child. For the first time in her life, she stood in fear of losing her father's regard altogether.

It was Jezreel and Loruhamah who changed things. They blundered into Diblaim's privacy as freely as they chose and found only welcome.

Diblaim spoke slowly and solemnly: "My daughter, I awoke this past night from a dream, a frightful dream." Gomer looked up. It was the first time he had called her 'Daughter' since she was married. He went on: "In my dream I came to your house. At first it seemed empty; no one was there. Then I looked in the far corner where the children sleep. They lay there, both of them, Jezreel and Loruhamah, their eyes wide open. I tried to speak their names, but I could not speak. I tried to go to them, but I could not move. They were dead. Both of them were dead."

Gomer gasped and put her hand to her mouth. She beheld her father's drawn face and impulsively uttered, "Father, it was a dream, only a dream."

"It was not the dream. I am no stranger to nightmares. It was the word against me; it lay like a millstone on my heart when I woke. 'You did nothing to help. *Your cold and selfish heart.*'"

"Father, you must not speak so. Your heart is kind and generous."

Diblaim waved her aside. "You have heard me say a thousand times that everyone has a right to live his own life — must be *free* to do so."

"Indeed I have," Gomer said in a soft, respectful tone.

"*You live your life, I live my life.*"

"All Samaria knows and respects it. You do not meddle in other people's lives."

"Yes, neither to hinder nor to help. That is the stone in the sandal. That is what tolled in my heart when I woke: Jezreel and Loruhamah lay dead and I did nothing to help them."

"They love you, Father! 'Papa-Papa' is Jezreel's favorite word."

"I know, I know. He throws himself in my arms. Loruhamah smiles like springtime when I take her up. All of that was in the dream. Yet, when I tried to draw close to them, I could not move. I could not speak their names. The moment I woke, the portent was clear as noonday sun: *You live only for yourself, you do nothing to help others.*"

"Oh, Father!" Gomer cried. "It is not you, not you. It is me. My sin. My selfish heart."

Gomer came close and embraced her father, the first time since he had turned cold toward her. "Forgive me, Father. I have been a wretched daughter to you, have brought shame on your name."

For some moments they stood thus, silent, embracing one another.

"I have made you a stranger, my daughter," Diblaim said with a catch in his voice. "You, the darling of my heart. And Jezreel and Loruhamah — I have not helped. How can I help?" he asked beseechingly.

Tears streaked Gomer's cheeks. She tightened her arms around her father.

2

In the first month of vine-tending Menahem died. His son, Pekahiah, became the seventeenth king to rule Israel.

During Menahem's reign, Israel's fear of Assyria had dulled. For a time the people hoped Pekahiah would lighten the rule of his father, and even throw off the yoke of Assyria. When he did not, the grumbling that had been against Menahem turned greater upon Pekahiah. In the marketplace, the Temple, and in the stone houses of Samaria's landowners — even in the army, no longer held together by Menahem's strong hand — the muttering was heard that Israel could not look to better days as long as Pekahiah sat on the throne.

* * *

What next happened with Gomer began when Loruhamah was near to being weaned, between her second and third year. One morning at the market, near the east gate of Samaria, she met Donath, the innkeeper whose marriage proposal Gomer had refused more than five years before.

"You never grow older. Always the beauty!" he said, smiling warmly.

"Your words never change," Gomer answered guardedly, smiling. "Always exaggerated."

"You have a skin of wine," he said, looking into her basket.

"The wine is not good this year."

"An innkeeper must take notice of such things, I suppose. The rest of us merrily drink whatever is sold in the vineyards or at market."

"I have some excellent wine in my cellar." He looked at her searchingly. "If you come by, I would happily fill your skin with something better than what you have there."

Gomer knew what he was saying, as certainly as if he had spoken the words straight out. It was how she imagined all men now regarded her: *Come by. Take love with me.*

"Tomorrow I must visit my mother," Gomer said on sudden impulse. "Your inn is on the way. I will stop by with an empty wineskin and test your honesty."

Thus it began. She went to his inn.

Her mother learned of it the third time Gomer went to Donath. Anna walked across Samaria by herself of a morning, when she supposed Hosea would have left the house. She greeted the children with a spiritless embrace and quickly herded them to the door.

"Go across to Deborah," she said. "Play with Jonathan."

Jezreel bounded out the door and Loruhamah toddled after him, always instant at a word from Mama-Mama.

She fell on Gomer with no hint of gentleness. "What are you thinking?" she shrieked. "You plead forgiveness of your husband and your father and me for the shame you have brought upon us, only to heap fresh shame on us! Do you want to be stoned? Is that your mind?"

Gomer stood white-faced in the middle of the room. She wore the sky blue linen robe Diblaim had given her on the fourth year of marriage, not a workaday garment. She made no attempt to lie or excuse herself; that had never been the way between them. She bowed her head, said nothing.

"Have you nothing to say?" Anna demanded. "Are you prettily dressed to go whoring already in the morning?"

"That is what he called me," Gomer said bleakly.

"Called you?"

"When he found me at the palace. He called me Whore."

Anna took a step toward her. Her voice gave up some of its edge. "You said things were better between you. What is this foolish thing you have done?"

Gomer sank to the floor, covering her head with her hands as though to ward off a blow. Anna sat beside her. For a time, neither spoke. After some moments, Anna laid a hand on

Gomer's arm. Gomer covered the hand with her own. They began to speak, mother and daughter again.

"It has been more peaceful between us," Gomer said quietly. "But never the same. Never as it was."

"He comes to you?"

"Sometimes. Only in the dark. Not as often. And not — not as before."

"You must lead him."

Gomer shook her head and spoke her pain: "He takes me as one takes a whore. Only to have me. Not to love me. There is no play between us like before, no careless laughter."

"That then is your pain, Daughter. Make it your own and count it light payment. He has taken you back. Many Yahweh tether would have turned you out or had you stoned."

"I speak the same words to myself, but they give me no comfort." Gomer lifted her head and looked pleadingly to her mother. "I cannot live only by words."

"The innkeeper? He gives you more than words?"

"I am beautiful to him, not blemished. He wants me."

"As he would want any Temple harlot. He pays you with lies and gifts, cheap coin, and will cast you out when he tires of you."

Gomer looked away. She had no answer. The words her mother spoke were the same words repeated over and over in her own thoughts. Shamed in all Samaria, a shame to her mother and father, a shame to her husband and the father of her children, skulking from his bed to — to what? Shame, more shame, and no way back. How had she come to such a day?

"Do you think me a good wife to your father?" Anna asked suddenly.

"You, Mama? A good wife? How else could I think?"

"You think me a good wife?"

"I do."

"Have you always thought so?"

"Sometimes I thought — thought you wanted too much to have your own way with him. You did not always show him respect."

"That gossip I know well, in all the city. 'Diblaim does not rule his own household.' Your father rules differently, by giving or holding back himself."

"I know," Gomer returned. "If I displeased him, he withdrew, even when he gave me my own way."

"How, then, have I held his love these years, though I want my own way and quarrel wildly? How do I still hold his love?"

"I know he loves you, Mama. He cannot let you walk by him without reaching out to touch you."

"That is some part of it. We bed well together. But I am more than his bed woman and the mother of his children — the sons who died, and you, the darling of his heart. I *help* him."

"Help him? How help him? Where? In what?"

"In whatever concerns his well-being — tending important relationships, advancing his leather business, punishing his enemies. When I can, I help directly. Four leather merchants twice combined to cut off his leather supply from Bashan. They were half successful at first. Things went badly with us for a time. On their second try I shrewdly located new supply north of Tyre, among my grandmother's people, the Sidonians: cheaper and better quality. Mostly, I encourage him."

"Encourage him? How encourage him??"

"I shared his world those dark days. I believed in him when all Samaria prophesied his defeat."

"I am no encouragement to Hosea," Gomer said distractedly.

"Not in the public street. Perhaps not in his bed, for a time."

"What else is there?"

"What else? His life, Daughter! You must become part of his life, blood and skin. He is a priest. Some say a prophet. I do not pretend to understand Hosea. Baal has done well for me and is god enough for me. But if Hosea is truly a prophet — no prophet in Israel ever labored under an excess of encouragement. He will always need encouragement."

"He thinks me a harlot. What help, a harlot's encouragement?"

"He has kept you his wife. I do not understand it in him. He is an Israelite who hates adultery. I would better understand him if he turned you out or had you stoned, according to Israel's Law. In some way he continues to love you, in the face of all that has happened openly.

"Who is left to encourage him? When friends desert him, when Samaria laughs at his word, when he comes disheartened to his house, be there to encourage him. Believe in him. Work for him. Punish his enemies. You are a prophet's wife, as I am a leather merchant's wife. Turn your will and your skill to advancing your husband's cause. A wife rises or falls with her husband."

Gomer took Anna's hands in her own, kissed first the right hand, then the left. "Can a whore ever become a wife again?"

Tears brimmed in Anna's eyes. "Child, you are not a whore."

"I have acted the whore."

Anna nodded slowly. Some of the edge returned to her voice: "Then act the wife. Redeem yourself." She rose to her feet. "Save your sky blue robe for your husband."

Gomer stood up slowly, strangely strengthened by her mother's rebuke. She stepped out of her sky blue robe, folded it carefully, and put on a rough gray robe, twice stained.

"Let Donath be a stranger to you, nothing but a stranger," Anna said as she stood at the door to leave. "He has some secrets of his own he would rather keep buried. I will make certain he is reminded."

Gomer embraced her, whispering, "I would be like you, Mama."

Anna gripped Gomer at arms' length. "We are already too much alike. You must be what I could never be — Yahweh tether to the soles of your feet."

3

Gomer did not return to Donath. In the following weeks she stayed close to the house, spending much time with Jezreel and Loruhamah. Sometimes she sent Jezreel to fetch water so she would not have to be seen in the streets. He was not yet four years old, but he rose happily to the task, fetching a half-bucket of water, man of the family when Hosea was gone.

Diblaim had taught Gomer to read when she was little older than Jezreel. She never thought it peculiar that she, a girl, could read and write. If her father decided it was good, she was free to do it. That was an end of it. Neighbor women came asking her to write letters or make records for them. She was the only woman in the street who could read and write. Now, when the children slept or went out to play with neighbor children, she read from Hosea's many scrolls.

When Hosea came home from his altar or from the city, she asked him careful questions about the stories and teachings in the scrolls. She seldom had to take a scroll in her hand; with two or three readings she could recite the words from memory.

"You know the scroll better than I do," he said when she once asked him about the story of Lot's wife leaving the city of Sodom.

"The words stick with me," Gomer said, "but not always the meaning. I want to know the scrolls as you do, both words and meaning."

One spring afternoon Melohim, a cousin of Hosea's helper Odenjah, planned to celebrate the naming of a son at Hosea's altar. Gomer was invited to participate in the celebration, along with the children. When she and the children arrived at the altar, they found Hosea in a heated discussion with Melohim's father-in-law. The mother-in-law stood close by her husband. After the naming ceremony, she wanted to have a small Baal festival to insure the yield of a vineyard they were giving Melohim, in honor of the first grandson.

"No festival of the Baal can be held at this altar. This is an altar of the LORD, only the LORD," Hosea told them.

They spoke some more, arguing and gesturing. Gomer could not understand what was said until Hosea raised his voice and spoke clearly, "It is the first Word of the Law: *You shall have no other gods before me.*"

The mother-in-law whispered to her husband.

"It can be a few paces down the hill," the man said. "Another altar, lower down."

Coming into the circle, Gomer knelt down beside Jezreel, seeming to answer him in a loud whisper, "It is against the scrolls."

The mother-in-law spoke angrily to Gomer: "Is this now a matter for women and children?"

"Pardon me, I beg you," Gomer murmured. "I wanted to quiet the child."

The father-in-law broke in. "What mean you, 'against the scrolls?' What is against the scrolls?"

"I thought only of the word of Moses in the Torah," Gomer said softly. "'The LORD is God; there is no other alongside Him.' Even downhill, it would be an altar alongside the altar of the LORD."

Melohim broke in. "Let there be an end to this," he said, looking directly at his mother-in-law. "We are here to name our son. The vineyard can wait until another time."

The woman tossed her head and turned away. Those gathered broke out of the tight knot they had become and moved toward the altar, muttering to one another. Gomer moved to the back, her eyes on the ground, holding Jezreel in an iron grip with one hand, Loruhamah with the other. Hosea stared after her in some wonderment.

4

A fear came to trouble Gomer. What would Hosea do if he learned of the visits she had made to Donath, even though half a year had passed and it did not seem to be known in the street?

In the scrolls she read prayers King David wrote when Nathan the prophet came to him, after David had committed adultery with Bathsheba. She learned all the beautiful words. She recited them aloud, even making up a melody with one, singing the words to herself when she was alone in the house. Some of the words troubled her, some comforted her.

When I declared not my sin, my body wasted away through my groaning all day long. For day and night your hand was heavy upon me. I acknowledged my sin to you. Then you forgave the guilt of my sin.

Against you, you only, have I sinned, and done that which is evil in your sight. Create in me a clean heart, O God, and put a new and right spirit within me.

When King David owned his guilt before the LORD, he did more than plea for mercy; he looked to the LORD to put a new spirit in him.

When Gomer went to Shallum, and then to Donath, she thought little of guilt. She feared being found out, being punished. Guilt came to weigh on her more slowly, when she saw the grief she brought on people she most loved — her husband, her father and mother, her children.

And something more. King David said, "Against you, you only, have I sinned." Who was *You*? It was the LORD. She had gone against a word in the scrolls, the seventh Word, adultery. She had thought only of keeping her trespass hidden, or, when it became known, of escaping punishment. But behind the scroll, behind the Word, was Him who spoke the Word, Him whose word it was: the LORD.

Two thoughts warred within Gomer. She feared Hosea's judgment. That was familiar. But something new began to stir within her — a longing to be clean of guilt before the LORD, to have a new spirit, as King David had prayed, and him guilty of the same sin.

As weeks and months went by, Gomer came to see her life as a walk on two narrow planks — her standing with Hosea on one side, her understanding of the LORD and His ways on the other. Every step on one side seemed to call for a balancing step on the other. When some tenderness began to grow again between her and Hosea, she longed to find something akin to it in her understanding of the LORD and His ways, especially His ways with her.

Should she confess her sin openly? Could there be new life for her?

She came to Hosea one evening, after the children had been laid to bed. He reclined by the table, neither reading from the scrolls nor writing, seemingly lost in thought. Most of the room was in darkness. The oil lamp cast a dim light and shadows. Gomer knelt by his feet, not speaking, though she had planned her words with great care. After some moments, Hosea reached out and laid a hand gently on her shoulder.

She took it as a sign she might speak. "My husband, I would speak with you."

"Some new word you have read in the scrolls, I imagine," he said, smiling.

"A word concerning me. I have long wanted to tell you."

"This wife is almost a stranger to me, so solemn," Hosea said with a laugh. "Speak on."

"Before Loruhamah was born, I sinned greatly against you," Gomer began, halting almost with every word. "You showed me great kindness, took me again into your house."

She waited, not certain whether he would speak. He remained silent but did not remove his hand from resting on her.

"More than three years have now passed. I live happily in your house, happily with our children, most happily with you, my husband."

"I live happily with you," Hosea responded, almost as a question.

Slowly Gomer spoke the words she had practiced so carefully. Six months earlier, she told him, she had gone three times to Donath. She was without excuse. She gave in to temptation. She sinned, sorely sinned. Better he hear it from her than in the street, if that should happen. She wanted no falsehood to stand between them. Would he forgive her, though she deserved judgment?

"Why do you tell me this now?" Hosea asked after some silence between them. "Is there yet something between you and this man?"

"Nothing between us. Nor shall there be. I have not laid eyes on him in many months."

"Why then have you told me?"

"That no evil secret stand between us, whatever you may do."

Hosea dropped his hand to his side, too bewildered to speak further. Gomer remained silent. After some time Hosea said, "This is no common speech between wife and husband."

Gomer spoke words from King David's prayer, "'Cast me not away from your presence.' If you find it in your heart, have mercy on me."

Hosea rose to his feet, took the lamp and walked out of the house to the shed, his common retreat when he and Gomer clashed.

Gomer remained in the darkness, not moving. More than an hour passed. She had not known how Hosea would receive her words. There had been good months between them, but when she spoke to him now and looked in his eyes she saw great dismay.

Telling the secret lifted a burden from her heart. For the first time since that dread afternoon at the palace, she felt strangely at peace within herself. Her confession went beyond her words to Hosea. The prayer of King David brooded in her thoughts, *Against you, you only, have I sinned, and done that which is evil in your sight.*

5

I stood in the middle of my carpenter shed, surveying unfinished projects that lined the walls. I spun a hammer in the air and caught it behind my back without a thought. Was this to be the endless cycle of our life? Sin, rebuke, tears and promises, reawakening love, another wandering from home and marriage bed, reproach, more tears, more broken promises? What would I come home to discover next month? Next year? The good months we had known blew away like morning mist.

I sat down on the dirt floor, holding my head in my hands. An hour must have gone by. "What can I do?" I asked myself. "What hope is there for us?"

I had not overheard the voice of the LORD in more than three years; not since the day He spoke the name of Loruhamah.

"What am I to do?" I whispered.

In the silence of my carpenter shed I suddenly heard the notable Voice. The word was not spoken directly to me but pronounced a decree spoken in divine council: *Strip her naked and make her as in the day she was born.*

This was the language of divorce; the words for turning out an adulterous wife. It was not a strange word. It was a common word whispered about in Samaria by my foes and followers alike.

The word brought me no peace. "Loyalty to family and friends stands above all else." A word from my mother. I could not think of myself and Gomer except as husband and wife. Gomer owned my life and affections.

Was I setting myself above the Law of the LORD? Did I push the Law of God aside in clinging to Gomer? That would be a high order of sin.

6

When Hosea returned to the house, Gomer knew at once the fragile scaffolding of trust between them had collapsed. She had thought of thwarting judgment, of cleansing between herself and Hosea, between herself and the LORD. She had not imagined that her confession would haunt his days with fresh doubt.

There were no harsh words as before, nor tears and pleadings from her. His voice was disheartened, empty of anger and bitterness. He told her, in the formal way of a judgment, lest his words be misunderstood: "This one time I receive you back into my house, and then no more. If you again play the harlot, I will turn you naked into the street."

Gomer knew Hosea would not waver from his word. He had withheld punishment for the last time. There began between them a cold and sorrowful time, marked by fear that their life together could not long endure.

Chapter 22

A Birth, a Death

1

When Gomer's adultery with Shallum was first shouted aloud in the Temple, it drove Hosea to humiliation and silence. When she privately confessed her adultery with Donath, the outcome was opposite. He prophesied more urgently.

Israel became like a second wife, vexing him with unfaithfulness, crying out for judgment, tormenting him with a love he yearned after, remembered, and could not surrender.

When not at the countryside altar, he was much in the city — preaching in the open, speaking in the gate. He came to be called prophet more than priest. For a time the priests of the Temple tried to vex him with words about his wife and shouts of 'Wittol' and 'Whoremonger' from the edge of the crowd. Mostly he bore their taunts without retort. Israel and Gomer became as one. The judgment of one spoke judgment on both. After a time the priests grew silent about his wife. He ignored their taunts, and the people seemed loath to take issue with Hosea in the matter of his wife.

Hosea came more and more to see Israel's worship as a marriage. The LORD chose Israel as a man chooses a bride. She owed to the LORD the faithfulness of a bride. She wandered forty years in the wilderness, knowing only the LORD, faithful to Him only.

It was not enough to worship the LORD and observe fast days. The LORD was Israel's husband. The LORD *alone* must be worshipped. Here lay Israel's sin — mixing worship of the

229

LORD with festivals of Baal and Ashtarte — claiming marriage to the LORD and whoring after other gods, as Gomer went whoring after other men.

'The LORD, whose name is Jealous, is a jealous God.' This word came down from Moses. Few in Israel took account of it, save the Rechabites, who dwelt in tents and lived a hard and simple life on the far side of the Jordan. They alone worshipped the LORD God according to the covenant made with Moses. Hosea had always thought the Rechabites a queer and fanatic folk, still dwelling in tents, with strict laws for eating and dress. Yet for all of that, they had clung to a word all Israel should remember — a word that spoke to the heart of the evil that plagued Israel.

'I, the LORD your God, am a *jealous* God.'

The LORD's jealous claims on Israel found pitiable echo in Hosea's dejected yearning for Gomer. All Israel kept feasts and holy days, but they walked careless of the First Word of the Law, *You shall have no other Gods.* Gomer lived as wife in his house, but what else — who else — laid claim to her affections?

Hosea gained fewer offerings at his countryside altar — sometimes barely enough to keep food on the table. Long hours would go by with no person coming to make offering or sacrifice. Hosea came to dislike these lonely times; his thoughts rankled in a pasture of empty hopes.

Diblaim and Anna came by less often, mostly when Hosea was away from the house. They found it hard even to make talk with Hosea. They knew he and Gomer had fallen on hard days and were a mumbled byword in Samaria: *Open adultery and the prophet took her back.* Gomer's shame stood like a wall between her parents and her husband. Hosea never spoke the charge, but they took it on themselves, the common notion that blame for a bad wife came back to rest on the wife's father and mother. Diblaim devised ever more artful excuses to bring gifts for the house or for the children. Spirited talk between mother and daughter, theirs since Gomer's childhood, dwindled away. In the last purposeful talk they had, Gomer told Anna of her confession to Hosea, and Anna replied, "You spoke too soon. You should have waited."

Diblaim and Anna knew that no one dared disdain Hosea openly; such was his stature and the regard in which he was held in Samaria. In this they found some comfort.

2

One mid-morning, as Gomer was preparing to go to the market with Jezreel and Loruhamah, Obed, the husband of Hosea's sister, came knocking at the door. In the first three years of their marriage, Shania had not conceived. Twice she and Obed came to Samaria to visit Hosea and Gomer and to make sacrifice and prayers at Hosea's altar, that she might be with child. Some weeks after the second visit they sent Hosea and Gomer the joyful news that Shania was with child.

"Obed!" Gomer exclaimed. "How good to see you. And how is my sister? Her time is near."

"Yes, near for certain, and the reason for my journey."

Gomer brought him into the house, making greetings between Obed and the children.

"Is all well?" Gomer asked.

"With Shania, all is well. She is troubled about the birth."

"What first time mother is not?"

"It is not about herself, but the midwife."

"The midwife?"

"Four babes, now, have died under her hand. People are saying a spirit of death has come upon her, and Shania believes it may be so."

"She is the only midwife in Dothan?"

"For some years already. Shania asks if you would come and be midwife to her."

"Me?" Gomer said in astonishment. "I have never been midwife for anyone."

"I said exactly what you have said: that you have no experience as midwife. But you have had two children of your own. Shania brushed everything aside, even stomped her foot, 'If Gomer is by my side, all will be well.'"

Gomer answered with an impulsive nod, "Then I will come!"

"Can you come back to Dothan with me?"

"So soon, you think?"

"She is large."

"It will slow us, but I must take the children."

"We can still reach Dothan by early evening. I can carry Loruhamah some of the way."

Gomer thought to leave word with Deborah, but Deborah had gone early to the well. Gomer scratched a message for Hosea on a scrap of wood she found in the carpenter shed and laid it on the table in the house: *To Dothan with Obed. I am midwife for Shania.*

Jezreel ran ahead like a horse released from the stall, excited by the adventure. Loruhamah was too little to keep up walking and too heavy for Obed to carry all the way without resting. They arrived in Dothan three hours after sunset.

Shania leaned forward to embrace Gomer. "My sister, my savior!" she exclaimed. "Now I am at peace."

Gomer laughed, "Women have been having babies forever and ever. You could do it all by yourself."

"Better with you beside me."

* * *

Two days later Hosea came to Dothan. He had spent anxious moments when he came home and found the house empty. He did not at once see the message Gomer had left. The neighbors, Ebarth and Deborah, knew nothing. He went to

Diblaim's house, but she and the children were not there and her parents knew nothing.

In a hushed voice Anna asked, "Is all well between you?"

"All is well," Hosea answered hastily, pushing aside the fear that she had left his house, together with the children — with whom? He set out across Samaria at a trot. When he arrived at his house, Deborah stood at his door holding up the wood scrap with Gomer's message.

"Does this tell you anything?" she asked.

Hosea read the words and gave a shout, "My sister! She has gone to be midwife! I must go."

Deborah picked up his relief and the fear that stood behind it. "Exactly what I would have expected," she said forcefully. "Always ready to help others. That is always her way."

Four days went by. Each morning Obed and Hosea stood by, looking at Shania before they went out to attend to Obed's wine business, as though their helpless stares might hasten the birth.

Gomer and Shania carried on cheerfully, content that babies come when they are ready to come. Shania wanted to know everything. Gomer's labor with both Jezreel and Loruhamah had been brief. She recounted every detail she could remember, Shania sitting by, asking some questions, but mostly listening.

Mid-afternoon of the fifth day, Jezreel and Loruhamah went outside to play and climb trees in the olive grove. Shania ventured an uneasy word with Gomer. "Is all well with you and my brother?"

Gomer did not answer at once. What could she share with Shania? "Have you heard anything amiss?"

"Heard? I have heard nothing. It is only what I see. I mark a coldness between you." Distress showed in her voice.

Gomer nodded. She leaned down and drew a circle in the dirt of the floor, then stroked a line through the middle. "We have come on hard days. We are divided."

"Gomer!" Shania broke into tears, her worst fears rising like a specter between them. "How can you be divided? You are husband and wife. You have Jezreel, Loruhamah."

"Samaria is close. I thought you would have heard. Or suspected it, the last time you came to our house, before you were with child."

"Hosea spoke hard words against Israel, like the prophet from Judah. He was intense. He has always been so."

"His hard words are for me also."

"No!" Shania cried. "You are the darling of his heart."

Gomer knelt on the floor and settled back on her legs, leaning away from Shania. "You have become dearest sister to me," she said with tears. "Now you must hear my shame. I have gone to two other men."

Shania's mouth fell open. She sat down beside Gomer, shaking her head from side to side. "How . . . ?" she whispered.

"It was a festal celebration," Gomer said, "at a new vineyard of the king." She told Shania the whole story without excuse, speaking against herself as though she were another person. She paused when the story was done, then said, "Now you will hate me."

"Never, dear my sister." She reached out and laid her hand on Gomer's hand. "He took me back and bore the taunts. Things went better with us for a time. He did not know about Donath, the innkeeper."

"Someone told him?"

"I told him. I wanted no dark secret between us. I had dwelt on the confessions of King David when he sought new life with the LORD. I dreamed it might be so with us. I spoke too soon. Love had grown warm between us again, but his trust was more fragile than I knew. When I confessed, it drove a wedge between us. He fears I will go again."

"He took you back." Shania spoke it like a word of pardon.

"How well I know," Gomer answered, catching Shania's meaning. "Yet I live in fear."

"Hosea will not go against his word."

"I fear my own inconstant heart."

"Oh, Gomer! You love him. I know you love him."

"I am wife to the most admired man in all Israel, and I took pleasure with men who do not come up to his sandals. What kind of woman am I?" Gomer buried her face in her hands.

Shania circled her arm around Gomer's shoulders. "Hosea was the star of my life when we were growing up," she said. "More even than our father or mother. We were closest in age and heart. If I did something wrong, he scolded me like a father. He was more Yahweh tether with me than our parents. His anger never lasted. He found ways to put it aside. Love and kindness always won out."

Gomer returned Shania's embrace and kissed her cheek. "Dear sister, we know and love the same man — you his sister, I his wife: anger and judgment woven together with love and kindness. Sometimes I have thought, *If only he would punish me proudly, as a man, with beating and railing and un-repenting rage.* But no, on the heels of outrage — soft pleading, words of love renewed, tenderness. Until now. If I go aside again, he will turn me out. That he has sworn."

"Gomer, you must not go aside. Your love is for Hosea."

They sat in silence for a time, still embracing one another.

"'Your love is for Hosea,'" Gomer repeated sadly. "It has never been otherwise. My heart has never gone aside from clinging to him."

"Your love is *only* for Hosea," Shania said softly.

Again silence. Then Gomer spoke: "That is my sin. I have lived with a divided heart. Married to Hosea but secretly giving my heart to another man. I am caught in a snare of my own making."

"It is no snare," Shania responded. "Obed is a hedge of protection for me."

"You? You have faced such things?"

"Obed has known ridicule all his life because he is small. It does not disquiet him. He is every cubit a man. When we were married more than a year and I did not conceive, men made brazen suggestions to me at festivals and out in the country-side. Some were well-favored men; you would little expect such rudeness. When they suggested themselves to me I made my voice hard as iron and said Obed ben Jeshurun was more a man at three cubits than they would be at six." Shania stood up awkwardly, leaning on Gomer. "I stand under his name. His name protects me."

"I have dreaded telling you these things," Gomer said as she stood up beside Shania. "I feared I might lose you."

Shania embraced her with both arms. "You are closer to me than my blood sister. I love you."

* * *

When the men returned to the house in mid-afternoon, Gomer set Hosea to work building a birthing stool, should the birth be prolonged. Four days later Shania went into labor. The pains came, and then they ceased. She slept through the night. The pains came again in the morning, more severe. Gomer's children had come quickly while she knelt on the bed. With Shania it did not go quickly, and Gomer realized with fear that she was no midwife. She asked whether they should send for the midwife. Shania clutched Gomer's hands.

"I want only you," she begged.

Gomer put her on the birthing stool and sat beside her. Shania was in great pain but made no sound.

"It happened quickly with me," Gomer said weakly. "I don't know how to help you."

"Stay beside me. You love me. You are my greatest help."

Gomer spoke vainly but in a commanding voice, "Come, little baby, come!"

For some moments the pain lessened, then came again

more than before. Shania rolled her head from side to side and spoke to Gomer between gasps. "You know the scrolls so well. Read to me from the scrolls."

"They are in Samaria. I have no scrolls."

A moan escaped Shania's lips, the first utterance of her pain. Gomer sensed Shania's resolve to bear the pain in silence as a thank offering for the child. Suddenly, Gomer heard herself speaking words from the scrolls. "You are like a tree planted by streams of water that yields its fruit in its season, and its leaf does not wither. In all you do, you shall prosper."

She needed nothing to read; whole scrolls were hidden away in her astonishing memory. The words flowed from her, thoughts and phrases from different prayers, spoken as words to Shania.

"Thou, O LORD, are a shield about me, my glory, and the lifter of my head. I cry aloud to the LORD, and he answers me from His holy hill. I lie down and sleep; I wake again, for the LORD sustains me. Answer me when I call, O God of my righteousness! You have given me relief when I was in distress. Be gracious to me and hear my prayer! Know that the LORD has set apart the godly for Himself; the LORD hears when I call to Him."

Gomer fell silent between Shania's birth contractions. When Shania nodded or squeezed her hand, Gomer continued to speak words from the scrolls. After more than three hours she spoke the words of Moses, his concluding blessing on the tribes of Israel, where he calls Israel by the name given to Obed's father. "There is none like God, O Jeshurun, who rides through the heavens to your help, and in His majesty through the skies. The eternal God is your dwelling place, and underneath are the everlasting arms."

Shania gave a sudden shout, and cried out, "He comes! Come into the world, my son!"

Gomer reached down and caught the hairy little head as it fell below the birthing stool. She dared not do more than hold her hand gently to the head. The birth was not yet complete. "Push!" she commanded Shania.

With a final effort, Shania gave birth. The child gave out a lusty cry. Gomer swung the babe into her arms. "A boy!" she cried. "How did you know?"

"When you spoke the name, I knew. He shall be named Jeshurun, for Obed's father."

Three days later, Shania lay abed with the newborn child. She reached up to embrace Gomer before she and Hosea returned to Samaria, the day before Sabbath.

"Beloved sister, look at the gift you have given us!"

Gomer ruffled the babe's abundant hair. "I! I sat by while you gave birth. I did nothing."

"You came a savior to me and the child. Now there are two of us to love you — will always love you."

"Come, little daughter," Hosea said as they were leaving. Loruhamah squealed as he swung her up on his back. "I will be your horse. You can ride me all the way home."

Loruhamah laid her head against Hosea's neck. It was the first time he had ever held her.

The day was warm and fair. They walked at an easy pace and came within sight of Samaria well before sundown. They had not spoken much during the journey. Hosea waited until Jezreel scampered ahead toward the city gate, then spoke quietly to Gomer. "Shania loves you. She expected to die until you came."

"It was I who had reason to fear — fear I might be the cause of her death, or the child's. I am not a midwife. She is the dearest friend I have."

"She knows about us, does she not?"

"I told her."

That night Hosea came to Gomer's bed in the dark. For a long time he held her in his arms. No words were spoken. Gomer wept and lay quietly in his arms, her head on his strong chest.

For some weeks Shania lingered like a silent presence between Gomer and Hosea. It did not last.

* * *

Half a year went by. The mood between Hosea and Gomer waxed and waned. Interludes of warmth gave way to brooding silences. The talk that once animated their life together seemed lost to them. The fear that their life together would come to an end hung over them like a deadly, invisible presence.

After the former rains a child was born, a boy, crippled in his right leg. Again Hosea overheard the LORD speak the prophetic name by which the child would be known: *Call his name Loammi, Not My People, for you are not My people and I am not your God.*

For nearly a year Gomer had stayed close to her house. Jezreel was now past four years. She herself was twenty-four, still lissome and youthful, though more drawn in the face and lackluster of eye.

In times of brooding silence, the misery of the past crept back to haunt and torment her. She was like two persons within herself, arguing now in her favor, now against herself.

As a child she had learned something of Israel's holy Law, passed down from the hand of Moses. Such was the heritage of any child in Israel. But in the house of Diblaim the words of the Law gave way to what seemed good and reasonable. Gomer grew up living according to the mood and temper of the times. Even more, according to her ties with those she loved, first of all her mother and father, then Hosea and their children.

Gomer knew the plain words of the scrolls condemned her, yet strangely she had come dearly to love the scrolls. They tied her to Hosea and his world. She did not dislove Hosea when she went aside with the other men. It was never that, she told herself over and over. Like her mother at a harvest festival, it was a pleasant interlude, no diminishing of her wifely love.

Shania had spoken the word she could not step around or forget. "Your love must be for Hosea *only*." Much as she loved Shania, Shania's bold, undivided love for Obed stood like the Seventh Word against her, a silent accusation against her divided heart. When the temptation came, she had foolishly given way.

Five years. Shallum. Donath. Was there no release from what had happened? Would the LORD never put a 'new and right spirit within her,' as King David had prayed?

She was lonely. When Hosea was gone from the house for long hours, could he understand nothing of her loneliness?

And the passion. Who should know better than he of that? It was he who first wakened passion within her and delighted in it. Can you put passion on and off like a garment?

In such ways Gomer brooded over her standing with Hosea, her standing with herself, and her growing awareness of a standing with the LORD.

Though in some ways she stood free of the Law, after the free ways of her father, Gomer could not stand free from Hosea and the memory of what her life had once been with him. Her brooding thoughts came back to this — here is where the pain of her adultery came to rest — not the naked guilt, but what the guilt had wrought: separation, the awful, awful separation.

It was wrong, yes, it *was* wrong. Wrong that it should not be with them as it once was, wrong to throw days of happiness carelessly into the wind — wrong, wrong. A woman should not let herself be property to any man who rouses her passion. A woman should be for one man alone — Hosea, only Hosea — as it was in their first days together, as it was for Israel forty years in the wilderness. They two, alone, the world outside — they two, and naught between them but love and happiness, and sharing together without shame. They two, alone, alone. If that day could come again — if all that had happened between them could be blotted out forever —

There were kisses still, and embraces, even tender words. But never would it be the same. Never. In the morning there was no quiet lying together, the foolish little kisses and nibbling, and the glow of what they had been to one another — nay, it was a turning away and cold silence, as though they had taken what was unclean. In the evening it was 'Peace' cold and weary — no latching the door with a laugh and sweeping her into his arms, no silly hiding and play, no dear, dear words whispered on her ear that she was all and all to him, no sitting at his knees, drowsy and content, his fingers combing through her hair, his voice tuning a song, low and sweet, no cradling him to her bosom as a child, no fingers stealing beneath her robe, shyly, as a lover, no gentle kiss upon her breast. Nay, such time was past. All was coldness now. And darkness. And silence. And separation.

Not only between herself and Hosea, but between Hosea and the children.

Loruhamah. Loammi. Their prophetic names stood like a wall between them and their father. Something in him broke briefly when he carried Loruhamah home from Dothan after Shania's son was born, but it did not continue. He was distant toward them, as with strangers. And the children, quick to sense the leaning of his heart as children do, held a stranger's distance from the man they called Father.

It was different with Jezreel. Hosea was fond of the boy. Often he took him along to the altar or down into the city. The two were strong for adventuring together in the countryside around Samaria, or even as far west as Mount Carmel. They looked not at all alike. Jezreel was slender and swarthy skinned, whereas Hosea was fair and thickset. Yet in his speech and walk and manner, Jezreel was the pattern of his father and a great joy to Hosea.

Jezreel sometimes wielded an impudent tongue with Gomer. At other times he would cling to her and want to be held by her. He was too young to know all that lay between Gomer and Hosea. He sensed something bad lay between his father and mother, and he took his father's side. In Hosea's presence he was respectful toward Gomer, but when Hosea was gone from the house he often vexed and angered his mother. He would set himself against Loruhamah and Loammi, worrying and provoking them however he could, so that it seemed to Gomer their house was ever at war, with the younger children and herself on one side, and Jezreel and Hosea on the other.

Loruhamah was now past three years, gentle natured and affectionate. Loammi was helpless, with the crippling in his right leg. Between these two and Gomer there came to be a kind of defensive concern for one another. Yet, it brought Gomer small comfort. As it had always been with her, all must be right or nothing was right. As a child, even the smallest untoward happening could darken her to despair, or the gentlest word of admonition rouse her to anger and defiance. Never was she one to bear patiently a pain or distress. When all was told, the younger children ministered little joy to their mother. Her thoughts dwelt on the estrangement from Hosea and Jezreel.

This one time I receive you back into my house, and then no more. If you again play the harlot, I will turn you naked into the street.

For months these words had hung between them, dark and threatening. For fear of these words, she had scarce spoken to other men. She harbored no thought toward another man, but she knew no claiming of it would breed comfort between her and Hosea. Her words were too poisoned by broken promises.

* * *

Anna, and sometimes Diblaim, still came by to see her and the children, but between them talk dried up. Gomer no longer sought her mother's counsel. Then, in the month of Abib, a wasting sickness came on Anna. In two months time she was shrunken and bedfast. Diblaim wandered about the house aimlessly, too distracted to attend to his work. He came to Gomer and reported that her mother's breath was weak; she slept most of the time. Gomer asked Deborah to care for the children. She went to her mother and sat at her bedside, holding her hand, speaking to her when she was awake, as though they were carrying on normal talk with one another. She stayed by the bedside night and day, barely eating or sleeping herself. Sometimes she quietly spoke words from the scrolls. On the ninth day, around noonday, Anna opened her eyes and smiled. She laid her own hand over Gomer's hand.

"We were often at sword's point, you and I," she breathed. She squeezed Gomer's hand. "Long past and forgotten. Peace. Find peace with your husband and children." Her eyes closed. In the evening she died. Gomer's voice keened through the house, a wailing cry that would not be comforted.

She stayed the night with her father. Hosea came in the morning. They walked back to their house. Gomer held tight to Hosea's arm and leaned against him, still weeping.

"She was a beloved mother, also to me." Hosea said. "I loved her."

"She was a voice of wisdom to me," Gomer said. After some silence, "You, she truly loved. She admired you. Her last words commended you and the children."

Chapter 23

Envoys From Egypt

For ten years the Pharaoh of Egypt had watched the movements of Tiglath Pileser in Assyria, hoping that some power or ill chance would stop his rise. When Menahem of Israel paid tribute to Pileser, Pharaoh saw the last sure wall between himself and the Assyrian crumble away. He knew that his vain hopes must give place to action, or Egypt would surely fall to the conqueror.

Pharaoh purposed more than a trade agreement with some small mention of aid in war. He hoped to create a firm alliance of Israel, Damascus, Judah, and the coastal regions of Tyre — an alliance which he himself would quietly support and control, and which would bleed the Assyrians to weakness. He dispatched to Israel the same envoy that sealed the fateful treaty with Shallum ben Jabesh, which Menahem had never honored. To this purpose Seremta, the son of Pith, had traveled northward to Samaria and taken up residence in a well-appointed house west of the king's palace.

* * *

More than two years had passed since the death of Menahem. The fields of Jezreel stood winter green. Pekahiah ruled in Samaria, the seventeenth king of Israel's northern tribes.

The night of the first full moon following the late planting darkened suddenly with heavy clouds scudding in from the south. An unseasonable storm broke over Samaria. The hard-packed streets softened to mud and slime.

* * *

On a dark rainy night at the east gate of Samaria, a woman's voice called up to the gatekeeper, seeking entrance into the city. Behind her was a train of twenty servants and seven heavily laden camels. Huddled against the lead camel, seeking some protection from the pelting rain, was a man in the dress of an Egyptian.

"Who are you, at such an hour, on a night like this?" the gatekeeper asked, peering downward in the near-darkness.

"Midemi, the son of Nemeneneh, from the court of Pharaoh," the woman replied.

"Are you a man?"

"Nay, it is I who am Midemi, son of Nemeneneh," said the man standing against the lead camel. "My consort and our servants beg you entrance. This rain —"

"Open quickly and let us in," the woman said. "This rain has delayed us already and will ruin our baggage. We are bound to the house of Seremta, the Pharaoh's trusted envoy to your king Pekahiah."

The gatekeeper called down and ordered the gate opened. The woman walked through first. Midemi came a step behind with a servant at his side, holding up a leather shield to give his master some protection against the rain. Then came a handful of servants, male and female, then the camels. Last of all came twelve giant Nubian slaves, bearing on their shoulders a burden hidden under heavy tenting and rising above the bearers more than twice the height of a man. When they had passed into the city, the gateman called up: "Saw you the size of them? Five cubits if a handbreadth — every one of them!"

"What was their burden?"

"Hidden under wrapping."

"Perhaps we should not have opened to them."

"It is no night to be outside the city wall. They bore no weapons."

"Yes." The gatekeeper turned back toward the little shelter he had set himself against the parapet of the wall. Crouching under the tenting, he muttered, "Strange, the woman seemed to be leading them —"

A quarter hour later the camels of the Egyptians were settled for the night against the low wall that surrounded the house of Seremta. Two Nubians stood guard of their wrapped burden, set down in the small courtyard. Within the house, the servants busied themselves with unpacking. Soaked blankets and robes and gowns were strung throughout the house. In a corner of the main hall, Midemi knelt over a robe of deepest blue, trimmed in gold. Carefully, he was smoothing it across the face of a low table. The woman came up at his side.

"Let the servants see to that," she said sharply.

"Ruined!" he said. "And not another like it in all Memphis. Their weather here is as vile as their food."

"Come," the woman said impatiently. "We must speak now with Seremta."

A frown darkened Midemi's handsome face. He brushed a hand through his dark red hair.

"Let it wait till morning," he said.

"Waiting will make it no easier."

"Tania, I like it not —"

Tania grasped his arm and spoke low and tense: "Think of us, Midemi. In six months time all this will be past. We will be back in Egypt with a high place in the court of Pharaoh."

"But Seremta —"

"Had Seremta any true wit about him, this alliance would be under way already. Let him look to his own fortunes in the court of Pharaoh."

"Nay, he knows these people well. Such things take time."

"Midemi, we have traveled this ground a thousand times! The matter is settled beforehand. We have the Pharaoh's letter. We need only show it to Seremta. He is replaced by you as Pharaoh's envoy."

"Yes, and with that he loses his stand in Pharaoh's court."

"No matter. Think on us, Midemi."

"He will take it ill from me. We are friends."

"Let each man look out for himself. There is no other way in the court of Pharaoh."

* * *

Midemi had been aide to Seremta when the treaty with Shallum ben Jabesh was made, more than four years before. When Menahem won the throne, the two men returned to Egypt. Menahem would have no dealings with them.

When Midemi appeared suddenly in the doorway of Tania's house on his return to Egypt, wearing the look of a little boy come to surprise her, a single thought flashed through Tania's mind: he has failed!"

He and Seremta were to have remained in Israel more than a year, to husband the Pharaoh's trade agreements. Here he came, returned to Egypt in less than two months. Surely they had failed to obtain the treaty.

The mission to Israel had been a vital step in Midemi's career, and so also in Tania's. Ever since she was smitten with the breathless good looks and boyish charm of Midemi, Tania had set herself to one purpose — Midemi's advancement in the court of Pharaoh.

In the tumble house of intrigue that was Egypt's court, Tania's father had been done out of great wealth and position by the scheming of Pharaoh's nephew. With what little he was able to salvage, he bought a small house and began to plan and scheme his way back into power. In a year's time, all his substance was gone. Only the house remained. Tania's mother hired herself out as a house servant to keep food on the table. Hunger was a frequent guest. They were poor, bitter poor, yet her father would turn his hand to no trade. He swore he would regain favor at court and wreak vengeance on those who had caused his downfall. Twelve and fourteen hours of the day he hung in the shadows of the palace, seeking favors and appointments, until at last he became a pathetic jest in the court of Pharaoh.

His craving for revenge drove Tania's gentle mother to her death. His schemes never came to fruit. He followed his wife to the House of Death, a lonely and bitter man. Tania was fourteen years old, the only child, heir to her father's shrunken wealth and withered dreams.

She took up her father's struggle and vowed she would one day sit mistress over the fortunes and power her father had lost. She spurned the offer of hospice with her father's relations, dangerous as it was for a girl of her years, blooming into womanhood, to live alone and unprotected.

Tania soon learned that her slender, attractive body and her sensuous lips could win favors that her father's endless scheming could never win. At eighteen she had the ear and the affection of men high up in the Pharaoh's court. It was then that she met Midemi and fell madly, hopelessly in love.

She brought him to her house the first day they met. If ever a man was pursued and won by a woman, Midemi was that man. She went to his arms boldly and without shame. She wanted Midemi as she had never wanted a man before. She took him, as she had learned to take what she wanted.

Midemi accepted Tania's passion with little surprise. His handsome features, and the hint of shyness in the cast of his eyes, roused a strange passion in women — something of the mother as well as the lover. Midemi had grown accustomed to it. It was jested in court that Midemi would be husband-slain seven times daily if the wives of Memphis were to make deeds of their secret dreams. Such was his charm.

Yet, he came to care for Tania in a special way, as he did not care for other women who offered him love. He came to depend upon her decision and authority. She told him what move would advance him in the Pharaoh's court and when the move should be made. She took from him the burden of choice, leaving him free to dream as he would and to charm all he met with his comeliness and winsome manner. He had only to follow Tania's bidding, and he would gain wealth and security in the court of Pharaoh.

How a dreamer like Midemi was born to Nemeneneh the Scribe was the source of endless talk. Some said he bore a resemblance to the cousin of his mother, in his nose, so fine and straight, in his wide-set eyes, and his dreamy, wistful expression. His mother and her cousin had been raised together as children. They were much of an age and devoted to one another, as the neighbors remembered it. Seven months before Midemi was born, the cousin left Memphis and was never seen in the city again; such talk was certain to follow. But the truth or falseness of the talk went to the House of Death with Midemi's mother. His father never doubted his wife's faithfulness and counted the child his own.

Midemi's father was chief scribe in the court of Pharaoh, a practical man, given to unvarying habits, and wholly without imagination. His face was homely, almost ugly. In every way, he and Midemi were as unlike as two men could be.

He hoped to teach Midemi the Scribe's profession, but at last gave up in despair. Midemi spent all his time making the figures beautiful and perfectly balanced, caring not at all for what he wrote, for speed, or for accuracy. So Nemeneneh won him an appointment in foreign service, where at least his good appearance would work to advantage. But even here Midemi made little progress, and at his death Nemeneneh held no hope that his feckless son would ever rise beyond the position of a court follower. Had he lived two months more, to Midemi's twentieth birthday, Nemeneneh's hopes might have risen. It was then that Midemi met Tania.

Tania used every cunning to advance Midemi's cause in the court of Pharaoh. In Midemi she saw not only a man she loved, a man desired by many women, but also the means of gaining the wealth and power once held by her father. Joined as she was to Midemi, by her love and by her pride in having won him, she could no longer play so loosely with the affections of other men. But she could guide Midemi's easy grace with people into profitable ventures, and as he rose in influence, rise with him. She bent every effort to this end. She chose the clothes Midemi wore and dressed him with great care each time he appeared at court. She planned rare midnight meals to entertain men of influence each time Midemi's career reached a critical pass. The chanciest remark or most innocent circumstance she could turn to Midemi's advantage.

Her efforts were not wasted. He rose quickly in the court. When Pharaoh looked about for an aide to the old and respected Seremta on a mission of great importance, Tania connived to have Midemi chosen over seven men who preceded him by length of service. It would mean their separation for more than a year, but the influence it could bring Midemi would more than pay them for the time apart.

So it was that when Midemi returned from Israel, Tania was more disturbed than filled with joy. It doubly upset her that he took the failure of their mission so lightly. In Israel he had let Seremta take the lead in all decisions. On return to Egypt, he seemed quite content that Seremta should carry the burden of their explanations to Pharaoh, and that Tania should again work out a plan for his life.

This rankled Tania. She had hoped Midemi would develop some talent for decision in his months with Seremta. Ambitious and gifted though she was, Tania yet yearned as a woman to be ruled over in some point of her relationship with Midemi. Midemi made no effort. Even in their love, always it was Tania who came to Midemi. His charm had so accustomed him to be sought after that he never knew what it was to pursue or rule a woman. So long as Tania came to him, he found no reason to change.

For a time, the fortunes of Seremta and Midemi fell in Pharaoh's court. But as the menace of Assyria loomed ever larger in the east, Pharaoh found himself in need of men with wide knowledge of affairs in the coastlands of Canaan. And so it was that when Menahem paid tribute to Pileser, Seremta was the man chosen for a mission that could mean the life or death of Egypt. Tania had tried again to gain an appointment for Midemi. But this time, by his own request, Seremta traveled alone. When they had gone to Israel five years before, Midemi had done little but complain of the food and smell and uncouth manners of the Israelites. Though he had come to like Midemi, as most everyone did, Seremta knew that the mission now set before him would allow no time to nurse Midemi through gloomy moods. Thus, none to his own displeasure — for he had no desire to go again to Israel — Midemi was left behind while Seremta traveled to Samaria.

For some months Tania was wroth with Midemi, for taking this blow to his fortunes without despair, even cheerfully. She goaded him with words, hoping he would rouse himself and make some repair of his fortunes. Then, one night when she desired him and cradled him upon her breast, she came to know that it was not in Midemi to look to his own affairs. He had entrusted such things to her from the day of their first meeting. And because he lay so quiet and childlike in her arms, and filled her with so deep a love, a plan began to form in her thoughts, which could turn this defeat into a great victory for Midemi. It was a harsh plan, a child of love and hate, born of her passion for Midemi and her vengeful ambition for power and wealth.

In the months that followed, Tania haunted the market places and trading docks of Memphis, seeking out every camel train and every merchant newly arrived from Israel. Like dry desert sand, she soaked up their language and manners, their customs and their way of thinking, their history, their opinion of present affairs, their petty quarrels, their hates, their beliefs. Each night she sat before Midemi as teacher and dunned into his ears the ways of Israel. Playing desperately against time, on the chance that Seremta would not be able to quickly accomplish his mission with Menahem still on the throne, Tania prepared herself and her man for the greatest venture of their lives.

When Menahem died, and Seremta still reported no gains at the court of Israel, Tania knew the time was ripe. She began to have it whispered about that Seremta was letting opportunities pass by; that he had grown old now, and no longer possessed keen judgment. Next came the whisper that Midemi could bring Pharaoh's alliance to swift effect. He knew the Israelite temper well, and he had a plan: Israel grumbled under the rule of the son of Menahem. The land was ripe for revolt. If the envoy of the Pharaoh had wit and daring, he could conspire to set on Israel's throne a man who would favor the cause of Egypt.

These whispers brought Midemi, at last, into the presence of Pharaoh. Tania had prepared him well. The nation of Israel, Midemi said, was but a single man of Israel many times over. What swayed the man would sway the nation — fear, flattery, gifts, hope of gain.

Midemi proposed to take to Samaria twelve giant Nubian slaves. They would throw up to the people of Samaria a symbol of Egypt's power. As a group, the Nubians would play subtly upon the Israelite's fondness for the number twelve, which carried with it a thought of completeness and power going far back into their history as a people.

Midemi would also take, as a gift to their Temple, a huge golden image of a calf. This was the steed of their storm god, Baal, LORD of seed and harvest. The gift of the golden calf would kindly dispose the people of Israel toward mighty Pharaoh. In Israel, more than in other lands, the people carried weight in the affairs of the kingdom.

Midemi and his consort must live richly in Samaria, for the land had fallen on hard times, and the people must be given to hope that in an alliance with Egypt they might come to enjoy the kind of life the Pharaoh's envoy displayed before them.

A faction in the army had been set against the throne from the first day of Menahem's rule. This faction provided a hard core of men who would set their swords against the throne if they knew mighty Pharaoh stood behind their revolt.

The plan was peculiarly the creature of Tania — direct, personal, and deceptively simple. So skillfully did Midemi argue his cause, and so thorough a grasp did he seem to possess of Israel's affairs, even lapsing at times, seemingly without thinking, into their speech to explain some issue, that he won the ear of Pharaoh. The Pharaoh set his own goldsmiths to fashioning a calf-image that Midemi had described in great detail. In two months time, Midemi and Tania were on their way to Israel. Pharaoh had denied them nothing.

* * *

Seremta's frog-like voice broke in from the doorway of his house: "What in Pharaoh's name have you set in my courtyard?"

"A gift for the Temple here in Samaria," Midemi said. "The image of a calf."

Before Midemi could say more, Seremta cut him off. "Whose notion was that?"

"It was Midemi's," said Tania coolly, glancing sidewise at him.

Seremta shook his head dolefully. "I know not what demon of folly possessed Pharaoh to send you here in this fashion — set out like a royal wedding procession. Our fortunes tip a delicate balance in Israel these days. I can scarce show my hand. Even to send Midemi as an aide risks misunderstanding —"

Tania spoke up with quiet decision: "Seremta, Midemi has something to say to you. The matter is not quite as we let you believe on first meeting, that he is to be your aide again —"

She took Midemi's arm and looked up for him to continue. Never, Midemi thought, had he seen so keen and burning a light in her eyes. He reached slowly into the leather wallet that lay against his skin, underneath his robe, and drew out the letter bearing the royal seal of Pharaoh So of Egypt.

"Your mission in Israel is completed," Midemi said hesitantly.

Seremta's eyes suddenly narrowed. His instinct for sensing intrigue, an instinct soon learned if one hoped to survive in Pharaoh's court, came suddenly alert. Midemi's sudden arrival, unannounced, his fumbling just now at words, though his skill in speech was legend, the letter in his hand, and Tania —

"How is it?" Seremta asked coolly. "Are you here to replace me?"

"Yes," Midemi said in surprise. He felt Tania's fingers tighten on his arm. All she had taught him, in the months before his audience with Pharaoh, came back to him — the plan, the details, even words and phrases. When he spoke in the court of Pharaoh, even though he spoke of Israel and of a plan that would send him there,

Israel had seemed far away. It had all been unreal, somehow — a kind of play-acting. Tania had given him words, and he had spoken them. But now it was no play-acting. With Seremta standing opposite him, the words were real. Midemi had come to believe in the plan Tania set before him, yet he thought it ugly that the plan had been used to betray a friend. There would be unpleasant words between them —

Midemi said the same words he had said before Pharaoh, laid before Seremta the same plan, the same careful details —

"I had not thought you remembered so much from four years back, or that you ever observed so much," Seremta said, his voice still quiet.

"It is a fair plan, is it not?"

"If the times were ripe, there would be points in its favor."
Tania spoke up: "And how are the times unripe?"

"In many points: The army — it is yet loyal to the king. The landowners and merchants are divided among themselves. The priesthood — it is beset by a man called a prophet, who calls their worship of Baal unclean. Your gift to the Temple would only increase division among the people and do nothing to unite them in love for Egypt —"

Midemi looked to Tania, helplessly. But her eyes were fixed hard on Seremta. "Ah, Seremta, you are old and used-up in service and have grown over-cautious," Tania said. "Why would the army not be loyal to the king, with no plan for a successful revolt yet offered them? The landowners — surely they are divided among themselves, as they have been and always will be in Israel, always looking for a way to get the best of one another. That is their way — the way of all merchants. But in one thing they are united: their hatred of Pekahiah's rule. And this prophet — we know his name, Hosea — his following is with the rag and rabble of Samaria and some of the country folk. The priesthood needs just the show we will give them with the golden calf, to catch the eye of the people. We gain the favor of the priesthood and favor for Egypt at a single stroke."

Seremta looked quizzically at Tania. "It is one thing to devise a plan in comfort half a world away. It is another to bring the plan to action when every day and every hour it must be reshaped to meet the new and the unexpected — reshaped in a moment, in the heat of battle, and reshaped without flaw, or all be lost."

"When such a moment comes, Midemi will be equal to it."

"Midemi?" Seremta said, looking straight at Tania. "Will you, Midemi?"

"Yes, surely," Midemi answered.

Seremta shook his head. "Nay, you will not. There is no subtlety in these Israelites. When they intrigue, it is all blood and entrails. You would not have the stomach for it."

Tania spoke tensely, as a mother defending a child: "If he had the wit to devise the plan, he will have the stomach to carry it through."

"I think he had no wit in the plan at all," Seremta said sharply.

"What you think is no concern to us," Tania replied.

"Nay," Midemi said, disturbed by the tone their speech was taking. "It is that we — that we must do things each in his own way."

"You could do nothing without me," Seremta said.

"I must. Pharaoh has ordered you to Jerusalem."

"Jerusalem, you say?"

"Yes, to lay groundwork for Judah's part in this alliance. Pharaoh believes — foresees —" A happy thought came to Midemi quite suddenly, and he wondered why he had not struck on it before. "He foresees some difficulty with Judah in this alliance and wants a man of your experience to — to spend some time there to see to Egypt's interests."

The forced calm went from Seremta's voice. It was all bitterness and anger now: "Or do you mean that Pharaoh wants me to spend some time there until he can strike on a fair scheme to put me away altogether?"

"Nay —"

"Nay? Was I born to this business yesterday, Midemi? Any dock drudge knows Israel is the keystone to Pharaoh's alliance. He would never take his most experienced and trusted envoy from Samaria, except that you have turned him against me — you and your consort."

"We spoke no word against you, only laid out a plan —"

"Why do we trade words with him?" Tania said, snatching the letter from Midemi's hand. "Here is Pharaoh's letter. Read for yourself."

Seremta took the letter and read it. When he spoke again, the calm had come back to his voice: "So you have won. You have a commission from Pharaoh, you have servants, you have a house better than most in Samaria . . . and a foul-smelling, vermin-infested people to strike a bargain with."

Midemi grimaced.

"May you find it more pleasant than I have," Seremta said, gesturing his arm in a wide arc. Then, bowing low in mock servility, he said, "May we meet again, one day."

"You need not leave at once," Midemi said, "in this rain."

"When one is done, one is done."

Seremta threw a cloak over his shoulders and walked to the door. Turning, he said, "Who knows? Perhaps another ruler will have some use for an old, used-up servant of the Pharaoh."

"You go not to Jerusalem?"

"Jerusalem? Nay, Midemi. Keep this for a day in your own life: there is no stepping down in the court of Pharaoh — only up, or out. I have come to that last step."

He walked out into the rain. For a moment there was quiet in the house, and then suddenly Tania leaped toward the door.

"Stop him!" she shouted.

"Why?" Midemi asked, taking a step after her.

Tania paid no heed to Midemi. She flung open the door and called to the Nubian standing closest the gate.

"Tongo! Stop him!"

The Nubian stepped across Seremta's path and seized him by the arms. Without waiting to throw on a cloak, Tania ran out into the courtyard. The rain beat down, soaking her gown, matting the hair against her neck and cheeks, but she seemed not to notice. Her eyes burned with animal-like fury.

"Kill him," she said. "Kill him, Tongo!"

The Nubian grinned and wrapped his arms around Seremta. In his last moment, Seremta could only ask, "How — how did you know?"

"The way you would have known, Seremta."

"Then it *was* you — the plans — not Midemi —" Ironically he smiled. "With you, I give the plan fair chance of success."

The Nubian caught his arm around Seremta's throat. Seremta's face went purple. He gasped twice, fitfully, and slumped in the giant's arms.

Midemi stood in the doorway. "What is happening? What are you doing?"

The Nubian let loose his grip and Seremta slid to the ground. Midemi gasped. He ran back into the house, found a cloak to cover himself, and came into the courtyard. He stooped beside Seremta's body.

"Tania, what have you done?" he whispered.

Tania seemed not to hear him.

"So, it is done. The first step," she said low.

Midemi stood up and took Tania by the shoulders. "What have you done?"

She looked up at him, not speaking. Her eyes burned. Midemi struck her across the face.

"Tania, he is dead! You have killed him!"

"Fool," Tania said low and harsh. "Heard you not what he said — 'Another ruler might find some use for him?' He was about to betray us to the king of Israel."

Chapter 24

The Golden Calf

1

Something new will be accepted for a time, if only because it is unusual. But there comes a time when newness wears off, and people begin to look more closely, and suspiciously.

During the month of barley harvest all Samaria seemed an anxious host to the newly arrived Egyptians, with their many servants and twelve giant slaves. The golden calf stood brazenly in the outer court of the Temple, and Tania and Midemi were frequent guests of Anakah the high priest. Pekahiah had received Midemi and Tania at the palace. Wealthy landowners and merchants invited them to their houses, and Tania returned hospitality.

But from other quarters came rumblings of disapproval. Country folk, living close to starvation to pay levies said to keep peace with Assyria, now heard nothing but talk of Egypt when they came to the city — and grumbled that no word could be trusted in Israel these days. In the east gate of the city the prophet Hosea was a voice of derision —

"Israel herds the wind and pursues the east wind all day long, bargains with Assyria then calls to Egypt, a dove is Israel, silly and without sense!"

The army feared that the Pul of Assyria, Tiglath Pileser, would look askance at any show of friendship between Israel and Egypt. Pekah ben Remaliah had even spoken sharply with Pekahiah when the envoy of the Pharaoh and his consort had been received graciously at the palace. Pekah was now chief captain in the army of the king, standing next to Pekahiah himself. No man in Israel looked with greater suspicion on ties between Israel and Egypt than Pekah.

"While Pileser lives, Israel must be virgin to all but him. Even a sidewise glancing, Pekahiah — even that — could bring him down on us."

Pekahiah laughed that Pileser was not *so* jealous a lover, but afterward he allowed to himself that perhaps Pekah had spoken some truth.

Important though the priesthood and the people and the landowners were, Tania knew that in the end a faction within the army must rebel against the king. A small group of landowners led her to Remaliah. His son Pekah was close to the king, they allowed, yet it was likely that Remaliah could be persuaded to spearhead a revolt. He had resentment of long standing toward the house of Menahem.

Remaliah still held some power in the army, but he had grown old. Tania saw him more driven by bitterness toward Menahem, now turned on Pekahiah, than by a soldier's cool planning and determination. Tania found herself fascinated, rather, by Pekah, the son of Remaliah. That Pekah was said to hold nothing but scorn for Egypt, and that he was called Twin and chief captain to the king, caught Tania's interest less than something Remaliah let drop: that there lay between the Twins a rivalry of long standing. In the privacy of their house, Tania said to Midemi, "With families reared up as they are in Israel — son in the very footsteps of father — it would be strange indeed if some of Remaliah's ire has not rubbed off on Pekah."

Quietly she set herself to discover if Pekah ben Remaliah indeed stood as staunchly for his king as it seemed.

Two weeks later it was arranged that Tania and Midemi were invited to a great banquet in the king's palace. More than two hundred people milled about in the great hall. Tania moved gracefully among the guests, stopping to speak here and there in flawless Israelite tongue, quite as though she had lived all her life in Samaria.

For a time she was separated from Midemi. When she saw him again, he was standing against a wall, beautifully robed and groomed, and alone. Tania shook her head in disgust. Midemi made no attempt to win favor from the people in Pekahiah's court who might serve their ends. The charm that came so easily to him in the court of Pharaoh withered away in this land that Midemi held in contempt. He longed only for the day they would return to Egypt and be quit of this people with no manners, loud talking, and an unlovely tongue. It rankled Tania that Midemi took so little responsibility for their mission, that always she must act the part that better belonged to a man.

Yet this night too much lay at stake for her to be wroth with Midemi. She had been pointed to Pekah, the son of Remaliah. The chance came to speak with him somewhat privately. Pekah stood alone to one side of the banquet hall. Tania approached quietly. Some steps away she stopped and bowed her head.

"Peace, son of Remaliah."

"Peace," Pekah said in response. Then, coldly, "Yes, you are the consort of Egypt's envoy."

"If it pleases, yes," Tania said. She raised her head and looked at Pekah directly. He had the same animal grace of Pekahiah but a less handsome cast to his features, heightened by the deep furrow standing straight above his nose. Tania pursed her lips, half smiled. "They do the son of Remaliah injustice to set him as Twin to the king. You are more handsome."

Pekah smiled with embarrassment, as he always did when spoken to intimately by a woman. Yet the smile hid something of pleasure. Tania knew her flattery had found a mark. They sat together on a low couch, and Pekah muttered that he and Pekahiah had often been said to look alike, though he himself had never much seen it.

"Only men would call you twins," Tania said. "Women see differences."

A blush colored Pekah's cheek. His shyness with women was a common jest in the army. The wife of his youth had died in childbed more than two years before, and Pekah had not married again.

"You — you speak our tongue well, for one newly arrived in Israel," Pekah said, making some show at friendliness.

"Do you think so?"

"Indeed."

"I think —"

She stopped herself.

"Yes?"

"It was nothing, only that I deemed your king little liked my way of speaking."

"Why not?" Pekah asked, a little hotly. "You speak as well as a born Israelite."

Tania lowered her eyes, playacting shyness.

"Pekahiah is a great one to pick fault," Pekah said peevishly.

"I meant him no offense."

"I took it not so," he assured her.

Tania sensed that Pekah found some satisfaction in setting himself apart from Pekahiah. As they spoke on, she played it into their talk. "Now the king would not understand such a thing as this, but do you tell me . . ."

Almost without his knowing it, Tania drew Pekah into confiding some of his feeling against Pekahiah. Always it had been expected that Pekah would nod to any word of Pekahiah. And now with Pekahiah on the throne, even more so: Pekahiah spoke, and Pekah's agreement was taken as a matter of course. That he most often did agree with the king mattered not to Pekah. It was that the agreement was too much expected. Fond as he was of his Twin, and as many rollicking good times as they had enjoyed together, this ever setting them together annoyed

Pekah. It was as though he had no wit of his own apart from Pekahiah. He found it good to talk with someone who seemed to care for his judgment, his opinion — even though she was an Egyptian.

Tania dwelt not on affairs between Israel and Egypt. She knew Pekah's opinion in the matter. It was not this that first concerned Tania, but rather how it stood between Pekah and his king. Tania looked first to the personal loyalty. If that could be turned, the other would follow in its time. Only one mention did she make of Israel and Egypt. "What a pity that our nations cannot be as you and me, just man and woman to one another —"

Again, Pekah blushed. Tania hinted that she would welcome a more personal acquaintance with him, and then she took her leave. A few steps away she stopped and turned. He was fairly devouring her with his eyes. She smiled and nodded, then walked away. It was as she thought: beneath his shyness lay a well of passion.

Pekah touched a finger to his lips, for they seemed to be trembling. He found himself thinking that perhaps he had spoken too hastily with Pekahiah in the matter of Egypt's envoy.

2

The golden calf came to be a sight that drew worshippers to the Temple in Samaria. Its workmanship was stunning. Set on a stone platform half again as high as a man, it towered fourteen cubits above the paving of the outer court. In the setting sun it cast blinding reflections westward into the city.

The first word spoken against the calf-image was a word of ridicule, spoken in the gate by Hosea: "In time past, Israel kissed the Law of the LORD, carved on her doorposts. But now — men kiss calves! Sacrifice to this, they say! Ah, Israel follows any wind that blows — like chaff that swirls on the threshing floor, like smoke from a window, so is the house of Jacob."

But as the months of summer passed, Hosea saw that words of ridicule little moved the people. The golden calf seemed to have enthralled their fancy. As harvest drew near, greater and greater crowds thronged into the Temple to lay offering and sacrifice at its feet. Anakah had not felt so content in many months.

Often in the late evening, when the streets of the city lay deserted, Hosea would stand across from the Temple and gaze on the image of the calf rising starkly against the night sky, and there would well up in him a wistfulness and deep sadness. "Israel, O my Israel! Running after lovers for your bread and your water, your

wool and flax and oil and drink. Know you not that the LORD gives you the grain and the wine and the oil? And the silver and gold, which you use for Baal?"

At first Hosea had thought the golden calf a senseless folly of the people. Now he came to see it as something deeper: open and unashamed idol worship.

"It is no god-image," the priests said smoothly, "but only his steed."

Hosea saw beyond the clever speech of the priests. Simple worshippers did not make fine distinctions. When they laid their offerings at the foot of the calf, in the hope of plentiful harvest, they worshipped the calf. Idolatry, nothing less.

In recent months, Hosea had been driven to ponder the traditions come down from Moses. Together with Odenjah he had gathered the traditions wherever they could be found in written scrolls, song and legend, or remembrances of aged patriarchs. More and more they came to see that Israel held to the letter of the Law but had lost its spirit altogether.

This worship of the calf was linked not with the LORD but with Baal. Here lay the root of the evil. Israel had drifted from obeying the very first word of the Law: *I am the LORD your God, who brought you out of the land of Egypt, out of the house*

266

of bondage. You shall have no other gods before me — nay, not *before*, but *beside* me!

Here was the true meaning of the word — no other gods *beside* me! It was not enough that the LORD be first: He must be *only*.

This calf worship was the same unfaithfulness to the LORD that had become the burden of Hosea's preaching — the same whoring after other gods.

Hosea felt himself like a tanner's skin, stretched tight on a rack, held fast on the one side by his caring for Israel, but on the other side by anger at her wanton idolatry, anger at the priests who led her astray, anger — yes, anger at the golden calf that now stood in the Temple.

How much longer would the LORD withhold punishment? Would not Assyria soon swarm over the land and lead all Israel into exile?

Hosea at last determined that ridicule and even soft pleading must give way to sterner words. In a way he felt, though he could not fully understand, the coming of the golden calf had brought to a crux his struggle against Israel's worship of Baal. And Hosea, not one to lie in wait, carried the struggle into the very courtyard of the Temple a month before grape harvest.

"In days of old, when Israel spoke, men trembled — he was exalted among the nations! What now is Israel? A dead branch. Aliens devour his strength, and he knows it not. Gray hairs are sprinkled upon him, and he knows it not. Yet he sins more, turns to molten images, idols of gold, the work of craftsmen and not your God! Ephraim mixes himself with alien peoples; Ephraim is a cake not turned, joined to idols is Israel! A band of drunkards, given to harlotry, loving shame more than their glory, Who is the LORD!

"But hear this word of the LORD, O Israel: a wind has wrapped you in its wings, and you shall be brought to shame because of your sacrifices!"

Every day for a week Hosea preached in the outer court of the Temple. His words had little effect with the people. Still they made sacrifices and offerings to the calf. Hosea's words turned darker. He summoned the specter of Assyria —

"Israel shall return to the bondage of Egypt! Assyria shall be her king, because she refused to return to me, says the LORD. The sword shall rage against her cities, consume the bars of her gates, and devour her fortresses. My people are bent on turning away from Me, says the LORD, they are appointed to the yoke, and none shall remove it!"

The priests of the Temple found fault in Hosea's words and railed against him when he spoke. Still he preached. Each midday for three weeks his voice rang out in the Temple courtyard.

Anakah grew concerned, lest Hosea at last win some people away from the Temple. Tania, too, feared that his drumming of Assyria could work harm to her plans. They met in the high priest's chamber and laid a plan to draw the people away from the prophet.

When next Hosea appeared at the Temple, no priests came out to speak against him. The people, with their Israelite love of argument, felt cheated of their midday pleasure. Hosea found himself preaching to a silent and sullen crowd.

Within the Temple, in the high priest's chamber, Midemi stood waiting, dressed in his finest robe, a bright girdle drawn about his waist, his hair oiled and carefully arranged, polished sandals on his feet. Tania drew back from him and smiled with satisfaction. "The prophet will cut a poor figure beside him!"

"The words will count for more than the figure," Anakah said drily.

"Midemi will have his words. See that your priests are ready to join words with him at the right moment." Then, to Midemi, "You know now exactly how to proceed against him?"

"Yes," Midemi said wearily.

"Disdain him, ridicule him. Show him what it is to match words with one trained in the court of Pharaoh."

Midemi nodded and dusted a fleck from his shoulder. He had little stomach for these doings, but anything to speed their return to Egypt —

"Bend the knee to no image of a god!" said Hosea in the outer court. "Did Israel drink the Law of the Lord with his mother's milk, and will he yet bow to the calf?"

"Even I know more than that, and I am no Israelite!" Midemi spoke from the archway that led to the inner court of the Temple.

A sudden murmuring went up, almost a gasp — so arresting was the Egyptian's appearance. Hosea found no words on his tongue. Midemi was an unusual and handsome figure of a man.

"The calf is no god-image," Midemi said smoothly, "but only his steed."

Hosea was silent a moment. Then he said, "So say the priests of this Temple. But the ones who lay sacrifice at the calf's feet think straight on the harvest. It is worship of the calf."

"'Can any but the Lord look on the inward parts?' Comes this from your writings?"

"I know it not."

"Then were you better to apply yourself to wisdom, for I am no Israelite, yet I know it."

A rippling of laughter went up, led by three priests who had slipped quietly into the crowd. One of the priests called out: "Does the country priest now learn of the Lord from Egypt?"

The laugher rose higher. Before Hosea could reply, Midemi turned to the people, and with arms raised said, "Friends in Israel, this day I make wine offering in the Temple for your harvest — seventy jars of finest wine. Your high priest ministers at the altar, the woman Shifra performs the ritual dance, the wine is shared with all and the calf of Samaria stands witness to your worship!"

From within the Temple came Tania's twelve Nubian slaves in a double file. "Does Egypt now minister to Israel?" Hosea asked mockingly.

Midemi disdained to answer. Speaking still to the people, he said, "The ritual begins. Follow the steed of Baal!"

With a loud groan the Nubians raised the golden calf from the platform, and setting the iron runners on their shoulders, moved into the inner court.

"What! Will the calf defile the Temple itself?" cried Hosea.

"Follow the steed of Baal," the priests chanted.

The people took up the chant and began to move toward the inner court. Hosea ran to the archway and stood against the crowd. "Has Israel forgotten his Maker?"

The people paid him no heed, streamed around him and into the Temple. Within, the Nubians came abreast of the altar and set the golden calf on a platform higher yet than the one in the outer court. Anakah stood at the altar and began to chant the worship.

A hot rage swept over Hosea. He ran to the rear wall of the Temple, tore a trumpet from its brackets, and sounded a blast that echoed through the inner court. Then came his voice like a thunderclap: "Set the trumpet to your lips, for a vulture is over the house of the LORD!"

The people who had turned around at the trumpet blast now saw Hosea break suddenly into a run, coming toward them.

"They have broken the covenant, transgressed the Law!" he called out, as he ran. He flew past the edge of the crowd that was gathered in front of the altar. Coming alongside the platform of the golden calf, he swung himself aloft and came to a stand on the platform, under the head of the idol. Looking down on Anakah, he cried, "You chant, 'LORD, we know Thee!'

You know me not, says your God! *Were I to write my laws by ten thousands, you would find them strange things.*"

"Throw him down!" shouted a priest.

"Blasphemer!"

Hosea held up his hands. "Let no one contend, and let none accuse, for with you do I contend, O priest! My people are destroyed for lack of knowledge, says the LORD: you have rejected the knowledge of your God, and so I reject you from being priest to me — you have forgotten your God, and I also will forget you!"

"The calf of Samaria be your destruction, soothsayer!" called a man from the crowd.

Some few voices went up in a shout. Hosea spoke above them, his voice laden with scorn: "Who utters mere words and empty oaths? Already the judgment springs up like poisonous weeds in the furrows of a field. Let the inhabitants of Samaria tremble for their calf of vanity — for they shall mourn over it and idolatrous priests shall wail over it — over its glory, which has departed from it. Yea, the thing itself shall be carried to Assyria as tribute to the great king. Israel shall be put to shame for her idol!"

"No idol, but steed for the god of harvest!" cried a priest.

"A workman made it. It is not God. The calf of Samaria shall be broken to pieces!"

For a moment there was utter silence in the Temple, save for Hosea's heavy breathing. Then, from the side of the Temple, came the voice of Midemi, weary and contemptuous: "The calf of Samaria will be standing when your foolish words are long forgotten, when you yourself have wandered like a wild ass to Assyria to chase after your fancies."

"Well spoken, well spoken!" Anakah said, forcing a harsh laughter over his words.

The crowd murmured agreement and broke into shouting and clapping. Hosea looked down on them, anger and pity bringing a thickness to his throat.

"O Israel, Israel," he murmured.

His hand brushed back against the leg of the calf, then suddenly tightened on it. A strange light came into his eyes. "The calf of Samaria shall be broken to pieces!" he cried.

He stepped quickly to the back of the idol, set his shoulder against the leg, pushing against it. His foot slipped, and he fell to his knee.

"Does your prophet fancy himself twelve Nubians strong?" Midemi asked. A shout of laughter went up. "The prophet is a fool!"

"The man of spirit is mad!"

Hosea's face went deep red. Never since his youth had a person dared make light of his strength. He pushed against the calf but could find no footing and fell again. The laughter screamed in his ears. The faces below him blurred into a mass. All the world seemed to fall away, except the golden calf that towered above him, set to crush him to the earth.

Then, on the far edge of the platform, Hosea saw that every third stone was raised to form an edging scarcely more than two-fingers high, but raised, nonetheless. He set his foot against the last stone and leaned once more against the leg of the calf. The idol seemed rooted on the spot.

"Bring him down!" came a shout. "Throw him from the Temple!"

"Send the Nubians after him," Midemi said low to Tania.

"Nay — yet a moment. Let him taste well the bitters of humiliation."

Hosea moved his foot a stone closer to the rear of the idol, to gain a shorter stand. With all his strength he heaved himself against the molten image. The veins bulged from his neck and forehead. His head throbbed with pain.

The calf moved, slid forward a hand's breadth on its iron runners. Again he set himself against it. Again. And again.

The crowd gasped and backed away from the altar. The golden calf tipped on the edge of its platform, balanced for a moment, then crashed to the stone floor of the Temple and broke into pieces.

Hosea swayed dizzily on the platform. His voice came low, in fitful gasps: "As you have spurned me, says your God, so do I spurn your calf, O Samaria."

There was quiet in the Temple. Hosea let himself down from the platform. He stood at the front of the people, the golden calf broken in pieces at his feet. The face of the people mirrored fear and hate and wonder. Hosea said, "In one month's time comes the Feast of Weeks. Prepare yourselves against that time, that the LORD may minister forgiveness for this abomination. I myself will be priest to you."

He walked through their midst. No hand brushed against him.

At the side of the Temple, Tania dug her fingers into Midemi's arm until he winced and half pulled away. He looked down at her. Her eyes were on Hosea, disappearing through the archway into the outer court. Almost soundlessly her lips moved. "He has named his own fate. Let him be one to prepare."

Chapter 25

The Scheme of Tania

1

Now was the struggle between Hosea and the priesthood beyond argument and preaching. Anakah knew it. If the people turned against Hosea, all would be well. If not — and if echoes of discontent began to stir in the palace and gained the ear of the king — Anakah and his priests might be overtaken in a bloody cleansing the priesthood had not felt since the days of Jehu, a hundred years before, when Jehu lured the priests and worshippers of Baal into the Temples and slew them to a man. Such was the memory and fear the priesthood held of any man who gained the ear of the people by raising his voice against Baal. Such now was their fear of Hosea.

Tania cared nothing for the fate of Anakah and his priests, except as they worked into her own plans. But in the matter of the prophet Hosea, she was one spirit with Anakah, and that spirit was set on revenge. The smashing of the golden calf was more than an insult to her beloved Egypt. It was a blow against herself, for the calf had been her own creation, the child of her planning. The revenge she began to shape against Hosea was kin to the vengeance of a mother bear robbed of her cubs.

Tania brushed aside the plans of Anakah that would deal with Hosea only as a prophet set against Baal worship. Tania saw Hosea as a man, and it was as a man she deemed he could be brought down. She learned all she could of the prophet before she struck on a plan that would bring him low.

In two points Tania found weakness in Hosea: his strength and his marriage.

When she came alone to Anakah, he first scoffed at her plan. Hosea's strength and prowess was known in Samaria, indeed throughout Israel. Tania herself had seen him move the golden calf. And his marriage? His wife was known for adultery — what more could befall?

Tania bid Anakah hold judgment while she laid out her scheme. Hosea's very reputation of strength pointed to a weakness. If he could be lured into a contest he was sure to lose, he would he humiliated before the people and would lose standing. And in his marriage, if he should lose his wife not merely to her own lust, but to someone more the man than Hosea himself — and a foreigner, moreover — then the wound would be deep. In careful steps, Tania showed how her plan could work.

Though the scheme was devised by a woman, the high priest grudgingly allowed it fair chance of success. Even one as plain thinking as Anakah could see how Tania had struck on a truth. It was not as a prophet that Hosea was vulnerable, but as a man.

Tania left Anakah's chamber and returned to their house to set afoot that part of the scheme least to her own liking.

Tania paused on the threshold of Midemi's room. The careful order and arrangement stood in contrast to the usual disarray of her own room.

Midemi sat cross-legged on the floor, a clay bowl across his knees. He was painting on it a scene from the Nile, a flock of geese settled in among the rushes, quiet and peaceful, out of the river's current. He nodded to her and asked with little interest where she had been.

Tania came to her purpose carefully and with some reluctance. Scheming and ruthless she could be, but Tania was yet a woman. She little relished putting her own man into the arms of another woman, even when it was a planned thing. Tania feared a lack in herself. Though she was winsomely attractive, she sensed something unwomanly in her driving will and ambition. If ever Midemi, with his quiet withdrawn way, were to fall into the arms of a soft, yielding, utterly womanly creature, Tania feared she might lose him.

She had lingered near the well to catch a glimpse of the prophet's wife. At the sight of Gomer she all but drew back on her plan. The wife of the prophet was a fair woman to look on. Yet Tania dared risk no moment of weakness when so much hung in balance. She pushed aside her own misgiving, as she pushed aside anything that stood in the way of her schemes.

Midemi drew back in disgust at the thought of taking an Israelite woman. "It is vile! I will have no part in such a scheme."

"We are too deep in this thing to fall back now," Tania said coolly.

"I will not rub against an uncouth Israelite."

"You will find it none too unpleasant. She is a comely woman."

"How are you so strong for this? Have you no care that I should lie in the arms of another woman?"

"We must do what must be done. So long as your heart is given to me, and mine to you, it matters not if we lie with others to gain our purpose here in Israel."

"Yes, lie with others," Midemi said with a sharp nod of his head. "You with the son of Remaliah!"

"I have not lain with him."

"It is a matter of time. I have seen you these weeks, always finding a way to meet with him and he with you." Midemi said this with little passion. It mattered less that Tania should lie with Pekah than that she force him into the embrace of an uncouth Israelite woman.

"Midemi, this is for us, our life," said Tania warmly. "What is a kiss, a caress — even one's body, if given without the heart?

It is nothing — a coin, a barter. Our smallest kiss carries more of passion and giving than all the body, used by another. The truth of love lies in the heart, not in the loins." She spoke with strong feeling, as though she must sway not only Midemi but herself as well.

"It is crude. Vulgar."

"Yes, and so it is. But life itself is crude and vulgar when you possess neither wealth nor power. You know nothing of this. You have never known want.

"In the streets of Memphis they threw camel dung on my father when he fell from Pharaoh's favor. They burned the porch of his house and stacked the wall with skulls so he would not forget his place and the nothingness into which they cast him. We were poor, bitter poor, to the day of his death. Food was scarce and often foul. All the clothing we owned you could wrap in a bundle the size of a shock of wheat and was patched and mended many times over. Never shall I return to those days. Never."

"It is crude to use the instrument of love basely, to lie in the arms of one you do not love."

"Yes. But better than meanness. Better than hunger. Better far than what will come to us if we return to Egypt, our mission undone."

"But why this way," Midemi sighed, "why this lying abed with them?"

"We take them where they are, in their point of weakness. In the matter of his wife, the prophet is weak."

"I cannot —"

"You must," Tania said fiercely, "and you will! This world does not give up its treasure at a song. You must plan and labor and yield up — yield up even that which lies closest to your heart — if you would gain the treasure you seek."

Midemi shook his head ruefully. "I could better lie with a whore of the docks — at least she would be Egyptian."

"You will find the prophet's wife more a woman than I care to think," Tania said, turning down her eyes.

Midemi took her to him.

"Tania, you want this no more than I."

She nodded, but yet would not look on him. "Yes — I want no woman to know you as I know you. Yet neither do I want to return to Egypt and find banishment the due of our efforts. This thing must be done."

"Why should this woman lie with me, only because we have come to it?"

"Such has never been a difficulty for you," Tania said wryly. "If reports of this woman are true, it will come none too hard."

Midemi pulled away from her and let fly the clay bowl from his hand, smashing it against the wall. "The day we set foot out of this land will be the best of my life!"

2

The Feast of Weeks was near its end. I had stood at the altar of the Temple, the golden calf broken in pieces at my feet, and pointed the people to this day.

"I myself will be priest to you," I had said.

There could be no mistaking the meaning of my words. I had challenged the authority of the priesthood in Samaria to act as priests.

In the wan light of early morning, within the house, I leaned back against the south wall. Two weeks had passed since I destroyed the golden calf. All Samaria eagerly waited the coming of this day. Never before had the priesthood been challenged so boldly. Every man in Samaria knew that Anakah the high priest could not let such a challenge go unanswered.

I found myself longing for the company of Amos. Surely Amos had felt this same thing when he set himself against Amaziah — the fear, the uncertainty. What counsel would

Amos give? Had I indeed overreached myself, as the priests of the Temple darkly hinted in the marketplace and gate?

My eyes drifted back across the room to where Gomer lay. She no longer slept. Her eyes were open, looking at me. Her voice was drowsy and languid, deep in her throat, like the cooing of a dove. "Good morning, my husband."

"Have you been long awake?" I asked.

"Umm — for a little. I have been watching you."

"I woke early."

She crept out of her bed quietly, so as not to waken the children, and came to my side. Wordlessly she laid her head against my shoulder and kissed my neck and cheek. Her hands moved slowly, in aimless caresses, over my arms and chest and belly. After some moments she said, "It was like a long ago time, to have you lie next to me all through the night."

I tightened in her arms but leaned my head down against hers.

"Never was it more blessed with us," she said.

"Yes."

Silent we stayed for some time. Then Gomer spoke: "Hosea?"

"Um?"

"Hold you any regrets?"

"Regrets?" I asked. The question puzzled me.

" . . . of last night?"

"Nay."

"May I speak of something?"

"Yes, speak what you will."

"What I spoke of yestermorning —"

"Of going into the countryside?"

"Yes, just we two and the children." She raised up in my arms to face me, her eyes eager and bright. "Just to be out of the city for one day, away from the noise and bustle, and together. Could we not, Hosea? Could we not?"

"Nay, I think not," I answered. "People still gather at the Temple altar. I must warn them of God's judgment."

"Let it be another day! We have had no day in the country during all the Feast of Weeks. I am so weary of the city I could die."

"This thing between me and the Temple priests is bringing many families to the Temple, making sacrifice —"

"You could let it pass for a day, if you wanted."

She turned away from me with a toss of her head and a moment later got up and went to the far side of the house and began grinding the lentil seed for our morning meal. She seemed to have no care now for waking the children. I rested an elbow on my knee and leaned my head against my closed fist. For a time I watched Gomer at her mill, and then my eyes lowered. I looked on the earth floor of the house, packed hard by many thousand footfalls.

"How hard has this floor become," I thought, "how hard and unyielding."

Yes — it was the picture of our life these last years. It has become hard between us.

Softness came only by moments, precious moments, as in the night now past.

There had been cruel words over supper, some foolish thing between Jezreel and Loruhamah in which I took Jezreel's part, and Gomer said that Jezreel could do every evil in the Law and I would still judge him in the right. There followed sharp words between us, and then angry silence. When dark had settled upon the house, and we lay in our separate beds, such loneliness came over me, and a kind of sadness, that I slipped out of my own bed and came to Gomer's side. For a moment I knelt there in the darkness, hesitating to waken her. Then her voice had come, cold and distant: "What do you wish?"

I touched a hand awkwardly to her shoulder, but I could find no words to speak. I lay down beside her. After a time I put my arm around her. She was stiff at my side, and there was no warmth between us.

Tears came to my eyes, tears of emptiness and longing for a day now past, when there had been a sureness of love between us, and the pathway set before me by the LORD was yet unclouded by the uncertainties of these latter years. The tears brimmed over, and some fell on Gomer's cheek. And then tears came to her also. She turned toward me and gave me her mouth in a long, aching kiss. She wept more, and I as well, and her arms went tight about my neck, and low in her throat she sobbed and sobbed. But she spoke no word, nor I either.

Then she was no longer in my arms but above me, unclad and waiting for my touch. And there began a night such as never before between us, not even in our early days, with murmurings and low pleadings and breathless surrender. Our passion knew no bounds — each touch and motion and caress was a fire, consuming us with thrill and abandon again. We met, and yet again — nothing could quench us but utter weariness, and with it a blessed forgetfulness of all that stood between us. It was no yielding to desire alone, but to a deep bond that held us together despite all — a love that yet could find no speech or sure way of life, but must tell itself in wordless giving and surrender.

When the first light of morning slanted through the window, waking me from a light sleep, the sweetness of the night gave way to troubled brooding. Gomer lay in the bend of my arm, sleeping peacefully. A tenderness welled up in me, and I would have leaned down and kissed her, gently wakened her. But I did not. I went quietly from her side and sat alone against the far wall of the house.

I bethought myself that many another man, having passed such a night with the wife of his youth, would content himself that all stood well between them. Such I could not do. Even when Gomer abandoned herself to me in passion, I could not be quit of uncertainty and doubt — not a doubt that she was now faithful to my bed, but that she would have it so of her own choice.

The thought rankled with me that only fear bonded Gomer to me — the fear that I would turn her into the street, as I had sworn. I could scarcely brush against her without the thought that her heart might be elsewhere, except for the threat I had laid upon her. Her faithfulness I held captive. But her heart — who could hold captive a heart?

This cut deep — to keep her in my house, sharing her passion, yet ever uncertain of her love. If one day she was all warmth and tenderness toward me, another day she would turn cool and distant. Never did she so free me of doubt that the thought of love was certain.

Gomer —

No woman in Samaria was as fair as Gomer — three times a mother, yet still the blush of youth in her cheek; her face comely and well-shapen, and no line in her brow.

Fair she was, passing fair. There was wonderful warmth in her, and dearness past knowing. When Gomer made love, it was with her whole heart. She never gave her love piecemeal, but recklessly and without stint, everything — or nothing. On a day when her heart was turned to me, she would work about the house like one driven under a slave master's whip — cleaning, washing, grinding meal, baking — waiting for my return. But if bitterness rose between us, she would sit whole days on the housetop, alone, and brood on days past. When I returned at eventide and found the ladder pulled up to the housetop, the children hungry and unattended, I knew there would be silence and coldness in the house that night. But when she stood in the doorway and sighted me far down in the city and ran out to meet me — then I could think myself the envy of any man.

For such moments and such days I bore uncertainty, bore the bitterness and silence and jealousy, bore doubt even of my own right rule in clinging to her. Others imagined that I had forgiven Gomer, and that in these years mercy had worked its way with her. Odenjah once said as much.

I could not shake myself loose from the thought that Gomer remained in my house only out of fear. What good that her feet walked a straight path if her heart walked wayward? Here was the evil — the heart, the wayward, false, inconstant heart.

Here was the pain. To have her in the house, never knowing when smoldering discontent would surface.

I wanted her — could bear no thought of yielding her up, even though she filled my days with doubt and uncertainty — yes, and even if the Law of God itself stood against me.

When we were youths in Dothan, Obed once said to me, "If ever a woman wins your heart, you will be her slave." Was it so? Gomer fetches me mockery in Samaria. I cry out for purity and keep an adulteress in my house. I preach judgment on Israel but lay no hand of punishment on my wife. My preaching speaks one word, my life with Gomer speaks another. How else could my prophecy be so forsworn, except Gomer has enslaved me?

And now this day was announced and upon us. I will call Israel to repentance. How does it stand with the heart of my wife?

My eyes had came back to rest on Gomer. When she woke and came to my side and nestled to me, my troubled brooding seemed to melt away. I dared not, and could not, plumb the thoughts and purposes of my own heart. I only knew my life lay in the circle of her embrace. Even now, as she worked grimly at preparing the morning meal, and I knew that this would be a day of bitterness because I could not go with her into the countryside, I knew that nowhere else but in her arms could I be long content.

At the meal Jezreel teased Loruhamah that he was to go to the Temple altar with me, and she must remain at home. Gomer turned and spoke angrily: "Is it not enough that the two of you leave us here when all Samaria goes into the countryside? Must he vex her with his words, besides?"

"I meant nothing," Jezreel said, his ebony-black eyes wide and innocent. He turned to me. "She takes my words amiss."

I said nothing. It seemed to me that Jezreel looked triumphantly at Gomer and Loruhamah.

Loruhamah was now past her third winter, a slender maid, dark of skin, high-cheeked, her blue eyes large, seeming to command her entire face. She made no retort to Jezreel. As her way was, she spoke little when things were wroth between Gomer and me, unless it were some word that might bring things to a better pass between us.

"I want to go into the countryside," she said to Gomer with unaccustomed determination.

"Who would want to carry you all the way to the country?" Jezreel said, pushing at her leg.

"You said we might go," Loruhamah persisted.

"Yes, and so I did — before I spoke with your father," Gomer said grimly.

"Jezweel," Loruhamah said quietly, "we could play on the housetop."

"What kind of adventure can I have with a witless girl?" Jezreel taunted.

"Be silent, Jezreel," Gomer said sharply.

"I said nothing —"

"Be silent!"

"Let there be an end to this," I said.

"Yes, an end to his brash tongue," Gomer answered.

Loruhamah made a pinched look at Jezreel. Jezreel slid a foot out to kick at her until I stopped him. "Enough, Jezreel."

"She makes faces at me."

I shook my head and went back to my eating.

After some moments of quiet, Gomer spoke, her voice now soft and wheedling: "Still, might you take all of us to our countryside altar, Husband. If not many come, we could have a day of adventuring thereabouts."

I turned to her. The words came slowly, for I yearned that she might understand what I myself but half knew. "Gomer, it is a solemn occasion. There is a mood upon the people, something to do with Baal-worship in the land. I dare not — each day more people have come to my altar, making ready for this day. I dare not —"

"Yes," Gomer cut in bitterly, "dare not show yourself at the altar with your wife!"

"Nay."

"Nay? What then — the children you have named bastard, though they are not?"

"You speak too boldly."

"You think I have not seen it," she said hotly, "your brooding about these last weeks? Looking askance at me and the children on every occasion, going early from the house, and returning long past sunset? Yes, you fear that we will shame you before the people now that you have made this bold stand against the priesthood."

I found no answer. I dropped my eyes and held a hand over my brow.

"Father fears nothing," Jezreel said brashly.

I looked up slowly. I glanced across at Loruhamah. She lowered her eyes quickly, hiding tears.

"You make your children weep with such words," I said.

"Well they might, for the barren life they lead in this house. Jezreel goes whenever he will, and we never at all."

"Every priest in Israel takes his firstborn son," I retorted.

"I am the oldest, it is my right," Jezreel said.

"Yes, take him!" Gomer said, rising suddenly from the table. "Take him and go to the Temple till the Feast of Weeks is come and gone. Go, go —"

"We shall go," I said with determination. I rose to my feet. "Come, Jezreel."

"I care not if the two of you ever return," Gomer said wildly.

I stepped forward and gripped her roughly by the shoulders. "Curb your tongue. You are still wife in this house."

She turned her face aside, her jaw set hard. I let drop my hands. I nodded Jezreel toward the door. Loruhamah still sat at the table, with Loammi lying at her side. I turned and walked from the house with a heavy step.

* * *

At the Temple a handful of worshippers showed themselves. I waited with Jezreel into the afternoon. No more came. We trudged home near sundown. There would be no light talk in our house this night.

Chapter 26

The Plot Against Pekahiah

1

Gomer lay alone on the housetop in the shade of a tenting set against the west parapet. Hosea had been gone to his countryside altar scarce an hour. A soft knocking came at the door of the house.

She heard the low speech of a man and Loruhamah saying that Hosea was gone to his altar west of the city wall. The speech was not that of an Israelite. Curiously, Gomer went to the edge of the housetop. Below stood the Egyptian she had seen some few times in the city, clad in a knee-length robe of bright crimson, drawn at the waist with a girdle of Tyrian purple. She had never seen him so close. Indeed, he was handsome —

"Peace, sir," Gomer said.

Midemi looked upward. A fetching smile crossed his lips. "Peace," he said, barely to be heard.

"What is it you seek?"

"Some small knowledge from the one called Hosea. I am the envoy to Pekahiah, from the court of Pharaoh."

Gomer nodded him recognition. "My husband is not here."

"Yes, that I have now learned." He paused, glanced at Loruhamah standing in the doorway, then again to Gomer. "Mayhap you could supply me —"

"Sir — ?"

"May — may I come up?"

Loruhamah looked up at Gomer, a sudden frown darkening her brow. Gomer hesitated.

"It is somewhat private, not for all ears," Midemi said. "Then come atop," Gomer said with odd suddenness.

She lowered the ladder and then returned to her place beneath the tenting. She laid a hand to her breast. Her heart beat fast. It was bold to receive him on the housetop, Hosea being absent, yet what harm — and the day was drear, drear —

Midemi came up over the parapet and stepped onto the housetop. He began to pull the ladder after him.

"Nay — leave it down," Gomer said quickly. A drawn ladder would start talk for sure.

Midemi stood before her, outside the tenting.

"What is it now you crave?" Gomer asked, holding her voice cool.

Midemi seemed not to hear. He looked down on Gomer and the tenting over her. Indeed, she was not swarthy like most Israelites, he thought. Her skin was fair.

"It is good cunning against your Israelite sun," Midemi said smiling, pointing to the tenting.

"Yes, it shades a little."

Midemi stooped under the tenting and knelt an arm's length from Gomer. "Your sun is too hot for me," he said.

Despite herself, Gomer smiled. Now she saw him face to face, she thought the Egyptian something almost too handsome. Hosea she had always thought handsome, but this man was more — almost beautiful.

He seemed not hurried to come to the purpose of his visit. They talked for a time of indifferent matters. First she had been loath to say more with him than she must — for she feared neighbors might take it amiss if he remained overlong on the housetop. But as they spoke on, she found herself liking the way he lingered at talk. Hardly had she spoken to a man in the last months, it seemed, so silent and brooding had Hosea become. And he had a warm and friendly way about him, this Egyptian.

Midemi could feign what mood he chose — interest, friendliness, anger, concern — whatever the circumstance required. Such was his training in the court of Pharaoh. Yet, as he spoke with Gomer, he warmed to friendliness quite unfeigned. She asked him something of life in Egypt. He was soon relating to her memories from life along the Nile, half lost himself in reverie, and quite forgetting the dislike he had built up for any person not born Egyptian — and this woman especially, whom he had thought would cause him unpleasantness. She seemed well content to listen as he spoke, quiet and attentive. It was something pleasant to have a woman listen as he talked. Tania listened but little. She was ever rushing here and there, bent on some plan or duty. And she was fair to look on, this woman. Truly, for an Israelite, quite fair.

In not long a time they were talking and laughing together like good acquaintances, though Gomer mostly looked away from him, or downward, when she spoke. It was as if each one's life had been a wandering in barren wasteland, and in meeting together they came on sudden verdure and refreshment. Indeed, not until Midemi made ready to leave did it return to Gomer that it was Hosea he had first asked after, in coming to the house — and he had not yet come to his purpose.

Almost regretfully she asked him of it. The purpose had been a devisement, and now Midemi deemed it could be set aside. He laughed that he had forgotten it altogether, so fine had been their talk.

"Nay, but you must tell me," Gomer insisted, for she would have some word to tell Hosea, should he learn of Midemi's visit.

"Well then, it is a matter with one of my servants," he said.

"How does it take in —" She stopped before the words 'my husband' came out, and flushing, said only, "— him?"

"The fellow wants to take an Israelite maid to wife — a young thing, living with her uncle not far from my house. My man is a good one and free — would give her fair keep. For my part, I hold nothing against it. Yet I think you in Israel look somewhat askance at wedding a foreigner. If some offense would come of it, I will send the man back to Egypt before he does the maid any mischief."

"Why come you to —" Again Gomer flushed, at the near-mention of Hosea. "The priests of the Temple could give you answer," she said.

"Yes, I imagine they could," Midemi said carelessly. "I heard your husband spoke with greater authority in such matters. It was only a thought." Then, looking on her with some boldness, "What think you? Might an Egyptian and an Israelite have somewhat to do with one another?"

For the first time their eyes met and held. "Perhaps they could," Gomer said low.

2

The last day of the Feast of Weeks dawned surprisingly clear in Samaria, after a week of drizzling rain. In the early morning hours, Pekah ben Remaliah trudged his way across the city toward the palace, still heavy with sleep, and not a little angry to be summoned before the king at so early an hour.

In the throne room of the palace, Pekahiah walked slowly back and forth before the windows that looked eastward toward the Temple. He muttered low to himself, trying over the words he would use with Pekah. He little liked bringing reproof against his Twin, for Pekah seemed to take offense at any stray word these days. Yet some trouble lay afoot this day, and Pekahiah deemed he must warn Pekah, lest some harm come to the throne.

Pekahiah turned as Pekah entered and greeted him without waiting on ceremony. "Peace, my brother. Well met this day."

"I come in answer to your summons, my king," Pekah replied stiffly, grudgingly.

"Away, away —" Pekahiah motioned the two guards who stood at the door to leave. "Stand not so stiff with me, Pekah. I am still your friend, though they hang this robe on my shoulders."

Pekah answered nothing.

"We have grown apart these months, friend of my youth."

"Indeed? I had little noticed, my king."

Pekahiah made an impatient gesture. "Will you forget that I am your king — think of me only as your Twin, if I speak to you forthrightly?"

The troubled look on Pekahiah's countenance somewhat softened Pekah.

"Yes, if you wish," he said.

Pekahiah began slowly, feeling carefully for each word. He knew it to be a matter of some jealousy with Pekah that his Twin now sat on the throne of Israel. Gentle rivalry had dogged them from the day of their birth. At times it even flared up in anger and fighting, as between brothers. But Pekahiah did not yet perceive how deep Pekah's jealousy had become, and he had no knowledge how it had been fed these weeks past by Tania and Remaliah. He saw only coolness between himself and his Twin. It troubled him.

On this day he had special concern for what Pekah might do. In the month of barley harvest Pekah had taken to Baal worship, along with some drunkenness. Somehow this was linked to a companionship with the consort of the Egyptian envoy, for the two were seen often in the Temple together. The drunkenness itself cumbered Pekah's duty. More than this disturbed Pekahiah. It tokened a deep change in Pekah. Pekah was never one to join in Baal festivals, nor was he much given to wine drinking. And for women, he had not even turned aside to harlots since the death of his wife.

"This worship of Baal and much drinking — this is for the people," Pekahiah said, with a hint of sternness.

"My command has not suffered. My chariots still outrun all in Israel."

"That I know, and is the very reason I bring this to you —" Pekahiah thought fleetingly of the messages he had received from Hoshea ben Elah at the court of Pileser — the growing pressure for war against Israel, from certain Assyrian captains. "The day is not far distant when our tribute to Pileser will have no more effect, and we must lay a sword on the border of Galilee. When that day comes, Israel will have greater need of you than of me. I would not have you lose authority."

"I lose authority?" Pekah said contemptuously. "Have no fear."

"Oh, put away your airs," Pekahiah said, his voice falling into the familiarity of earlier days. "I am your friend. Let this be as between brothers."

"Well enough, brother. Then let my private drink and worship be my own concern."

"When it endangers Israel, it is no private concern."

"I endanger Israel?" Pekah laughed.

"You keep too-frequent company with the consort of the Egyptian envoy, for another matter."

Pekah reddened with embarrassment. His shyness with women was well known to Pekahiah. A nervous trembling came to Pekah's lips. He spoke angrily to cover his embarrassment: "Now must I have you choose my women as well as my worship?"

"Egypt tends no good to Israel. They would have us renew the folly of Shallum ben Jabesh, against which my father took the throne."

"This is nothing to me. I am not king."

"You have authority, and that is enough. I fear she may have it in mind to use you —"

"You think I am so unwitting? She is a woman, and I find pleasure with her. It starts and ends with that. I am no fool to be used."

"If that be true, answer me: what have you planned this day?"

"What?" Pekah asked, startled by Pekahiah's abrupt challenge. "I have planned nothing — nothing —"

"This is the end of the Feast of Weeks, a festival day in the Temple. Have you planned to take some part in the worship?"

"Perhaps I have —"

"Then hear well what I say: some plan is afoot — some sort of contest between the high priest and the prophet Hosea. You may know of it yourself —"

"No —"

"It is rumored about, though the plan itself seems secret. Yet, some clash will come between them this day for certain — the prophet set himself against Anakah the day he smashed the golden calf. And the Egyptian envoy has a hand in the plot too, it is said."

"What is all this to me?"

"You are closer to me than any other, and that is well known. Your attendance at a Temple festival is taken as my approval. It is better that I am linked with neither the Temple nor the prophet."

"Your father thought not so," Pekah said warily. "He skimmed handsome levies from the Temple coffers."

"Yes, and so do I — but quietly. In my father's day, the man Hosea had not so great a following."

"Do his prophecies frighten you?" Pekah spoke now with some insolence. "These are matters better left alone. If the high priest is in some kind of agreement with the Egyptian envoy, it bodes no good for Israel. We are better having no part in it."

"I think you begin to see plots hatched in the walls."

"Be not deceived by a woman's wiles, Pekah. You yourself once warned me against showing ourselves too friendly to the Egyptian envoy and his consort, and in that you spoke some truth. Neither he nor his consort came from Egypt to enjoy our sweltering Samarian summer."

"You take me for a child. I am not sheep-led by a woman."

"Then see that she does not take you to the Temple this day."

"I am not *taken* by a woman," Pekah said vehemently. "She takes me no where —"

"You will not be seen in the Temple. Is it understood?"

"It is my own affair."

"You speak now to your king."

"And still it is my own affair! Was ever a man in Israel denied wine or worship or woman by order of his king? You overstep yourself, Pekahiah ben Menahem!"

"Pekah, I speak as your brother. You have looked on no woman since the death of your wife. Why now this one, suddenly — and she no Israelite?"

"No concern to you."

Pekahiah sighed heavily. He had feared it would fall out between them. He had no smooth way with words. Always he must come on things with the blunt tongue of a soldier. And Pekah wary for his own standing —

"Have you aught else to bring against me?" Pekah asked coldly.

"Nay —" Pekahiah said wearily.

Pekah spun on his heel and strode angrily out of the throne room. "It was as Tania said," he muttered to himself. "Every day Pekahiah is more given to folly."

3

In her room Tania bent over a chest of polished ebony, bordered about with carvings of Egypt's history and glory. She straightened suddenly at the sound of Pekah's voice behind her. He had vaulted the wall and come to the side entrance to her room, not entering the main house. He paused on the threshold — always it seemed that he stepped into another land when he came to Tania's room. Disarrayed though it was, the spirit and charm of Egypt breathed itself into the very air.

"Pekah! You frightened me!"

"What is this business with the prophet Hosea?" he asked bluntly. Tania shrugged carelessly and turned back to the chest. "Come — help me find the girdle to go with this gown."

Pekah came into the room with a slow step. He ground his teeth, as was his habit when Tania set him ill at ease with her whims and moods. The words stuck in his throat.

"Here, now I have found the one," Tania said.

She slipped a bright colored girdle from the chest and wound it about her waist, snugging in her ocean-blue gown, and turned for Pekah to see. "There. Does it suit?"

"Yes, it suits well." He clasped his hands to her waist and pulled her toward him, roughly.

"Nay we have no time," she said, holding against him.

"Never do we have time," Pekah said wryly. "What is this plan you have with Anakah the high priest?"

"Where have you heard of it?"

"From the king."

"The king — he knows?"

"By rumor only. Is it some plot against the prophet?"

"Yes — it is that."

Tania half turned aside when Pekah asked some knowledge of the plot. She inquired something of his meeting with the king. When she learned what had passed between them, and read in Pekah's eyes the anger Pekahiah had roused, something new came to her.

She had thought to make Pekah no party to her scheme against the prophet, for she knew that Pekahiah would stand against it. Jealous though Pekah was of Pekahiah, underneath remained a core of loyalty and love for his Twin. Tania had deemed she would need some time yet to poison their friendship.

But now she saw the chance to draw Pekah into open disobedience of the king, and so hasten the breach. When the breach was widened beyond all mending, Pekah would be left with no comfort save among those who stood against the king. He would have no course but to swing over to the Egyptian cause.

Carefully she laid before Pekah the scheme against Hosea. The prophet was to be lured into a contest of strength in such a way that his very prophecy hung in the balance. When he was defeated —

"Do you know the man?" Pekah broke in. "He is strong and quick. There is not his match in all Israel."

"Yes," Tania said proudly, "but in Egypt —"

"Midemi?"

The woman laughed aloud. "Midemi! Nay, fighting is not for him. He has quite another part in our plans. Tongo, my Nubian slave."

"That would be no fair contest," Pekah said a little sharply. "Your Nubian is near five cubits."

"Did not your king David set himself against Goliath the Philistine, and himself but a stripling?"

"Yes —"

"Come to the Temple with me. It will be worth the seeing."

Pekah bit on his lip. Something of the soldier returned to his voice, a note of challenge: "Why are you so set on bringing the prophet down?"

"He destroyed the golden calf given to Israel by Egypt," Tania said coldly. "He stands in our way."

"How are you so sure the people will not side with him in this unequal contest?"

"I care not who the people side with. The prophet himself will be humbled. And when, to top it, he discovers that his wife has played him false again — with the handsome envoy of Egypt — then will he have small heart indeed to prophesy more in Samaria."

"Pekahiah says it is better these things be left between the prophet and the priesthood."

"Pekahiah would say such a thing. He has not the wit to rule."

"Oh, let us have an end of this everlasting talk against the king."

"Yes, rather would you scrape your forehead at his feet all your days," Tania said, goading him.

"I scrape before no man — nor him either!"

"He tells you to stay from the Temple today like a child."

"I told him it was my own affair."

"Will you come then?"

"I — I have not thought on it, whether I care to —"

"You do scrape to him."

"Let us forget this business." Pekah tried at laughing — put his arms awkwardly around Tania and drew her toward him. "You are too full of scheming and too sparing of caresses."

He tried to kiss her, but she turned her mouth aside and pushed his arms away. She stepped back, a hint of anger flashing in her dark eyes.

"No. I do not trade my affection lightly."

"You trade it not at all," Pekah said, looking aside at her, now with embarrassment because of her rebuff.

"To one who feared not to take the due of his birth and gifts, I would give myself willingly."

"I fear nothing —"

"Then will you come with me to the Temple?"

She moved a step nearer, laid her hands on his broad chest. His voice trembled, as always it did when she touched him.

"Yes, if you wish it."

She smiled, a pleased, inviting smile, and stretched up to kiss his mouth. He grasped her tightly in his arms, and for a moment she let him press himself against her as he would.

"We have too long played at this," he said thickly.

"Soon we need play no longer."

"Now."

"Nay, first you must . . . prove yourself."

"In what?"

"I must know you are the man I believe in."

She kissed him again. As if in promise, she pressed herself against him until his hands tugged at the back of her gown.

"You are a king," she breathed, close to his ear.

"Tania!"

"You shall one day rule this land of Israel."

He did not hear the words, and she knew he did not hear them. But they would lie in his thoughts and take quiet root.

"Lie with me," he said crudely, passion now overwhelming him.

"I must know — I must know of a certain that you lack not the courage to claim your destiny."

"I lack nothing, nothing — only you —"

"We shall see."

Tania slipped from his embrace and stood apart. He reached out for her.

"Nay," she said, smiling. "Not yet, not yet —"

Chapter 27

A Contest of Strength

The sun had barely come in sight over the walls of Samaria before the crowds began to gather at the Temple on the last day of the Feast of Weeks. By midmorning the outer court was full, and the people spilled out into the street. No one knew for certain what lay afoot — what either the prophet or the priesthood intended. But certain it was that some clash would come between Hosea and Anakah this day, and no man in Samaria meant to miss it.

At midday the cry went up: "He is here! He comes now!"

The tall angular figure of Odenjah led the way, and behind him came Hosea, followed by four of his closest disciples.

"Let us through. Clear a path," Odenjah said to those who blocked their way.

"Take care for the high priest," a squat little man said intensely, grasping Hosea's arm as he passed.

"They have plotted against you," whispered another.

Hosea nodded to each that spoke and pushed on toward the outer court. There his disciples hoisted him to the platform on which the golden calf once stood and remained below, on either side, holding back the crowd.

For a moment Hosea paused, then his voice broke loud and clear: "There is hatred in the house of God against the one who speaks the word of the LORD. The prophet is the watchman of Israel, but you would set a snare for him. Yes — you have plotted against him, and it is known!

"The Lord shall protect his prophet, but those who have deeply corrupted themselves with hatred shall fall because of their iniquity. I shall remember their sins, says the Lord!"

The crowd tensed. Some few priests stood in the archways of the Temple, in range of Hosea's voice. He had challenged them — dared them to carry out any plot against him. If the rumor had any ground, it would soon come into the open.

Hosea swept his glance over the crowd. Now he spoke straight to the people, less harshly, earnestly. It is the end of the Feast of Weeks, he told them, a day of dedication to the Lord. Israel had sinned, and no house was free of guilt. The empty rituals of the Temple would not atone for Israel's sin. The cry of God was for true repentance — steadfast love, not sacrifice; the knowledge of God rather than burnt offerings. Beyond the walls, north of Samaria, was God's own Temple, the Hill of Cedars. There was an altar now raised where Israel could truly worship the Lord this day.

Hosea paused and measured the effect of his words upon the people. Even the eager faces, proud of their loyalty to the prophet, clouded with doubt. So this now was his purpose: to lead them away from the Temple altogether. But the Temple was the house of the Lord, from early days. And this was no Baal festival but a day set apart for the Lord.

Some heads nodded agreement. To what depths had worship fallen in the days of Pekahiah? Drunkenness, blasphemy, harlotry — sin added to sin. "Surely the Lord of hosts dwells not in temples made with hands," Hosea cried out. "The very heavens are his Temple —"

A ripple of agreement whispered through the crowd, and one voice cried out: "Lead us! We will follow!"

Within the Temple, Tania, Pekah, and Anakah stood in a tight circle around Abiel, the tall priest who was to challenge Hosea.

"You know the words?" Tania asked tensely.

"I know them well. But I — I fear we begin too soon. The ritual should be started —"

Wait another quarter hour, and he will have the people led out of the city," Anakah growled.

"Those below me are picked — our own people?" the priest Abiel asked.

"Set your fear aside," Tania said contemptuously. "You will not be pulled down by the followers of the prophet."

"Take your position," Anakah said.

Abiel followed seven priests to a small stand opposite Hosea. He stepped up, and his powerful voice rang out in challenge: "You call yourself a prophet of God?"

The people turned. Abiel repeated his challenge, a faintly mocking tone edging his voice.

"You have said it," Hosea answered, turning toward the priest.

"It is said the LORD stands close to those whom he anoints. Is it not so?"

The priest was speaking in the traditional manner of public contest — careful question calling forth careful answer or counter question.

Hosea simply answered, "It is so."

"There is one here who does not believe," Abiel said, seeming to suggest himself. "He can match his strength against any man, be he prophet, priest, or king."

"The LORD speaks in truth, not in strength."

"Did not the LORD send young David to battle Goliath? Or was it not the LORD?"

"It was the LORD that sent David —"

"And the LORD that restored Samson's strength when he was led into the Temple of Dagon? Or was it not the LORD?"

"Samson called on the LORD."

"And did the LORD answer?"

"You know this," Hosea said warily. "Why do you challenge me?"

"There is one here who does not believe. He vows David was a sure slingsman and Samson a man of strength, and the LORD looked on."

"The LORD lent courage and purpose —"

"In their victory was the LORD glorified?"

"The LORD was glorified."

"And if they had failed?"

"They would not fail. God stood by them. He prepared them. He called them."

"Then the LORD does speak sometimes in . . . strength, for you have said David and Samson glorified the LORD in their victory."

"The LORD speaks how He will," Hosea said with grit. This priest spoke with a smooth tongue, not blustering like the others.

"Then tell me, if you be a prophet, and one knowing the ways of God, why did God send David and Samson against the Philistines, speak to them in . . . strength?"

"The Philistines scorned the name of the LORD, scorned the people He had chosen. They knew no language but the sword."

"There is such a one here today. He scorns the power of the LORD. What shall the prophet do when challenged by such a one?"

Was it to be this? It never came to Hosea that the plot against him would be a contest of strength. "The LORD calls His prophet to declare His word, not to a contest of strength."

"Is this so? Even when the LORD has endowed His prophet with power and strength and grace?"

Hosea bit his lip hard between his teeth. The words of the priest sprang up like snares from the ground.

"The LORD fears not idle threats," Hosea answered. He little doubted his own strength against this tall priest. It was but a boast.

"And the LORD's prophet?" Abiel asked mockingly. "Fears he no threats?"

"Neither he."

"Think well what you say. These be no idle threats."

"Then let the idle boaster do what he will. The word of the LORD stands firm."

"The idle boaster, as you call him, would pit his strength and his god against whoever dares stand against him this day."

Hosea glared searchingly at Abiel. An awful stillness lay over the outer court of the Temple. This he had never done, nor even thought. The LORD had given him strength above other men. If this man dared boast that he had cut himself off from the LORD and now served another god, then the LORD would strike out punishment in the arm of His prophet. Anger lent Hosea purpose. His blood pounded with resentment to see the mocking priest, sworn by sacred covenant to serve the LORD, now openly flaunt his unbelief.

"I stand for the LORD God of Israel!" said Hosea.

"I fear you shall not stand for long. Let the unbeliever come forth."

The figure of Tongo hulked suddenly through the archway from the inner parts of the Temple. Tania and Anakah came at his side.

"Does he understand well?" Anakah whispered tensely. "Let him be hurt, but not killed. We want no slain hero made this day."

Tania nodded. She stopped Tongo and spoke to him in the Egyptian tongue. "You understand now what you are to do? Hurt, but do not kill."

"You show me," said Tongo, grinning, "— I kill." *I kill* were the only words Tongo knew in the Israelite tongue.

To the surprise of those standing by, Tania stretched her arm upward and struck Tongo a stinging blow across the face.

"Do not kill," said Tania fiercely, as though speaking to a cur. "Hurt — not kill." The Nubian nodded grimly. The slender woman who struck him wielded authority. Raised a slave from childhood, Tongo yielded obedience to what he recognized as authority.

"Keep the others close by," Tania said back to Pekah. "He may not stop —"

Tania took from Tongo's hand the short club he always carried and pushed him into the outer court. Tongo lumbered across the courtyard toward Hosea. The crowd shrank back from his path.

"What is this you send to me?" Hosea asked fiercely.

"The unbeliever," Abiel replied.

"What of yourself?"

"Myself? I am a son of Israel. I named not myself. But what now of the prophet? What of his trust in the LORD's strong arm? Does the prophet now tremble?"

Hosea clenched his teeth. So this was the plot. And like a child he had played into their trap. He could not turn back. He had set out the honor of his God, and he could not leave it to be trampled beneath the feet of even this unbeliever. Nor could he hold his head with honor if he turned away. The monstrous hulk of the Nubian loomed within feet of Hosea's stand, atop the platform. A great hand swept out to seize his feet. Hosea leaped quickly to one side and sprang to the court.

"Hosea, stay back! It is a trick!" Odenjah shouted.

"This must be done," Hosea answered grimly. He backed off, crouched at the waist, measuring the speed of Tongo's plodding advance.

The tight-packed throng of people in the outer court pressed closer together, clearing a circle around the two combatants. Tongo swung out at Hosea with one of his great arms. Hosea ducked underneath and drove a closed fist into the Nubian's belly. Tongo grunted in surprise.

Hosea continued to back off slowly, waiting for Tongo to make the first move. By cleverness and fast movement he thought to counter the Nubian's great strength. Tongo backed Hosea to the steps of the Temple and lunged at him with both arms outstretched. Hosea stepped aside, seized one arm, and hurled him forward down the steps of the Temple. A ripple of excitement passed through the crowd.

"A shekel of copper that the prophet triumphs!" called out a bandy-legged man on the edge of the circle, waving a pouch in the air.

Tongo stumbled back up the steps. Before he could fully recover, Hosea smashed a closed fist into the side of his face and hit him again in the belly. Tongo mumbled a curse and came after Hosea at a run.

Hosea dodged, stepped quickly behind, and kicked him a glancing blow that sent the Nubian crashing headlong against a pillar of the Temple.

Tongo shook his head. He turned on Hosea, eyes narrow and vengeful. His long arm snaked out with surprising speed and grasped Hosea's right forearm.

Hosea kicked the Nubian below the knee and dug an elbow into his ribs. Tongo roared with pain and let loose the prophet's arm. Hosea hit him again, a sharp, quick blow high on the breast.

"I kill!" Tongo raged.

The giant lunged at Hosea. Hosea snapped him back with a sharp blow on the side of the head. Tongo shook it off, drove Hosea into the edge of the crowd. There he laid his great hands on the prophet and hoisted him overhead.

"Unh! I kill!"

Hosea wrenched backwards and seized the Nubian by the neck, dug his fingers into the thick flesh of his throat. Tongo howled with fury and hurled Hosea to the ground.

Hosea clung fast to the neck and brought the giant down on top of him. Before Tongo could act, Hosea kicked free and staggered to his feet. He leaped on Tongo's back and banged the giant's head against the paving of the Temple courtyard. The Nubian wrenched an arm backward and grappled Hosea's leg. He pushed to his haunches with his free arm and jerked Hosea from his back. Hosea spun around on his back and kicked out at the crouched hulk above him. Tongo lost his grip. Hosea rolled out of reach and regained his feet.

Tongo pushed slowly from the stone paving of the courtyard. His dull eyes blinked, befuddled. Never had he encountered a creature he could not seize and crush in his great arms. He wiped a trickle of blood from his forehead and started toward Hosea in a half crouch.

Hosea backed off, jabbing at the Nubian with his fists but dodging backward, out of reach. Tongo shook off the blows. He drove Hosea to the steps of the Temple. Hosea moved cautiously out of reach, but when he stepped aside in an attempt to get back to the courtyard, Tongo lunged forward and caught him with both arms.

"I kill!"

Hosea's face went purple in the giant's crushing grip. With one free hand he dug his fingers into the Nubian's eyes and nose, trying to force back his head. Tongo howled with pain, but he would not release his death-grip on the prophet.

Hosea felt his senses swim dizzily. He thrust the giant's head backward with his last strength and then went limp.

"I kill! I kill!" shouted the Nubian.

He swung Hosea over his head and hurled him to the ground. The prophet's body thudded against the steps of the Temple. Tongo was on him like a wild animal. He pounded his great fists against the prophet's ribs, raised him up over his head, and flung him back into the courtyard. Hosea landed on the shoulders of one of the onlookers and slid to the ground, limp and unmoving.

"It has gone far enough," Anakah said to Tania. "He will kill him."

"Tongo, stop!" Tania commanded in a shrill voice.

"I kill!" Tongo roared, stumbling back up the steps after Hosea. The sharp crack of a whip sounded from the Temple archway. Tongo halted uncertainly.

"Tongo, come back," Tania said, brandishing the whip in her slender hand.

The giant turned slowly from the crumpled figure of Hosea and slunk back across the courtyard toward his mistress.

"Go inside with the others," she said.

Odenjah pushed through the crowd to where Hosea lay.

"What think you now of your mighty prophet?" Abiel mocked.

Odenjah glowered at the tall priest. He and two others picked Hosea up in their arms and pushed through the crowd.

Hosea had barely come to his senses when Odenjah and the two others bore him through the door of his house. At the click of the latch, Gomer rose startled from the sleeping mat where she lay, half-clothed. Flushing red, she drew a robe hastily over her shoulders. Not a quarter hour had passed since she lay abed with Midemi, and the Egyptian was gone from the house but moments.

"Set me down, set me down," Hosea groaned.

"Hosea?" Gomer half rose from the mat. She stifled a scream with her hand when she saw the bruised, bleeding form of her husband. She flew to his side. "My husband — Hosea — what happened?"

"He was attacked," Odenjah said tersely.

"Set me down."

"Where can we lay him?" Odenjah asked Gomer.

"Here, on the bed."

"They set the Egyptian slaves on him," said one of the others.

"The Nubians?"

"Yes, the biggest."

They eased Hosea onto the bed. He rose up on his elbows, his eyes wild and frantic.

"I must go back . . . go back —"

"Lie down," Odenjah encouraged him. "Fetch towels and water —" he told Gomer. "Wash his wounds."

"Yes, yes —"

Gomer hurried to the water jar and returned with a bowl of water and two towels. Two of the men held Hosea's shoulders.

"Take your hands off me," the prophet screamed. "I must return. I have betrayed the honor of my God —"

"You are hurt," Odenjah said soothingly.

Gomer dipped a towel in the water and washed the blood from a gash in Hosea's side.

"Agh!" the man cried, "Get away — let loose on me!"

"My husband, I want to help —"

"The LORD of Israel lies trampled in the Temple court! Take your hands off me — I must return!"

Hosea wrenched free of the two men who held him and lunged from the bed.

"Thousand demons!" Hosea cried out. A sharp pain doubled him at the waist.

Odenjah caught him in his arms.

"Let me be!" Hosea shrieked. "I will return — I will!"

"You are sore wounded."

Hosea lurched toward the doorway, convulsed with pain. "The LORD of hosts will not be mocked!"

He retched blood. He reeled into the center of the room and collapsed to the floor. Odenjah sped to his side.

"Quickly! Help him to the bed again. Gomer, wine —"

Hosea lay on the bed, tossing fitfully, his eyes rolling.

"Drink, my husband," Gomer coaxed, tipping the wine cup to his lips. Hosea spit it out and fell back to the mat.

"LORD of hosts, have mercy," he whimpered. "Stay Thy hand, O God —"

A blackness overtook him. He struggled to open his eyes. The faces above him swirled in clouds, the room fell away, and then he sank back on the bed.

After a time his breathing grew more quiet, and it seemed he slept.

"Stay close by his side," Odenjah told Gomer. Then, looking about, "The children — ?"

"They are at the house of my father," Gomer said quickly, averting Odenjah's eyes. Two days earlier Midemi had taken Gomer to his house. When she left, she told Midemi she would be alone at home two days hence. She went on, making explanation to Odenjah, "The children and my father — we were to go all together to the Hill of Cedars. I was preparing —"

Odenjah cut her off. "Send word by the wife of Eharth if you need me."

Gomer nodded. Odenjah and the others left quietly. Gomer stood at the foot of Hosea's bed, clutching her hands to her bosom.

"Oh my husband, my husband," she moaned, her eyes flooding with tears.

So helpless and wretched he lay before her, his beloved face bruised and swollen, his strong body discolored and beaten — cut and wounded defending the honor of his God, while she had dishonored the vessel that was his alone, given to a stranger and alien —

O LORD of hosts, what kind of woman was she! What sort of creature could deceive without shame — deceive and deceive and deceive . . .

Was it true, what she had feared and never dared believe, which haunted her dreams even before she was wed? That she was a lewd and heathen woman, seeking only her pleasure? Her love for Hosea — it was deep and real — yes, it *was*. And yet, beneath lurked her divided heart. When he was out of sight, she could turn without qualm to another — vent her passion like a temple harlot.

Again, she had dishonored Hosea, dishonored him with her hateful, inconstant heart. She was a daughter of Israel. And yet — was the blood of her father not sufficient? Did the passion of her mother so master her that she was a heathen woman despite her birth? Did her sin choke out her birthright, cut her off from the inheritance of Israel?

For the first time in her life, Gomer spoke to the LORD as to another person — in her own words, not words from the scrolls. "O LORD God of hosts, have mercy," she sobbed, "For I am an evil woman."

Hosea stirred on his bed. Gomer returned to the jar to fetch more water to bathe his wounds. The cup she had drunk with Midemi stood beside the water jar, half filled yet with wine. This, too, was her evil that she inflamed her passions with wine. A wedded woman should drink wine only with her husband. Yes, she reached out for evil — sought it with purpose. She had done so with Shallum and Donath, and now with the beautiful Egyptian —

Hosea moaned on his bed. Gomer filled the water bowl and returned to his side. Gently she bathed his feverish face and neck. He did not waken at her touch.

The next morning Hosea wakened early, after a fitful night. He struggled out of his bed and dashed himself with water from the bowl that stood nearby. Moments later, Gomer appeared in the doorway behind him, a whisper of beauty in the half-light of early morning. She bore a fresh jar of water.

"My husband, you should remain abed," she said gently.

"Gomer — ? Where — where are the children?"

"They stayed the night at my father's house. I would not have them see you thus."

"I have failed, Gomer," Hosea said despairingly. "I have failed my God."

"It is not so, my husband. You were set on unfairly."

"No, no. It is so. The Feast of Weeks is passed — the day the LORD would have had me lead the people away from the abomination of the Temple. It has passed, and the name of the LORD is scorned because of me."

"How can the LORD be scorned that a giant was set on you to do you harm?"

"I took the challenge foolishly but in the name of the LORD. When I fell, it was for the name of God."

"If it were the will of God that you should triumph, it would be so."

"Nay, I stood in the way of His will. I trusted in my own strength and prowess and not in the hand of the LORD."

Hosea drew on his cloak and limped to the door of the house.

"Where do you go?" Gomer asked worriedly. "You should rest."

"These pains and bruises do well to remind me of my folly. I go to the house of Odenjah."

Gomer spoke uncertainly: "My husband — all is not lost. Your work, your people — they will not forget —"

"This day I trow they will not forget," Hosea said wearily.

"You must take care. I — I faint to think how you were brought here yesterday."

She hid her face from him, for the thought of Midemi crowded in on her, and she deemed the shame must tell on her face.

"If God has use for me still, I shall have no cause to fear. If not —"

Gomer looked up. Such an emptiness of spirit shown in Hosea's eyes that she wept to look on him. She ran to his side and kissed his bruised cheek.

"Be comforted, my husband. The LORD shall not leave you."

Hosea touched Gomer's arm awkwardly. That this word of assurance should come from her was curiously heartening. He smiled a strange, ailing smile.

When he was gone, Gomer stood at the door, her hands clasped together. The look of wretchedness in his eyes, looking to her for comfort —

Often had he wanted her, and often given her of his strength. Yet now it was something new: he gave her of his weakness — he needed her. It was something strange to be needed thus — for something more than the service of her woman's body. Something strange —

Chapter 28

A Fateful Tryst

1

In the days that followed, Hosea walked the streets of Samaria with downcast eyes. Never before had it come to him what store he set by his strength. The pain of his defeat by the Nubian went deeper than bruises and cuts.

Not since Shallum ben Jabesh mocked him in the Temple with the first knowledge of Gomer's harlotry had Hosea known such humiliation. Yet, from that humiliation he found some respite. When all fell out, it was Gomer who stood more accused and humbled. When he set himself to keep her, despite the Law of Israel, still was he a man who could stand up as man to any in Israel. Yes — so much the man that he could cling to Gomer, despite law and custom. Another man might have lost all hearing if he kept a wife openly branded a harlot; such was the respect and fear of Hosea that not even his own followers dared gainsay him in the matter of his wife. But in the contest with the Nubian, it was himself alone who bore the humiliation — and there seemed no escape.

Odenjah and the others minded him that the match with the Nubian had been a trick — was no fair contest. This counted for little with Hosea. The Nubian was not *so* strong. Another day the victory might have gone to him —

The humiliation went deeper: he had taken the challenge *in the name of the LORD*. He had staked his prophecy on his own strength — and he had lost. Never could his word ring out with authority again in Samaria.

Hosea came to see his defeat as a judgment against himself. Somewhere he had failed the LORD, and the LORD had wrought this punishment against him. Perhaps he had gone against God in clinging to Gomer — or prophesied too much from the turmoil of his own heart and been deaf to any word the LORD might give him — or spoken too harshly against Israel — or not harshly enough. He found no clear answer.

The thought clung to him that all his life to this day stood now against him, and soon there must come a change in the times.

* * *

Two weeks later Hosea learned of Gomer's adultery with Midemi. He got it from Deborah, and quite by chance. She deemed he knew it already, for it was common gossip at the well. She drew him aside to her doorway when he came home one evening. In her blunt way she asked if he meant now to turn Gomer out, and if so, what of the children — must they be made to suffer for the sin of their mother? When Deborah saw that Hosea knew nothing of the affair, she burst into tears, begging Hosea to forget her words — belike it was only gossip and evil slander.

Hosea had only to mention the Egyptian's name in passing talk, and he knew Deborah had spoken truth. Gomer flushed deep red. Her voice trembled. She could scarcely speak. A moment Hosea was silent, and then quickly — almost desperately — he turned their talk to other matters. One thought only swept over him: he must turn her out, as he had vowed.

He could not. He could not!

A week went by. Hosea lived with a hopeless sense of judgment hanging over him. He must put Gomer away once for all, according to the word he had overheard the LORD speak: *Strip her naked and make her as in the day she was born.*

He blocked Gomer from his thoughts. He scarcely spoke to her and the children, fearing any stray word might bring their family and their life together crashing down upon them. Vainly he strove to blind himself to what now seemed certain truth: in clinging to Gomer he had separated himself from the LORD; the LORD had abandoned him.

Yet, still he could not yield her up. He cast about for things that could turn his thoughts to other matters, forestalling the judgment.

In the affairs of the kingdom, Hosea found solemn cause for concern. Samaria was a-whisper with rumors of revolt and overthrow. He saw Israel slipping toward another fruitless alliance with Egypt, sure to release the Assyrian hordes upon the land. In another day he would have raised his voice in the city, calling king and nation to account before the LORD. With the double weight of humiliation that lay upon him, he had little heart to prophesy. He turned to a plan for Israel's weal, which he himself could help bring about. It offered some escape from all that weighed upon him in Samaria.

* * *

One morning, before the sun was yet up, he wakened Gomer.

"What is it?" she asked, rising up suddenly, her voice thin and half-frightened sounding.

Hosea spoke low, in a half-whisper, so as not to waken the children. "I shall be gone for some days. I travel to Assyria."

"To Assyria? For what purpose?"

"I mean to call Hoshea back to Samaria."

"Hoshea? But why?"

"There is mischief afoot — plans and devising against the throne. He is needed." Hosea had lain awake half the night searching for a right course to follow.

317

Tension in Samaria mounted day by day, as did shouting against the king. "Why must we starve to feed the Assyrian," cried the people.

"Egypt is our friend! Egypt buys our corn and barley!"

Hosea deemed it would not go much longer before there came a thrust against the throne. How such a thrust might come, or from whom, Hosea did not know. But if there were plots afoot against Pekahiah, the one man to prevent it would be Hoshea ben Elah.

Gomer clenched her hands together and tried to appear calm and untroubled. Yet within, a wild fear raged. She had deemed by Hosea's silence these days that he had heard some report of her adultery with Midemi. Something kept him silent. Gomer dared think that he still had a passion to keep her, despite all. So long as she could remain in his house, ever close to him, and could work her charm and wile with him, Gomer held some hope of winning through this pass. But if any chance should take them apart, and Hosea had any days for quiet thought, Gomer little doubted he would turn her naked into the street, as he had sworn.

"Must you be the one to go?" she asked hesitantly. "Cannot someone else — one of the king's own men? Surely this is his affair."

"Some who are close to the king may be thick in the plot — such is the talk. Belike the king himself knows not who he could trust with a message to Hoshea — or indeed, if Hoshea himself is against him —"

"But if Hoshea —"

"Nay, Hoshea was never one to set himself against the throne — that I know."

"I — I do wish you would not go —"

"Less than a month will see my return."

"Yes, and then?" Gomer burst out, as though suddenly she would have it done now, once for all. But straightway she caught a hand to her mouth and would have bidden the words unspeak themselves.

Hosea rose up and drew a cloak over his shoulders. It was still near dark in the house, but Gomer could tell by his quick and heavy breathing that hot anger lay close to the surface.

"Hosea, Hosea," she said low and despairingly, "so silent we have been these days. I — I would not have us part unfriends."

Hosea tied a sack of provision on his back and a skin of water at his waist. He stopped at the door, but he spoke no word. A moment later he was gone.

2

From the Feast of Weeks onward, the plans of the plotters moved apace. Five weeks had passed since the prophet Hosea was brought down in the Temple courtyard. The Temple priesthood quietly took lead of the people, setting them against the king. Anakah stood ready to anoint the usurper. Remaliah had gained the pledge of four outlying garrisons to give quiet support to their revolt, not coming to the king's defense. A band of Gileadite warriors had bartered their services to the plotters for fifty shekels of gold. Pekah now leaned heavily to the Egyptian cause. Four days following the next Sabbath, if all went well, Israel would have a new king. The first link in Pharaoh's alliance against Assyria would be forged.

In these weeks, few words passed between Tania and Midemi. More and more Midemi had withdrawn from the scheming against the throne, leaving all to Tania's judgment. Tania made excuse for him, allowed that he was taken up with the wife of the prophet, and moreover it was better that he be seen not too close to the plot. But in truth, Tania could not look on Midemi some days without giving way to secret despising — so loath was he to play the man.

She found him late one afternoon in his room, winding a long linen scarf into a cone-like headdress. She paused in the doorway, watching. She marveled that he could sit thus so calm, winding that scarf as if it were all in the world that weighed on him — when everything they had striven for lay now but seven days hence.

"Have you taken to the Israelite manner of dress?" she asked, making a show at lightness.

Midemi shrugged and let the scarf fall to his lap. Tania pressed her hands down along her legs, smoothing out the blue gossamer robe she had slipped into moments before. Unwittingly, she would assure herself of her own womanly charm before coming to Midemi with anything that touched on the wife of the prophet.

After a few moments Tania came to her purpose: she asked Midemi what he knew of the prophet's departure from Samaria. Midemi owned that he did not know the prophet was gone from the city.

"Has she said nothing of his going?" Tania asked.

"Nay —" Midemi turned aside, averting Tania's gaze.

"A priest of the Temple learned today that he was seen departing the city more than two weeks past."

"What matter?"

"His going bodes no good. These prophets have a way of going off into the wilderness for a time to hold counsel with their God and then returning with fire on their tongue."

Midemi laughed, to cover his unease. "I think rather he has gone off to lick his wounds."

"It may be," Tania mused. She smiled a little to think how well revenged she was on the prophet for his destruction of the golden calf. "Yet, still I like it not that he is out of our sight. Does he know of you and his wife?"

"I do not know."

"Nay? Speak you nothing to one another?"

Midemi glanced away and did not answer. Tania had craved little report of his affair with the wife of the prophet. She feared what she might discover if she over-questioned him — might find the woman was to his liking. But now Tania deemed that something else lay afoot with Midemi, so sullen and uneasy he behaved himself.

"What is it with you and her?" Tania asked sharply.

Still Midemi made no reply.

"You have prevailed with her?"

"Yes!"

"What then?"

"What then, what then! What more would you have?" Midemi spat out irritably.

Tania bit hard her lip. Now she was sure that all was not as she had planned between Midemi and the prophet's wife. Even in the streets, as she now thought on it, the whole affair was too little gossiped about, too secret.

"Methinks this should be brought more into the open," she said.

"It is known already."

"Yes, by shadow and whisper. But it must be shouted aloud in broad daylight."

"Then spread what gossip you will," Midemi said angrily. "I have done my part."

"Nay, you must be *seen* — walking with her in the streets of the city in full daylight. When the prophet returns, we must leave him no doubt."

"She will not go —"

"What?" said Tania mockingly, "have you lost your charm with her?"

"I have not known her since the day her husband fell."

All play at jesting fled Tania's face. "You have not been with her these past weeks?"

"No."

"Why?"

"She would not speak with me after what happened to her husband."

"Because of the Nubian? She held you to account?"

"I forswore all knowledge of it. But after he was beaten, she seemed regretful that ever she went aside with me — would have no more of it."

"And you took her at her word and nevermore returned to her house? You, Midemi?"

Midemi looked downward and fingered the bright scarf in his lap. It shamed him some that Tania should see him thus spurned by an Israelite woman. But more lay to it than that. He might have prevailed with Gomer again, had he set himself to it. Indeed, he had wanted to. He found himself drawn to Gomer. She had given him — it was more than passion, though it lacked none of that. It was, beneath, a kind of warmth and tenderness. Never had he found that with Tania. But when he came to Gomer's house after that day, he deemed she was much grieved by the wrong she had done her husband. Midemi stood to cause her much sorrow — had caused her sorrow already. He did as Gomer craved of him and came no more to her house.

"Have you forgotten altogether what brought us to Israel?" Tania asked bitingly.

"I have not forgotten."

"Yet for weeks gone by you have set our plans aside, saying no word."

Midemi stood to his feet. He affected a weariness of tone: "I deemed the plan had run its course, and so it has."

"What do you know of our plans?" Tania asked angrily. "You sit here by day and by night dreaming and moaning for Egypt. Our plans could be set on by a thousand spears, and you would sit there idly winding your turban!"

Midemi shrugged carelessly and turned away. Tania grasped him by the arm and whirled him back to face. "Care you nothing for our success?"

"I care nothing for your scheming," he said bitterly.

"Yes, you care nothing for my scheming. But well content you are to reap its fruit. Always is this your way — heaping the burden on me and taking the victory as your due. If you were the man, it would be you who had an eye to risk and danger."

"If you were woman, would you —"

Midemi stopped his words. Tania went ashen in the cheeks, and her lips trembled. "Yes, what? What?" she prodded in a thin voice.

Midemi thrust his hands into the girdle of his robe and strode away from her. Tania stomped her foot in rage.

"Yes, walk away and shell up in silence," she said hotly. "Always is that your way. Never can you face a thing cold in the face."

"I scarce think you would like it if I did," he said.

Tania held her head high and spoke in strained quiet: "Why? Because you would say I am too hard — not enough the woman, soft and yielding? Well enough. Say it then —"

Midemi looked downward but spoke nothing.

"I know what I am," Tania said, a quaver coming into her voice. "But I know, too, what I would be. And that comes not by dreaming. If hard and scheming I must be to win for us in Israel, then hard and scheming I will be. Better the stench of scheming for a season than a lifetime of meanness and no-honor in the commonwealth of Pharaoh."

Tania held her hands to her sides, gripping her thighs to quell her trembling. Midemi said nothing.

"Have you forgotten all our plans and dreams?" she asked.

"No."

"It is only for this I plan and scheme —"

Midemi ran a hand through his dark reddish hair. Never for long could he set himself against Tania. In the end, he knew that all his fortunes in the court of Pharaoh hung on her planning and scheming — little though he liked owning it.

"You still think this prophet a danger?" he asked, smiling weakly.

"No caution is too small," Tania said, coming to his side. "These Israelites regard marriage differently than we. It is no light thing for a wife to be caught in adultery."

"It is no uncommon thing in Samaria these days. And what of your fabled charm?" She forced a little laugh.

"Still, it seems cruel to . . . misuse the woman."

"What is she to us?" Tania said, touching his arm. "What are any of these Israelites to us, except they further our purpose?"

"Yes —"

"You will do this thing?"

Midemi looked down on her.

"Will you?" the woman asked again.

He nodded, slowly.

"Our waiting and planning nears an end," Tania said low. "Come kiss me, my love. We have known too little of love these weeks."

Midemi bent and kissed her, but with little feeling. His thoughts were suddenly on Gomer, and the tears that had come to her eyes the last time he saw her, when she begged him to come no more to her house.

* * *

Gomer sat cross-legged beside the fire pit, staring into the dying embers of the evening fire. A single ribbon of smoke curled lazily to the ceiling, flattened and billowed around the cedar beams, drifted toward the smoke hole, and then slowly escaped into the night air. Jezreel sat by Hosea's table, laboring over a written scroll, painfully tracing each character with his finger and muttering over and over its meaning, as one did in learning to read. Across the room Loruhamah played with Loammi. Two weeks Hosea had been gone. He left barely enough food to see them through six days. Gomer had gone to her father's house and carried back food.

Yet, almost more than his continued absence, Gomer feared Hosea's return. Sure she was that everything would be done between them when he came back. She had thought hopefully that she might win through with him again, with pleadings and promises. But she little believed it. Patient Hosea was in many things, despite his sudden temper. But when he set his solemn word on something, he seldom swerved from it.

If you go again into adultery, I will turn you naked into the street.

Gomer glanced across at Jezreel, bent low over his scroll. It was the practice in Israel that children must strip naked their mother when the father turned her out for adultery. Loammi gurgled a little chuckle across the room in his play with Loruhamah. A cold shiver trembled through Gomer's breast.

What might become of her if Hosea did turn her out? Gomer scarcely dared think on that. Yet beneath the stark fear lay something else besides — a sorrowful foreboding. For it was not only this house and safety she would lose, but Hosea himself. It was strange. When she went aside with other men, Gomer had it in mind that she would return again to Hosea when it was done with . . . and that he would take her back. This feeling bound her close to Hosea, and in a curious way it deepened her love of him. She came to depend upon his strength to redeem her weakness. With him she felt secure not only from hunger and want, but from herself — from the wildness in her blood. Food and shelter she might find, by one means or another. But Hosea — him she would lose utterly, and in losing him, lose herself as well.

A soft knocking came on the door. Jezreel leaped up and drew the latch. Without, Gomer heard the muffled accent of one not at home in the Israelite tongue, and a sudden tenseness gripped her.

"It is the man of Egypt," Jezreel said low, turning back into the house. He yet knew nothing of Gomer and Midemi, but his brow was drawn into a dark frown, and he looked on his mother with questioning eyes.

"What does he want?" Gomer asked in faint voice.

"He asks for you," the boy said coldly, returning to Hosea's table. Gomer rose hesitantly to her feet.

"Mama —" Loruhamah looked up at Gomer with fearful eyes. Gomer shook her head and smiled weakly.

"What do you wish?" she asked, coming to the door.

Midemi stood without, attired in the same blue robe he had worn the day Hosea fell, the same red girdle. The oil of his hair glistened faintly in the moonlight.

"Gomer, I must see you," he said, low and warm.

She stepped half through the door to keep her words from the children. "You must go. I cannot see you."

"Send me not away again," he pleaded. "My anguish these weeks, apart from you — you cannot know it —"

"You have no care for me," Gomer said in a kind of challenge, "to come here at night, when my husband would be at home."

"He is gone from the city. I learned it," the man said quickly. He stopped, then came again compellingly, "Oh my Gomer, I struggled against myself like one in fever, to keep my word with you and come no more to your house. But you have haunted me by day and by night. My dreams are nothing but you, and my days lost in thinking of you. Food and drink turn bitter on the tongue, for the memory of your kiss."

"You bring only sorrow on us both," Gomer said a little sadly.

"Not sorrow — say it not. But joy —"

Gomer shook her head and half closed her eyes: "You have your own consort, and I my own husband."

"I cannot look on her for thinking of you," he said vehemently. "When one has glimpsed heaven, all earth is drear to the eye." He took her hand and lifted it to his lips. "Oh Gomer, send me not away," he whispered, pressing the palm to his lips.

"No, no," Gomer breathed. But she could not draw back her hand. So lonely she had been and so full of despair. And now came his words — wanting her — wanting her more even than his own beautiful Egyptian woman. The thought came of the wilderness in springtime, burst suddenly to bloom in profusion of color, after the barrenness of winter —

"There is only we two, in all this world," he said.

"Would that it were so," she answered.

He drew closer to her. The scent of his hair wafted to her nostrils. Still he held to her hand, and his voice spoke caressingly, close to her ear: "Say you will not send me away."

"I must. The children are within. Already we speak overlong."

"Later, when they sleep —"

"Oh Midemi, I know not," she said despairingly.

"Know only us, only us."

She closed her eyes and leaned against the door. His kiss brushed across her lids. She held to his hand, squeezing it.

"When the children sleep," she whispered, not opening her eyes. "On the housetop."

When he was gone, she stayed a time outside, half fearful to enter the house again. Jezreel had looked on her so strangely. Perhaps he knew of her and Midemi. Perhaps heard it in the streets? What matter now? All would soon be over between her and Hosea. Midemi wanted her.

It was strange what she felt toward Midemi. Never had she known one with such ways of love! His manner of touching and playing with her — kisses she had never dreamed — foolish and loving little caresses. And yet there was so much of the child in him, wanting comfort and nestling like a suckling babe. Three times only she had been with him: their first meeting on the housetop, the day following when he watched for her at the well and took her to his house, and the day Hosea fell. In those three times she deemed she knew Midemi better than others she had known for years. Midemi wanted to be with her. In his own house they had done nothing but talk and talk and talk. He had but kissed her once on the mouth, as she left. There was such sweetness and restraint in that kiss that it lived with Gomer more than passion.

Then, in her house on that fateful day, she had held his head in her lap. And he had begun to caress her and do things such as never before she had known, so gentle and fleeting his touch that she must arch to it. And then suddenly sharp and hurting, yet no pain. His eyes burned upon her, his soft hair caught in her fingers. Kisses and kisses and kisses. Aching and reddened her breasts. Words she could not remember, urging, urging. And a soaring dizzying lostness.

Never, never had she known such ways of loving. And yet, in the days afterward, she marked it strange that the memory of it roused no passion in her. Always before it had been that passion begot passion. It was so even now, with Hosea. In these last months, when he came to her bed of a night, all the next day was an anxious waiting for his return. But her passion with Midemi seemed almost never to have happened — empty and futile. It was more their quiet moments she remembered, with a kind of wistfulness — their talking together or holding him childlike to her breast.

She wondered that she had consented to meet with him again, except that he seemed so lonely for her — and no harm could come now, for all was over between her and Hosea. And — the thought came on her suddenly — perhaps she could go with Midemi. Yes! Maybe she could!

Jezreel appeared in the opening of the door behind her. "He has left?" the boy asked.

"What?" said Gomer, startled from her thoughts. "The Egyptian? Oh, yes — he — he left some moments ago. Only wished some knowledge of your father's return. I remained out to enjoy some of the night air."

In the darkness Gomer reddened with shame, that she must lie and explain herself to her own son.

"It is time you children were in bed," she said severely.

Jezreel backed away sullenly, and Gomer followed him into the house. Loruhamah looked up at her, her eyes wide and questioning, somehow hinting sadness. Gomer looked away and set herself to rolling out their beds and making ready for sleep. When the children were abed, she lay down and stared up into the darkness.

Some time later, when the children's breathing had grown low and peaceful, she crept quietly across the room and outside. Moments later Jezreel rose up from his bed. He went to the doorway and stood there, listening.

Gomer found Midemi already on the housetop.

"How long have you waited?" she asked as she came to his side under the tenting.

"A moment — a lifetime," he laughed.

She kissed him lightly on the cheek, and soon he laid his head in her lap. They talked quietly for a time.

His hand lazed beneath her robe, here and there, touching her skin. When he pressed more against her she allowed him, until she deemed his passion was roused. Then she said to him, "Know you what will come of me, if my husband learns of this?"

"He threatened to turn you out, you said."

"Yes — naked into the street."

"I trow he would repent of it when the time came."

"Not he," Gomer said evenly. "He has sworn it."

"It is an idle threat," said Midemi. Then, as though it came on him suddenly, "Let him know of you and me! Then will you see how soon he draws back his threats. And you can do with him as you like."

Gomer shook her head and spoke with a hint of fearfulness: "Nay, you know not the man. He will do as he has sworn. It is his way."

Midemi feigned a show of strong feeling. "Gomer, the man is not living who could turn you out, once he has known you."

"Say you so, Midemi? What of yourself?"

"Myself?"

"Yes, could you turn me out?"

Midemi saw her purpose and thought quickly what he must say. She was set on this way — that he must take her himself when the prophet cast her off, and likely she would continue with him on no other ground. So now he must misuse her doubly — yet there was no other way.

"Nay, never could I turn you out," he said slowly, "were you mine."

"Is it so, Midemi? Truly?"

"Truly."

She kissed him warmly on the lips. And then, to make certain her ground, she said, "If ever I come to you, will you take me?"

"Might I hope that you would come to me?" he asked.

"Perhaps you could," she answered low.

"For more than this once — for always?"

Gomer nodded. Midemi looked downward as next he spoke: "And will you be unashamed of me — be seen with me?

"Yes, if you wish it."

"O my Gomer —"

She lifted his head and kissed him. Then slowly he lifted the robe over her head.

"It is chill," she whispered.

"Too chill?"

"Nay."

He was slow with her, holding back, rousing her and playing with her by turns. They lay a long time afterward with no cover in the chill night air.

Chapter 29

Tania and Pekah

1

Two days following, Gomer was seized with a raging fever. She woke in the night far gone from her senses, calling for Hosea and her children. Loruhamah came first to her side, speaking low in the darkness. But Gomer heard her not and cried the more. The child went across and fetched Deborah, who came with lighted lamp and laid cold towels on the fevered woman's head.

The next day the fever mounted. Gomer lay sweat-drenched on her bed, hot and shivering by turns and seeming not to know who came and went in the house. When she was not asleep, her eyes rolled in her head and she broke into raving senseless words and phrases — or she cried out that the heavy hand of the LORD was upon her and sobbed piteously, begging forgiveness, pleading stay of judgment. Deborah scarce left her side and wept and wept, crying that the fever would bring Gomer to her death, as it had her own sister two years past.

Midemi came the third day to the house. Jezreel would have prevented him at the door, but he pushed his way in. At the sight of Gomer he caught a hand to his breast. Deborah told him that she lay at the door of death. He stood a moment over the bed, struggling to speak, but the words stuck on his tongue. Gomer stared up at him, unseeing. He departed the house with an aching dryness in the throat.

The children kept mostly to the house, or fetched water or wood for the fire, as Deborah directed them. Loammi cried much, and Loruhamah held him in her arms, speaking softly to him, comforting him like a mother. Jezreel sat stiffly at Hosea's table, his face grim, and no tear in his eye; or he would creep to Gomer's side and seek to lie in her embrace.

2

The day following the Sabbath, Tania arranged her room with great care, dressed herself in a crimson robe gathered loosely at the waist, sprayed a delicate perfume into the air, and lastly laid her bed with a robe of ermine, spotless and caressingly soft. Then she sat on the edge of her Egyptian-carved chest and waited the arrival of Pekah.

Each wedge she had driven between Pekah and Pekahiah had to work past Pekah's stubborn reluctance to betray his Twin. He had long nurtured jealousy of Pekahiah. But there was fierce loyalty in him, too. Angry as he himself could become toward Pekahiah, Pekah resented the word of any other against his Twin. It was no easy thing to forget that more than once they had risked their lives for one another in battle and stood shoulder to shoulder against the Syrian desert raiders a whole day stretch. They laughed and shouted to one another with every Syrian felled, trumpeting their own prowess and mocking the other's in that way of belittlement that can pass only between closest friends. Not without some heart-sickness did Pekah yield up such memories. Yet, yield he did.

Each time they met, Tania cunningly played on Pekah's rankling against the king — goaded his ambition to allow one more deceit, one small betrayal. Little by little she had weaned him from his loyalty to Pekahiah and to Israel until he stood, now, agreed to seize the throne for himself. Agreed to the cause of Egypt. One last hindrance remained — the slaying of Pekahiah.

Pekah thought to simply set Pekahiah aside. But Tania knew the folly of such doings. A man who has tasted power rests not easy without it, save in his tomb. Nor would the land rest easy with an unthroned king about, hankering after counter-plots. Pekahiah must be killed.

For this, Tania had saved a last weapon. Never had she allowed Pekah to possess her, in nearly half a year's time. With uncanny wile she withheld her favor and yet kept his passion alive — promised without fulfilling, suggested but never agreed, tempted and yet did not yield, drove him at times to near-madness and still held back, asking yet one more favor, one last surety. If she won his agreement this day, she could well allow Pekah his conquest of her: her own triumph would be but a sword's thrust away.

Pekah drew back the moment he entered Tania's room. Its very order roused a sudden animal caution in him.

"I have waited for you." Her voice floated to him like a warm desert breeze.

"Why do you invite me again to your house?" Pekah asked stiffly. He had left in anger two days before. She had teased and tempted him beyond endurance and then shamed him into his old embarrassment. They had not spoken since.

"You are in danger," Tania said, rising and coming toward him.

"I? What kind of danger?" Pekah could not take his eyes from the crimson gown that swirled about Tania's legs, showing the whiteness of her limbs through its gossamer fabric.

"The king has learned something of our plans."

"Ah! I feared this, I feared this!" Pekah said with sudden vehemence. He paced to the window, almost as though he thought to see Pekahiah's guards marching across the city to seize him.

"We have moved the time ahead by two days," Tania said.

"What?"

"Tomorrow," she said evenly.

Pekah turned back toward her, clapping his hands behind his back.

"Yes, yes, it is good," the man said jerkily. "If he suspects some plot, delay but increases our danger."

"Your father and Midemi left early for Gilead to bring back those we hired."

"Good. Yes, good. They must have time to learn the lay of the palace and our plan of attack."

Tania pursed her lips thoughtfully and half turned away from Pekah as she spoke. "Have you thought what you will do with Pekahiah?"

"He must be held in the palace until our authority is secure," Pekah answered crisply. "He is not over-fond of ruling, may even welcome the overthrow."

"Such is not the word that reaches my ears," Tania said silkily.

"What is that?"

"That he will kill every man and his family that is thick in this plot rumored against him."

"That itself is a rumor," Pekah scoffed. "It is not Pekahiah's way."

"Little do you know, little do you know," the woman intoned darkly.

"Know I not my own Twin?" Pekah blanched at his own words.

"When a king's throne is threatened, his own brother is not safe," Tania said, turning suddenly to face him. "He would slay you in a moment if he knew the truth."

"You prattle like a fish monger," Pekah said angrily.

"It is true, what I have said — mark it." Tania glided to his side, spoke soft at his ear. "I fear for your safety."

"You fear needlessly."

"He sent one of your own charioteers to spy on you."

Pekah's fingers closed tight into the palms.

"Where did you hear this?" he asked.

"From the guard who stands at the door of the throne room and trades his ears for Egyptian gold. The words he heard were these: 'Watch his coming and his going. He has been strangely distant.' And when your man left, the king laughed to his scribe, 'It would be a pity for so good a man to die.'"

"It is false, false! Who is this man, this man sent to spy on me?" Pekah demanded, his cheeks and neck flushing with color.

"The guard knew him not, and no name was spoken."

"It is a false rumor — a lie!" Pekah said vehemently.

"Dare you be so sure? What does your friendship mean to him, now he is king of Israel? Nothing. From the day he stepped to the throne he has missed no chance to humble you."

"Ah, but to kill — kill his own Twin — this is not Pekahiah."

"His own words convict him. From this moment your life is endangered."

"No — I cannot believe it."

"My loved one —" Tania put her arms about Pekah's neck. "What is past is past recalling. This thing between you and the king — it is dead. He has turned from you."

"We are brothers —"

"No longer. He has sworn your life."

"It is madness!"

"Oh Pekah, Pekah, we have so little time." She tightened herself to him. "I must know you are here, in my arms, safe."

He took her lips in a sudden, cruel kiss.

"I could teach you love," she breathed against his lips, "love you have never known."

"Play not with me now," he warned.

She stopped his words with her lips and twined her fingers with his. "I must not lose you," she said low.

"Nay — our plan will yet succeed —"

"The king must not have his way against you."

"Nothing will go amiss." He strained against her hands, which held his arms to the side.

"If you were killed, this would all end —"

"Tania, it will not end. I will prevail."

335

She gripped his hands fiercely.

"You must kill him," she said.

"Kill him — ?"

"Yes, before he kills you."

"Nay, not this."

"The land can not bear an unthroned king. If you let him live, he will be your death," Tania said grimly.

"I cannot —"

"Then are you no man for me! Your destiny awaits you — if you shrink from it, you lose all."

"But to kill —"

"It is kill or be killed — that is the choice."

Pekah groaned aloud and drew away. Tania held to him, came against him. "Let me know that I have not misknown you — let me know —"

She stretched herself against him the length of her body. He seized her in his arms and buried his face against her neck.

"Will you?" she whispered, one last resistance still in her body. His teeth sank against the soft flesh of her shoulder.

"I will," he moaned.

Chapter 30

The Twins

1

Three years in Nineveh had changed Hoshea ben Elah but little. Still he wore the simple dress of a soldier, carried himself with leopard grace, spoke in the fast, clipped accents of one long accustomed to command, and smiled in that easy way that sped a quiver of tiny lines from the corners of his eyes. But a dark frown clouded his blunt, handsome features when Hosea told him what lay afoot in Israel. He paced the bare length of his quarters while Hosea pressed him to return to Samaria and seize command of the king's army. The last time he set his hand to court intrigue, Hoshea came out second to Menahem. He was not eager to risk again such humiliation.

The bare truth of Hosea's report stood plain before him: a revolt in favor of the Egyptian faction would lay Israel open to grave danger. With a single word Tiglath Pileser could launch an attack that would blacken every village in the land. If he saw Israel consorting with Egypt, that word would not stay long unspoken.

"Yet . . . someone must remain here in Nineveh," Hoshea said cautiously. "Our cause rests on sandy ground. There are those who press Pileser for war against Israel. A shifting of the winds could turn a hundred thousand warriors against the borders of Israel. I have come to be on close terms with Pileser. He would grow suspicious if I left."

"He will grow more than suspicious if Israel turns to Egypt," Hosea said. "Pekahiah knows how things stand. Each month I have sent him word."

"Hoshea! Pekahiah must see," Hosea cried out. "He will lose his throne, and likely his life, if this plot against him is not thwarted. What good then are your words to him?"

"He has good captains at his call," Hoshea said stiffly.

Hosea looked hard at his boyhood friend. "Hoshea, if I knew one captain to trust, I would have brought him to Nineveh with me."

"Think you the king's army would align with Egypt?" Hoshea said, laughing. "They are not so foolish. They know where the danger lies."

"You yourself fell near persuading them to side with the Egyptian alliance of Shallum ben Jabesh," Hosea said, knowing that his words would cut.

"To back Shallum, yes," Hoshea answered back, red with anger, "but an alliance with Egypt, never. Israel has one enemy to dread — Assyria."

"Yes, and that gives the very reason you must return to Samaria. Israel no longer cares for the hardness of Menahem, and now Pekahiah. They cry out for the softness of Egypt."

"I trow the king could send for me, if I were needed," Hoshea said, kicking at a pebble that fell from his sandal.

"I believe he sees the danger but partly."

"And you see it more clearly? How this concern of yours for the governance of the kingdom, Hosea? You have said a prophet has no part in the intrigues of the palace."

"It is the very reason I come to you. This is a soldier's business. Your name still carries weight in the army of the king. I see the danger. You can quell it."

"Pekahiah would little welcome any help from me," said Hoshea suddenly. "He stood against me when I contended with Menahem."

"He could not well stand against his own father."

"Pekah did. Yes, Pekah — there is one closer to the king than me. Let Pekah look to the king's interests."

"Pekah may himself be thick in the plot."

"Against Pekahiah, his Twin? That I could never believe!"

"He is taken up with the consort of the Egyptian envoy."

"Now there is a fair sounding rumor! And the envoy himself has it with the wife of Pekahiah, no doubt. And Remaliah is in it too, I trow, with the back entrance to Pharaoh's harem."

"They are seen together openly," Hosea said. "It is more than rumor. And it is no secret that she wields the club over her own consort. She is in the center of it."

"Ah well, that leaves the envoy free with Pekahiah's wife," Hoshea said, still scornful.

"With my wife, more likely," Hosea said, flushing painfully in his try at speaking lightly of the matter.

"Gomer — ?" Hoshea's countenance went sober.

"Yes, Gomer," Hosea answered low. "It is soon over between us."

All his way to Nineveh Hosea had fought down the choice he knew at the bottom he could not escape — until at last he had no more will to struggle. Turn her out he must, as he had sworn. Perhaps then some power of the LORD would return to him, though Hosea thought on it with little joy.

Hoshea spoke now in cold earnest: "This thing then with Pekah and the consort, it is no rumor?"

"So far as one can see, it is true."

"Yes — he has always nursed a kind of jealousy of Pekahiah — from Remaliah —"

"I know not how far it is gone, nor for sure that Pekah is caught up in it. But the throne is in danger, that I know."

"That would be a pretty chance," Hoshea said hotly, slapping his hand against his sheath, "turn to Egypt, and take the sword of Assyria in our back."

"Israel needs a strong hand," Hosea said with a strange beseeching note in his voice.

"I know not — I know not —" Hoshea muttered, covering his eyes with a hard calloused hand.

"No man in Israel except you is equal to the time."

Hoshea paused and looked through the tiny window of his quarters toward the great palace of Tiglath Pileser. Strange — other men wanted to rule, craved it, would plot and murder to gain it. He had never wanted to be anything but a soldier. "A soldier's destiny is linked too closely to his nation," Hoshea thought futilely.

"This time we dare not fail," he said.

Hosea looked at him searchingly. "You will come?"

"I fear I must."

2

A thick fog blanketed Samaria on a morning two days following the Sabbath. It drifted sluggishly through market and alleyways, massing and swirling with gentle wind gusts flowing down from Carmel, mantling each house and street in dim secrecy.

The day had good cause to be gloomy, Pekah thought, as he made his way toward the king's garrison, hard by the palace. How many days had passed since he made his promise to Tania? How many years? How many lifetimes? He could go back on such a promise, made in passion. But she had sound wisdom on her side, and from that he could not turn away. Israel could not abide two kings.

Pekahiah was hard. His rule was harsh. *It is for Israel I do this thing*, Pekah told himself. Only that could deaden the thoughts that gave him no peace and the words that drummed in his thoughts — coward, back-slayer, murderer, brother-killer, Cain.

A burly figure loomed suddenly out of the fog, an arm's length distant.

"Foul weather, captain," said the corporal, in greeting to Pekah ben Remaliah.

"Too thick for any good soldiering, Jacob. How many men stand quartered?"

"Eighty-seven with myself, sir. Seven gone home, and six on replacement to Bethel make the hundred."

"And the palace guards?"

"Eighteen or twenty, I would say."

"Twenty? Yes, they are enough. Dismiss your own men for the day. Keep one or two on hand for running messages and the like."

"Dismiss them? The fog will lift by midday, sir."

"Yes, but we drove the men hard last week. They have earned some rest."

"Seems it wise to turn them all out?" Jacob asked with some concern.

"Wise? How mean you?"

"This talk of revolt, sir, it is whispered about —" The corporal looked at his captain a little askance for some of the whispers mixed the name of Pekah in the plot.

"Pah! Such talk goes on the year around. The palace guards are equal to any trouble. Dismiss the men."

"As you say, sir. And tomorrow — ? Duty as always?"

"Tomorrow? Yes, duty as always."

The two men parted and vanished into the fog. Pekah headed toward the west wall of the city, to the flat-stone mansion of a wealthy oil trader, thick in Tania's plot. In the man's stable he met with Remaliah, Midemi, Tania, and fifty Gileadite warriors to lay final plans for the overthrow of Pekahiah ben Menahem.

* * *

Ner of Gilead stood four cubits and half a span. He could snap an oaken spear in his bare hands. He seldom spoke, yet in Gilead his words counted for much.

He and fifty of his warriors had arrived in Samaria in the late hours of the night. They lay carelessly about the stable with not much show of interest in the plan set before them. A treacherous lot, Pekah thought uneasily. The plan would get under way early in the morning, at the Temple.

Anakah had devised a riotous Baal-ritual to draw into the Temple a loud and boisterous crowd — the kind that would bend well to their purpose. When wine and reveling had set a mood on the people, the priesthood would begin to stir them up with harangues against the harsh rule of Pekahiah. As the people took up the chant, the priests would lead them out of the Temple and swing them toward the palace in high fury against the king. While the chanting, milling crowds spread confusion, the Gileadites would slip inside the palace walls and overpower the king's guards. Pekah would slay the king. When the angry chanting of the crowd reached a fever pitch, Pekah would throw the body of Pekahiah from the balcony and hail himself king of Israel to the wild cheering of the people.

"A clever plan," said Ner the Gileadite. "The high priest — he is able to carry out his part?"

"Have no fear of that," Pekah replied. "See well to your own part."

"Yes. I see now *what* a part we play in your schemes —"

"We have little more than two hour's time. The crowds will surge on the palace at noonday, if all goes according to plan."

"And you yourself will open the gates of the palace to us?" the Gileadite asked.

"Yes," Pekah replied.

"I hope we shall be able to enter . . ." Ner said slowly.

"What do you mean, 'be able to enter?'"

"There is the matter of some gold yet to be settled — we have received but thirty shekels."

"The other twenty you will receive when the job is finished," said Remaliah, breaking in. Remaliah had struck the bargain with the Gileadites.

Ner glanced aside at Remaliah, but he continued to speak to Pekah. "I deem fifty shekels of gold somewhat too little payment — for so valuable a service."

Pekah's cheeks flushed with anger at the Gileadite's haughty manner. "You have made the bargain."

"I would make another bargain."

Tania took a step toward the Gileadite. "What kind of bargain?" she asked.

"Double the amount — one hundred shekels of gold."

"Nay, you shall not have it," Pekah said fiercely.

"You have not seen such gold in all your life," said Remaliah in a sneering tone.

"You have not seen a throne so close at hand in all of yours — one hundred shekels of gold."

"You shall have it," Tania said.

The others glanced sharply at her. Her eyes burned: " . . . when the job is finished."

"We take half the second fifty now," said Ner.

"You get the whole seventy when the job is done," Tania replied coolly.

Ner looked at her for a moment, half-smiling. "As you say. When the job is done."

"And keep your men out of sight until we move toward the palace," Pekah said viciously, covering his shame that a woman had settled his contention with the Gileadite.

* * *

Outside the stable Midemi swung a cloak over his shoulders and headed toward the gate. As he left his own house, a young boy had brought him a message from Gomer. "Come to me. I need you."

When Midemi saw Gomer on the fever-bed, wild and raving, it came on him that she was far dearer than he had thought. For two days he had gone about in a heavy mood, supposing her

343

now to be dead, and grieved that he had used her ill and now had no way to make right the wrong he had done her. But now came this message. All morning he had sought the chance to slip away.

"Where do you go?" Tania called after him.

"My work is done."

"Pekah will need your help to place the Gileadites in position."

Midemi set his arms akimbo. "Is it not enough that I fetch them — must I lead them also?"

"Have no fear," Tania said with some contempt, "you will not be put in any danger."

"Well enough," Midemi said, matching her tone, "I will return before the time."

"Where are you bound?"

Midemi paused a moment, then looking downward he said, "To the wife of the prophet."

"You said she died."

"So I thought. She lay close to it, but not yet, it seems."

Tania's eyes narrowed with jealousy and anger. Plain it was that Midemi meant this visit as no part of their plan.

"Why do you go now?" she asked.

"She has sent for me."

"Our day has come. The prophet no longer endangers our plans."

"It will do no harm to see to her need — for the ill we have done her," Midemi said. The dismal duty inflicted on him by Tania — an affair with an Israelite woman — had turned out differently than he expected. The woman was clean and fair to look on. She knew the ways of love, but differently than other women. She drew him on, seeking more his pleasure than her own. He wondered at himself that he longed to be with her.

Tania looked on him coldly, and coldly she spoke. "You grow soft, Midemi. We have better things to do than see to the needs of a dying harlot." Then, in sharp command, "We risk no folly at this hour. You remain here with us."

For a moment Midemi made to reply, but Tania's harsh tone brooked no argument. He followed her back to the stable, sullen and resentful.

3

An hour before noonday Hoshea and Hosea rode through the gate of Samaria, hot and dusty and bone weary from their journey. The sun had dispelled the fog and now stood high and glaring in the heavens.

The rumble from the Temple had met them as they came up toward the city. Within the walls it became a thunderous chant.

"The king is hard! Our food is scarce! The king is hard! Our food is scarce!" Hosea and Hoshea pushed through the crowd.

"I like it not," Hoshea said uneasily. "They are in an ugly mood."

In front of the Temple itself Hoshea caught sight of an old soldier, a man who had fought under him in Syria. The old soldier, unarmed and dressed in a simple loose-flowing robe, leaned against a merchant's fruit cart and watched the milling crowds with some humor.

"Kenath ben Orth," Hoshea said sharply, taking the man's shoulder. "My old eyes deceive me!" the man exclaimed. "The son of Elah!"

"What is this celebration?"

"Mostly drinking and shouting," the man replied, laughing. "What brings you back to Samaria, sir?"

"Serve you no more in the king's army?" Hoshea asked, paying no heed to the old soldier's question.

"Indeed I do," he said.

"Why do you stand here, alone and unarmed?"

"Pekah dismissed us for the day — said he had worked us too hard." The old soldier chuckled, showing crooked, yellow teeth.

"Pekah dismissed you? How many?"

"All but one or two."

"None of the king's army is at quarters?"

"No, they are here, many of them — scattered through the crowd. They thought to join in the festival — the younger ones." The old soldier made a wry grin.

"This smells of trouble," Hoshea said briskly. "Now listen well, Kenath. Move out into the crowd. Find every man of the king's army you can. Pass the word to return to quarters."

"You — you believe this rumor, sir?"

"What rumor?"

"This talk that puts Pekah against the king."

"Know you aught of that?" Hoshea asked.

"I know nothing of it. I turn my ear from such old-woman talk. The day the Twins fall out, the River Jordan will flow back to Galilee."

"There is more to this than old-woman's gossip, I fear."

"You know something?"

"I wish I knew more, but it is enough. The king is in danger."

"I am with you, sir," Kenath said, with a sharp nod of his head.

"Round up as many men as you can. I will be at quarters in . . ." Hoshea glanced out over the milling crowd, " . . . in an hour's time."

"I will bring them if I must drag them bodily," the old soldier said decisively. He pushed out into the crowd.

Hoshea turned quickly to Hosea. "You still bear some influence with the people?"

"I — I know not," Hosea answered uncertainly.

"This chanting against the king is no mere chance. I like it not."

"I might gather some of my own people —" Hosea began.

"Time is too short. Can you challenge these priests — quiet the people?"

"I have spoken little these last weeks," Hosea said weakly.

"It is a chance we must take," Hoshea said with sudden decision. "A surly crowd is like a wounded bear. Quiet them. Send them to their homes."

"I know not whether they will listen. They are not my people —"

"Do what you can. If you cannot send them away, try at least to keep them near the Temple."

"I had wanted to see my wife —" Hosea said a little haltingly.

"No time, Hosea. This might break loose at any moment. I must see Pekahiah and prepare what defense we can."

"Is a plot afoot for sure?"

"The smell is foul," Hoshea said darkly.

He turned and strode through the chanting throng toward the palace of the king. After a moment Hosea pushed toward the Temple, scraping his memory for words and phrases to capture the ear of a crowd.

* * *

A quarter hour later a fat priest came puffing into the stable where the Gileadites were quartered.

"Pekah ben Remaliah," he cried, "the prophet has found out our plan!"

"What is this?" Pekah asked, turning to face the red-faced priest.

"He has raised his voice in front of the Temple — said the LORD knows of the plot against the king —" the man gasped.

"Fool! All the city knows of the plot, by rumor," said Pekah.

"Yes, but the prophet was seen with Hoshea ben Elah."

"Hoshea?" Pekah said, with a sudden tremor in his voice. "Hoshea returned from Assyria — ?"

The priest nodded vigorously. Pekah glanced uneasily at Tania and Remaliah. "The high priest fears some counter-plot is afoot between them. He craves you to send eight or ten of your hired warriors to seize the prophet, before he ruins our plans."

Pekah shook a fist in the priest's face. "You go to Anakah and tell him that the prophet is his concern. I have trouble enough on my own part without taking him on as well."

The priest mumbled lets and hindrances until Pekah screamed out "Go! Go back to your idols and incense and empty chants! And if the prophet prevails this day, it will be the blood of priests that pays. Tell this to Anakah!"

Tania moved quickly and stopped the priest at the door of the stable. "Challenge the prophet on the point of his wife. She has gone aside with the Egyptian envoy."

"I have done so," the priest wailed, his jowls quivering with fright. "He brushed it aside. He has a way with the people one cannot match. This is frightful, frightful —"

Tania glanced a moment at Pekah and then said coolly, "Tell Anakah I will send my Nubian against the prophet again. This is too dangerous."

The priest nodded and scurried out of the stable.

"How did Hoshea learn of this?" Pekah raged, smashing a fist against his leather shield.

"Who is this man Hoshea?" Tania asked.

"The highest man in the army of the king until Menahem won out over him. He has been at Pileser's court in Nineveh these three years past."

"What can he do? The army is dismissed."

"I know not. But if any man in Israel can stop us, he is the man."

"Then we must move at once," Tania said, "before he can gather a force against us."

"We cannot move until the crowd comes on the palace." "If some counter-plot is afoot, we can risk no delay."

"Our plan is useless without the confusion of the crowd."

"We have fifty warriors. We must chance it."

"This thing turns sour," Pekah said gloomily. "We need wait now until Hoshea's plans are known."

"So he can learn our plans and have our necks for conspiracy?" Tania said bitingly. "We have come too far, Pekah. Gather your men. I will see to the prophet." Tania whirled on Midemi, who stood off to the side with no seeming care for all that was happening. "Fetch the wife of the prophet," she said. "Bring her to the palace so we may hold her up to ridicule before the people." Midemi looked unbelievingly on Tania.

"The wife of the prophet," Tania repeated harshly, "bring her to the palace!"

"She lies near death," Midemi said.

"I care not if she be a corpse. Bring her to the palace."

Tania turned back on Pekah. "Hold the Gileadites until Tongo and I have reached the Temple, then move into position west of the palace. I will set my Nubian on this prophet and then rejoin you. If the prophet somehow prevails with the crowd, we still have his wife to use against him. He will not brush her away so easily when she stands naked before the people."

"What if Hoshea has a force drawn up against us?" Pekah asked tremulously.

"If thrones were easy to come by we should have nothing but kings," Tania said scornfully. "Lay by your fears. Think now of victory."

She turned and started toward the door of the stable. Midemi stood unmoving in his spot.

"Why are you not gone?" Tania demanded.

Midemi shook his head and looked away from her wild, blazing eyes.

"Come —" She grasped his arm and started him toward the door. "This is no time for quiet dreaming!"

Outside the wall of the house they parted. Tania headed briskly toward their house where the Nubians were quartered. Midemi trudged south toward the house of the prophet.

A few steps from the outer gate of the mansion he stopped. He glanced backward at Tania, vanishing into the city. His jaw took on a strange set of determination.

"Nay," he said low to himself, "I will *not*."

Then he continued on toward the house of the prophet.

* * *

For more than half an hour Hosea had stood against the crowd that milled about the Temple. Hesitant at first, he had warmed to the struggle. There came again the sense of God's presence at his side, His blessing on the words Hosea spoke.

The priests shouted insults and arguments against Hosea. The crowd chanted heartily on both sides, caring little for the argument, but hoping for some open clash between Hosea and the priests.

Then Hosea overheard the notable Voice: *Israel is a silly calf running to Egypt, toying with Assyria!* How long had it been since he overheard the Voice of the LORD? Hosea repeated the words boldly: "Israel is a silly calf running to Egypt, toying with Assyria!"

"Egypt buys our corn and barley!" shouted the priests. "Corn and barley!" echoed the crowd.

"None for Israel!"

"None for Israel! None for Israel!"

"The king's rule is hard. We want back the days of Jeroboam!"

Hosea raised his voice: "Like an angry fire their hearts burn with intrigue. All night long their angry plan has smoldered, and now it blazes like a flaming fire. They would devour their ruler, let fall their king. 'Give us the days of Jeroboam,' they cry. Cry for the days of Joshua, when Israel loved the LORD! Cry! Your destruction is at hand, O Israel. Set the king aside; raise up new princes. Seal your folly with Egypt. Spurn the truth and the enemy will pursue you. Your new princes will die by the sword of Assyria because of the insolence of their tongues.

Cry then to Egypt, house of Israel. Cry for the armies of So. The laughter of derision shall ring out of Egypt in that day, so the LORD has spoken!"

A quarter-hour before noonday, the priests urged the people who yet remained inside the Temple out into the court that faced toward the palace. Anakah himself paced their grumbling chants.

"Give us the coin of Egypt! The king's rule is hard! To the palace! The king is cruel! The palace, the palace! Give us the king! The king is hard! The palace, the palace, the palace!"

Slowly the great throng of people pressed westward toward the palace. But in the market square, hard by, the crowd held fast, caught up in the struggle between Hosea and several priests.

Hosea leaped up on a cart to command a view of all the people. He waved his arms in the air, clenched his fists against the heavens.

"Cry not for Egypt! Hear this word of the LORD!"

For a moment the tumult subsided; the people listened.

"Here one cries for Egypt, and there one cries for Assyria. Where are the cries to the LORD?

"The LORD has a controversy with the inhabitants of this land. There is no faithfulness or kindness and no knowledge of God in the land. There is swearing, lying, stealing, killing, and committing adultery —"

"That should you know well enough!" cried out a priest. "Whoremonger! Wittol!"

Hosea paid him no heed. "My people are destroyed for lack of knowledge! Their scheming breaks all bounds, and murder follows murder. Go now to the palace! Go tomorrow to Egypt! Give us new princes! Give us the days of Jeroboam! For this the land mourns and all who dwell in it languish. The beasts of the field and the birds of the air and the fish of the sea are taken away. For this you cry, O Israel — the destruction of the LORD! You have sown the wind, and you shall reap the whirlwind!"

"The king is cruel! Give us the riches of Egypt!"

The priests on the steps of the Temple took up the chant and crowded the people out of the Temple courts. But a strange quiet fell on the crowd — a soberness.

"Louder, louder," said Anakah to his priests. "They have taken his words."

"The king is hard! To the palace! The king is cruel! The palace, the palace!"

"To the palace!" Hosea echoed in derision. "To your destruction, house of Ephraim! Nay — but return to your homes. Return to the LORD you have forsaken." The people balanced delicately, half persuaded by the prophet's ringing words. And then, suddenly, a murmuring arose on the edge of the crowd. Above the heads of the people rose the towering hulk of Tongo, the Nubian slave.

Hosea tensed. Tania and Tongo pushed toward him. The crowd fell back, giving wide berth.

"O LORD, be now my right arm," Hosea prayed fervently. "Gird up my loins with strength and breathe fire into my soul. Let your name be glorified this day, LORD God of Israel."

Hosea girt his robe up about his loins, keeping his eyes all the time on the figure of the giant approaching him. The crowd shouted with excitement.

"Now they come against the prophet with a giant," Hosea thundered. "They think him sufficient where their words are weak!"

"More than sufficient on last remembrance," howled a priest.

"Come —" Hosea cried out. "Send him again. I would have my revenge!"

Tania caught sight of Anakah across the heads of the people. He waved his arms in the air, nodding his head wildly. Hosea's first defeat had dealt his following a crushing blow; the second would be his end.

"Go," Tania said to Tongo. "Kill!"

The giant lumbered toward Hosea, dangling a short club in his one hand. Hosea tore an arm-length plank from the cart he stood upon and sprang to the ground. The crowd cleared a wavering circle around the two.

Tongo swung his club at Hosea, a blow that would fell an ox. Hosea ducked underneath and swung his plank into the Nubian's side. Tongo gasped, and stumbled sideward. Hosea drove after him, slashing blows with the edge of his plank. Tongo caught his balance and crouched facing Hosea, his eyes narrow and vicious.

"The Nubian is beaten!" shrilled a little man, standing on the circle's edge, behind the giant.

Tongo whirled on the man and crashed the club down on his head. The little man collapsed to the ground with a startled yelp.

"I kill!" Tongo shouted in the Israelite tongue.

He leaped at Hosea, swinging his club wildly. Hosea stepped back, off balance.

He lost his feet and tumbled into the dirt. Quickly he doubled his legs and thrust out blindly with both feet. He hit the Nubian at the thigh, drove him to one side. Straightway he was on his feet, but his plank lay in front of Tongo.

Tongo heaved the plank out into the crowd and howled with laughter. He rushed at Hosea, his head lowered like a ram. Hosea stepped nimbly to the side and drove a closed fist against the side of the giant's head. Hosea let out a cry and clapped a hand over his knuckles. The giant's head was like rock.

Tongo turned and lunged at Hosea, caught one foot, and fell forward into the dirt, clinging to Hosea's leg. Hosea smashed his locked hands down on the back of Tongo's neck and straightened him with the savage kick of his free foot. He wrenched free of Tongo's hold and backed off, catching his breath in gasps.

Tongo stumbled to his feet and drove after Hosea, brandishing his club. Twice he swung and narrowly missed. A third time he struck a glancing blow off Hosea's shoulder. Hosea fell to his knee, struggled back to his feet, and dodged clear of the relentless giant.

Unwittingly he backed between a fruit cart and the wall of a weaver's shop. Too late he found himself in a short, narrow alley with the giant closing in the only entrance.

"I kill! I kill!" Tongo roared.

He swung a vicious blow with his club, aimed at the prophet's neck. Hosea bent double, felt the club whistle past his ear. Suddenly, from underneath the cart, a hand shot out and slapped Hosea's plank back into his hand.

"God save you!" said a voice.

Hosea drove the plank into the giant's belly, less than three handbreadths away. Tongo doubled up with a moan and staggered back. Hosea caught him under the chin with a second thrust and heaved him backward. Tongo caught himself with one arm, struggling to gain his balance. Hosea swung full arc with his plank, smashing it against the giant's head. Tongo shook his head, but did not fall. Again Hosea struck him, and yet again. The giant stumbled away, shaking his head dazedly. He turned, half raised his club, and looked on Hosea with the sudden pleading of a frightened child. The club slipped from his grasp. He whimpered and collapsed face forward into the dirt of the market place.

Hosea stood for a moment above the fallen giant, swaying unsteadily, breathing deep gulps of air.

"Let him alone," said the prophet.

He let loose his grip on the plank and stumbled toward the well of the city, two streets away.

* * *

Even while the battle between Hosea and the giant raged, and the sound of it carried westward to the palace, Tania had departed the market square and hurried across the city to where the Gileadites were moved into position outside the palace walls.

At midday Pekah walked up to the gate of the palace with a slow, uneven step that little concealed his unease.

"We are locked against all men!" called a guard through the oaken gate. "Open, you fool. I am Pekah ben Remaliah."

"My order is to open to no man."

"Who has given order to bar the gate against the chief captain in the army of the king?" Pekah called out with severity.

"Hoshea ben Elah."

Pekah ground his teeth in anger.

"You shall pay for your words!" he said.

He retreated in haste to where the Gileadites lay hidden, west of the palace, behind a low garden wall.

"We are foiled!" he said, coming around the wall. "The gates are locked against us."

"How are they locked against you?" Tania demanded.

Pekah slumped down against the wall. "By Hoshea's order. He has found us out."

"Fool! He could not have found us out," the woman said hotly. "It is a trick."

"It is no trick that the gates are barred."

"Who is this man Hoshea to foul our plans at the last moment!" Tania raged, hitting her two fists down on the wall.

"What can we do?" Remaliah whined. Tania dropped to her knee beside Pekah.

"We must gain entrance," she said, "we must!"

Ner the Gileadite stood to his feet and spoke, his voice low and calm. "The walls are no more than a tall man's reach. We shall need no gate-opener." He looked down on Pekah, eyes laden with scorn.

"What?" Pekah asked, stumbling to his feet.

"We have ways of vaulting a wall — when twenty-five shekels of gold wait on the other side —"

"How?" Tania asked uncertainly.

"Half the second fifty — we shall have it now," Ner insisted quietly.

"You shall have it," Tania said. She fumbled in the girdle of her robe and brought out a pouch of gold. "Twenty-five shekels, honestly weighed," she said, dropping the pouch into Ner's outstretched hand.

Ner smiled wryly. Never in his life had he bowed to the whim of a woman.

"Tania, we cannot chance it," Pekah said. "We have no count of the men Hoshea has gathered inside the palace wall."

"We know well enough the count of men he will gather against us tomorrow if we falter now."

"What of the prophet — the crowd?"

"My Nubian has set down the prophet, once for all."

"Midemi is not here," Pekah faltered.

Tania looked on Pekah with contempt and thought fleetingly that he was not much different from Midemi after all.

"We have no need of Midemi now," she said. "But if we fail —"

"We fail not! Gather your men, Ner of Gilead."

Ner swept an arm over his men, the proud gesture of a warrior who knows his mettle. "What say you, men? Shall we have some sport with these Israelites?"

The Gileadites eased to their feet as a single man. Ner gave commands in low, easy tones. Six men set themselves out from the others, ran crouched around the edge of the garden wall, and headed for the west wall of the palace. Three others followed at twenty paces. At the wall the six men paired together two-by-two, locked hands on their half-bent knees, and braced themselves back against the wall. The three who followed drew daggers, clamped them in their teeth, and raced toward the palace. The men at the wall caught the running foot of the men who sprang to them, and with a single heave sent the three Gileadites flying over the palace wall.

Before the two men at the gate could gather their senses, the Gileadites were on them, flashing their daggers — a thud, a muffled cry, and the guards crumpled dead to the ground.

The gate of the palace swung open, and the Gileadites poured into the enclosure. Even as they entered they broke into two companies and circled the palace from opposite directions, falling out by twos and threes to cut down the guards who circled the palace. Last of all came Pekah, Tania, Remaliah, Ner, and the four warriors who were to take Pekah to the throne room of the king.

On the south side of the palace Hoshea spoke earnestly with two of his men. Six soldiers had returned to quarters at the order of the old soldier, Kenath. By midday the word had reached seven more. These thirteen and the nineteen palace guards gave Hoshea thirty-one men. When a company of Gileadites swarmed around the west wing of the palace, Hoshea saw at once the folly of his plans. He had thought they would try the wall with ladders. He had posted his men all around the enclosure, to sound the alarm when the ladders were raised. Now, against the massed force of the Gileadites, his men were hopelessly spread out. He ripped the sword from his sheath and raced down the south wall of the palace, away from the Gileadites. He shouted for his men to follow, trying desperately to form a solid company to meet the thrust of the Gileadites. At the east end of the palace Hoshea gathered eleven men — five soldiers and six palace guards. Two cordons of Gileadites, still thirty men strong, rounded the palace almost together from opposite directions.

"We are lost!" cried one of the palace guards.

The Gileadites halted and looked on their opponents scornfully.

"What shall we do with these Israelites?" they called out mockingly.

"Spare us! We are defenseless!" said another of Hoshea's men.

A palace guard threw down his sword and prostrated himself before the Gileadites. A second and third followed. The Gileadites roared with laughter.

"What for the rest of you? Will you bow or die?"

Three soldiers and the remaining palace guards threw down their swords and fell to their knees. Hoshea and two soldiers alone remained standing.

"Three who wish to die? It is a poor day, men."

The Gileadites closed in on Hoshea and his two men.

"Put your backs together," Hoshea growled. "Make them pay dearly —"

"I do not want to die —" The younger of the two men who stood with Hoshea threw down his sword and fell to the ground.

"Oh ho!" cried the Gileadite leader, "now but two. What say you, men — who has the more cause to die, the cowards or the two?"

The Gileadites shouted hearty agreement. A palace guard half raised up at the shout and caught a sword thrust in the breast. His eyes bulged with horror and disbelief, and he fell back to the dirt with a groan. Six Gileadites leaped forward and seized Hoshea and his one soldier before they could resist. While they stood helplessly at the side, the Gileadites slew the kneeling guards and soldiers to a man.

* * *

In the throne room of the king Pekahiah faced Pekah, Tania, Remaliah, Ner, and four Gileadite warriors. Outside the door two palace guards slumped against the wall, dead.

"So it is true," Pekahiah said. My Twin has turned against me and seeks my throne."

"Your rule is hard," said Pekah, looking away from the king's intent gaze.

"Yes, it is hard," Pekahiah replied, raising himself to full height, "as my father's rule was hard — as your own rule would be hard if you stood in my place. Those who stand in the shadow of a powerful enemy must live in lean times, my brother."

"Egypt stands ready to make alliance to secure our defense."

Pekahiah stood still on the step of the throne. He looked down on Pekah with hard, cold eyes. "Have you heard these words from honeyed lips so often that you now believe them yourself?"

"I believe naught but what I know!"

"And what do you know? That Pileser has taken to the plow, and the Assyrians have beaten their swords into rakes? In a day gone by you showed more wit."

"He shows more wit in his finger than you have shown since you took the throne," said Tania, stepping close to Pekah. She caught a hint of wavering in Pekah's sidewise glance.

"Ha!" Pekahiah glared at Tania. "In choosing the reek of tawdry Egyptian promises he has shown little wit — yet he always was clumsy with a woman."

"Finish this business," Tania said fiercely to Pekah, wincing at Pekahiah's words.

"You mock easily," said Pekah slowly. Long nurtured bitterness crept into his voice. "Always you have made light of me."

"Made light of you?" said the other. "Made I light of you when I carried you wounded from the battlefield in Moab — carried you back to the safety of our camp without arms? Made I light of you when I rode straight into the camp of the Syrians, disguised and without arms, and rescued you from their hand? Never have I made light of you when you were my brother. But now you play the fool."

"I play not the fool!" Pekah screamed.

"When you play with Egypt, you play the fool."

"Silence his proud tongue!" Tania demanded.

Two of the Gileadite warriors drew their swords.

"No!" the woman said. "He will do it with his own hand."

"What! You would take my life as well as my throne?" Pe-kahiah broke into a high laugh.

"Make not light of *this*!" Pekah cried, drawing his sword.

"You dare not," said his Twin.

"Never have I lacked courage, Pekahiah. I have stood as well as you in any encounter."

"It takes little courage to strike down a friend — a coward could do as much."

"Keep silent!"

"Ah, Pekah, what has it come to that you stand with drawn sword before the friend of your youth?"

"No more are we friends."

"She has made you the fool."

"I do what I do on my own authority!" Pekah said vehe-mently. "No longer are you fit to rule."

"And are you fit better? Conspiring with foreign nations against your own people, your own brother —"

"I know what is best for Israel."

Pekahiah took a bold step toward Pekah. "You know what you are told by a scheming woman."

"Kill him!" Tania hissed.

"Yes, kill him, Pekah ben Remaliah! Kill him who speaks the truth and incline to her who fills your ear with stinking falsehoods."

"I do what I do for Israel."

"You do what you do for vanity! You imagine hurts and slights. You grumble because another wins something ahead of you or shows you up in some little way. Like father, like son. Yet I never deemed your vanity would drive you to such a pass — and would not have, except for her."

Pekah glared angrily at his Twin. "You know nothing of my cause —"

"Your cause stands beside you," Pekahiah said with con-tempt. "The sweet words of a woman, a night of love, and the brave Pekah, captain of the king's chariots, creeps up the back stairs of the palace to lay low his king, his Twin. You are weak —"

"No more will I listen to your arrogant speech!"

Pekah lunged forward with his sword out-thrust and drove it with violence into Pekahiah's chest. The king gasped and fell back against the step of the throne, clawing at the sword that hung from his body. Pekah stood over him, the sword gone from his hand, his face writhen with horror. Pekahiah raised his head with great pain and looked into the face of his assassin.

"Pekah —" Sorrow and hurt hung heavy in his voice. "My brother, my Twin —" The king fell backward with a groan and rolled over on his side, dead. For a long, tense moment no sound was heard, save the short, heavy breathing of Pekah.

Tania walked quickly to the window and looked eastward over the city. Below, the crowd from the Temple was gathering. She noted not that a silence had fallen on the people.

"The crowd is below," she said. "All is as planned."

Pekah stood over Pekahiah's body, unmoving.

"Finish this now, once for all," said Tania ungently. "Let fall his body over the balcony. The people wait now to hail you king."

"What?" Pekah spoke as one in a trance.

Tania turned from him and motioned two of the Gileadite warriors. "Quickly! Pick up the body and throw it to the crowd."

The Gileadites dragged Pekahiah's body across the room. Tania took Pekah by the arm and pushed him toward the balcony. The Gileadites heaved the body of Pekahiah to the courtyard below.

"Remaliah — your speech now!" said Tania.

Remaliah stepped to the window. "Israel, hail your king! The hard rule of Pekahiah is ended!" He raised up the hand of Pekah, standing at his side. Then, from the street below, thundered the voice of the prophet. "Pekah ben Remaliah! The LORD has numbered your days from this hour!"

Tania raced to the window. The prophet stood at the fore-front of the crowd. Midemi! Where was Midemi with the man's wife?

Again came Hosea's voice. "He who murders the stranger faces judgment, Pekah ben Remaliah — but he who kills his friend faces the wrath of the LORD God! You shall eat and not be filled, lie down and not sleep, run and never arrive. The crown of Israel shall weigh on your head like a millstone, so the LORD has sworn by His righteousness!"

Pekah fell back from the balcony, clutching at his eyes. The words of the prophet came on him like the tiny iron darts he once faced in battle with Edom, with Pekahiah at his side. He shook his head, as if to drive the words away. He turned and faced Tania and the Gileadites, trembling. Then he fell to the floor of the throne room and wept, the eighteenth king of Israel.

Chapter 31

Begone From This House!

Hosea walked with a weary step southward from the palace, toward his house. He looked skyward and thought grimly that the glaring heavens should soon darken with shame, to look on the treachery that had passed this day. Yes, and with foreboding, that Israel had turned her back on the chariots of Assyria. Darkened indeed should the heavens be, as they were darkened when Israel last set aside her king in violence. Yet the slaying of Shallum ben Jabesh had some good cause behind it. Shallum was himself a murderer and promised Israel little good, allying himself with Egypt. The son of Menahem was no conspirator. And though he cared nothing for the word of the LORD, he had some concern for the protection of the land.

Hosea wiped a sleeve over his brow, still running sweat from his encounter with the Nubian. Perhaps it had come to this, he thought, that Israel was past knowing any shame for unrighteousness or any fear of judgment.

How strangely silent the city had fallen, Hosea thought, even stopping and looking eastward toward the market. It was as though Samaria had paused to bethink herself and ponder on the things that had passed so swiftly this day.

His steps further slowed as he drew nearer the house. He did not know how he would bear himself toward Gomer. On the journey back from Nineveh he had plagued himself with new doubts and wonderings. He still drew back from turning Gomer away. Did he set himself against her with too high a hand, demand more of her than she could rightly bear? Why should the daughters and brides of Israel bear punishment? The men themselves go aside with harlots and sacrifice with cult prostitutes, and what is laid against them?

Yes, but the LORD had spoken a word. *Strip her naked and make her as in the day she was born.* No real proof had come to him, only the word of Deborah. And she forswore herself straightway she had spoken. If it were forgotten, forgotten and not spoken between them — A smarting of tears came into Hosea's eyes. He thought tenderly on Gomer — what treasure she was to him, and joy, yet ever the wildness and evil. How could the one and the other lodge so close together? Why could not the good overcome the evil? It was past knowing.

He came to the gate of his house. A moment he paused. Here too the silence — no sound of the children. Of a sudden the ache and tiredness in his body weighed on him like a lintel. He held himself against the wall. He breathed deeply and then slowly walked through the gate to the doorway of the house. The door stood a little ajar. Hosea entered quietly.

Jezreel was the first to see him. He let out a cry and ran to Hosea, throwing his arms around his father's knees. Hosea scarcely paid the boy heed. Across the room on the bed lay Gomer, Midemi kneeling by her side.

Gomer half rose up, her face deathly pale. "My husband," she said weakly.

Hosea leaned back against the door, pushing it shut. His eyes closed. "Call me no more 'my husband,'" he said, his voice low and trembling. Gomer broke at once to weeping.

"Yes, weep," Hosea said, coming toward her, "weep for your shamelessness — that consorts now openly in the face of your children."

"Nay," Midemi said, standing to his feet, "she is ill — has lain close to death these five days."

Hosea stood above her, looking down. Loruhamah huddled against the wall holding Loammi, across from Jezreel.

"It is so, Father," Loruhamah said timidly when Hosea looked at her. "Deborah said Mama would die."

All too fast this came on Hosea. He could see naught but the Egyptian standing over against him.

"How come you to be at her side?" Hosea demanded.

Midemi opened his mouth to give answer, then shook his head and looked downward. Came Gomer's voice in forlorn wailing, "It is me, it is me — he came at my bidding. You will have me no more — you are done with me —"

"He has known you?" Hosea asked, with a break in his voice.

"Yes, yes —"

Gomer buried her face against the matting of her bed and sobbed mournfully.

"Have you known her?" Hosea demanded of Midemi, as though he would prove Gomer false. "Speak truly —"

Midemi glanced up and nodded.

Hosea looked wildly to Loruhamah and Loammi, then to Jezreel.

"She was with him on the housetop," Jezreel said in an excited, half-frightened voice, for never had he seen such a look from his father. "She thought we all slept, but I heard all —"

"Aah!" Hosea cried in a long piercing wail. "No more!"

With a sudden move he seized Midemi by the arms and flung him back against the door.

"Begone from my house!" he cried.

"What do you intend — with her?" Midemi gasped, reaching backward for the latch.

"No matter to you. You have drunk your fill."

"She is yet ill."

"Begone!" Hosea shrieked.

Midemi looked with a strange and frightened longing once more on Gomer and then backed through the door. Hosea caught a hand over his eyes and groaned aloud.

"Hosea — my husband —" Gomer said faintly. Yet would she cling to some hope.

"Nay," Hosea said, turning to her, "you are not my wife, and I am not your husband."

Gomer gasped, catching a hand to her lips, for these were the words feared above all others by a wife in Israel: the words of divorce. Hosea looked down on her. His legs trembled. Suddenly he reached and grasped her by the shoulders and jerked her to her feet.

"Oh no —" she cried.

"Why?" he demanded wildly, crushing her in his grip. "Why? Why?"

"Oh my husband, never again, never —"

"Harlot!"

He threw her down in the center of the room. Loruhamah gave a cry and ran to her side.

"Leave her!" Hosea said.

"Mama, Mama," Loruhamah cried.

"Leave her, I say."

Loruhamah backed away.

Hosea now spoke with terrible calm, looking down on Gomer: "Adulteress you are and adulteress you will always be. As I swore I would turn you out, so I will — naked into the street, as befits an adulteress."

He motioned to Jezreel.

"What would you, Father?" the boy asked tremulously.

"Do the duty of the Law —"

"Oh have pity, have pity," Gomer pled.

Hosea lifted her to her feet. Jezreel approached uncertainly. Hosea pulled the robe from Gomer's shoulder and down over her breasts. She clutched at the garment, but he pushed her away with his free hand. With a mournful cry he thrust the gown into Jezreel's hands.

"Do the duty of the Law," he said. "Strip your mother naked."

Jezreel pulled on the gown. It fell to Gomer's feet. She crouched down helplessly, trying to shield her nakedness from her children.

"No, no," Loruhamah cried out. She ran at Jezreel, hitting him with her fists.

Jezreel pushed her away.

"I must do the duty of the Law," he said in a faltering voice.

He looked down at his mother. "I heard all," he said, half pushing her, half clinging to her.

Hosea bit his teeth hard together and turned away.

"Do it quickly," he muttered to Jezreel.

"You must begone from this house," Jezreel said, through his tears.

Gomer stumbled toward the door. Loruhamah ran to her side, clutching her arms about Gomer's waist.

"What — what of the children?" Gomer asked brokenly.

Hosea spoke with his back to her: "Their mother has acted shamefully. As they are named, so shall they be."

"Can you be so cruel?"

"Cruel!" Hosea cried, whirling to face her. "You lay the Law of God upon my neck — drive me to stand by and watch my own son strip you naked before my eyes — and yet you speak of cruelty as if you have no part in it? Go, go —"

He waved her away with his arm and bent his head weeping into his hands.

Slowly Gomer turned and started out.

"Mama —" Loruhamah cried, so frightened and timorous she was scarcely heard. "Mama, come back," Loruhamah pleaded, still clinging to her mother.

"Nay, I have naught to give you, child. Stay, and care for Loammi —"

She pushed the girl from her and backed through the door. The bright sunlight caught her in the courtyard, and she covered her eyes. She looked about like a frightened animal, uncertain which way to turn.

Jezreel's voice sounded behind her. "Mama, where will you go?"

From within Hosea spoke, "It is enough, Jezreel."

Gomer ran to the gate. A sudden dizziness came over her, and she wove unsteadily on her feet.

"Oh where can I go, where can I go — my father cannot take me," she whimpered to herself.

She rested a moment and then came through the gate out into the narrow street. A voice called to her from across the way.

"Gomer —"

She looked up, at once trying to cover herself with her hands. Midemi came toward her from behind the house of Ebarth.

"Midemi?" she said unsurely, as though she saw not aright. "Midemi — Oh Midemi!"

She ran to him, collapsing into his arms, sobbing wildly.

"He has turned me out, he has turned me out. Take me, Midemi, O take me — save me —"

The Egyptian drew off his cloak and wrapped it over her shoulders and around her body.

"Will you take me?" she sobbed. ". . . as you promised?"

He took her by the arm and helped her gain her feet.

"Come," he said gently.

He held her about the waist and walked slowly with her down the street.

Hosea had come to the door of the house and watched after them. Jezreel stood at his side.

"Father," the boy said, "Will all be well with us now?"

Hosea looked down on him. His face, drained of feeling, showed neither anger nor sorrow, only a wretched emptiness.

"All be well with us — ?" he repeated after Jezreel.

He shook his head and stumbled back into the house, making no answer.

Part Three

Famine in the Land

Behold, the days are coming
When I will send a famine
on the land;
Not a famine of bread,
nor a thirst for water,
But of hearing the words
of the LORD.

Chapter 32

The Silence of God

1

In the first month of the rule of Pekah ben Remaliah an unseasonable cold swept into Israel from the north. Fires burned night and day in the houses of the wealthy, and in the homes of the poor whole families huddled together at night to share the warmth of their bodies. Snow lay almost to the foot of Mount Carmel; twice snow had fallen in Samaria and remained on the ground till past noonday. The oldest people in Samaria could remember no such cold so late in the season.

Some among the devout read it as a sign of God's disfavor. The LORD in His anger had taken away the warmth of the sun. Certain it was, they said, the LORD had small cause to love Israel in these days. A kind of mad revelry had seized the people.

For a time Israel had submitted to rigorous discipline and girded herself for battle. But now, with the iron rule of Menahem and Pekahiah cut short, people returned to the pleasures they had enjoyed in the days of Jeroboam.

Pekah blinded himself to the threat of Assyria and established an alliance with Egypt. Israel let slip surpluses of wool, oil, and lumber at cheap exchange. For a time food showed up more plentifully in the market places of Samaria and Bethel. The taxes Menahem had imposed to support his army slowed to a trickle, and Pekah made no move to enforce them. The young warriors who had rallied to Menahem's banner drifted back to their homes. Israel's army withered to a skeleton. Five months time remained before the next tribute was due the Pul, and no one in all Israel, it seemed, looked beyond that day.

Wine houses offered the people, besides an evening of pleasant forgetfulness, some relief from the unseasonable cold. Men and women warmed themselves beneath blankets with friends or strangers. Soberness seemed to pass from the land. In the marketplace a mood of strained jesting replaced the grimness of Pekahiah's rule. Like a drunken man Israel reeled, laughing and shivering, toward the brink of a catastrophe it would not see. The life Israel had nurtured from the days of Joshua — Israel's purpose and destiny — lay abandoned by the wayside.

2

I have been rising early. I have not known the city at this early hour. In the half-light of early morning a gray mist, rising from the valleys and the sloping hillsides, creeps over the city like a great gloomy blanket.

The beginning of another week: the fourth since Gomer left. What will it bring? More sorrowful days? The dread silence of early morning . . . aimless jobs in the carpenter shed . . . trudging to my altar outside the city . . . tossing on my bed at night . . . troubled dreams . . .

One thought stands always at my shoulder, never leaves me — my wife. Even yet I call her nothing but 'wife'.

A late carouser down there. Staggering along the lower street, bellowing a tuneless ditty. Lurching from building to building. Cursing when he misjudges his position and careens into a wall with a thud.

A mallet there, across the passage to the carpenter shed. What's it doing there? Useless. Could not pound a straight peg if it tried.

Half finished jobs lay scattered about the shed. The top of a nearly completed table needs to be planed. My hand is lazy and inconstant on the plane. I skim over rough places and gouge into smooth ones. My master, Ebarth, would shake his head at such careless work. I switch to the repair of a web-bottom chair. I weary of that and wander aimlessly to the entryway and lean against it, looking out toward the street.

She would be preparing the morning meal now . . .

The sun rises above the mountains, chasing the fog before it. In its slanting rays the city rises up, uglier and drearier than the dank mist that shrouded it at dawn. The streets begin to clatter with people and beasts and all the noise of the first day of the week in the city of Samaria. A dirty, noisy, foul smelling city.

Another job catches my eye and hand for a moment, then another, and another. I finish nothing, it seems. The rasp of the file, the crack of the mallet, the hoarse whisper of the saw — every noise and effort beats into my thoughts the dull rhythm of her name. I file harder, pound faster, saw more furiously, as though to frighten the dumb planks and pegs into silence. They only speak more constantly. When I stop, suddenly, even the silence beats out the rhythm of her name in the beating of my heart.

Go-mer, Go-mer.

Shortly before noonday a shadow fell across the doorway. I turned to see Hoshea standing on the threshold. Like some hardy desert scrub, Hoshea weathers storm after storm of upset and palace intrigue. Pekah kept him in a position of authority because Hoshea knew so well the court of Tiglath Pileser, the Pul.

He entered a bit hesitantly and greeted me with the courteous peace-blessing, a strange formality for Hoshea. We spoke of indifferent matters for some moments. Neither of us seemed to listen to what the other said. Other thoughts, deep and disturbing, hung unspoken behind our unmindful words.

I tried to smile, but the drawn lines around my mouth held like fired clay, hard sorrow etched into them since the day Gomer left.

"You are still preaching?" Hoshea was asking.

"O yes," I answered without taking thought. Then, "Somewhat less. You can see, I have things to repair."

Hoshea nodded. He seemed to hesitate. "You have heard about my wife?" I asked.

"Yes, somewhat —"

"You need not be polite with me, Hoshea. Of course you have heard. Everyone in Samaria knows about it."

Hoshea nodded. "I did hear some talk."

For a long moment neither of us spoke. I stared off into space. I felt a tear slide down my cheek. "I miss her. Is that not mad, Hoshea? No better than a temple harlot — worse — and I miss her. Is that not mad?"

"Not so mad."

"I never knew what loneliness was until she left."

"Has it been long?"

"New moon to full moon, and new moon again. It could as well be a year, or a hundred." I looked away from Hoshea, out the door of the shed.

"You have divorced her then?"

I did not answer. The words repeated themselves in my thoughts, then I turned to Hoshea. "The law of divorcement. I turned her naked into the streets." Slowly I shook my head. "Yet still I call her 'wife' . . ."

"You never could do things by halves, could you?"

"I am empty, Hoshea. When she left, something inside me died."

"You did what the Law requires."

"What the Law *allows*. The word I spoke bound me. The LORD spoke it to me. I swore to turn her out if she played the harlot again." I shook my head slowly.

"You love her, do you not? You still love her."

"Yes, I love her." I shook my head. My own words puzzled me. "I think I loved her from the first moment I saw her. It drew me to Diblaim seeking betrothal."

Hoshea said nothing, only touched a hand to his ear, as often he did when we were growing up, to mask a fear or uncertainty.

"It is not only that I loved her from the first moment," I told him. "Before the betrothal agreement, the LORD spoke a word that settled on Gomer. I was to marry her. It was a strong word, a command. It likened our marriage to the LORD's 'marriage' with Israel, a marriage of harlotry."

"Then you knew Gomer to be — ?"

"No, no. The word was strange. Gomer was an untouched virgin. I understood the word only for Israel."

Hoshea again touched his hand to his ear.

"The LORD saw it all from the beginning," I said, "yet He commanded me to marry her. To what purpose? To turn her naked into the street, as I have done? I do not know. He has hidden His ways from me.

"Yes, I love her. When she went aside, I loved her still — whether because the LORD had joined her to me or because of the love itself, I do not know."

I looked fondly on my childhood friend and spoke slowly. "What kind of a man am I, Hoshea? When we were boys — you remember — I was always a leader because I was strong and quick. Son of a priest, never to be a soldier, yet always a leader in our little contests and games of war. Some of that respect stuck to me when first we were grown, but no longer. I have become a laughingstock. Any spindle-legged man in Samaria could put away a wife for burning his bread. What kind of man am I, that I cannot — and her a harlot? Who ever linked love with joy? They never knew each other. It is torture."

"You will smother the life out of yourself if you go on like this," Hoshea returned. "Have you signed a bill of divorcement? Better to sign a bill of divorcement and have done with it."

"Yes, sign a bill of divorcement. Everyone speaks these sage words to me. Even Diblaim, her own father.

"I never truly understood the word, 'I the LORD your God am a *jealous* God.'

Why jealous? Why not divorce wayward Israel and choose another bride? He cannot. He is a jealous God. He chose her and He holds fast to her. In anger. In judgment. In mercy. Even in loneliness."

Hoshea looked into my face with calm and wonder. He had no words. After some moments I spoke again, quietly. "Jealousy masks a love that will not give up the beloved. He has laid His mantle of jealousy on me."

"Then why do you not get her? Find her. Bring her home," Hoshea asked.

"I can not."

"Holy God, man, she is your wife! What man in Samaria these days has a wife who has not bedded with others during the barley harvest — and he keeps her still. You will kill yourself."

"Hoshea, you cannot take a woman, lock her in a cage, and say: 'Love me!' If I had her in the house, and every time I looked into her eyes were to see smoldering passion for another man, that *would* kill me."

I lifted my hands with the thought that I still had something to speak, but no words came and I sank to my bench.

Neither of us spoke. I reached out and picked up a hammer, listlessly. I pushed myself up and shuffled toward a half-finished table.

"So, what do you do?" Hoshea asked at length.

I shrugged. "I do not know. Perhaps a time will come when she returns and we make a new start. Or the LORD may give a word, where he has given none. I do not know. Who knows, my friend? Who sees into the future except the LORD? Perhaps I will forget, in time. I do not know."

"What of your call from the LORD?" Hoshea asked again, after some moments of silence. "Is that dead as well?"

"No . . ."

Hoshea gazed intently at me. This had been the purpose of his coming, I suddenly realized: to speak to me about my priesthood and prophecy. He seemed to pause, now, uncertain whether he could go on. He touched his ear.

Hoshea had never been a man of religious passions, but slowly he picked out words he had been pondering — words that brought him to see me. He saw the deadening effect of the Baal cults: they sapped the people of energy and the will to fight. They made Israel a weak and spineless people, easy prey to the savage warriors of Assyria.

Since the fall of Pekahiah, with no voice calling them back, the people had turned to Baal gods without restraint. For the first time, Hoshea began to see that the danger from Assyria was part of the picture, but not the whole. What was Israel in herself? She closed her ears to the word of God to pursue the pleasures of Baal. That was the other part of the picture, the part that troubled Hoshea.

He saw me as one who could cleanse Israel of the moral rot of the Baal cults, call the people to a hard life that would prepare them for the struggle that stood now at the threshold. But I could only shake my head when he urged me to return to prophesying.

"Is it that you are afraid to speak God's word now?" Hoshea asked, earnestly and not unkindly, ". . . afraid the people will scoff, because of your wife?"

"Do you really believe that?"

"I do not want to."

"Hoshea, you stop too short. Scoffing! Do you think I care whether people laugh at me or not? They have laughed at me since I first came to Samaria, snickered behind my back when she went to Shallum ben Jabesh, and now the Egyptian. No, friend, it is not that simple."

"What is it then?"

"God has . . . left me."

"*Left you* — Man! What are you saying?"

"Hoshea, I do not know! Something has gone, something has suddenly left me. The word of the LORD burning in my breast — it has lifted away, as it lifted from Amos the night he spoke his last words to Amaziah. The word no longer burned in his breast. He returned in peace to his flocks in Tekoa. Only with me there is no peace, only emptiness and a longing for the way of the LORD. I have tried three times to preach in Samaria, but every word I speak I must push past my lips. The words stop up. The power is gone."

"This is madness."

"I do not know what God wants any more. I am lost. I pray, but I cannot think of anything but her. Again and again and again I try to throw her off, but she comes back to plague me. When she stayed in my house, and I fretted that I kept her against the Law and against the will of God, I did not preach either. But that silence was my own, my own confusion. Now, with her gone, it is a frightening silence, Hoshea. It is God's silence. I do not know if He is angry with me for letting her go or punishing me for holding so long to her. I do not know. It is not what is out there in the city that stops me from preaching. It is what is in here —" I thumped my own breast and shook my head in great weariness.

Hoshea left some moments later, troubled and uncertain. In a strange way my bewilderment seemed to shake his confidence that Israel could achieve her destiny, even if her armies were restored.

* * *

At midday, Deborah, the wife of Ebarth, came to the entrance of the shed and called me to the meal. Since Gomer left,

Deborah had prepared the midday meal and taken over much of the care of the three children. Jezreel trotted ahead of her, hopped over the threshold, and ran over to me.

"Father! Father! Deborah baked fish cakes, fish cakes!"

I set down my tools and swung Jezreel up in my arms, laughing at the boy's excitement. Jezreel brought me what little joy I found these days.

"Well, we love her for that, do we not?"

"Yes, yes!"

Deborah carried the young Loammi on her hip. Loruha-mah hung at the side of the entrance, looking at me, and Jezreel skipping beside me.

"The little one is out of sorts this morning," Deborah said. "I set some water to boiling. It is his stomach. Boiled water the best thing for it. Same with my own."

"I would be hard put to take care of these three without your good help, Deborah."

"Nothing. Nothing at all." Deborah flushed with pleasure.

Loruhamah looked after me when I passed through the door. She always tried to copy Jezreel. She followed after us with a kind of rolling, hopping step, the closest she could come to imitating Jezreel's bounding gait.

At the meal Deborah chattered as she usually did. Ebarth seldom returned home from his carpenter shop for the noon meal, and I spoke but little, so she had no one to divide the talk with. But this day she spoke more slowly and carefully than was her wont. She said she had lain awake at night, planning how she could tell me what she felt it her place to say. Knowing I had no mother, Deborah liked to think she filled that place in my life.

She tried to come to the subject from the side, which for Deborah proved difficult. In the end she blurted it out plainly: "You are young and well favored. You could find another wife with small trouble. For the children, if not yourself."

"It is an unfair burden for you, I know."

"Psh! That is nothing. It is for yourself. Your own life."

"I do not think I could look well on another woman. Not yet."

"Now I say this: I always liked her. Even when I knew what went on. She was as good a neighbor as one could ask for. Never full of gossip and foul tongue like Esther bath Halachai, on the other side of us. I would not believe a word she said. Last week she tried to tell me the husband of Miriam bath Eben took up with another man's wife south of the market. Disgraceful. She had no way of knowing. She only overheard it. I found out. Not a word of truth in it. Not a word. Gomer was never like that."

"One can hardly spread gossip when she is more the subject of it."

"Well, now it is over and gone. You should look ahead."

"Perhaps I will, in time."

"The sooner you take on a new wife, the sooner you will forget her. You have to forget her, now she is gone."

I bit my lip in silence. For all her good-hearted intentions, Deborah's ways could be meddlesome.

"Have you seen the youngest daughter of Josiah, the stone cutter? She is past sixteen winters. Beautiful, too. A little thin, but she will get fatter."

"I am not interested in another woman." I think I spoke curtly.

"You cannot just wish yourself a wife. There are ways —"

"I want no — want no wife. I have — have a wife."

"She is gone."

"No difference. It makes no difference."

"You cannot raise children without a wife."

"If they — if they overburden you —"

"No, no. Do not be angry. The children are no burden to me. I love them as my own. I do. I — I think of you."

"Then leave me in peace. This thing —"

"You still love her." Deborah said with quiet finality.

"Let it be."

I stood abruptly from the table and walked to the door of the house. Jezreel and Loruhamah sat tight-lipped, watching after me. I was used to that. They had learned not to speak when their father's face turned red and he stuttered his words.

Deborah shook her head sadly, yet a warm glow shone in her eyes as she came over and touched her hand to my shoulder. It moved her that a man could go against all custom and tradition for the love of one woman.

3

In a crumble-walled inn, hard by the east wall in Bethel, in a small grimy room, Midemi stood facing the doorway, his hands clenched fiercely together behind his back. Behind him, on a narrow bed, lay Gomer, blue-lipped and pale.

True to his nature, Midemi had taken Gomer from Samaria with no practical regard for where they would go or how they would travel. He took no thought for the money they would need or how they would make any kind of life, cut off from everything of the past. He thought only that he was breaking free of Tania's grip, striking out toward something new and free and beautiful.

Ugliness and disappointment surrounded him. Gomer had taken ill, rising too quickly from her sick bed, and living now in the unnatural cold that had come on the country. She lay on the narrow bed, her whole body shaking with the cold. Midemi's small purse of money had dribbled away during the four weeks they stayed in Bethel, until they were forced into the harsh, unlovely room where they now lived. Ugliness, ugliness, ugliness — crushing out all joy in living.

In Egypt he still had friends, even if he were barred from Pharaoh's court. At least they could eat and live in quarters not crawling with vermin.

She could not travel, she told him. She was ill and weak. Midemi suspected, and soon convinced himself, that more lay behind it than her illness. She hesitated to leave her own people, clung vaguely to her tribal folkways and their God. Clung, perhaps, still to her husband, though she would not admit it.

"If you loved me truly, you would go with me to Egypt," he said angrily.

"Midemi, do not plague me. I — I am weak and cold. If only I could have another blanket, please?"

"The innkeeper has no more blankets to give us."

"I am so cold, so cold."

"In Egypt you would be warm."

"Please, please — I cannot. I am ill — weak. Oh, Midemi, get me blankets, I pray you. I shall freeze. I am chilled in all my bones."

"Can you still not understand — there are no blankets for us!"

"In Samaria there are blankets lying unused in the corner. It is cruel, cruel."

"Yes, you would like to return to Samaria, would you not? Go back to your husband."

"No, no! I did not mean it so. Be patient with me, Midemi. I shall be well soon. Oh, if only I might get warm. I am so cold, cold."

"You have moaned the same song these four weeks."

"Oh my love, please. It must be as we said — lovely and beautiful."

"Look around you! Do you see any beauty? Any loveliness? It is ugly, horrid!"

Midemi slammed out of the room in disgust. Gomer buried her head in her arm as she had done every day since she left Samaria. Shivering with the cold, and wretchedly unhappy, she wept. The image that floated before her vision was not Midemi or herself or their waxing misery, but a dreadful dream she remembered from childhood of a stone altar and sacrificial knife.

* * *

At the entrance the greasy-skinned woman who kept the inn halted Midemi on his way to the street. She asked for the rent, eleven days past due. Midemi had hoped to avoid her. The woman had taken a fancy to his handsome looks, and her fawning attention sickened Midemi more than the shame of not paying her.

"I — I shall have it soon," he muttered. He had but three shekels left, and they must go to buy food. After that, he did not know. Midemi had never in his life faced through an unpleasant problem.

"Do not hurry away," the woman said with pinprick sweetness. We must settle this matter more definitely."

"I shall bring you the money by tomorrow."

"Why do you look away from me so . . . shyly?" The look was one of disgust, but the plump woman chose to fix pleasanter notions behind the Egyptian's disarming features. "Am I so ugly to look upon?"

"No. You are not ugly."

"I am a bit fat. But men like women who tend to plumpness, is it not so?"

"What?"

"Do you not like a woman who is fleshy?"

"Yes. Yes, certainly."

"This life is lonely for one like myself, with no husband. My husband died two years gone. It is lonely for a woman."

"I must go."

"I like to do things for a man. I have good wine in my rooms."

"I — I must see to matters in the city."

"Will you come?"

"What?"

"To my rooms."

Midemi grimaced with disgust.

"We could see if the rent might not be extended."

"I will get the rent!"

"Do not be haughty," she said with sudden ferocity. "You are no better than me. If you do not come up with the rent — or make no arrangements — out you will go. You, and your woman, too!"

4

Early in the morning, two weeks later, a sharp rap sounded on the door where Midemi and Gomer lived.

"Who is it?" Gomer called out feebly.

"I have a message for the Egyptian called Midemi." It was the boy who tended the stable.

"He — he is not here."

"Where may I find him?"

"I think he will be in the room of the innkeeper." Gomer's voice trailed off to a whisper.

"Where did you say?"

"In the room of the woman who keeps the inn."

When his money was gone, Midemi had no choice but to hire himself to the innkeeper. He had no trade. He had never mastered anything beyond what was given him at birth.

The stable boy knocked on the innkeeper's door and told in a quiet voice that a slim young woman waited outside.

"Tania!" Midemi thought instantly.

He dressed quickly in a crumpled woolen robe. With a mumbled excuse to the still sleepy innkeeper, he hurried to the entrance of the inn. Tania was someone secure and dependable, someone to help him out of his plight. Not until he stood face to face with her did he fully think on the circumstances that stood between them.

"How did you find me?" he stammered uncertainly.

"Does it matter?" Tania's voice was throaty, subdued, as after much weeping. She wore a simple blue gown, gathered at the waist in the manner of Egyptian women. It gave the appearance of softness to her body.

"No, no. I suppose it does not matter."

"Oh, Midemi! What are you doing in a place like this?"

"I — I have no money," he admitted dejectedly.

Tania shook her head and had to blink back tears. So like a little boy he was — could not even dress himself properly if she did not pick his clothes.

For Tania, the sweet victory she had won turned bitter in her mouth when she discovered Midemi had gone away with the wife of the prophet. If she were to win a struggle in Man's world of warring and intrigue, only to lose her woman's hold on the man she loved, the victory would turn to ashes in her teeth. She had to have Midemi or the victory would have no meaning.

She sent word through the network of palace servants and slaves, posting a reward for word of Midemi. When word came, she sought him out in Bethel.

"Our train is waiting outside the city walls," Tania said. "Seven camels to take us back to Egypt."

"Egypt?"

"Yes. To all we have dreamed of."

The treaty with Israel was renewed. Tania had sent a message to the court of Tiglath Pileser, warning that So of Egypt stood with Israel. Egypt had no plan or power to do battle with Assyria, but Tania supposed that Egypt's past glory could still loom as a threat in the reckoning of Pileser. She had planned well. It was accomplished. Midemi's fortunes stood at a crest in the court of the Pharaoh.

"She is ill," Midemi said feebly.

"The wife of the prophet?"

"Yes."

"You think of her, Midemi? Have you forgotten the water lilies on the Nile, the warmth of the ocean breeze, trunks and trunks of fine clothes, and the life of contentment that awaits us in Egypt? Look at this place — is this where you mean to spend your life?"

"No!"

"You have nothing here, nothing. In Egypt you have everything."

"What can I do with her?"

"Leave her."

"She is ill, weak from her sick-bed."

"Leave money, then, for her care."

"You have money?" Midemi seized on Tania's suggestion with desperate eagerness.

"Yes, of course."

"And everything — everything is arranged, back in Egypt?"

"Everything."

A quarter-hour later Midemi and Tania mounted the camels that waited outside the city walls. As his camel lumbered to its feet, Midemi thought one last time of the sick, shivering figure of Gomer, lying on her bed, waiting for him to return. And he knew, as he rode off beside Tania, that he left behind the only person who had ever drawn him outside himself.

Chapter 33

Judas ben Ishbaal

1

The unseasonable cold gave way to warmer days and the approach of olive harvest. Pekah's reign was in its fourth month. The heathen altars of the bull lay heavy with sacrifice, and no voice in Israel was raised to call the people back to their God. From the border of Judah to the mountains of Lebanon, and from the Great Sea to the easternmost plains of Bashan, it was the shadowless noon of the great god Baal.

In a cellar wine-house west of Samaria's market place, Hosea hunched over a small table, alone. His robe was crumpled and dirty, loose at the middle. His face had grown the stubble of a beard and his hair hung matted about his ears and neck.

Doubts, doubts.

Why should he struggle to serve a God who brings only misery and regret? He could count on one hand his days of happiness since he fastened a prophet's rope around his middle. Why cry out for the people to return to the LORD? What could he offer them but a cup of bitterness and grief? What man not possessed of a demon would pay heed and turn to such a God?

What fool of a man imagines himself in love or fancies himself favored of God, except he be caught in the toils of a demon? What conceits drive his twisted soul?

Hosea took no interest in another woman, nor could he. He sought to blot the very thought of Woman from his mind. He came to the wine-house to be near other people, to escape the awful loneliness of his own house or the countryside altar. He stared at the half empty cup before him. He seldom drank a second cup of wine, but this day he emptied the cup and called out, "More wine. Another cup of wine."

The owner himself answered the summons. Hosea recognized the man who had once contended for Gomer in marriage and with whom Gomer confessed she had gone aside, the wine merchant called Donath. Hosea had not seen him on previous visits.

"Now here is cause for scoffing," Hosea said. "I am served by the man I thought once to have bested — but you got the better of it, you did. Far the better of it. I should serve you."

Donath slid the wine jar across the table. Drunken customers were so many posts, not to be paid any heed.

"Here, do you not know me?" Hosea asked.

"Two coppers for the wine."

"Sweet irony. A copper for each two years she lived with me, and not with you."

"Heh!" Donath started in spite of himself when he looked closer and recognized Hosea. "The prophet. The husband of Gomer bath Diblaim."

"Sit with me, and let us drink a glass of wine to . . . Gomer bath Diblaim."

"I never drink." Donath's tone was cold.

The name of the prophet whispered through the wine house from the table nearest him. People turned to see for themselves if it was indeed the tall young man who preached in the Temple and the market place.

Yes, it was he. You see: it is all a lie. Everything is a lie these days — soothsayers, seers, priests, prophets. They are all the same. This one looks even worse.

Donath turned from Hosea's table. He shook loose his sleeve and dusted it as though he had brushed against something unclean. It gave him a strange satisfaction to humble Hosea openly. He had not forgotten how Hosea had bested him, gaining Gomer in marriage five years before. It had pleased him when Gomer came to him secretly after her marriage, but the affair had been short lived. Gomer's mother knew well the secrets and intrigue that swirled through the streets of Samaria. She warned Donath to keep silent about his affair with Gomer or she would dredge up and noise about Donath's false testimony against a wine merchant from Bethel, a dealing that had gained Donath considerable profit.

"You never knew how fortunate you were when Diblaim gave her to me rather than you," Hosea blurted out.

Donath faced Hosea from three cubits, bitterly sarcastic: "If she had married me, she would not have become common property in Samaria."

Hosea dropped his hand to the table, upsetting the cup of wine. He took no offense. He would soon leave and head back to his house. After wakefulness that seemed never to end, his eyes would finally close, and the vision would again trouble his sleep — the cloud, the thunder, the lightning, and the beckoning hand.

2

Pekah closed his ears against war-rumblings from Assyria. Assyria had threatened for years. Nothing ever came of it. Israel had her alliance with Egypt.

Hoshea returned from Memphis and reported that the promise of help from Egypt was an empty hope. In a month's time another tribute would be due the Pul. If it were not paid, Assyrian hordes would overrun Israel.

Pekah laughed at the sober-faced counseling of his captains. A strange, unnatural laugh — high-pitched and distracted sounding. He boasted that he needed no help from Egypt, nor did he need to squeeze his own people for a tribute to the Pul. An easier way lay open to him.

Against Hoshea's counsel he conspired with Rezin, the king of Syria, to send an army against the Southern Kingdom of Judah. In the Temple in Jerusalem was gold and silver enough to satisfy the Pul for many months. Israelites locked shields with heathen Syrians and besieged the walls of Jerusalem, breaking fifty years of peace between the two kindred nations.

Ahaz, the king of Judah, sent a messenger to Tiglath Pileser with gifts of gold and silver from the Temple.

'I am your servant and your son.' The message spoke in the courteous, flattering words common to Eastern courts. 'Come up, and rescue me from the hand of the king of Syria and from the hand of the king of Israel, who are attacking me.'

The Pul answered Ahaz's plea because it matched his own plans. He marched his armies against an undefended Damascus and took it in two days' time. The leaders among the Syrians he carried off to his own land, to the province of Kir, as was his habit with conquered peoples. With no one to lead them, a conquered people had no means of revolt. Rezin, the king, he killed openly in the market place of Damascus for all the people to see.

Pileser had grown weary of the Syrians. Rezin paid his tributes tardily with much grumbling. And this offered the double chance to parade Assyria's power before Israel — to remind the new king of his tribute-duty and to show Israel with the clash of steel how trifling he accounted the posturing of Egypt.

Israel and Syria withdrew hastily from the walls of Jerusalem. The Syrian warriors, hapless boots of an already conquered people, returned quietly, each by his own way, to family herds and tents in the desert. The ragged army of Pekah marched sullenly back to Samaria, grumbling at the king's folly. No people, not even the Syrians, now stood between Israel and the armies of the Pul.

3

Two soldiers stood arguing outside the crumble-wall inn that stood near the east wall of Bethel. The taller of the two, a young faced, gangling boy, objected doggedly to paying three copper shekels for a woman. A harlot could be had in the Temple for a flask of cheap wine.

The shorter man, thickset and older, contended that the woman who called herself Miriam was worth a score in the Temple. It was not that she was beautiful — oh, she was comely enough — but it was the way she loved.

"You would think she sought to kill you! She loves with a passion that sends you reeling."

"But three copper shekels. A single copper were more to my liking —"

"Last night you were agreed to come and see for yourself, and now you back away."

"Last night I was full of sour wine."

"Go to Miriam and you will be drunk for a week — drunk with loving. Come — are you afraid?"

"Three copper shekels for a woman? You can get the same thing in the country with idle promises. It is foolish."

"You can get nothing like this anywhere in Israel. Come. When we laid around the wall of Jerusalem you talked of nothing but women. Women, women, women, day and night. Here is your chance."

"I should have said 'No' from the beginning," the boy said stoutly. He dared not admit that, for all his boasting, he had never had a woman, and he was more than a little anxious at the thought.

"Come, I will go first, and then I will tell her you are coming and are a special friend of mine. You will never regret your three shekels."

"I would enjoy it more at one shekel."

"If you feel cheated, I myself will pay two of the three."

The gangling boy shrugged and followed into the inn, still murmuring that no woman could be worth three copper shekels.

Gomer received the thickset soldier and sated his passion with an unsatisfying quickness. The soldier feared he might well lose two coppers if she offered his friend no more.

He told her that his best friend waited below, that he had heard so much about this Miriam that he could hardly contain his passion, that he was somewhat young and foolish, and needed to be . . . shown.

"I am tired. I can see no more today."

"I have promised him. I told him about you till he cannot sleep — you must."

"Tell him to come tomorrow."

"He will not come tomorrow — cannot. He — he is leaving."

"I can not see another man today."

"You must! I had a demon's time getting the boy here at all — promised him everything under heaven!"

"You said his passions were past control."

"It is true, but the boy is . . . shy. Will you not take him, this once? You have made enough from me for this one favor."

"I am weary. Please leave me."

"I will see the innkeeper. I am a paying guest. I deserve consideration. I will see her at once."

The soldier stomped out of the bright room, muttering a curse at the inconstant ways of a woman. Gomer sank back to her bed, trembling with weariness.

She was driven to sell herself. Midemi deserted her before two months had passed, leaving her a pitiful pouch of coins. When that was gone, no other way lay open if she meant to go on living. The innkeeper would have thrown her into the street.

When she recovered from her fever, Gomer sought to shake herself loose from regrets and cheerless remembering, as her mother would have done. Anna was seldom low-spirited. She told Gomer to look on life with an honest eye, trained on the day ahead: *Look on yesterday without fear or excuse. Fashion a scheme for today.*

Gomer had always been well in her body, almost never sick. When the fever left she quickly regained her strength and youthful look. She took a false name, the custom if one became a hired harlot. It was thought a woman saved her family from shame if she hired under a name not her own, though a harlot herself might be regarded with little reproach. Gomer called herself Miriam, and her name spread through Bethel and beyond. In ten days, the innkeeper moved her from the wretched hovel where she had lived with Midemi to the largest room in the inn because she brought good income.

Gomer gave herself with mastery and seeming abandon. Her native passion found a wretched kind of pleasure in rousing the passions of men who came to her bed. In each man's embrace she mimed a passionate pleasure with him, only him. It was the only thing left to her, the one thing that gave her place in the world of men.

The innkeeper stormed into Gomer's room, her fat cheeks red with anger. "Slut! What do you mean, turning away a customer!"

She received half of Gomer's charge in turn for her lodging.

"I am tired. I can take no more today."

"Tired? Pish! Lie on the bed — no work in that. I will not see good coppers go begging."

"You receive five times the worth of my lodging, and well you know it. Today, no more."

"The boy is waiting below."

"He can come tomorrow or find someone else."

The innkeeper swore an oath and stormed out of the room.

In six weeks Gomer began to command private income. The word went around to leave her silver shekels, or a special gift, besides the coppers paid to the innkeeper. She carefully hoarded her treasure, hiding it in unlikely places. She ventured into the city, bought things in the market — colorful gowns, sweet breads, wool, oil, good wine. Tradesmen came to recognize and greet her. She had money. Whispered words, and directions to her inn followed after her. She was known only as Miriam.

She had lived in Bethel half a year when a man of notable appearance came one evening to her room. She saw by his costly clothing that he must be a man of some wealth. She received him as she did others, but more slowly, spending more time in giving him pleasure.

Two days later he came again, and twice the following week, each time leaving more generous payment. Gomer never sought the names of those who visited her. Each encounter had a life of its own — birth, growth, and death. On his fourth visit the man asked, "Do you know who I am?"

Gomer spoke lazily. When those who came sought to make talk with her, she had learned how to engage them. The words came slowly as though she were forming them one by one, though her thoughts were instant: "I would give you a name like Joshua — a commander, a conqueror, a man who could stop the sun in the heavens to finish what he has begun." She smiled as though in inquiry.

The man smiled unnaturally in return. It was not his usual way. He made his face a mask when he engaged with others, showing neither agreement nor disagreement, keeping others off balance and easier to command. This woman Miriam. He wanted to know her, and wanted to be known by her. Drinking wine with three friends late one evening he had said, "Wives and concubines weary me. They lie there like a board and think to pleasure me. And they cannot put two words together." Eladon ben Joseph, near him in wealth, challenged him to visit the woman called Miriam, who, he assured, was no board. "If you live, she will delight you. Else the doing of it will kill you, and you will die happy."

"My name is Judas ben Ishbaal," he told Gomer.

She replied at once, but with ease, no hint of fear or awe, "Everyone in Israel knows the name Judas ben Ishbaal." He was the richest man in Israel.

"Do you find me pleasant?" he asked.

"Exceedingly pleasant," she answered, adding, "likewise generous."

"Are you content here?"

"Contentment is a fickle lover. When you come, I am more content." Since becoming a harlot, her mother's words were never far from her mind: *His greatest pleasure comes in knowing he gives you pleasure.*

"Would you like to live in my house?"

"And be lost among a hundred wives and concubines? I would grow fat and lazy."

"You could have done with oafs and dolts, have only me."

"My life here is not bad. Better since you have come, Judas ben Ishbaal. But here I am free. That counts for much."

Judas knew when to leave a matter hanging, let them ponder what they might lose. "Think on it," he said as he left.

Think on it, Gomer did. He was a pleasant man, no need to flatter him with a made up story. He was a lonely man, as rich men often were. She had seen it in her father and in men who did business with him, ever employed to get the best in a bargain, trusting no one, on guard against false dealing from every quarter.

She supposed him to be past forty years. What could she be, coming late to his life? If only a bed companion, it would not last. If she learned what occupied his days, learned what troubled him, saw ahead of time what profited him or endangered him — *if they spent time together, talked together, entwined their lives with one another* — a life with Judas ben Ishbaal might be secure.

Judas had never met a woman like this harlot Miriam. Three weeks went by. She did nothing, said not a word to pursue the offer he had made. One day she remarked that he seemed disgruntled and asked if anything were amiss. He said one of his camel trains had been attacked by brigands as they approached the borderland of Egypt. They overpowered his drivers and made off with more than half his baggage. Gomer sat silent for a time, then spoke slowly and with uncommon confidence for a woman. "Perhaps Egyptians should undertake a share in the protection of your caravans. Offer them a better price, but at the cost of a band of guards to meet your train half way and see it safely to Egypt."

Judas continued to visit her. They talked with one another, sometimes more than half their time together. He told her things that troubled him and listened to her words, always slow and measured. He asked again if she would come to his house. When he said it a third time, she answered, "You do not need another concubine. I have no desire to be one."

"What then?"

"What we now are — lovers and . . . friends."

"Friends? You would have me be *friend* to —"

"To a *woman*? A woman who is a friend is a lover twice over."

"You would have me come to you, keep coming to you here?"

"In your house, perhaps."

"Then you would be a concubine."

"No, a harlot. A friend. But free. Give me spacious quarters in your house. Hire me as you do now, generously. I will be there for you . . . as long as both of us desire it."

"A private harlot . . ."

"If you like."

* * *

Summer was past, grain for the new year planted; clouds laden with former rains scudded in from the Great Sea. Gomer waited until she found a caravan from Egypt that had discharged its cargo. The night before their return to Egypt she hired seven soldiers from the caravan to move her belongings to the house of Judas ben Ishbaal in the dead of night, leaving no witness in Bethel who could testify to her whereabouts. Gomer knew Judas longed to have her in his house, but knew also he did not want their arrangement widely known.

Spacious housing awaited her according to their agreement. Three large rooms, bright and airy, facing east toward the cool morning sun, shielded from the heat of the afternoon sun in the west.

Summer lay yet five months hence. Neither Judas nor Gomer would know another summer in Israel.

Chapter 34

An Uneasy Truce

1

Hoshea paused stiffly outside the arched entrance to Israel's throne room. He thought quickly, one last time, of what he must say. Then he nodded to the guard and waited to be announced into the presence of the king.

Pekah stared idly out a window of the throne room, toying with the ivory-knobbed tie of his heavy velvet cape. He did not bother to look up to acknowledge Hoshea's homage. Hoshea's daily visits had become ordinary and boring — a new account of Assyria's might, a new plea to strengthen Israel's army, and finally, another royal promise to give the matter careful thought.

"What dire warnings do you bring me today?"

"No warning, my king." Hoshea spoke in a flat, unmusical voice that spoke his deep concern, overlaid with doubt and fear of the outcome. "I ask you to send me into Israel to collect the tribute-tax for the Pul."

"Hm . . . you are no longer content to harangue me to have this done. Now you must do it yourself?"

"The tribute is due in ten days time."

"Hm . . ."

Pekah looked out the window again, seemingly deep in thought. Tribute to the Pul. Build up the army. Train more officers. Recruit new soldiers. This man Hoshea was growing more and more wearisome.

Pekah had wheedled Hoshea into remaining chief of captains after the murder of Pekahiah. He thought it would cover his bloodguilt to have a man of stature serve him. But it was not to be. Others he might fool, not himself.

In cutting down his dearest friend, Pekah killed something in himself. He could not wash from his mind the last, stricken look on the face of Pekahiah. It hounded him by day and haunted his dreams by night. He had turned violently from Tania, the symbol of his guilt. He agreed to anything she demanded, only to have her gone from his sight. No matter which way he turned, Pekah could not escape the haunting guilt that plagued him.

In the end, it strangely twisted his imagining and brought all Israel to the brink of disaster. He laid his own guilt, and his secret want of punishment, on the Israel he ruled. His life as a soldier had taught him better than most the danger of Assyria. Of a purpose he ignored the warnings of Hoshea and his fellow captains, waiting stubbornly for the day the armies of the Pul would raze Samaria to the earth.

"Let us see," Pekah said, as though carefully weighing Hoshea's words, "ten days time, you say. The journey to Nineveh requires two and a half days, or three perhaps. Menahem raised the tribute in four days time. That makes seven days, a full week. We have three days, then, before we need begin."

"We cannot raise the tribute as Menahem did."

"Have you grown squeamish?"

"No. But neither have I grown foolhardy. Israel can ill afford to spill her own blood."

"Yes, that has always been your way, Hoshea ben Elah — like a tiger in battle, gentle as a kitten at home. Never raise the sword against your own people, and never, never, never against your king, however evil he might be. I well remember the day you stood against Menahem, in defense of the ruthless Shallum ben Jabesh."

"Can you, Pekah ben Remaliah, push the word *ruthless* through your lips when you speak of another?"

"Why? Because I did what you would never have the courage to do? Because I saved Israel, even when it meant the life of my closest friend?"

"Israel blunders toward destruction, and you do nothing to halt it. You have weakened her to the point of death. Our armies will not last a week in battle with the Pul.

"What do you know? You know nothing! Nothing! I know what is needed for Israel, I know. Be gone from my presence."

"I ask you once again: give me the authority to go into Israel to collect the tribute-tax. If you do not —"

"What? What will you do?"

"If you do not, Israel will he lost," Hoshea said evenly.

"Ha! Israel will he lost. You know nothing. Nothing! Be gone! I will see to this myself."

Hoshea flushed angrily. He was not a man of speech. He had no words to counter Pekah's taunt that he lacked courage. He turned and strode from the throne room.

Hoshea's thoughts tumbled over one another. Pekah — he was — what? Blind and deaf? Did he truly not see the menace of Assyria? All his life Pekah had been a soldier, yet now his hands hung limp at his side. He refused to do anything. Hoshea trembled to think what he himself must now do.

Pekah watched Hoshea leave. A leer spread across his face — contempt. A coward was no better than a murderer.

Now, for Hoshea, no middle way remained. Left to himself, Pekah would dally on his throne while Israel hurtled to destruction. The man seemed not well in his mind, so easily provoked to anger and screaming. Yet for Hoshea to take the step that might save Israel — to himself seize the throne — this fell not to his liking.

Since the days of Joshua, thirty generations gone by, Hoshea's people had borne arms in Israel. From the reign of Saul, Israel's first king, no ruler in Israel had lacked a warrior of the blood and lineage that came down to Hoshea. They had served faithfully and well, never conspired, never plotted. In this they took great pride. When he was a small boy, Hoshea's own father said to him, "My son, serve your king and your God with a strong arm and a stout heart. Leave to others the bickering and intrigue of the palace." Hoshea grew up with angry scorn for anything that smacked of 'plucking at the throne.'

Yet, Hoshea wondered painfully whether something more lay behind his misgivings. Was it fear that held him back, fear of a duty too large for any one man to bear? Dread of shouldering an authority that might save — but more likely destroy — Israel? Far easier to make a judgment, or offer advice, if the burden of failure rested on another's shoulders! What if Israel, under his hand, were to fall into the grip of the Assyrian? What if he, in all the history of Israel traced back into the mists of time, were to lead his people not to glory but to destruction? How would his name be remembered if Israel, under his rule, tumbled into the abyss of nothingness?

No man in Israel, except himself, could wrench power from Pekah. But to what good purpose? Eighteen kings had mounted the throne, some for years, some for mere days. Did Israel now need a nineteenth king? Pekah once knew the threat of Assyria. He had lost that vision, or if he still held it, no longer cared. The same thing could happen to himself, Hoshea thought. Is that what happened when a man took up the scepter? Was the Assyrian monster too much for any ruler to face? Yet, if he dared not chance it, what then?

Hoshea saw — if not clearly, painfully — his long held understanding and way of life crumbling away. He doubted his own ability to rule Israel wisely. Yet no man with experience and understanding stood ready to do what must be done. With disquiet in his heart, he turned himself to do what he had sworn never to do. He began to lay a plan that would overthrow the rule of Pekah ben Remaliah.

2

In ten days time, Hoshea could not hope to raise a revolt against Pekah, wrench a thousand talents in tribute-tax from the people, and travel to Nineveh in time to halt the armies of Tiglath Pileser. He struck on a different scheme, one for which his service under Menahem had unwittingly prepared him. He saddled a horse, took two more in lead for a fast journey, and started early the following morning for the court of Tiglath Pileser.

The Pul was a shrewd, practical ruler. He could have overrun Israel long before, had he wanted. He preferred tribute to conquest. If he knew a strong and stable man could seize and hold Israel's throne, he would bargain with such a man. The unrest in Israel's palace was a nuisance to the Pul.

At noon, the third day after leaving Samaria, Hoshea rode into Nineveh, hot, dusty and tired. An hour later, dressed in a clean robe, he presented himself before the king of Assyria.

Pileser squinted down his straight, thin nose and tapped the arm of his deep-cushioned chair with a slow, methodical beat. He seemed to have grown more frail and gaunt, and he spoke with a kind of wheeze.

"So it is my old friend, the son of Elah called Hoshea. We have missed you at our court this half year."

"The months away from the grandeur of your presence were as years, and the days as weeks." Hoshea intoned in the stately manner expected at court.

"Do you come, now, to bring the greeting and tribute of your new king? He is over-long in paying his respects to so close a neighbor. But some days ahead with the money. A good balance, all in all." Pileser chuckled at his own wit.

Hoshea moved a step closer to the Pul and squared himself firmly in his stance. He spoke bluntly. "I come, rather, to strike a bargain with the Pul."

"Does your bargain involve a thousand talents of silver? If it does, I will listen to you."

"That and something more."

Hoshea outlined his scheme to seize power from Pekah. The men of the army would support him if he would be given time to assemble them. The tribute money could be raised, if he be given time. Hoshea asked only that of the Pul — time. One month's time.

Pileser wound the gray, wispy strands of his beard around his little finger as he listened to Hoshea's proposal. Hoshea was the kind of man the Pul would have on the throne of Israel . . . almost too much the kind of man. Pileser could detect a hint of Hoshea's intention, someday to break free of vassalage to Assyria. Yet he offered what the Pul wanted in Israel — a sensible ruler with whom he could make sound bargains. The shifting tides in Samaria inflicted a measure of uncertainty on his broader plans. He had long dreamed of moving southward. He would have to concentrate his forces. He could not continually look back over his shoulder to the current state of affairs in Israel. Against the risk of Hoshea building too strong an army, Pileser weighed the advantage of a stable, sensible rule in Israel that would free him, for a time, to concentrate his forces southward, toward Babylon. It seemed a fair gamble.

"If I give you this month's time, how am I to know you will not use it to assemble an alliance against me — Judah, Egypt, Philistia? When your new king took the throne, I received a message from So of Egypt, warning me that he stood with Israel. How am I to know you would not seek such alliances?"

"The Pul knows that I lived two years in his court. I know the might of Assyria, and know as well the hollow reed Egypt has become. No alliance Israel would make could stand up to the power of Tiglath Pileser."

"Ha! Now that I like in you, Hoshea the son of Elah. You do not profess false love and fealty but recognize the brute truth of the matter. We can bargain with one another!"

"Then I have your promise of a month's time?"

"Yes, a month's time to take the throne and deliver to me one thousand talents of silver. Those two things. You agree to both?"

"I shall deliver the tribute myself."

"I have never set a man on a throne in quite this manner. One can sometimes accomplish as much by inaction as by action."

"May I take my leave at once? I would enjoy your hospitality a courteous length of time, but I have work to do."

"You are a clear-minded man, Hoshea son of Elah. Such a man as I would have near me if you came of different blood." A dark frown clouded Pileser's brow as he spoke. Then his voice took on a strange note of fondness, and he leaned forward. "We two understand one another. A war that must yield sure victory to one nation should never be fought. What has the weaker to gain but defeat? What has the stronger to gain but hollow triumph? Better the weak offer tribute to the strong and save itself the humiliation of defeat. Better the strong make gain by simple agreement than wrench it out at the cost of blood and treasure. Men stumble into war without cause, more guided by passion than wisdom. War is a last choice, a final step to take when a threat is no longer heard."

"Indeed, we understand one another to the final letter." It abased Hoshea's pride to hear the weakness of Israel spoken of so lightly, yet he could not gainsay the truth of Pileser's words.

"I tell you this because it is much on my mind. I am an old man, Hoshea son of Elah. Seventy winters I have seen, and I look now to the day another hand will rule the kingdom I have built. It is strange that the one man capable of holding together this sprawling, bickering people of mine should be a man so little like myself."

"You speak of Shalmanezer?"

"Yes. He is a man of great strength and ability. He has the blend of certainty and decision to hold together this nation. Yet there is a foolish ruthlessness in the man. He has long hounded me to move against Israel and bring your people into subjection. He suffered some sort of embarrassment with an Israelite woman when we warred in Galilee. It caused him humiliation before his men, and he cannot forget it. He is much guided by his passions."

"I see no waning of Tiglath Pileser's strength. You have many years yet."

"It may not be so. Strange things happen to the body with the weight of age. Strange pains and disturbances that become so much the dot of a man's attention that he loses touch with any future except his own."

"I see none of this in the Pul."

"Today is a good day for me. And better for having seen you, Hoshea son of Elah. I think of you more as friend than vassal. As long as our agreement is kept, and I am yet alive, you need not fear the sword of Assyria."

"May you live many years."

"That is known by one only."

"How is it known by 'one?'"

"You, who are an Israelite, should have no need of such a question. In the years of my father, a strange man from Israel appeared in Nineveh. Nineveh is a great city, three days journey across. He walked a day's journey into the city and cried out, 'Yet forty days and Nineveh shall be overthrown!'"

"The story of this man is known in Israel also."

"He should have been laughed at, even killed, but he was not. The king himself, who sat an uneasy throne in Nineveh, arose from his throne, removed his robe, covered himself with sackcloth, and sat in ashes. He issued a proclamation calling every man, woman, and child to repent before the God of Israel, and so it happened.

The words of the king were recorded. He said, "Who knows, God may yet repent and turn from his fierce anger, so that we perish not?"

The people of Nineveh, even unto the king, believed this man. Why did Nineveh believe the God of Israel? Why did the God of Israel show mercy to Nineveh? Have we a common destiny?"

The Pul touched a finger to his chin and gazed thoughtfully at the high ceiling of his marbled palace, the palace raised to trumpet the wealth and glory of Assyria. He had taken it from the man who ruled before him and built it yet larger. Shalmanezer would add still further to its sprawling wings and gardens, as would the one who followed him — until some new people, greater than Assyria, rose up and toppled the fluted columns and returned the watered gardens to desert. "I think if I were to live again I might spend more time learning of God and less time quibbling with men. In seventy years one grows weary of men."

"The Pul is a wise man."

"I speak from knowledge. Wisdom —" A strange wistfulness clouded Pileser's dark eyes, ". . . I do not know. I will look for you in a month's time. You, and a thousand talents of Israel's silver. We are agreed?"

"A month's time."

3

Hoshea greeted me warmly, though with some stiffness. He told me his bargain with Pileser and his intention to seize power from Pekah. He spoke slowly and with some unease. He seemed anxious for my approval but unsure of it. He remembered our last meeting, when I put his words aside.

"I sometimes wonder whether God much cares for Israel any longer," I said sadly. "We see-saw this way and that, turn again to the Baal altars, unseat king after king. I wonder . . ."

Now sworn to a plan that brooked no retreat, Hoshea was seeking practical steps to gain success. Israel's road ahead lay scattered with boulders and hidden faults. Only a hard, lean people could make the passage. Hoshea believed that the words I once spoke would strengthen Israel if they were re-kindled and heeded.

"We cannot wish away the armies of the Pul. Pekah heads us toward sure destruction."

"Yes, yes. Maybe I wonder more for myself."

"I have no doubts for you. You still have the power, if you will revive it and use it."

"I am a weak man, Hoshea. When I shout my voice over the market place, I can see people whisper to one another, 'He is a prophet of God; his word is sure.' They know nothing of the uncertainty within me. Do you know where I have spent the last three months? Do you know?"

"No. I have not seen you."

"In wine houses of Samaria! Running from the God I cannot escape, and a wife I cannot forget. I am weak, Hoshea. And I am a sinful man. What is the will of God? Do not ask the prophet. He cannot see God's will for himself, cannot keep himself free from sin. How is he to see it for Israel?"

"You persecute yourself needlessly, dwelling on this thing of your marriage at such length. She is only one woman —"

"Only one woman. Yes, Israel is only one people, too, but chosen, betrothed, wed, mated. It is different, Hoshea, to have a woman for one night, as soldiers do — different to be wed, to raise up children from her loins. A wife is not easily forgotten."

"Some wives I have seen might better be forgotten. Why is this so great a matter? Other men have had wives light-foot it to another man's bed. They turned them out and found another. Are you so different?"

"If some men can shrug off a wife like an old cloak, then I am different. I cannot."

"And can you shrug off your God? What of that? More than your own life and destiny is concerned. All Israel hangs in the balance. What of that? Is it the will of God that you squat in your little carpenter shed, brooding for a whore of a wife who left you, while Israel clatters to destruction?"

I took his words without retort. "You cut deep," I told him.

"Is it true? Is it? You are learned in the will of God. What say you?"

"I know, I know. I have tormented myself with these same questions, suffered the bitter silence of God, and wonderings about His call on my life. I know . . ."

"We have little time, Hosea, little time. The death of the Pul will be the keening of Israel unless we are ready for battle. Without   without the fear of God, Israel never can be ready for battle!" Hoshea blurted it out, and having done so, his lips trembled with what he had said.

"You have come to know this?"

"I — I need you, Hosea. I need every help I can muster — the LORD's, if He will give it. This is hard business."

"I want to. Desperately I want to, if only I can — if I can be forgiven for my weakness, my sin. It is grief to be separated from my wife, but to be separated from God is death. He is a strange God, Hosea. You remember the prophet Amos?"

"I do."

"I once thought when he thundered the wrath of the LORD over Israel that I saw God as clearly as I see you, with understanding. What I saw, and understood, was . . . a grain of sand in the desert. One little grain.

"Two nights ago I dreamed a strange dream, Hoshea. I stood on a high mountain, and in the valley below, on a narrow road, a woman lay fallen among the rocks by her own folly. The LORD was on the road, and when He came to the woman, He leaned down and lifted her in His arms, lifted her gently." I gazed through the door of my little shed. After some moments of silence I said in a low voice, "There is a tenderness in the LORD, a puzzling tenderness."

"Solomon himself spoke of God's mercy."

"Yes, mercy and forgiveness when a people repent and return to the LORD. But the LORD came down to the woman. He Himself lifted her in His arms. She was there by her own folly. I am not sure she even knew it when He lifted her up. It was strange."

"Will you try?" Hoshea asked, returning to his purpose. "For the LORD, for Israel, and . . . even for me?"

"If the LORD will have me prophesy again, I will. It may be He will use his own words to . . . take away the sin and the loneliness that plagues me."

4

Hoshea hoped to seize power from Pekah while half of the Pul's month still remained. That would leave him two weeks in which to collect the tribute-tax and carry it to Assyria. He could hardly do it in less time.

His plans edged forward slowly, methodically. Hosea moved back into the life of Samaria and regained some following. One by one Hoshea gained the support of well-placed captains in the king's army. The thrust against Pekah was carefully planned, and the basis for the tribute-tax laid down. Hoshea checked each step of the plan with cautious care.

Two days before the planned revolt, a runner from Ijon, north of Galilee, stumbled through the gates of Samaria with news that Assyria had crossed the borders of Israel. Janoah and Kedesh had fallen. Galilee lay in peril.

Hoshea's face drained white when the news first reached him. The soldier in him rallied. His slow cautious planning gave way to sudden dispatch. Two causes of the Assyrian invasion seemed possible. Either the Pul had gone back on his promise, or he was jabbing at the borderlands to remind Hoshea that time was fleeting. Whatever the cause, Hoshea knew he had to deliver his thrust against Pekah at once. If

Pileser did not stop, he would be at the gate of Samaria before the week was out. Together with two captains and three soldiers, Hoshea marched briskly across the palace yard, heading for Pekah's private quarters.

Pekah gave a short whinny of a laugh when Hoshea entered his front room with the two captains and three soldiers. "So you have heard the news," he said.

"You see now what your rule has brought to pass," Hoshea said bluntly.

"I hope to see more, much more!"

Pekah's eyes lit with the gleam of a madman. When the news he had waited and hoped for at last came, Pekah lost all possession of himself.

"The armies of the Pul are already in Galilee," Hoshea said, a little unnerved by Pekah's strange frenzy.

"In a week they will descend on Samaria, on this nation of *murderers*," Pekah returned wildly.

"He is mad!" one of the captains breathed to Hoshea.

"I must take the throne," Hoshea said in even tones. "You are no longer fit to rule."

"What! Ha! You would seize my throne in my hour of triumph? Israel is no longer fit for any rule — a land of murderers!"

"Come with us," Hoshea said.

"Take my throne you shall not. Guards! Guards!"

The door to Pekah's chambers swung open. Two guards started into the room. Hoshea's three soldiers, standing at the opposite wall, sprang on them with drawn swords, forced them into the room, and slammed the door. "Guards! You fools, fools!"

Pekah made a dash for the door. Hoshea drew his sword and blocked his way. "I must take the throne if Israel is to be saved. You are my prisoner."

"Israel will not be saved, will not be saved! I will see the walls of Samaria razed to the earth!"

"You are mad."

"What will you do? How will you save her? You cannot!"

"Take him to the soldiers' quarters," Hoshea ordered. "Hold him there. Treat him well."

"No, you shall not! Ha!"

Pekah dodged back a step, and before Hoshea could move his arm, lunged forward, impaling himself on Hoshea's upthrust sword. Hoshea gasped and jerked the sword back. Pekah collapsed to the floor, clutching at his belly.

"Now — now you shall see. Now you will know what it is to slay the king — suffer for your royal murder!"

The breath caught in his throat. He gasped and rolled onto his stomach. The eyes seemed to bulge from his sockets for a moment, and then, with a wheezing gasp, his head thudded against the floor.

The months of guilt-torture were ended. He died believing in his last wild moments that he had passed on to Hoshea his own sin against Pekahiah.

Hoshea became the nineteenth, and last, king to rule Israel.

5

For the tribute money Hoshea had no time to raise a tax. He resorted to the Temple. In the reign of Pekah the Temple had done brisk business. Deaf to the shouting and condemnations of the priesthood, Hoshea moved his soldiers into the Temple and carried out sixty great sacks of silver. With an escort of seventy chariots, he headed northeast out of Samaria, toward the plains of Galilee, to meet the armies of the Pul.

The chariot tracks of the Assyrian stopped short halfway through Galilee and turned back toward the East. In Gilead and Naphtali the story was the same. Without seeming cause, the small, fast chariots of the Pul had withdrawn, headed back toward Nineveh.

The moaning cry of new-made widows and the wailing of motherless children rent the sky over Israel's borderland. The sudden, vicious attack of the Assyrian, and his even more sudden retreat, left the people dazed and bewildered. In four bloody days, village life in the borderlands was wrenched from its quiet routine, never to be returned. The village elders were gone, led captive to Assyria. The merry shouts of children at their games gave way to frightening silence. In Kedesh, one pregnant woman remained alive. Hid in a tiny closet, she escaped the marauding invaders. Others were dragged from their houses into the streets and ripped open from belly to throat with the sword of steel. Wherever he sped with his escort of chariots on his way eastward, Hoshea heard the keening of mourners, the whine of the funeral lute, piteous weeping, and low-toned curses for the king who had let this horror descend upon them.

In Nineveh, Hoshea found the Pul close to death.

"You must forgive me." The Pul spoke haltingly from his broad high-pillowed bed. "This faintness came on me of a sudden. I had not shown the good sense to tell Shalmanezer of our bargain. When the time for the tribute came, he mounted an army against your people on his own authority. I was in a death-sleep."

"Our borderlands are laid waste," Hoshea said bitterly.

"Yes, yes. When I woke and learned of the move, I recalled my armies at once. It is a sad stroke."

"Does . . . the Pul have long to live?"

"Heh! You are still the blunt man, Hoshea son of Elah — quick to size your position. There is still some life in this old man. Still some life."

"What of my people, led captive to your country?"

"Were there many?"

"I do not know. The elders of every village I passed through were said to be captive."

413

"It is a bad stroke."

"Will you return them? I have brought the tribute money."

"I cannot. Money has already changed hands on them. Not even the Pul can intervene when money has changed hands."

"My rule begins under a cruel omen."

"Return and establish yourself. Our peace shall not be broken as long as I live." The Pul reached out and grasped Hoshea's arm with a pale, blue-veined hand.

Hoshea drove his chariots out of Nineveh at a gallop, half expecting the armies of Shalmanezer to rumble to life behind him even as he raced for the border of Israel.

Time was desperately short. Israel's fate hung by the slender thread of an old man's dwindling life.

Chapter 35

O Gomer! O Gomer!

1

"When Israel saw his sickness, he went to Assyria and sent tribute to the great king!"

Hosea called out over the market place in the early morning. The shock of Assyria's assault on the borderlands awakened a respectful fear for the words of the prophet. He had foretold the happening.

"The Pul is not able to cure you or heal your wound. For I, the LORD, will be a lion to Israel; I, even I, will rend and go away. I will carry off and none shall rescue. The LORD it is has done this thing, the LORD of Hosts!

"Return, O Israel, return. The day is far gone toward evening. The dove has sought its nest and the marmot its hole. Turn from the altars on your high places, and from harlotry in my Temple. The night shadows touch you. Return to your God, O Israel!"

A close knot of four priests moved toward the market place from the Temple. Hoshea's looting of the Temple silver and Hosea's sudden re-appearance had plunged the high priesthood of Anakah into dangerous crisis. The Temple had come to support a hundred and twenty-two priests in the sumptuous days of Pekah ben Remaliah. They could little afford to stand by and watch Temple offerings drop away. Anakah had a plan.

The unaccountable attachment of the prophet to his unfaithful wife was known throughout Samaria. His strife with the priesthood had hinged on that strange relationship almost from the beginning. Whenever a crisis arose in his own home, the prophet fell into a period of silence. This knowledge lay at the root of Anakah's plan. Three of the priests buzzed with anticipation as they followed the fourth, a heavy bearded man, newly arrived from Bethel.

"Like grapes in the wilderness I found Israel! Like the first fruit on the fig treein its first season, I saw your fathers. But they came to the high places of Baal. They gave themselves to false gods. They became detestable like the thing they loved. Israel's glory shall fly away like the bird — no birth, no pregnancy, no conception! Even if they bring up children, I will bereave them till none are left. Woe to them when I depart from them, says the LORD! Your sons will be led forth to slaughter. Your daughters shall have miscarrying wombs and dry breasts. A people of unclean lips, a land of drunkenness and harlotry is Israel. Your daughters play the harlot. Your brides commit adultery.

"Why — why should I punish your daughters when they play the harlot, and your brides when they commit adultery! The men — the men themselves go aside with harlots and sacrifice with Baal prostitutes — a people without understanding shall come to ruin."

The heavy bearded priest seized on Hosea's sudden stammering: "Is this how you excuse yourself for your wife, who now sells herself in Bethel for three copper shekels?"

Hosea's jaw went rigid. Color rushed to his cheeks. It was the first word he had heard of Gomer since the day she walked from his door with the Egyptian.

Whispers raced through the crowd. Hosea stood trembling atop the small platform from which he spoke. Then he plunged into the crowd and headed across the market place toward his house.

Gomer — in Bethel! How could it be? What of the Egyptian? Was she a harlot in the temple of Bethel? Or in one of the inns?

Since Hoshea came to him, the LORD had returned the word of prophecy to Hosea's lips. Two times he had overheard the LORD, so long silent, again speak words, the same words Amos had spoken his last night in Israel. *You He will bruise, but unto healing.* And a second word, *The* LORD *will draw you close to His heart.*

The months of painful separation from the LORD ended. New strength sprang to life on his lips. God gave him words. Even a kind of happiness returned, as the people hearkened to his words. But then, suddenly, came again the name of Gomer. *O Holy One of Israel! Would it return? Would the torture come again?*

Gomer . . .

Lips curved like a gentle seascape, promising life. Ebony hair tumbling loose to the shoulders. Cream white skin. Eyes of fire. And words. Words, words, words about everything and nothing — cheerful reports of an ordinary day, bold questions about the ways of the LORD, proud encouraging words when enemies pressed in, somber words about the God of Israel whose words she could recite from memory, yet be angry at His ways. Laughter like the rustle of wind in a high palm. Arms enfolding and caressing. The soft voice whispering endearment. A lap cradling the weary head of one beloved.

O Gomer! O Gomer! Why do you return to plague me?

Had not the LORD spoken the word that should quit him of Gomer? The word had fallen hard for Hosea. He embraced it reluctantly, not with desire. When finally he spoke it, he despaired ever having said it. He sent her from his house, but his heart went with her. He wanted her still — wanted her with a longing he could not name or understand.

The unplanned words he had spoken in the market place — 'Why should the LORD punish the brides who commit adultery more than the men who sacrifice with harlots under terebinth, poplar, and oak?' — whence came these words? Did he suppose it would lighten the judgment of an adulterous wife if judgment fell equally on men?

As he strode to his house, he thought, "I must gather my thoughts in a single line. Gomer was my wife, an adulteress. I turned her out. Was that the beginning and end of it? Much lay at the root. I took her from Diblaim's house an untried girl, too much pampered by her father. I left her too much alone, knowing her to have warm passions. I withheld affection when she came back to my house. I forgave, yet a shadow lingered on. I held out my hand but withheld the honest embrace of my arms."

As he approached the house he turned aside to the house of Ebarth and Deborah, where he supposed the children would be. Then he heard voices in his own house and recognized Jezreel's high laughing. He turned to his own door and stood a moment outside. A familiar woman's voice lilted in the air, "You have both grown, but this little one — he is like a weed."

Hosea stepped into the house where he was greeted with a shout from Jezreel. "Father! Shania and Obed are here, and Jeshurun!" Jezreel rushed to Hosea and gripped him about the knees.

Shania rose and embraced Hosea with one arm, holding little Jeshurun in the other. "Dear, my brother."

"So early you come," Hosea said, puzzled by their sudden appearance. They knew of Gomer's leaving a week after it happened; Obed's cousin brought word to them, and Shania came to Samaria by herself to inquire of Hosea what had happened. She returned home in dreadful sorrow, thinking Gomer had gone to Egypt.

"Look first at your little nephew!" Shania said, passing the child into Hosea's arms. "He has given up walking — he runs the day long."

Hosea lifted Jeshurun high, tossed and caught him. "So! You will follow your father, run like the wind." Despite his size,

Obed was swifter on his feet than all his comrades. He could almost outrun Hosea.

"Throw me too, Father," Jezreel cried.

Hosea lifted Jezreel and threw him high. Loruhamah looked on.

"What brings you to Samaria?" Hosea asked.

Obed came close and spoke in a whisper, as though he would keep it from the children. "We have heard word of Gomer."

"She is in Bethel," Hosea said bluntly.

"You know?"

"Even this morning."

"We learned that she lives there under the name of Miriam," Obed said.

Shania passed Jeshurun to Loruhamah, sitting against the wall, and came beside Hosea. "We come with a question and a request," she said.

"A request?" Hosea repeated, uncertain of Shania's word.

"You set her aside according to the Law. I know your sorrow, dear brother. It is my sorrow as well."

"You speak of a question. What question?"

"What now of us, Gomer and me? She is my sister, dear to me as life."

Hosea nodded in understanding.

"Can we seek her out?" Obed broke in.

"That is our request," Shania said. "Can she live with us for a time, if she is willing?"

"That would be strange," Hosea said quietly. "Half a day's journey from her husband and children."

"She is not divorced from us. She must build a new life. She has no good life in Bethel." Shania spoke the last almost as a gasp.

"My very thought as I came now from the Temple," Hosea said, almost to himself. "I cast her into the life for which I cast her out — an impossible life."

"You did what the Law requires," Shania said. She would not set herself at odds with Hosea.

"The LORD wants more than what the Law allows," Hosea said mysteriously.

Shania looked up at Hosea, fastening her eyes on his eyes. Plainly she did not understand what he meant.

"I know the Law, little sister. She knows the Law, knows the whole Law better than I. Something between us is greater than the Law, or other than the Law."

"What is it?" Obed asked.

"I do not know. But the LORD put it there."

"You love her still, do you not?" Shania whispered through her tears.

Hosea circled his arm around his much loved sister. "I would have her back," he said quietly.

* * *

For two days Hosea searched for Gomer in the city of Bethel and could not find her. He tramped through the streets and alleys of the city, inquiring of every merchant and beggar he encountered for advice of the woman called Miriam. Toward evening of the second day he had all but given up hope. The lengthening shadows crept eastward across the city. He grew fearful that if he dared inquire at the Temple he would learn of a raven-haired woman who had plunged the sacrificial dagger into her own belly.

When they were first betrothed, Gomer once told Hosea about the recurring dream she had since childhood. In the dream she was running toward a stone altar with a great sacrificial knife upon it. She would wake up screaming and crying. She told him the dream when they sat in Diblaim's garden, hiding her face in her hands, trembling.

At dusk, Hosea drank and washed himself at Jacob's Well. A crippled beggar hobbled toward him. Hosea had waited near the well for more than five hours. It was said one could find any man in Bethel by waiting at Jacob's well.

"You are the one who seeks the woman called Miriam?"

"Yes. You know of her?"

"I did not know of her when you asked me this morning."

"I have spoken to so many."

"I troubled myself to look for her, which proves some difficulty for one with legs like mine."

"I will pay you."

"How much?"

"Whatever you ask."

"A shekel?"

"Copper?"

"Silver."

Hosea dropped a silver shekel into the man's outstretched talons.

"You will find her in the cellar inn and wine house of Armalath, in the south of the city."

Hosea found the Armalath Inn. The mistress told him the woman called Miriam had left two weeks earlier. According to an elderly gardener she departed at night in the company of Egyptians. The innkeeper whined that she had showered great kindness on the harlot Miriam — saved her from starving — only to have her desert the inn without word or warning, consorting with Egyptians.

2

In the grand house of Judas ben Ishbaal, Gomer was known to all as 'Miriam.' It was the way everyone in the house addressed her, when they had occasion to speak to her. A cloud of uncertainty shadowed exactly who Miriam was, or why she was in the house. A serving maid, Rebekka, attended to her needs and slept in a small, adjoining room.

Miriam kept mostly to her own rooms, according to her agreement with Judas. She looked forward to Judas' visits two or three times a week. It broke the monotony of her days. She had not fully reckoned how alone she would be.

One crisp morning, in the second month of late planting, she awoke early and stood out of bed before the sun had fully risen. She dressed herself in a common gown, brown, indistinct. She pulled on a short woolen coat over her gown, drawing the hood down over her head, hiding her face in its shadow.

She walked undisturbed through the marketplace near Bethel's west gate, every street familiar from her earlier days at the inn. She paused at a stand of colored cloths, fingered some of the material, and moved on without speaking. She stopped at a fish stand where the fish were being laid out, looked on only moments, and went on. At a table of sweetbreads she bargained for two loaves in a high squeaky voice. In all, she walked unrecognized through four streets where Miriam was known on sight by the tradesmen.

She returned to her rooms in high fettle. Her disguise worked. It would give her freedom to leave the house from time to time. When the walls of her rooms crowded in on her, she could walk by herself in the countryside. She could go to Jacob's well and enjoy the gossip, remaining aloof from too much questioning. She could watch caravans from distant lands arrive and unload their baggage, tuning her ear to unfamiliar speech. She could acquire attractive goods, mostly unneeded, in the marketplace.

* * *

The fourth time she ventured out she saw something only she would have recognized. In the marketplace she stopped by a seller of leather goods. She looked down at three breastplates, such as soldiers wore, protective against a sword thrust. Her eyes were drawn to the center one. *She recognized at once: it came from her father's store of leather.* It was thicker than the other two, and its coloring was uniform. Diblaim had once told her in a rare show of boasting that they would never be poor; anyone who understood leather knew that his was the finest leather in Israel. He showed her two stretches of leather, one from cattle herds in Bashan where his competitors purchased their hides, then one from herds in distant Sidonia, where he secretly bought most of his hides.

A man from the country crowded in and began to size up the breastplates. "How much for these?" he inquired. He held an ivory carving of a lion prominently in one hand.

"Eight silver shekels," the owner answered.

The man shrieked that a breastplate at such a price would be worthless — he would die of starvation before it would ever protect him from an Assyrian sword. The bargaining ground down to four silver shekels; the buyer seemed close to assent.

The owner picked up the breastplate on the left side of the three and held it out: "Three silver shekels, two coppers, and your miserable ivory lion," he declared.

Gomer whispered to the man from the country: "The cow in the middle fed on richer pasture. Look at the thickness."

The buyer took the outthrust breastplate, lifted it up and down as though weighing it on invisible scales, set it down and picked up the middle breastplate. "This one. Three silver shekels, my ivory lion — the work of a master carver. No coppers."

"Done," the owner agreed. He had not heard the exchange between the buyer and the woman at his side.

The buyer took the breastplate under his arm and started off. He stopped and turned back to the woman. He was about to speak a word to her when he saw she was weeping. He shrugged indifferently and walked away. "Strange," he thought. "Crying over a breastplate . . ."

Gomer walked away from the market, through the west gate, and continued walking into the countryside, aimlessly.

Her remarkable ability to seal herself off from the past and the future and live in the present moment suddenly weighed down on her. Since moving to the house of Judas ben Ishbaal, she had thought less often of her life in Samaria. Now, suddenly, the past had rushed in on her again, filling the present moment with itself.

She sank to her knees in the small shade of three terebinth trees. Her quiet weeping gave way to sobs and a wailing cry, like the keening of funeral mourners.

What had become of her life?

Father. What of him? According to custom, a divorced wife lost standing not only with her husband but with her own family as well. Who was there to watch out for Father now, with Mama gone? Would he marry again?

Samaria. Was there anything for her in Samaria? Could she return, crawl back to Hosea, beg him to take her in? When Midemi left her in Bethel, the thought was never far from Gomer, waking or sleeping, *I will go and return to my husband. It was better with me then than now.* The hope that someday she could be reunited with her children and her husband haunted her day by day, but it was a hollow hope. He would not have her. Who could love a woman paid to lie with any swineherd and dung-shovel in Israel?

Loruhamah. She would have grown these past months. Soon four years, always chattering on after Jezreel.

Loammi. Soon a year. A sickly child. He might have died. No! He must live.

Jezreel. More than five years. A little Hosea in his speech and actions. She would hug him to her breast when he allowed her.

During the first days in Bethel, were it not for the memory of the children she left behind and each day craved to hold again in her arms, and the husband she longed for in her wretchedness, she might have given way to the impulse that hearkened always at her elbow, to escape into the quiet mystery of death. The dream of an altar and a dagger came often, and it no longer held great terror.

Her fortunes improved. She prospered as a harlot. She could buy sweetbreads and raisin cakes and wool and flax and oil and wine. Then Judas ben Ishbaal came and enfolded her with riches and security. For the first time since leaving her father's house, she was again surrounded with the belongings of wealth. Was this to be her life?

Gomer dried her tears on the sleeve of her robe. She struggled to her feet. How could she have so banished those she loved from her life and thoughts?

Hosea had turned her out; to return was not possible. But Father. He took the Law more lightly. She could visit him. Perhaps he would receive her.

* * *

When she returned to the grand house Judas was waiting in her quarters. "Where have you been?" he demanded.

She had not told him of her ventures into the city. She steeled herself to speak quietly, without fear: "You come early. It was a lovely morning. I walked in the countryside."

"I do not want you out and about in the city."

Gomer drew off her coat, taking time to smooth her gown and run fingers through her hair. "I am not your wife or concubine," she said.

"You belong to me," Judas stormed.

"I belong to no man except for the hour I am hired."

"I will set a guard on your door!"

"Then our agreement is at an end. Our words to one another were plain: *as long as both of us desire it*. If you lock me in my rooms, you will find no desire in me when you come."

"Who are you to speak such insolence to me?"

"I have honored your wish, that our life together not be known in the house or the city. I have never spoken of it in the house. I have never left the house without good disguise. I am unknown, unrecognized."

"What is this!" Judas roared. "I furnished you these rooms so you would be here for me."

"So I am. Two or three times a week you come. I am ready for you and will not disappoint you. The other hours of the week are my own. I will not spend my days as a caged animal."

"This is madness! I come to your quarters, maybe you are here, maybe not."

Miriam did not answer. She sat down on her spacious bed. At length she said, "I am ready for you, Judas ben Ishbaal."

"You are at an end," Judas returned harshly.

Miriam spoke with quiet finality: "I will leave word with Rebekka. You will know where I am at any hour. Waiting will not be often, and our bed that much better for the wait." Judas stood looking down at her, his face set, wordless. She added in a kindly tone, "And have no fear: I will not be hired by any other man. I am content to be for you alone."

"You do not know with whom you think to bargain." Judas said evenly. He strode out of the room without a backward look.

3

Judas had found his visits to Miriam at the inn a pleasant refuge. He had no need to be on guard. No one sought to get the best of him. In Miriam's embrace he found simple comfort; when they talked together about his undertakings, he enjoyed a peace and freedom otherwise unknown to him.

In his own house, and in Bethel overall, no sanctuary of peace distracted him. He must be ever on guard, suspicious alike of those who sought his favor or sought his undoing. He had shown a hard side of himself when he learned of Miriam's goings — the only side known to his women and slaves and herdsmen and camel drivers and indentured servants and unfortunate debtors. Miriam knew another side of him and chanced he would not lightly abandon it. She stayed in her rooms, waiting for him. Four days passed. He did not come to her. She began to fear she had overreached herself.

Gomer determined to carry on boldly with her side of the agreement, behave like herself, ignoring any break between them. She knew the hard words leveled against harlotry in the scrolls, yet she continued to observe many of the rituals of Israel. She once told Judas laughingly that she was Yahweh tether, from head to foot. She stayed in her rooms until after the Sabbath, when journeying was forbidden. The day following Sabbath she stood up before sunrise, dressed in a rough gown, and knocked on Rebekka's door.

"If the master asks for me, tell him I have gone to visit my father. I will be back before the week is out."

Walking at a brisk pace, away from well-traveled footways, across open country much of the time, she arrived at the bank of a small river by noonday, having seen only two herdsmen and their flock all morning. The river lay half way between Bethel and Samaria; three hours further on she would wade through another slow river that wended to the Great Sea. She sat down to rest and eat the small meal of bread and cheese she carried with her. She fell asleep by the riverside for a short time, then awoke and corrected her direction slightly to the west, according to the path of the sun.

When she first caught sight of the walls of Samaria, she stopped abruptly and clutched a hand to her breast. Would anyone recognize her? Would her father receive her? She pulled the hood of her coat lower over her face.

She entered the city by the small west gate and turned at once toward the north wall, away from the marketplace, the palace, and the Temple. She walked past the street leading to Diblaim's house so she could approach the house from the rear, walking through smaller streets — less chance of being seen.

She came to the house and circled around it to the entrance. The sun was still in the sky, hanging red and low above the horizon. Should she ring the large bell at the gate? She shook her head at so witless a thought. Had she ever had to gain entrance at this gate? She opened the gate and walked through the double row of evergreen oak to the main door of the house. Again she paused and again shook her head. She opened the door and walked into the house. The front room was empty except for the elderly servant, Abraham, who stood to his feet. His face lit with sudden recognition. Gomer put her fingers to her lips and pointed to the door across the room. The family usually gathered in the next room, around the eating table, at the side of the kitchen. She crossed the room, opened the door to the kitchen and stepped in.

She gasped. Her hand flew to her mouth. Sitting around the table were her father, her two older children, and a woman she did not know, who held Loammi in her arms.

The first to recognize her was Jezreel, then Loruhamah.

"Mama! Mama!" they cried. They rushed to her and threw their arms around her legs. She knelt down and embraced them. Jezreel's bitter memories had long since given way to a child's longing. He clung to her, a five-year-old boy happy in his mother's embrace. Loruhamah buried her face in Gomer's gown, crying out, "Mama! Mama! You came back."

Holding each child by the hand, she stepped toward the woman who held Loammi. The woman held Loammi out. Gomer took the child in her arms, enfolding him in a close embrace. Loammi reached up and pulled on Gomer's ear and gurgled a laugh, his little trick whenever he was content in his mother's arms, something Gomer had done in Anna's arms many years before.

Gomer moved sideways, coming to stand before Diblaim. "My lord, I do not mean to discomfort you. I came to the house by back streets. No one recognized me. I have thought much of you in recent days. I only wished to see if you are well."

Diblaim stood speechless before her. After moments he stuttered, "Gomer. Daughter. We — we heard you had gone to Egypt."

"I am in Israel."

"It is like a dream — a happy dream turned real!" Diblaim exclaimed.

The woman at Diblaim's side spoke to Gomer: "We have never met. I am your aunt."

"Jasimine? Father's sister from Tyre?"

The woman nodded. "I came after I heard Anna — your mother   had died. My husband has also died. I thought to be some help to my brother."

"The children? They are with you?" Gomer asked, looking from Jasimine to her father.

"Hosea is gone for some days, gone to Bethel." Diblaim answered.

"Bethel!" Gomer exclaimed. She was about to say she now lived in Bethel, but stopped herself. "For how long is he in Bethel?"

"Not long. A week. Perhaps ten days. He went there with Odenjah and some other of his followers. Deborah has been sickly. He asked if the children might stay with me in his absence."

"My visit is doubly blessed," Gomer declared. "That you are well, and I see my children."

"Surely more than — more than a visit," Diblaim stammered. "You have come back. You must stay."

Gomer looked down. "I have been turned out. I no longer have a home in Samaria."

"Father wants you back!" Jezreel said.

Gomer smiled, thinking, "He tones his words exactly like Hosea."

"We shall see," Gomer said, her familiar words when she wished to set a matter aside.

Later she slept between the children, cradling Jezreel under one arm, Loruhamah and Loammi under the other. When they woke, she kissed them each. Jezreel hugged her about the waist as hard as he could, as she had done with her father when she was a child.

After a hearty morning meal Jasimine took charge of the children. Gomer and Diblaim walked in the garden and sat down at their favorite place. He urged her to stay, assuring her that the word Jezreel had spoken last night was more than a child's zigzag desire. Hosea had said it to his sister, Shania, and had said the same to Diblaim himself.

"My life has greatly changed," Gomer said evenly. "When Hosea turned me out, I thought I would shortly die. The Egyptian left me before six weeks were out. I did not die. I am young and strong. I became what a woman can become. I gained the favor of men. I gained some wealth."

"Daughter, I have wealth. You may have it, as much as you need."

"It is more than wealth. A gap lies between wife and harlot. They live in two different worlds." Gomer sat silent beside her father. She took his hand in her own. "You gave me a virgin bride to Hosea, Father. I was wife and mother. I have become a harlot. I live in a different world." She gripped Diblaim with both hands. Tears flowed down her cheeks. "It grieves me, Father, that I have disappointed and shamed you."

"Your mother was no Israelite, yet she believed you could return to the world of your husband and children."

"Those were her last words to me," Gomer allowed. Squeezing her father's hands she said, "I do not see how it could ever be. We lived that way for a time. Too much lay between us."

Some of the overseer crept back into Diblaim's voice: "A harlot's days are few. What will happen when youth and beauty fade? What will happen when men no longer come to you?"

"My life has changed already. I am no longer a woman in the open. I live with one man."

"His concubine?"

"No. I would not have it that way. I am his woman, only that. We are friends." They sat in silence, subdued by the brutal testimony of the years. After some moments Diblaim lifted a hand to Gomer's cheek and turned it so he looked straight into her eyes, a gesture more tender than had ever passed between them. "This man you now live with — you love him?"

"Love? In my world you speak of desire and pleasure, not of love. Love is what I held in my arms through the night — my children. And you, my father. Mother, when she lived." Her voice hushed to a whisper, "Hosea, my husband. We had love."

"He loves you still, my child."

"He put me out according to the Law. I live in another world."

"For how long?"

"I do not know."

"Who is this man you now live with?"

"He wishes it kept secret. The knowledge of it is not open — even the servants in the house only guess at it."

"Servants? He has many servants? He must be a man of wealth."

"Considerable wealth. Great wealth," she added with a mirthless smile.

"You will return to him?"

"Today. We have come to cross-purposes of late. I must not remain overlong."

"Will you come to us again?"

Gomer clutched her father's hands. "I must. The children — I must know how it goes with the children. I will find a way."

"You are fond of this man?"

"He has been good to me."

"If so it must be, then so it must be," Diblaim said, then added with a dry laugh, "So long as his name is not Judas ben Ishbaal."

Gomer gasped. "Why do you say that name? It is a name known in all Israel."

"I only meant it as an ilk not to be trusted. No better example than Judas ben Ishbaal. I once did business with him. He dealt falsely with me, promised a price for my leather, then cut it by a third when I delivered the goods, on the testimony of two scoundrels he paid to lie for him. He is not a man of his word."

Gomer started to speak further, then bowed her head and said nothing more. She reached out and embraced her father with both arms. "Forgive me, Father, for the pain I still cause you. It is not much good you receive from me."

"Dear my daughter —"

"The ear of the LORD is little turned to the words of a harlot, yet I pray for you. Is that not strange?"

"Not strange."

"When I think of you and the children and Hosea, I pray that the God of Israel watch over you."

"The LORD has been more kind to me than I deserve. I have never been a man of prayer."

"Hosea taught me the scrolls of Israel. They condemn me, yet they also comfort me. Especially the songs and prayers of distress."

Diblaim returned Gomer's embrace and held her head to his breast. How different it was between them, she thought. As a child he shut her out and retreated inside himself when they were at odds. Now he embraced her and her shame-filled life. "You have brought me my happiest day," he said.

Gomer remained the day and slept the next night with the children held close. The next morning she left early to return to Bethel, uncertain what awaited her with Judas ben Ishbaal.

Chapter 36

Israel's Dark Hour

1

Hoshea swung a heavy, gold-encrusted cape over his shoulders, muttering that no right-thinking man should wear so uncomfortable and sweltering a garment. The royal velvet robe pleased him no more, with its pearl necklace and ermine trim. He shuffled through the dim-lit corridors of the palace toward the throne room, unattended by any guards or scribes, a strangely lonesome man in his royal trappings.

Hoshea walked slowly, not anxious to hurry his audience with the seven merchants who waited in the throne room. They would demand an easing of their tax burden, as they had done before. And they would present the demand in such a way that he would be hard put to refuse them some concession. In the first five months of his rule, Hoshea had learned that a king's authority in Israel rested on shifting ground. Kingly plans could be curbed, even reversed, as conflicting pressures in Israel showed strength or weakness.

Hoshea had launched a dangerous plan for the defense of Israel. When the Pul died, Shalmanezer would ascend the throne and send his chariots against Israel. That Hoshea knew. But if the Pul survived for as much as a year, even nine months, Hoshea clutched the hope that he could raise an army to halt an Assyrian invasion.

He summoned into Samaria all but a fragment of the king's army. The supply of trained soldiers had fallen so low during Pekah's reign that Hoshea could not spread them over the

435

kingdom. He left the borders of Israel defenseless, should Assyria strike. Within Samaria's walls he worked long days to increase and train a band of soldiers that could harass and slow the Assyrian until he turned back to his homeland, as he did in the borderlands.

For a time the people responded to Hoshea's stern rule, but when the fear of immediate invasion faded, a kind of languor settled on the land. The cry of Assyria had been sounded year after year and the armies of the Pul had never come beyond the borderlands. The people came to doubt that such a blow would ever fall. The God of Israel would protect them. The harvest had been good. Food was plentiful once again.

In Menahem's day the army had grown to some strength. It dwindled to a shadow under the rule of Pekah. The people, it seemed, had no desire to return to the stern days of Menahem and Pekahiah. The Baal priests lured people back into the Temple and helped spread the word of discontent. In the countryside young men paid little heed to Hoshea's plea for warriors. In the marketplace merchants agreed with a nod that Assyria was a phantom, conjured by the king to frighten Israel.

Israel no longer stood together as a people. Each person lived to himself with no vision beyond his own threshold. Hoshea's rule raised not loud complaint but indifference. A stupor settled on the land.

Hoshea walked into the throne room unannounced, as a captain would walk into his garrison.

"Peace," he said gruffly.

The two guards at the doorway half straightened themselves, and the seven merchants who waited on Hoshea half bowed toward the throne.

The oil merchant called Zedechiah spoke for the merchants. He stepped forward and came quickly to the purpose of their visit. Hoshea's tax for the support of his army cut too deeply into the purses of the merchants. Craftsmen and farmers, because they lived from one day's earning to the next or one crop to the next, escaped the tax altogether.

"The poor pay well enough," Hoshea said sharply. "When you pay the tax they pay as well, for where does your wealth come from except you squeeze it from them? Israel has prospered you — and you shall prosper Israel. Those who have no money will serve with their bodies and arms."

"Your tax is unbearable," said a second merchant. "Money for your armies, tribute for the Pul — we can no longer endure it."

"Would you endure rather the yoke of Assyria? The times are hard for all. Each must do what he is best suited for."

"Assyria, Assyria," said a third merchant. "The same cry we have heard since the days of Jeroboam, and the Pul has not come." All seven nodded agreement.

"Travel to the borderlands! Ask the widows and fatherless in Galilee if the Pul has come."

"The borderlands are of small account."

"The 'borderland' will soon be the wall of Samaria if Israel does not gird for battle."

"So it has always been said, but we cannot believe it. The king must ease this burdensome tax."

"How can the tax be eased when in one month's time I must deliver a thousand talents of silver to the Pul?"

"That you must see to yourself. We can no longer pay tribute to the Pul and support a growing army as well."

"You have no choice. Without the tribute we cannot stall off the armies of the Pul. Without an army, we cannot meet the chariots of Shalmanezer that will strike when the head of Pileser is laid to rest."

"It is no affair of ours," said their spokesman, Zedekiah.

"You make it none of your affair by blinding your eyes. So you have done since the rule of Jeroboam. The tax will be set aside when Israel's danger is set aside."

"We are loyal subjects," Zedechiah said, turning suddenly soft voiced, "but that which burdens us overmuch gives us pause to consider . . ."

"Consider what?"

"If our money can support one king, it could support another as well."

"Speak straight off your tongue, plainly."

"The king must read it for himself. This much he can know — all Israel is not content under his rule."

"Israel is not content because Israel is blind, as you are blind. Israel cares only for wine and Baal and harlotry, as you care only for your precious storehouses of money!"

Hoshea's wrathful words told Zedechiah that he dared not flaunt the threat of rebellion any further. Kings sat guardedly on the throne of Israel these days and might strike out suddenly at any sign of uprising.

"Are we understood between us?" he ventured more meekly.

"We are well understood — shall be better understood yet, the day the armies of Assyria tear down the flat stone mansions you have built with your precious shekels!"

Hoshea stormed red-faced from the throne room. He could run his sword through the lot of them, yet could not because they held money. Money was power! Money paid his soldiers, bought their food, shaped their weapons. The purse was stronger than the sword.

It maddened Hoshea that he must build and maintain his army by tangled intrigues, balancing one party against another. Yet he saw no other way. Israel had come to think so lightly of its kings and so little of its own wellbeing that any company of men could topple the throne, if another group did not stand on the other side to prevent it. Hoshea could do no more than carry on a desperate, bitter-mouthed game of balancing and try to maintain a measure of royal authority around which to build Israel's army. But for how long, Hoshea dared not think.

2

"Where are you going?" Jezreel cocked his head charmingly to one side and looked up at me. I fastened my robe about me. "I am going to the palace," I answered him absently.

"May I go with you?"

"I think you must stay at the house to welcome Papa-Papa when he comes."

"Loruhamah can welcome Papa-Papa. I would rather go with you," Jezreel protested.

"On another day you may go with me. Hand me the girth."

Jezreel picked the rough made girth from the eating bench and walked across to me, fingering the leather with his stubby fingers.

"Someday *I* may wear a girth and be a prophet, too."

"Yesterday when I came home you had a great wooden sword. You and Loruhamah were going to be soldiers. What of that?"

"Loruhamah is a girl. Girls cannot be soldiers. I want to be a prophet, like you." I tousled his hair and knelt at his side. "Give your father a kiss."

Since the children told me of Gomer's visit at the house of Diblaim, I found more occasions to hold and kiss them. I did not much ponder why; it happened of itself. Perhaps I felt more keenly the absence of a mother in the house.

The knowledge of her presence in Israel awakened a sudden hope, like a bright-colored desert bush in springtime. As quickly the bright color faded away, as in the heat of summer. She neither sought me out nor left word of where she lived. She had gone back to her lovers.

I went back to prophesying. Yesterday, a priest mocked the first word in the Law of Moses — 'You shall have no other gods beside me' — saying that Israel must also honor the harvest Baals. The people wondered whether I would speak against him, but I found nothing to say.

Loruhamah came alongside Jezreel and looked up at me. I took her in my arms and looked mock-sternly into her great round eyes.

"You will be a good child for Papa-Papa and Aunt Jasimine while I am gone?"

"I be a soldier, like Jezweel," she said solemnly. For all her tenderness, Loruhamah was always somewhat stiff in my arms, almost fearful. She seldom cried or gave way to temper, as did Jezreel, but waited quietly for me to show first attention.

"And you, also, be a good boy." I chucked Loammi under the chin and smiled.

Diblaim and Jasimine came at the third hour. I went to the palace to speak with the king.

3

Hoshea welcomed me into his royal quarters with little ceremony. His concern for my words had dwindled since he took the throne. He had even tried to mend his breach with the priesthood of the Temple. He discovered they were a force to be reckoned with. In suddenly facing the demands of ruling, Hoshea saw quickly the power wielded by various factions, but he understood too little the subtle authority a leader can wield by standing firm with sound reason, forcing the other party to an uncertain choice of action.

Hoshea knew I had come to ask that he take steps against the Temple priesthood — limit their activities to traditional religious rites and impose taxes on their income. Hoshea did not want to offend me, but neither did he want to endanger his standing with the powerful followers of Anakah the High Priest.

These days I seemed to shout into the wind. The people had grown weary of my words, weary of prophecies that warned woe and destruction. I had come to think that the times called for sterner measures than only words.

"How can the people heed the word of the LORD when the canting of the Baal priests fills their ears? The boot of Assyria wedged in our doorway, and Israel dances to the tune of the bull-god. It cannot continue, Hoshea."

"It is not in my power to prevent it."

"Consider well, Hoshea. You are king of Israel. You bow to no man."

"It is not so easy, I fear. Anakah's Temple contributes handsomely to Israel's treasury. If I took more, by force, he would begin to oppose and undermine me, and soon I would get less by force than I get now by agreement. I need Anakah's money. In three weeks time I must again load chariots with tribute to the Pul. I am short of finding the thousand talents."

"Hoshea, Hoshea will you be like all the others? A concession here, a secret negotiation there, and across the way a whispered promise to cancel the first agreement? Will such bargains save Israel?"

"Israel will be saved when she meets and bests the armies of the Pul in battle."

"Yes, on the battlefield — but under the banner of the LORD. I once said this to you, Hoshea, and afterward came to doubt it. I know now that my words were true. You must meet the thrust of Assyria by trusting and following the LORD, not by tortured intrigues."

"What do you know of governing a nation? I would have you spend one day on the throne of Israel. You would stagger home with your senses reeling."

"I know, I know. Ploughing a straight furrow is no easy task. Yet for Israel, the LORD's way is the *only* way. There can be no swerving aside. She is the chosen of the LORD, singled out from all other peoples for His peculiar purpose. The LORD is our life, our destiny."

"It is well for you to preach such words, but you bear no burden for bringing it to pass."

"Each has his duty — mine to speak the words of the Lord, yours to govern wisely in the name of the Lord. Move your soldiers against the High Priest, Hoshea. Let the people know that you stand for the Lord, and strength will well up in you like a lion. They need only to be led, to be shown. They are children."

"You have preached and shouted and condemned. Have they listened to you? Why should they listen more to me? You do not move people's hearts with the point of a sword. You yourself told me this, in speaking of your wife."

"Brother, if you do not stand strong for the Lord — do not move against this evil that is sapping the will of Israel — the prophecy against Israel shall be against you. You will not escape."

"Each in his own way, Hosea. You in yours and I in mine. I cannot yield to your request."

"Then the judgment is on you!" I cried with sudden passion.

Hoshea smashed the flat of his hand against his scabbard and cursed the Israel that drove him to so cruel a choice.

I wheeled from the king's presence and strode from the palace to which I would never return.

Chapter 37

Uncertain Days

1

Four months later, toward evening, Hosea sloshed toward his house through Samaria's muddy streets, returning from villages in the north where he had prophesied. A fine mist fell over the city, shrouding it in a blanket of shifting grays and silvers. The former rains had begun early, though winter still lay heavy on the land.

Hosea seemed little to notice the discomfort of his soaked garments. His eyes burned with weariness. Discouraging thoughts coursed through his mind. Idolatry held sway in the northern tribes, alongside indifference to the threat of Assyria. Hosea did not find a single countryside priest who turned aside Baal worship at his altar.

Hoshea had delivered tribute to Nineveh three months before. For three more months prophesies of destruction would fall on deaf ears. Hosea's words caused scarcely a ripple any more. Even in borderland villages that had felt the fury of the Assyrian less than a year before, the people did not care. They sacrificed to the Baal gods on the high places and paid no heed to the king's call for warriors.

How long could it continue, Hosea pondered? Israel was without sense, a land of sheep. The Pul lay half paralyzed on his bed, near death. Hoshea's army stood at less than a third the strength he would need to meet the chariots of Shalmanezer, and still the people turned to their Baals, reveled in the streets, and scoffed at the cry of the prophet. They listened

443

neither to warning nor promise, could be neither frightened nor lured from their idolatry or from their lethargy. How long, how long?

2

When Miriam returned to Bethel she expected to have hard words with Judas. To her surprise, he came to her rooms two days after she returned in a friendly temper and inquired after her father.

"Is he unwell?"

Miriam bowed her head in token of honor. "He is well. He is in grief at the death of my mother."

"Recently?"

"Some months already. They were very close. He grieves still."

"Does he live in Bethel?"

"He lives elsewhere."

Judas stood waiting. Miriam saw that she must contrive a story to keep her life secret. Haltingly she said, "My father barely received me. Others in the family would not speak with me. We live in different worlds."

"They know nothing of your life?"

"They know I follow a harlot's life, but I revealed no name or place. They accord me no place in their world and want none of mine. Our worlds are secret from each other, and best so."

Judas nodded in seeming agreement. He looked toward the bed.

"My bed stands quite unused," Miriam said, turning a fetching smile toward Judas.

Judas waited. Miriam came to him and wrapped him in the magic of her embrace, not hurrying. Afterward, they lay for some time abed, neither speaking nor anxious about silence. Their first days together at the inn seemed reborn. When Miriam at length ventured a thought, even an endearment, Judas gave no response. He seemed content, yet he held something away from her. She did not know what.

* * *

Two days later Miriam learned at what price she had provoked the displeasure of Judas ben Ishbaal by venturing alone from his house.

Shortly before noonday a hard knock came at her door. It would not be Judas; Judas entered without knocking.

"Who is it?" she called.

Again the knock, but no voice. Miriam went to the door and opened it. A tall, swarthy man stood at the door, dressed in a short leather tunic. His face and neck sweated heavily from recent work, alike his unwashed arms and legs. He smelled of strong drink. And of camels and sheep. He stomped past Miriam into the center of the room.

"What will you?" she asked, her voice harsh and unwelcoming.

"You are the woman Miriam?"

"I am."

He looked her up and down. "I am a camel driver for the caravan of Judas ben Ishbaal. We leave for Egypt in the hour. He said I might take pleasure with you before we go."

Miriam said nothing. She saw what was afoot. Judas had not forgotten her proud insolence before she went to Samaria to visit her father. His revenge was not to have her beaten or lock her in her rooms, but to humble and degrade her: give a filthy caravan worker leave to bed her.

"Have you the five silver shekels?" she asked coldly.

"Five silver shekels? For what?"

"For my bed."

"Are you mad?"

"That is my price."

"More than half my wages, to Egypt and return! Nothing was said about price. We finished packing the caravan four

445

hours early. Judas rewarded every man with an extra skin of strong drink for the journey. He bid the camel drivers cast lots, the winner to have you as added reward."

"So, you won me in a casting of lots — a gift to you from Judas ben Ishbaal?"

"I understood it so."

Miriam realized that Judas had planned her punishment with care. She could not turn the man away. She was his due. He would take her by force if necessary.

"Then welcome to my bed," she said, forcing a smile to her lips. She dismissed him from her room a quarter hour later.

* * *

Miriam said nothing to Judas when next he came to her room, nor did he question her. Their life together continued as before, but an unspoken understanding settled between them: if he suffered displeasure, he would visit displeasure on her. He would not be gainsaid in his own house. If he was displeased with Miriam, he went to wife number nine, a raven-haired beauty from Galilee. The fondness Miriam had felt toward Judas began to die.

She thought back on her life at the inn, the measure of shekel-freedom she had gained there. That was the blunt way harlots described their own fortunes: *shekel-freedom* — no father or husband to rule over them during the scant years of youth and beauty, then the later years of hunger and begging and early death. No future awaited her back at the inn. And she could look for no comfort or promise from Judas. The words of her father hovered in her thoughts, "He is not a man of his word." For the first time since coming to Judas' house, Gomer began to feel the slow crushing dread of her uncertain life.

3

Spent and weary, Hosea turned from pleading and lashed out at Israel with a forecast of doom. The time of repentance was past — judgment was at hand, and swift destruction would follow. Assyria would mete out God's punishment on a people stopping their ears against the calling of the LORD.

The Spirit of God raged in his breast. He spoke with a power beyond himself. He went without food and drink for days at a time, seeming to live by a strange inner fire that gave him the appearance of one almost mad. He preached the word of the LORD as it had never been preached in Israel before that day — but preached to people without cars, a land without hearing.

Chapter 38

Shalmanezer Strikes

1

Hoshea looked out over the city from his bedchamber. He mused that he had never before seen how dirty and ugly Samaria really was — building stacked close against building, rubbish heaped high in narrow alleys, offal littering the market place, and all looking yet more dismal in the drizzling rain that had held steady for half a week.

The early rains made collecting the tribute tax more difficult for his soldiers. The twice-yearly tribute was due the Pul in less than a month's time. More than three hundred talents of silver remained to be gathered. He had hoped the harvest tribute would be the last, but it fell short. And he had not begun to collect taxes to increase Israel's army. The army stood at less than eight thousand men, no match for Assyria's hordes.

Where was an end to the drain on Israel's wealth, he pondered wearily, where an end to the intrigue and bickering and bargaining of the palace? He came almost to dread leaving his bedchamber each morning. He prolonged his stay until forced to attend to some business of the kingdom.

When the Hebrew nation divided, following the glory of Solomon, the northern kingdom of Israel had known some days of greatness under Jeroboam II. That greatness and that rule had shriveled to a gloomy memory. Yet Hoshea dwelt more on the evil of overthrowing the king than upon returning Israel to greatness. From childhood his father Elah had taught him to honor the king. Seizing royal power by plot

449

and overthrow had been dishonorable. When Pekah lost his life in the undertaking, it turned more shameful still. When he mounted the throne, Hoshea found he was not deft in the ways of kingship. He was too blunt, too lacking in cunning. In the face of mounting resistance to his rule, he retreated into solitude.

Hunching under the heavy gold-encrusted robe of the king, Hoshea was a man torn from his natural place — a camel on a mountain crag, a bird without wings. Not until he donned his soldier's clean, simple tunic and rode chariot with his soldiers did the sharp ring of authority return to his voice. But he found no way to bring his simple, direct, soldier-authority to good purpose in the throne room of Israel.

A timid knock sounded at the door. Hoshea turned grudgingly from the window. The page who stood at the door was bled of all color. His voice trembled as he spoke, for he knew how the king's temper could flare at the report of unhappy news.

"O king, a messenger has arrived from the East." He paused a moment, as though his message were ended. Then, scarcely above a whisper, "Tiglath Pileser is dead."

"Pileser? Dead?"

"Yes, my king."

"Who told you this?"

"The messenger arrived bare moments ago from the outlands of Bashan."

"Who sent you to me?"

"Judiah, your captain."

"Is this some joke — some trick to play on me because I turned him out of my presence yesterday?" Hoshea seized the boy roughly by the neck of his robe.

"It is true, my king," the boy gasped. "I heard it with my own ears from the messenger. It is already known throughout the borderlands."

"Where is Judiah?"

"With the quartered soldiers."

"Send him to me — in the throne room."

"Yes, my king."

"At once!"

"Indeed, indeed!"

The boy dashed down the corridor, his heart tripping like the spatter of rain on a low roof.

Hoshea donned his captain's tunic and hurried to the throne room. Judiah arrived moments later. His words spilled out: "The men are greatly troubled by this news!"

"And well they might be! Here, now, is what must first be done: Take thirty of your best men and close the Temple."

"Close the Temple?"

"Yes. Seize the treasury and lock the outer gates. Cordon enough of your men around each entrance to make certain no one can enter."

"My king, this will greatly anger the priests."

"Before this is done, Judiah, we will anger every man in Samaria — must do so, or there will be not one of us left to anger."

"But the Temple — why?"

"I want no wild-eyed throng whipped into revolt by the priesthood. Their love for me runs shallow. We have trouble enough outside the walls. The city must be readied for siege."

"How can we meet the chariots of Shalmanezer? What do you plan?"

"That will somewhat depend on Shalmanezer himself. For now, the city must be prepared. Seal up the Temple."

"I pray this will not bring greater calamity on us."

Hoshea waved Judiah out impatiently. His thoughts were already leaping ahead, considering circumstances that might arise, dealing with each in the crisp, summary fashion of an experienced military leader. So absorbed was he in Israel's crisis that he did not consider how suddenly his soldier-instinct had resumed command.

2

Anakah, accompanied by seven of his Temple priests, stormed into Hoshea's throne room in high fury.

"What is the meaning of this? How do you send your soldiers to seal off my Temple?"

"The meaning is simple enough. Israel is on the brink of war. The people have no time for your festivals."

"Bosh! Where do you learn such a thing?"

"On better authority than your Temple soothsayers and seers who call themselves prophets — who speak with honey in their mouth."

"It has never been the right of the king in Israel to have authority over the priesthood."

"It has never been the custom of the priesthood, before your time, to fix like a leech on the people — sucking out their money, their will, and the fear of God from their hearts. I am long overdue in putting the whip to you, Anakah."

"You forget the money you skim from my coffers."

"Money! What will you do when the warriors of Assyria encircle Samaria's walls? Fire a handful of shekels down on them?"

"You will regret this day!"

"My regret is that I have been too long in coming to it!"

Anakah bit his lower lip but said nothing. Suddenly this king of theirs was a strangely different man.

Hoshea jerked his head, and the two guards at the door sprang forward to escort the priests from the throne room. Hoshea watched them leave; a look of grim satisfaction spread across his broad face. Hosea should have been there, he thought fleetingly.

3

Three tense, uncertain days followed in Samaria. Hoshea sent messengers to his garrisons in the North and East, with orders to fall back to Samaria when the blow fell, delaying the enemy as long as possible. Stores of food were carted in from the surrounding farmlands and cached in the Temple and palace enclosures. Triple bars were fixed on the gates. Tents and huts were set up in the streets and in the market place for the country folk who would stream into the city ahead of the invading Assyrians. A stern faced respect followed Hoshea wherever he went. Suddenly he was no longer a harsh, erratic ruler, but a trained warrior — Israel's hope in the face of the advancing Assyrian.

On the third day, shortly before noon, an Assyrian horseman rode up to the wall of Samaria and shouted to the gateman that he had a message for the king of Israel. The gateman admitted him, and four soldiers rode him escort through the crowded streets toward the gate of the palace. The people stared curiously at the copper skinned Assyrian, sheathed on each hip with a short, glistening sword. Word raced through the city that a warrior of Shalmanezer was in parley with the king. Before he reached Israel's throne room, the Assyrian had grown to five cubits.

Hoshea met the Assyrian with the practiced reserve he had learned in the court of Tiglath Pileser. He expressed condolences at the death of the other's ruler and inquired calmly what might bring him to Israel's humble court.

The Assyrian delivered his message with crisp formality: the new king of Assyria, Shalmanezer, demanded a four-fold increase in the seedtime tribute.

Hoshea nodded thoughtfully, as though considering the demand with great care. Such a tribute was impossible. Yet, if he could delay the chariots of Shalmanezer with the promise that Israel would pay such a tribute — delay them a fortnight, delay them even a week . . .

"Such a command must be the object of some consideration," Hoshea said slowly, as though weighing the issue even as he spoke. "Tell your king that I shall send him word in seven days' time."

453

"I give no promise he will wait," the messenger replied gutturally.

"If he follows the wisdom of Tiglath Pileser, he will wait."

"I shall deliver your message."

"Deliver also this gold ring, a token of Israel's friendship with the new king of Assyria."

Hoshea slipped the ring from his finger and laid it in the messenger's hand. The Assyrian nodded a soldier's leave-taking and departed. No sooner had he passed through the arched doorway than Hoshea summoned the seven chief captains of his army.

In the four days that followed, the wealthy merchants of Samaria came to know a different king than they had met and coolly threatened in Israel's throne room. Hoshea's soldiers reflected their leader's harsh determination to brook opposition from no quarter in Israel's hour of crisis. In every city and village, from the border of Judah to the hillside dwellings of Lebanon, from the summer mansions of Judas ben Ishbaal, the rich tradesman of Bethel, to the country houses of Adakiah ben Amer, who lumbered the cedars of Lebanon, the soldiers of the king pruned the wealthy of their money and possessions in a desperate effort to raise a part of Shalmanezer's tribute. By the fourth day, Hoshea had two hundred chariots laden with silver, jewels, and precious metal — just under three thousand talents.

Without the threat of Assyria, Hoshea would have been overthrown in a day for his ruthless looting. With the steel sword of Shalmanezer poised at the borders, not even the reckless and irresponsible dared band together to take Hoshea's throne. Hoshea found grim satisfaction for the humiliation he had suffered at the hands of the arrogant rich.

Hoshea dispatched Judiah to the court of Shalmanezer with the great train of chariots. Judiah was to present what treasure they had been able to raise on short notice, with the promise that the rest would follow in a month.

One captain, Alelyia ben Joseph, favored the treaty with Egypt and spoke the Egyptian tongue. Hosea sent him to Egypt in a feverish tactic to secure the aid of Pharaoh. Israel's treaty with So still held. In the despair of the hour Hoshea put aside his lifelong distrust of Egypt, clutching to a vague hope that Alelyia could gain a hearing with the Pharaoh and somehow Israel might be saved.

4

Eighteen days later Hoshea and Judiah faced one another in Hoshea's private quarters, in the east wing of Israel's palace. Alelyia had arrived back from Egypt two days earlier, Judiah from Assyria at sundown the night before. Hoshea's hopes for assistance from Pharaoh proved vain indeed. The alliance was sealed with Pekah ben Remaliah, the Pharaoh's minister reasoned smoothly. If Pekah was dead, then Egypt was free of obligation.

Judiah's report from the court of Shalmanezer added no encouragement. Shalmanezer accepted the partial tribute but answered with silence the promise that the remaining tribute would be delivered in a month's time.

A king never knew, Shalmanezer said after long moments, what . . . conditions might arise. Judiah confessed to Hoshea that he little trusted the new king of Assyria to hold back his armies.

"Shalmanezer is no man to bargain with," he said worriedly. "The words come out both sides of his mouth. I do not trust him."

"This is bad, this is bad," Hoshea muttered. "I had hoped we might delay him long enough for us to throw up some defenses outside Samaria itself."

"There is no defense in all Israel to match his chariots and the sword of steel." Judiah said. "I saw the power massed in Nineveh — impossible to defend against it. It is hopeless even to think of meeting the Assyrian in battle."

"A thin hope remains, Judiah, and the only one, I fear. I may yet be able to persuade Shalmanezer to follow the example of Pileser and leave off invading Israel."

"He will not listen to you."

"Perhaps not, but we must chance it. While I am gone, speed half of Samaria's garrison to the borderlands and mass what forces you can against an invasion. They must pay dearly of men before they reach Samaria."

"We were better to surrender now, before Israel's life-blood is spilled on the soil of Jezreel."

"Surrender! Are you balanced in your mind? So long as there is one soldier in Israel, it will not be 'surrender.' If we die, we die, but we will die with honor."

"You have no wife and children. You can say that more easily."

"Women and children must take the same fate that befalls their men. We are a people. Let there be no more talk of surrender. Leave with your men by noonday. I shall be gone within the hour. Are you well understood on your duty?"

"Yes," Judiah replied sullenly. "Well understood."

"We may yet avert this, though I fear Shalmanezer's love of power exceeds his love of silver."

5

Hoshea steeled himself to walk the length of Shalmanezer's throne room with the confident step of one who held no fear of the outcome of his mission. On a dais raised seven feet above the floor — twice the height set up by the Pul — slouched the surly, thick-chested hulk of Shalmanezer. Hoshea tried vainly to read the man's mood in the brooding deep-set eyes, and tight, thin lips.

"We are honored by the presence of Israel's king in our humble court." The sweetness of his voice belied his foreboding appearance.

"We are proud to recognize the worthy follower of Tiglath Pileser, Israel's friend of long standing."

Shalmanezer smiled with his lips. His eyes stayed cold.

Hoshea presented Israel's plea with carefully rehearsed reason. Given time, Israel could gather the rest of Shalmanezer's tribute. Israel was a wealthy land, but the wealth went quickly into hiding when the king's soldiers marched abroad. A king raised in Israel would know the hiding places of such wealth, as no foreign prince would ever know. An invading army would find Israel suddenly a nation of beggars.

Hoshea took heart from Shalmanezer's nodding attention to his argument. He harked to the rule of Tiglath Pileser and suggested, as boldly as he dared, that Shalmanezer would surely employ like wisdom.

"What use, O king, to risk men and arms to gain what you can obtain as a sheer gift? The Pul knew this well, and Assyria prospered under his hand."

Shalmanezer drew little circles in the air with his forefinger, as though he were carefully weighing each one of Hoshea's arguments. Then he said coolly, in a voice edged with granite: "The Pul was a fool."

The line of his lips hardened into a fierce grimace. He suddenly straightened himself on his throne, and all sweetness dropped away from his voice.

"Do you take me for a fool? Your talk of pleasant and peaceful relations between our two peoples — do you think I believe it? I had hoped you would speak to me in the same sweet tones you spoke to doddering old Pileser. Now it is known for certain that Israel is false, and deals falsely."

"What I say to you is the plain truth."

"The plain truth? Ha! Let us see."

Shalmanezer clapped his hands together. A man in long flowing robes entered through a side entrance of the throne room.

"Tell us, in a loud voice," Shalmanezer said, "from where you have recently returned."

"From Egypt, my king," said the man "And what is said in Egypt?"

"That Israel has sought her help, to make war on Assyria."

"Now . . . does Israel speak truly or falsely?" Shalmanezer looked hard at Hoshea. "Is it the action of a peaceful and friendly people to seek the means of war against my people?"

Hoshea clenched his fists tightly to his sides. Those clever in the dialogue of the court could find a smooth answer to such a query, could meet Shalmanezer's words blow for blow — even, perhaps, win their purpose through clever persuasion. But Hoshea had only a soldier's blunt honesty. Unless he spoke to a man who respected such honesty, the words fell like lead weights from his lips. He had tried to adapt himself to the wiles of the court, but when pressed against a wall, he had only the directness of a soldier.

"I sought the aid of Egypt because I did not know the intentions of Shalmanezer."

"And why did you not know his intention? What cause had you to think him different than Pileser? Who would advise in such a way?"

"Pileser himself," Hoshea said through clenched teeth.

"Ah, so Pileser and you had your heads together!"

"We understood one another."

"Then let us be understood as well! You, for your false dealing, and for the tribute you did not bring, will enjoy the comfort of my own prison. And your people — your proud and arrogant kinsmen — shall enjoy the edge of the sword of steel!"

"You will pay dearly for every foot of Israel's soil."

"Now we see the true man. I regret you will not see the fall of your people — your women ripped open, your children slaughtered, your wealthy and powerful herded like cattle into captivity. Ha! Now shall the haughty merchants of Israel bend their necks and the proud daughters of Samaria lose their robes to the warriors of Assyria.

"Take him away! Take him away! To my deepest dungeon . . . until I think of some delicious way of killing him."

Hoshea wheeled from Shalmanezer's presence and walked out of the marbled throne room between four heavily armed Assyrian guards, holding himself erect and proud. His stomach churned with the helpless, impotent anger that grips a man when he knows, beyond all doubt, that he has failed.

Chapter 39

The Fall of Samaria

1

The outlands of Israel fell quickly. In Galilee whole villages vanished before the marauding Assyrians. Israel's soldiers saw no end to the chariots and men flooding toward them from the East. Except for the rapacity of the invaders, Israel's army might have been destroyed altogether. The Assyrians stopped to plunder every village they passed through. They hobbled old men behind their chariots and dragged them through the streets, for they knew Israel venerated age. Young women they raped and brutally murdered, children they slaughtered with shouting and laughter. Another generation of Israelites would never raise arms against Assyria. No person, young or old, male or female, escaped the fury of the invader. Farmers and villagers deserted their homes, carrying with them what they could, and fled toward Samaria before the awesome, slashing sword of steel.

By the third day the streets of Samaria were jammed with refugees, and still they streamed in from North and East, each wave bringing more fearsome tales of the ferocity and might of the Assyrian. The city prepared desperately for siege.

Word of Hoshea's capture reached Samaria ahead of the advancing armies. The people floundered without a leader, bewildered by the awful calamity engulfing them. Dire warnings of Assyria had sounded within Samaria's walls for years, and nothing ever happened. The people learned to ignore the warnings, turn a deaf ear to unpleasant words. Now, suddenly, the verity of it loomed beyond the horizon. They found themselves unhappily without king or ruler.

The city became strangely silent in the desperation of the hour. Hosea moved among the people but he spoke no words. People crowded around him, pleading that he call down angels from Heaven to save Israel. A frail, bony-cheeked woman grasped his arm and babbled out the story that her husband and children were slain in Hazor of Galilee; only one son, seven years old, remained alive. She pleaded for Hosea to entreat the LORD's blessing on her only son, that she not be left helpless and alone in her old age. Country folk, who had heard of Hosea only by name, sought him out, hoping for some prophecy of encouragement.

Hosea had no word for them, except repentance and prayers for mercy. No prophecy or promise came to his lips, no word of hope that Israel could escape the onslaught of Shalmanezer's chariots.

2

On the sixth day the retreating army of Israel stumbled through the gates of Samaria, ragged and weary from their hopeless battle with the soldiers of Shalmanezer. Wives and mothers rushed to the gate when the word was called out, searching the columns of soldiers for the face of a husband or a son. Those who found the one they sought screamed hysterically and rushed to the loved one's arms, the horror of the hour forgotten in the sweet moment of reunion. Others grasped the arms of the warriors, glassy-eyed with fatigue, and inquired frantically after this or that certain man. Many turned tearfully to their homes. More than half of Israel's warriors lay slain or hopelessly abandoned on the blood-tracked road to Samaria.

The last soldier was not an hour through the gate before the chariots of Shalmanezer rode over the horizon. Quickly, the gates were triple-barred. The defending army mounted the wall to meet the first thrust against the city. The horizon blackened with the advancing hordes. Like unnumbered locusts they swarmed up the slopes of Samaria's high hill, some mounted, some in chariots, some on foot . . . all brandishing the glistening sword of steel.

On the north wall three great ladders were brought up and pitched against the wall. Foot-warriors scrambled up the ladders, swords drawn. Israel's defenders swarmed to the point of attack, smashing down on the Assyrians with heavy stone mallets. Two, three, and then six fell away, but still they came on. Two fought their way to the wall's top and slashed down three defenders before they were hurled back. The defenders fetched up a notched pole and toppled the ladders backward, crushing four Assyrians beneath the heavy timbers.

At the small west gate of the city the attacking army wheeled up a huge battering ram, wielded by thirty men. Israel's bowmen raced to the west wall, raining down arrows on the men at the ram. Assyria's bowmen answered the volley, felling the front rank of Israel. Answering Israelite arrows whistled through the air. In seven minutes time more than two hundred warriors, on both sides, lay dead or wounded. The Assyrian forces left the battering ram in the dust outside Samaria's west gate and withdrew out of range.

Six hours the fighting raged. The Assyrians arced flaming torches over the wall. They tried again, at other points, to breach the wall by ladder. They felled Israel's defenders by sword, spear, and arrow. But before nightfall the men of Shalmanezer withdrew and camped down in a wide circle around Samaria's walls. Seventeen hundred warriors lay dead around the walls of the city. Samaria was better defended than Shalmanezer had supposed.

3

All through the night and the following day the weary soldiers of Israel stood watch, catching short, fitful sleep when they dared, dreading the next onslaught of the Assyrian. A second day passed, and then a third. The watchmen could see the camp of the enemy and the warriors of Assyria moving about, half dressed, unarmed, showing little concern for the seizure of the city. A week went by and Shalmanezer mounted no further attack.

The Assyrian strategy became evident. Samaria could not long feed the mass of people crowded inside her walls. Shalmanezer had no need to sacrifice his warriors in an attempt to take the city by force. He had only to wait.

To amuse themselves, the warriors of Assyria raided villages and farmlands in the west of Israel and paraded their captives outside Samaria's walls. Israel's watchmen looked on powerlessly, as gray-bearded patriarchs were lashed to the back of chariots and dragged around the walls of the city until they were dead. Pregnant women were ripped open and left to crawl up toward the wall of the city, their lifeblood spilling out, wailing piteously for help that would never come. Virgins of Israel were violated in open sight of Samaria's walls. Young warriors, stripped naked, were sent running toward the wall, only to be cut down by spear or arrow before they reached the safety of the city's gate. Those who watched from the wall could only curse the Assyrian and wait helplessly for the day a like fate would befall those within.

4

A full moon came and went and came again. The tension of waiting grew unendurable. Not able to band together in a common struggle, the people of Samaria split hopelessly apart. Their stolid determination to join together and fight gave way to petty disagreements or common foolishness. They rioted in the city for any cause, or no cause at all. They raided storehouses in the temple and palace enclosures and recklessly wasted the food. They lived like a drunken man who knows he is about to die and flings one last challenge at the stars. Wine flowed in the inns. Cries against looting, murder, and rape went unheeded. Restraint gave way to lawlessness.

The people who first flocked to Hosea, pleading for God to save them, now turned to howl derision at his prophecies. Death and destruction gave up their meaning. The grim reality camped outside the wall of the city was strangely answered by passion and gluttony within the walls — each moment lived as though it were the last. No leader rose up to fire their hopes or capture their loyalty. Only the lonely voice of the prophet, and he was unheard in the tumult.

5

I felt driven to the marketplace, though the people mocked every word I spoke. The armies of Assyria camped outside our walls. I cried out to the people, but Israel would not listen.

"Howl in the day of the LORD!" I cried out over the tumult in the market place. "Howl, for the destruction is at hand. You have forgotten the law of your God, and I will forget you, says the LORD."

"Preach to the Assyrians, son of a madman!" shouted a beardless youth.

"Repent, says your God!"

"If the LORD would have us repent, let him destroy the chariots of Shalmanezer!"

"When the LORD would restore the fortunes of his people, the corruption and wickedness of Israel are revealed. The thief breaks in, bandits raid without mercy, Samaria is a city of evildoers, tracked with blood; robbers lie in wait, and priests band together. You have plowed iniquity; you have reaped injustice. You have eaten the fruit of lies. You trusted foolishly in your chariots and in the multitude of your warriors. Who can help you, who can help you now, O Israel? Where is your king to save you? Where are your captains to defend you?"

"Baal is our defender!"

"Where is Baal in the day of battle? Shalmanezer took the cities of Galilee. Mothers he dashed in pieces with their children. So will he do in Samaria. Samaria shall bear her guilt because she has rebelled against her God. You shall fall by the sword of steel, your little ones shall be dashed in pieces, and your pregnant women ripped open — so the LORD has sworn by his righteousness!"

"Here is 'righteousness' for you!"

A stone whistled through the air and struck me on the arm.

People knew that I suffered no one to attack me in the body. My strength was known.

"Let him step forth, this one who throws stones like an old beggar woman!" I shouted with contempt.

The crowd quieted. No one chose to join the young soldier who had thrown the stone. The tenseness in the crowd gave way to harmless mumbling. I made my way through the crowd, toward our home, heavy of step.

When would it end — the headlong descent to catastrophe, the reckless abandon of law and restraint?

When would the LORD lift from me the call to prophesy, when take away the words burning on my lips, the cries of doom, the foretelling of destruction? When would the awful turmoil be quit within my breast, and my aching soul find rest?

6

In the middle of the afternoon the day grew ominously dark. Lightning streaked across the sky, and roll after roll of thunder rumbled in the heavens. Pelting rains swept the streets of the city. Thousands of homeless refugees crowded into the temple, crept beneath carts in the market square, or huddled forlornly against the side of a building, out of the wind. Never had the latter rains continued so late into the heat of summer, or come so suddenly, with crashing thunder.

And then a deeper rumbling was heard, a rumbling that grew to an ear-shattering roar. The earth trembled and shook. Walls of houses collapsed to the ground. Two pillars of the temple cracked loose at the base and toppled the roof overhanging the outer court. Great fissures split the stone paving of the market place.

Earthquake!

The Assyrian hordes poured in through two giant gaps torn in the wall of Samaria. Screams of women and children rent the air.

"The judgment of the LORD!" went up the cry.

Deep-throated curses, in a guttural tongue, rasped across the market place, through the palace of the king, in the temple enclosure. The chariots of Shalmanezer careened through the streets, smashing to the ground those who could not escape the churning wheels.

A young mother clutched a child in her arms and ran frantically down the narrow street toward her house. Before she could reach it an Assyrian horseman rode after her, speared the child from her arms, and galloped off, waving the babe aloft on the blade of steel.

Anakah the High Priest cowered helplessly in a corner of his private quarters, pleading with seven of the invaders that the king had seized the temple treasury, and he had nothing. The leader spat in his face and pressed a steel point to his belly.

"Where is it hidden?"

Anakah led them to seven hidden caches of money, swearing that each was the last. But at each stop the insistent point of steel urged him to uncover another hidden store.

When at last he had exhausted his secret treasury, the Assyrians had become so satisfied of his dishonesty that they plunged the sword of steel into his belly when he would not lead them to more money.

"I do believe we got it all," the leader laughed. "He loved his life more than his wealth."

They lugged their booty out of the temple, leaving Anakah prostrate and bleeding on the floor of the temple. Anakah's blurred vision fixed momentarily on the one object the invaders had not bothered to take — the simple leather girth given him by his father the day he became a priest. Then his eyes rolled back in death.

A band of eighty Israelite warriors tried to set up a defense by the north wall of the city, jamming a barricade of carts and bales into a hasty, makeshift fortress. Word raced through the ranks of the Assyrians that some Israelites were making a fight of it on the north wall, and a thousand foot soldiers, horsemen, and chariots descended on the hapless Israelites. The chariots sped past the fortress, snagged the carts and bales with short grappling hooks, and opened a breach for the foot warriors. Seven abreast, the Assyrians slashed into the ranks of Israel. Once inside the fortress they fanned out, letting more of their comrades follow after them. They divided the Israelites, cut them down, and sent some of them rushing out of the fortress into the street of the city, only to be chopped down by waiting horsemen.

In every street and alley of the city was seen the flashing sword of steel. Women hid in their closets, frozen with dread, clutching babes to the breast with a hand held over the mouth to keep the babe from crying. Soldiers threw down their weapons and sought places to hide. Crowds of refugees, with no homes to hide in, bunched together in the market place, seeking protection in the heaving cushion of human bodies. Like a great tree, dead and hollowed by the eating of a thousand thousand insects, Samaria collapsed to the ground before the keen, hard blade of the Assyrian.

7

Jezreel, Loruhamah, and Loammi huddled against me, clutching at my robe. We made no move when four Assyrian warriors burst through the door of our house. The children watched, terrified, as the Assyrians stripped the house of everything they wanted and smashed what they had no use for.

"Money — where is your money?"

I could not understand their speech, but understood the gesture of the thumb brushing across fingers. I pointed to an earthen jar where our little money was kept.

"More?" the lead soldier said, turning the jar upside down.

"I have no more," I said, shaking my head. I rose to my feet, swaying unsteadily. I had barely eaten or slept in the last days of the siege.

The Assyrians growled their dissatisfaction at the poor loot. One of them seized Jezreel and threw him against the opposite wall. Jezreel fell to the floor, howling with terror.

I summoned my strength, stood to my full height, and lunged at the Assyrian, smashing a fist into the side of his head. Another soldier swung at me with his sword. I whirled aside. The blow whistled past my head. I kicked out, hitting the man in the groin.

"Kill him!" the Assyrian shrieked in his native tongue, doubling with pain.

Now in command of myself, I sprang behind the other two soldiers, gripping my arms about their necks. They crashed to the floor, I on top of them. I smashed their heads together and sprang to my feet.

The soldier I had first attacked raised his sword. I struck him a second blow full in the face. The sword clattered to the floor, the man fell face down on top of it.

The soldier I had kicked struggled to his feet. I wrenched the sword from his hand and pressed the point to his neck. "Out! Out!" I commanded. The Assyrian could not understand my speech. I swept the sword toward the door and said again, "Out! Out!"

I clamped the sword under my arm and picked up the two men I had driven to the floor. I carried them, one in each hand, to the door and threw them into the street. The soldier who was still standing swayed uncertainly on his feet.

"All of you!" I shouted, pointing to the soldier face down on the floor. The standing soldier reached down and grasped the arm of his fallen comrade, but he could not lift him. I picked the fallen man up by the scruff of his tunic and carried him to the door, dragged him out into the street and let him fall face down in the dirt, still senseless. I took the sword again in my hand. The last soldier stumbled into the street. He cowered back, his hands raised protectively. I shook my head, threw the sword to the ground where he could pick it up, and waved the soldier off toward the east gate. The soldier looked at his three fallen comrades and staggered away toward the east gate of the city, not knowing whether his companions were alive or dead. I turned back to the house.

I knelt to the floor, still heaving from the struggle. The children huddled together where Jezreel had fallen. Suddenly I overheard the notable Voice: *Say to your brother, "My people," and to your sister, "She has obtained mercy."*

Loruhamah huddled beside Jezreel, against the west wall, still trembling at the great violence she had witnessed. I held out an arm to her. "Come," I said. She edged cautiously toward me. "Come," I implored. She came slowly to my outstretched arm, her great eyes wide, strangely fearful. I drew her to myself. "No more *Loruhamah*," I whispered. "*Ruhamah* shall be your name. 'You Have Found Pity.' *Ruhamah*, 'You have found love.'"

Tears beyond her years or understanding coursed down her cheeks. She wound her little arms around my neck. "Father," she spoke the word uncertainly. Then pulling herself close to my ear, for the first time ever she spoke the word, "Dada," seeming to test the word that had always belonged to Jezreel, never to her.

I rose to my feet, still holding Ruhamah in my arm. I crossed to Loammi. I lifted the boy into my other arm. "No more *Lo*ammi," I said, looking straight into his eyes. "*Ammi* shall be your name. 'You Are My People.'"

"Ammi," I repeated, putting my lips against his ear. "'My people.'"

I turned and spoke to Jezreel. "You have heard?" I asked. "Call your brother *Ammi*, call your sister *Ruhamah*."

Jezreel stood silent.

"Have you heard?" I demanded.

Jezreel nodded and repeated, "Ruhamah. Ammi."

Part Four

Captivity

"Return, O Israel, to the LORD your God,
For you have stumbled because of your iniquity.
Take with you words and return to the LORD."

Chapter 40

Deported

1

The following day, four Assyrian soldiers stood guard on a great pile of loot stacked against the double row of evergreen oak that bordered the property of Diblaim. The shout and tumult of battle had died away; the Assyrian captains brought their men under discipline. The grim aftermath of conquest set in.

The conquerors designated Diblaim's house as one gathering place for the share of booty allotted to Shalmanezer. Diblaim himself they marked for deportation. Any person of rank — any potential leader — they carried back to Assyria so a vanquished people would have no person to spearhead a revolt. The farmers and artisans were left to produce their wealth for Shalmanezer.

Diblaim wandered aimlessly through the empty rooms of his house, looted of everything of value. The wall in the center room was split from floor to ceiling by the earthquake. Nothing left. Nothing. The prophecies of Hosea — they had been right, as he knew they were. Yet one can never truly imagine desolation and utter destruction until it stands naked before the eyes. Even then, part of it lies hidden behind a stubborn screen of denial.

"Might I go to the south of the city, to see after my grandchildren?" Diblaim asked the soldier who guarded the entrance to his house; some of the leading Assyrian warriors understood a little of the Israelite tongue.

"You are to remain in your house."

"It is only a short way. I will return in an hour."

Diblaim had regularly visited the children when they stayed with Deborah or were left alone for short periods by Hosea. A sense of shame oppressed him whenever he went there — shame of Gomer, and of himself. He knew that by his indulgence he had not been a proper father to her — indeed, had laid seeds that grew to bitter fruit in her marriage.

Yet now, when he found himself shorn of his wealth and property, he thought warmly of Gomer. Even a ruined family bond offered more hope than the nothingness that surrounded him.

A captain, walking quickly on tour of the house to see that nothing of value was missed, heard Diblaim asking if he might visit his daughter's children.

"Who is your daughter married to?" the captain asked brusquely.

"Hosea, the son of Beeri."

"What does he do?"

"He is a priest."

"An Israelite priest? Is he a soothsayer? A fortune teller?"

"He is a man of God, as we say in our land."

"A religious leader, then?"

"Yes, he is that."

"Very well. You may go and visit your grandchildren. Return back here within the hour."

"I shall! I shall!"

Diblaim pushed by the guard and out past the evergreen oaks before the captain might think to change his mind.

"Report to the commander's tent outside the city," the captain ordered the guard. "See if this man called Hosea son of Beeri is among those going to Assyria. If he is not, report that I have discovered he is a religious leader — that *I have discovered*, you understand?"

"I shall do as you order."

"If he is not among those already captured, take two men and bring him here yourself. Any beggar can be a priest among these Israelites, it seems."

"The captain is wise in seeking them out." The guard knew how to please the captain.

"It is a simple matter of asking the right question at the right time." The captain straightened his helmet and strutted out into the yard.

2

After the earthquake, Assyrian chariots wheeled to the west and south. They met no resistance; Israel's entire army had been assembled to defend Samaria.

In Bethel, according to orders, the Assyrian commander went straight to the house of Judas ben Ishbaal.

"This man has wealth," he was told. "Find it. Strip his house bare. Maim and kill as you must, but find it. All of it. Load the plunder on his own camels and oxen and wagons and put them in a caravan back to Assyria."

"And the man himself? What with him?" the commander asked.

"A leader. Attach him to the caravan."

The Assyrians surrounded the property of Judas and entered the main house. No struggle was mounted against them. Judas rose from his seat in the main hall and welcomed the commander to his humble dwelling. At his side stood a scribe who knew the Assyrian tongue.

Judas quickly learned that his lifelong habit of bargaining and coming to favorable agreements had no place in the plans of the Assyrians. He was told to set his servants to gathering all his goods, especially gold and silver and precious stones, and pack them into a caravan bound for Assyria. When he demurred, taking it as the first step in bargaining to an agreement, the commander stepped in front of Judas, drew his sword and pressed the point hard against Judas' chest.

"Assemble and pack the caravan in four hours time," he said. "Anything discovered after four hours will earn you stripes — uncomfortable companions on your journey to Assyria."

"My journey — ?"

"You have spent your last day in Bethel. You are deported to Assyria, you and thirty who exercise foremost authority under you."

Judas' face fell. "I — I can gain wealth — taxes — here in Israel," he stuttered. "I know the land. I will be no value to you in Assyria. I can do nothing —"

"Your value is that you do nothing — nothing to undermine our rule in Israel. In Assyria we will keep you under our eye."

The commander turned abruptly and strode away. "You have four hours," he repeated at the door.

"What of my family?" Judas croaked.

"What family have you?"

"Wives. Concubines."

"Take one or two wives with you. The rest remain — except for their jewels!"

* * *

The huge red circle of the sun hung low in the western sky when the Assyrians finished their looting of Bethel. Four caravans of Judas' treasure merged into one long train. In the face of the onsetting darkness the train began its slow, methodical journey eastward.

Judas rode a camel in the middle of his caravan, hoping to remain as obscure as possible. Twice they had searched him for any hidden stash of gold or jewels and found nothing. One cache of gold shekels they missed; it hung in a pouch between his legs, high up.

In an ox-pulled wagon behind him rode his number nine wife, Miriam, and the scribe who understood Assyrian speech. "They are my wives," he said to the soldiers who herded him into the caravan, "and my chief scribe, who knows your tongue."

He had gone to Miriam's rooms and hurriedly instructed her. She was the cleverest and would be the biggest help to him. "I can take you in the caravan as one of my wives," he told her. "In the high room, above the main hall, there are scrolls. Go there but keep out of sight. Look for the scroll with a blue stripe at the bottom. Behind it is a box of gold shekels and four rubies. Hide them in a pouch drawn up high inside your legs. It will be our only bargaining tool."

3

On his way to Hosea's house Diblaim met them — Hosea and the three children.

"I was coming to you —" Diblaim began.

"We were coming to you." Hosea said. "It is no longer safe for us." Hosea quickly told him of his fight with the Assyrian soldiers.

Diblaim reached inside his robe to a special pocket sewed on the seam so it could not be detected from the outside. He pulled out three gold trinkets: all he was able to hide from the Assyrians.

"Little to show for a lifetime of saving," he said with hapless irony. "I thought for the children — someday they may be able to use them."

Two soldiers turned into the street and stopped short.

"Are either of you the man called Hosea the priest?" one asked in halting Israelite tongue.

"Yes, I am he." Hosea answered warily.

"Come with us."

"He? He is only a countryside priest," Diblaim objected.

"A religious leader. Come."

Diblaim opened his mouth to speak. He had unwittingly betrayed Hosea.

Hosea shook his head gently at Diblaim. "Very well," he said, falling in behind the soldiers, motioning the children to remain with Papa-Papa.

"Your family as well."

"I have no family."

"The children are his?" the man said.

"They are his grandchildren," Hosea said. "Their mother is gone."

"All of you come," the leader of the two said. "Walk between us."

Hosea and Diblaim followed the leading soldier. Jezreel held Hosea's hand, Ruhamah nestled in his arm. Diblaim carried Ammi. They walked through the quiet, quiet streets of Samaria.

The rubble of the earthquake littered the streets. In the north and east of the city the captives going to Assyria — the high born, the wealthy, the priesthood, captains in the army — stood already in columns, flanked by the foot soldiers and horsemen of Assyria. The farmers and artisans, who all their lives had grumbled at the sharp practices of the rich, now saw them in the long lines of captives and wondered how they would survive without them.

Hopeless despair shrouded both those who began to snake out the city gate and those who looked on. After eight hundred years the children of Israel started their slow march back into slavery. The freedom they had won so dearly when they followed Moses out of Egypt was lost, forever lost. The root that nourished it had withered away. Fierce loyalty to the LORD God of Israel had given way to the gaudy promises of the Baals, blooming like desert flowers a brief season, then withering under the sun and falling back into the barren earth.

The captives marched out of Samaria in long, mournful columns. East of the city they combined with other lines of prisoners from the east and south of Israel. Like a great, slow-moving snake it wended north and eastward, through the verdant fields of Jezreel, ankle-high with grain, to the hills and valleys of Galilee, across the plains of Bashan, and into the barren lands of Syria. Twenty-seven thousand strong they marched captive from the land they once entered as conquerors — their portion in the Land of Promise and in the inscrutable purpose of their God, lost beyond recall.

4

Caravans from the south wended north of Samaria, adding stray captives to their trains before turning eastward. Villagers and country folk who remained behind pressed into line along the way, slipping food and water to those trudging to an unknown future with their captors.

The caravans of Judas ben Ishbaal joined a train of two other caravans traveling east of Samaria. On their third night from Bethel they made camp opposite the village of Dothan. Most of the captives brought too little food for the journey, and their captors supplied them nothing. Judas, with his wife and Miriam and scribe, had a greater supply. They sat in a tight circle eating their evening fare of bread and cheese and raisin cakes, their backs to the other travelers.

"Gomer!" A woman's voice cried out from the line of villagers who came with food and water.

Gomer looked up, startled to hear her real name. She scanned the line of villagers.

"Gomer!" Shania stood in the front, waving a white cloth.

Gomer jumped up and half ran to the edge of the caravan. A soldier moved across her path, his hand upraised. "Not yet! They come by tens when we allow them."

"It is my sister!" Gomer shouted. "Sister! Sister!" she pleaded; she had already learned some words of Assyrian speech.

The soldier scratched a line in the dirt with his sword at the edge of the caravan and a small circle on either side of the line. With his sword he pointed to each of the circles, indicating that each must remain on her own side of the line.

Shania ran to the edge of the caravan. Obed followed and stopped some paces behind her. At the line in the dirt both women dropped to their knees and embraced one another.

"Sister! Dear my sister!" Shania gasped.

"Shania! What good fortune brings you here to find me?"

"The whole village comes to bring food and water to the captives in train. This is the second day. I never thought to find you."

"You and Obed — you are free?"

"Obed is a vintner. Not important enough for them."

"And you are well. Your child — ?"

"Children, my sister! Jeshurun has a baby brother, Jarmel." Gomer squeezed Shania. "I am glad."

"You — you are not alone?" Shania asked.

"I am with a man — Judas ben Ishbaal."

"Judas ben Ishbaal! You are wife to Israel's richest merchant?"

"Neither wife nor concubine, only his woman. In his house I am called Miriam."

Shania took Gomer by the shoulders and held her at arms' length. "Hosea would have you back. He said it to me."

Gomer's eyes misted with tears. "Much has happened. I live in another world."

"You sat with me when I gave birth to Jeshurun and spoke words from the scrolls, many words."

"I remember."

"Some of the words I still remember, one especially: 'The LORD, the LORD, a God merciful and gracious, slow to anger, and abounding in steadfast love and faithfulness' — love and faithfulness . . ." she faltered.

Gomer supplied the missing words, "'Keeping steadfast love for thousands, forgiving iniquity and transgressions and sin.'"

"Yes! Words for you, as they have been words for me. I do not remember all the words, but they have been the bedrock of my life — with Obed and with the LORD."

"I think of you often, dear sister," Gomer said, hugging Shania closer to herself. "If only I had as little need of forgiveness as you."

"You know me too little!"

Gomer lowered her voice, though their talk was well out of earshot. "Do you know anything of my children? My father? Hosea?"

"Nothing. It all happened so quickly. We heard no word from Samaria," Shania answered, echoing Gomer's hushed tone.

"They could still be in Samaria," Gomer ventured. "Or captive in one of the caravans."

Gomer nodded and bit her lower lip. Her voice trembled: "The children — will you go to Samaria and see if you can find them?"

"I will!" Shania answered, sensing Gomer's anguish.

"If something has happened to Hosea — if the children are alone —"

"Obed and I will take them," Shania said straightaway. "And you — " Shania stammered, "How will it go with you?"

"Everything has changed. Judas lost everything."

"Is he good to you?"

"Sometimes. He chose me over his wives and concubines."

"Ten steps forward to the caravan border!" a soldier shouted, pointing to the line of villagers standing by with food and water.

"Here," Shania said, pushing three sacks toward Gomer. "Take it all — bread and sweet cakes, water, two skins of wine."

"Be blessed four times over," Gomer said, embracing Shania again. "You bring a happy beginning to our long journey."

"May the God of Israel go with you, dear my sister. 'Keeping steadfast love, forgiving iniquity and transgressions and sin.' Do I have the words right?" Gomer nodded and took the sacks of food in her arms.

"Move on, move on," a soldier shouted. He grasped Gomer's arm and pushed her back into the caravan.

Shania burst into tears and walked backward to where Obed stood, continuing to look after Gomer.

"Who was that?" Judas asked when Gomer returned to him. "What did she call you?"

"She is the sister of my husband. She called me by my name, Gomer."

"So you come from this village. And you have a husband."

"My husband once lived here. We are no longer together."

"What did she give you?" Judas asked, reaching for one of the sacks.

The guard who stood by grabbed the sack out of Judas' hands before he could open it and took the other two sacks from Gomer. He rummaged through the sacks, took out the wineskins, and threw the sacks to the ground.

"The wine is not for you." He grasped Gomer by the arm and pulled her to her feet. "Perhaps she gave you something else as well, now hidden in your robe?"

He ran his hands up and down her robe, between her breasts, down her legs to the bottom of her robe, then slowly up the inside of her legs. High up his fingers paused and flicked something side to side that hung between her legs.

He lifted the bottom of the robe and thrust it into Gomer's hands. "Hold it!" he commanded. He pulled a knife from his waistband and cut the string that held a small pouch high between her legs. He emptied the contents into his hands — more than twenty gold shekels and four rubies.

"Ha! This is from Bethel. Nicely hidden, but not nicely enough! You have earned yourself stripes!" He quickly pocketed ten of the shekels and two rubies. "Captain!" he shouted.

A captain he did not know came across from the other side of the caravan. The soldier reported that he had searched the woman after she received three sacks of food from the local people and found she had a hidden treasure pouch under her gown. He handed the half-empty pouch to the captain.

The captain stood face to face with the soldier, saying nothing. Some moments passed. He held the soldier's eyes in a stony stare, still did not speak. The soldier reached slowly into the pocket of his jerkin, pulled out seven shekels and a ruby, and dropped them into the pouch. The captain continued to look at him, not speaking. The soldier reached into his pocket again and came out with the rest of the shekels and the second ruby and dropped them into the pouch. The captain shook the pouch down. Now it was full. He tied it off and put it in his own pocket.

The soldier gulped a mouthful of air; he had been holding his breath with the captain standing silent before him. Most captains inspired fear by shouts and threatening. This one was dreadfully silent.

"Beat her," the captain ordered. "Fifteen stripes."

The soldier took a lash from his belt and ordered Gomer to her knees. He ripped the robe from her shoulders, baring her back. He swung the lash against Gomer's back with loud shouting. The first strokes Gomer bore in silence. Then she cried out and sank face down on the ground as the lashing went on to fifteen strokes.

"These are together?" the captain asked, pointing to the others.

The soldier said they were.

"Search them as well. If you find stolen treasure on any of them, beat them. Fifteen stripes. Bring them and their stolen treasure to me — all of it! Do you understand?"

"I understand!" the soldier said in a quavering voice.

The captain took Gomer by the arm and lifted her up. "Follow me," he ordered. He started across to the other side of the caravans without looking back. Gomer looked at Judas, her hands turned up in a helpless gesture. Judas looked away. Gomer limped after the quiet Assyrian captain.

Fresh from his search of Gomer, the soldier searched the scribe and wife number nine. He found no hidden treasure.

Last, he searched Judas. He found gold shekels in the same place Gomer hid her treasure, a pouch hung between his legs, high up.

Judas pointed to wife number nine and spoke quickly to his scribe. "Tell him he can take my wife as a slave if he overlooks the pouch."

"Show me your back," the soldier retorted. He would not trust himself a second time to deceive the quiet captain.

Judas pulled the robe off his shoulders and knelt in front of the soldier. The soldier struck him fifteen heavy blows. Judas stumbled after the soldier to the other side of the caravan, the richest man in Israel bereft of all but the robe and sandals he wore.

* * *

Shania and Obed observed all this across the span that separated the local people from the caravans. Even as she fell weeping to her knees, Shania began to form a plan for Gomer's rescue.

Chapter 41

Life in the New Land

1

In Assyria the captive Israelites were settled into compact communities along the Habor and Gozan rivers, south of the sharp rises to Mount Kasius and midway between the Tigris and Euphrates rivers. The new life they faced demanded skills and resources they had long forgotten. In Israel, with one shrewd exchange, a merchant could make as much money as a craftsman grubbed together in a whole year. But here, in the new land, they had no wealth to exchange, no merchant system, only scant substance to fend off starvation and exposure, if one had the will to work for it.

Men who had never handled a farming tool in their life found themselves wielding hoe and scythe with sore, blistered hands. Silver-haired elders, who never thought of a weaver or carpenter or smith except as someone to swindle to the lowest price, sat patient apprentice to the few artisans taken into captivity.

Women who had expended no greater effort than to raise their voice for a servant took up the tedious tasks of household — cooking, cleaning, mending, keeping after the children. Strangely, many found a simple contentment in the daily round of activity; a sense of purpose and usefulness they had forgotten. Female instincts, long buried, rose up with a sweet familiarity. In Samaria and Bethel, some rich women had looked on childbearing as a tedious inconvenience, an unpleasant intrusion into the round of activities. Now the conception of life in the womb fulfilled a longing in the captives, a sense of re-birth, a new beginning.

The first baby born into the East Gozan community brought a stream of visitors and well-wishers to the mother's bedside — friends, acquaintances, and total strangers welded together by a feeling of community, a sense that the newborn child established again their identity as a people. The radiant happiness of the mother, holding the babe to her breast, brought tears to the eyes of some of the women, who happily confided that they too were with child. Another betrayed a look of poignant envy that turned to a puckering smile when she took the arm of her husband and whispered as they walked home that she had saved the food; tonight she would prepare his favorite meal.

Slowly, and with toilsome hard work, the captive Israelites took up the threads of their new life. A late crop was planted and harvested, though it did not reach full growth. Mud brick houses rose up in place of tents and makeshift lean-tos. In each community stood a tent or shelter for the worship of the God of Israel.

An upsurge of faith spread through their communities. In the face of the Assyrian conquerors, one reality set them apart and molded them together — the God of Israel.

Now the deepest hurt of their tragic experience struck home: in so long mingling worship of the God of Moses with worship of the Baals, they had lost the liberty of serving Israel's God as a people. A note of sorrow marred the re-discovery of the LORD, a haunting awareness that while they might pray to Him and know Him as families, they wondered whether they any more counted as a chosen people in the purposes of God. To other hands would be entrusted the inscrutable purposes of the LORD. This was the melancholy of some who studied the writings.

2

In the East Gozan community, several hundred cubits closer to the river than the worship tent which stood at the center of the community, Hosea built a small house and carpenter shop. In the rush of harvest he had lent help in the fields and left the finishing of his dwelling for later. Now, in the sixth month after arriving in the new land, the house stood finished to the eye, though still unfinished in the final work of sealing the walls and coating the roof with tree gum.

Working early in the carpenter shop, as was his habit, Hosea one morning looked up quite without thinking. A woman stood in the doorway, the sun behind her, so that he could see her outline but not her features. His heart leaped. The small waist and gentle sweep of the hips was like Gomer. The woman stepped inside, and then he saw her face and knew he was mistaken. It was a slender oval face with quiet, deep-pooled eyes.

"Hello." Her low melodious voice marked her as not from Samaria, more likely from Bethel or perhaps a coastal village. "I am a near neighbor. I do not believe we have met."

"No, we have not. I am Hosea, a carpenter."

"Yes, I know. That is why I have come. I have a door that broke off the hinges. I live on the short west-running street just off your own, fifty cubits down. I am Rachel bath Ebenezer."

"Rachel?"

"Yes."

"That is odd."

"Why?"

"It was my mother's name. It is not often heard any more."

"I have been Rachel all my life," the woman laughed. A warm, friendly smile, Hosea thought.

"May I see to your door when I finish this wagon wheel? It is promised for today."

"Yes, most certainly." The woman lingered a moment, quietly surveying Hosea with a look midway between musing and proper reserve. "You are the prophet, are you not?"

"Yes." Hosea answered quietly and did not look up from his bench.

"I was from Joppa. I heard of you, before they came." The Israelites always spoke of their captors impersonally.

"Your husband was — what? A merchant?" Hosea asked.

"Yes. He is dead."

"Since coming?"

"He died on the way. He was not well."

"Then you live alone?"

"With my son, twelve years. You also have children and are alone?" Immediately she said this the woman felt she had been overbold in giving away the real purpose of her visit. Old manners and customs did not fit well in the new community. One had to be practical, lay old customs and manners aside when necessary. She was a widow, with a son to look after. This tall carpenter was also without a mate, with children to care for. She had loosed the door hinge with her own hand; it was as good a way as any to make the young carpenter's acquaintance.

"Yes," Hosea answered softly, "I am alone."

"It is strange, is it not, how half a year can so change our life?"

"Passing strange. And yet, they have not treated us badly, have given us a fertile strip of land, and leave us unmolested if we pay the tax without protest."

"Do you grow lonely for Israel?"

"More at some times than others. But carpentry is carpentry the world over." He laughed a little.

"When they took me from my home in Joppa, I thought I would die. Yet, one gets along somehow. Things that were so necessary and important are really . . . not so important. If — if I were not alone, I think I could be almost content here."

Hosea glanced at the woman to see if he rightly grasped her meaning. She parted her lips in a faint, half questioning smile. Hosea returned the smile but with reserve. She took this as passable gain for their first meeting and bid him farewell.

Hosea watched after her and thought she was a comely woman, though perhaps older than he by a few years. His sorrow over Gomer clung to him with stubborn severity. Another love would not easily dislodge it.

3

The Assyrian Captain had taken the Israelite woman as his personal slave. Throughout the fighting corps he was known as "The Quiet One," but with the silent afterthought, *Beware! He hears and knows everything.*

The Captain soon found he had more than a bedmate in the fair-skinned Israelite who called herself Gomer. She quickly learned the Assyrian tongue. When he came to her, he often fell to talking with her, sometimes for more than an hour. Oddly, though she was a foreigner, he felt no need to threaten her with his stony silences.

Gomer well knew how to talk with a man. She plied him with questions about his land and his people. She told him something of Israel's history and people, for he seemed endlessly curious to learn of the world beyond Assyria. And she possessed an unerring instinct for sensing when to steer the talk back to him, his family, his hopes and dreams.

The Quiet Captain stood high in the court of Shalmanezer because of his uncanny instinct for detecting weakness in an enemy. He would secretly spy out an enemy land before a military campaign, blending in with the people like a common workman, a master of disguise.

The Captain was not married. He had no concubines. When Gomer came to the house he had four servants: an armed trooper sworn to defend the Captain with his life, a stable hand to bring along the horses that followed him into battle, never less then three, and two female servants to see to house and food, both attractive and bed-ready.

Gomer soon became the Captain's favorite: the first one he sought out when he returned from a mission, which roused the ire of the servants, all Assyrian. They were little above slaves themselves, but she was lower. An Israelite. She did not belong.

Once Gomer thought to escape, simply walk away when the Captain was absent. She left early one morning, before the sun was up. By midday she was at a well drawing water, two communities to the West, weary and without food. She had not realized what a stranger she was in the land, how ill-prepared she was to survive on her own. She turned around and returned to the Captain's house. In Assyria she had nothing. She did not belong. In the Captain at least she had a friend.

She arrived past sunset, tired and terribly hungry. She went to the main house, where the food was stored. She found a box with bread and cheese and began to eat. Suddenly she heard a footfall behind her. Before she could turn, she felt a savage blow across her back, then another and another and another, driving her to her knees.

"What are you doing? Stealing food?" screeched Arian, the gardener and cook.

"I am hungry," Gomer cried. "I have not eaten today."

"Yes, where have you been all day? Out whoring in the city? I am the cook in this house. You eat what I prepare and when I prepare it, or you eat nothing."

She struck Gomer again across the back with the rod she was carrying. "You are a slave, never forget it," she spat out.

* * *

The Captain returned four days later. He sent for Gomer after he had rested.

"You walk stiffly," he said as she entered his room.

Gomer shook her head, as though to dismiss it as nothing. The Captain stood up. He faced her but said nothing. It was the first time he had met her with his stony silence.

"It is nothing," Gomer said.

The Captain did not speak. Gomer knew she could not out-stare him. He once held a soldier in stony silence for more than an hour. She turned and lowered her robe, exposing three cruel welts.

"Who did this?" he asked, his voice suddenly hard.

"It is no matter," Gomer answered.

"Tell me who," he demanded.

"Arian. I was taking food."

He strode to the door and called in a loud voice. "Arian, to me, at once!"

Arian came running. When she saw Gomer, naked to the waist, showing her back, she gasped in panic. The Captain looked her straight in the face, not speaking.

"She was stealing food," Arian quailed.

The Captain continued looking at her, not speaking. She knew she must say something more, or take a beating. The words tumbled out, "She was gone the whole day."

"Who gave you authority to beat my slave?" he asked with dread calm.

Arian sank weeping to the floor, covering her head with her hands. "She distresses the peace of your house. She is not one of us."

"Nor you either, any longer. Pack your belongings into a small trunk. You go to the slave market in Khorsabad in ten days."

"Oh! Give me hope!" Arian cried out. "I will serve you without fault."

"Stand to your feet. Fetch olive oil to soothe Gomer's welts. While you await Khorsabad, you are Gomer's servant, night and day."

"Oh yes! Oh yes!" Arian moaned.

The Captain walked out of the room without another word or backward glance.

* * *

Gomer waited each day for the Captain to come by, to see how she was, perhaps to talk. He did not come.

On the fifth day Arian reported the Captain had been dispatched by Shalmanezer to spy out the war power of Babylon in the south. Gomer never saw him again.

The Captain's armed trooper was left in charge of the household. He knew how things stood: Arian was to be sold at the next slave market in Khorsabad, leaving himself, the stable hand, the second female servant, and the Israelite woman.

Arian waited on Gomer, according to the Captain's last command, but ever more resentfully as the day of Khorsabad drew closer. The day she was taken away, she came into the Gomer's room and spit on the floor. "That for you!" she hissed. "You have come into this house and ruined my life."

"I meant you no ill," Gomer said quietly. "I would gladly have been your friend."

"Ha! What friendship between us born between the Rivers and you whipped dogs brought in from the West? You are not one of us. They should have killed you back there." The trooper's voice bellowed from outside. "Should have killed you all," she muttered as she stalked from the room, "but they want the tax."

The next day the trooper came into Gomer's room and threw off the blanket that covered her on the bed. Captains allowed servants access to their women, except a wife, and his Captain was unmarried. He began to take off his outer cloak. Gomer realized he was about to come into her bed and have her. "You cannot," she protested. "I am only for the Master."

"You are for any of us who want you," he said flatly, dropping to the bed beside her.

Two days later, the stable hand came to her bed.

* * *

In the days that followed, Gomer came to realize that Arian had more than disliked her — had truly hated her. From the other servants she now felt the same hate. The remaining female servant doled out food sparingly. Gomer went to bed hungry night after night. Two weeks went by. Soon Six. Seven.

"What have I to look forward to in this land?" she thought to herself as she lay in bed. "One man in Assyria has been kind to me, the quiet Captain. He has gone.

"Everything in my life is lost to me. I am lost to my land. Lost to my native tongue. Lost to my husband. Lost to Jezreel and Loruhamah and Loammi. Lost to Shania, my dearest friend. Lost to my lovers. Lost to Mother and Father, Mother already dead."

A wan smile traced itself across Gomer's lips. She knew beforehand where it would all lead. Since her days in Bethel, Gomer had come to behold the silent nothingness of death without fear; sometimes with longing. She nodded quietly, thinking with remorse of those that hovered on the border of her remembering. Hosea. The children. Father. Mother. "Forgive me," she whispered.

"In this land I am hated. In this land I will never belong. In this land I will die."

She began to eat only part of the small portions of food doled out to her.

4

For some time after the widow Rachel left his carpenter shop, Hosea did not return to his bench. A mood of quiet thinking settled on him, fairly gripped him. He mused that these moods had come more often in recent months.

Time, and the experience of captivity, had tempered Hosea. The memory of Gomer still disquieted his thoughts. He wondered whether in time he would forget his life with Gomer and build a new life in the new community. This was the advice of his friends, and even of Diblaim, also settled in the East Gozan community.

At night, as he lay awake on his bed and could not sleep, Hosea's thoughts went to Gomer. He wondered whether she still lived — in Samaria or down in Egypt, he supposed — whether she was lonely or in need, and whether she suffered. Imagining that she suffered, he felt suffering in himself. At times he hoped she were not alive, if her life were one of lonely suffering.

The deep instinct of Hosea to cling to those bonded to him, nurtured through years of grief and doubt and bitterness, had reached a flowering. His voice had grown quieter, more tender. Yet it lacked any note of cheer or happiness. Sorrow overlaid his quiet acceptance of God's will. Whenever for a moment he lost himself in something of his new life, the thought of Gomer returned to weigh on his mind and heart.

The LORD gave Gomer to him, then took her away. The giving was swallowed up in the taking. Surely this was the LORD's purpose in driving her away, finally to free him of her presence. Yet Hosea clung to her memory and an uncertain hope.

Why could he not let her go? Why?

Everyone urged him, "You must forget. Time will heal. Look forward, not back."

How simple it was for them, who thought only of her waywardness, knew nothing of her warmth and passion and loveliness. How could he forget the smile given to him alone, the rippling laughter that gave brightness to the dreariest day, the kiss and sweet caresses the night she became his bride? It was this, the unblemished loveliness of Gomer, to which Hosea clung. If only it could be returned, the crust of sin and guilt broken in pieces and swept away. He did not want to forget her, did not want to be quit of hope, though he had come quietly to accept that it was a hope he would carry to the grave.

So much of life stretched yet before him. Would each succeeding year lay another mark of sorrow and loneliness on his brow? Would he come to the end of his days with no greater wisdom than he now possessed? Would his prophecies be forgotten and he be remembered only as a man who could not forget a love any other man in Israel would be shamed to own?

Hosea gazed out the narrow door of his carpenter shop, where a slender shaft of morning light edged across the threshold. Tears blurred his vision. The old wound was open again. The pain and anguish. He fell to his knees and prayed for understanding and relief.

Chapter 42

Hosea's Prayer

In the months of captivity Hosea overheard no word of the
LORD, nor did he feel the presence of the LORD urging him to
speak to the people. Kneeling in his carpenter shop alone he be-
gan to pray, stumbling over words. For a time he remained silent.
Then the presence of the LORD came over him like in Samaria.
Words came to his lips, tumbling over one another as he spoke.

O LORD God of all this world,
Sun of righteousness and light of truth,
In my anguish comfort me with your presence;
Come near to me in my wretchedness,
Make Your table with my sorrow.

As a child, O God, even at my mother's breast,
You visited me,
And as a youth
I felt Your hand ever close.
Sometimes I wandered from you
And paid you slight heed;
Yet your hand was on me,
And your voice called me to return.

You called me to follow your prophet,
To heed his words and take them to heart.
Then You touched my own lips with coals of fire;
My tongue was a flame.

I spoke your word.
The fire rose in my breast
At the wickedness of your people;
Your wrath was kindled
Against their evil worship.

They went unfaithful from your bed
And played the harlot with Baal.
They fell from your covenant
And reveled in adultery.
Your right arm gave me strength
And supported me;
In all my speaking
The power of your Majesty supported me.

Then, O God, my heart was sad
And my spirit heavy.
I could preach no more;
Your wrathful words died on my lips.

A love I thought dearer than life
Turned bitter in my mouth.
A wife I thought lovelier
Than all flowers that ever grew
Corrupted the vows that made us one.
The vessel that was mine alone
Became the mug of all Israel.

My heart fails within me!
I cannot put her from me.
I cannot give her up.
Though she committed the sin before my eyes
I would want her.

What shall become of her?
Does she suffer?
Does she yet live?

If, in anger, I could condemn her
And put her away once for all,
Would you send me peace?
My heart wrenches within me.

O LORD, I am lonely, lonely, lonely.

Hosea collapsed to the floor of his little carpenter shop with no answer, no understanding — only bitter, bitter loneliness.

The old vision came to him again: the dream that frightened him from childhood — the cloud, the thunder and lightning, and the beckoning hand. And Hosea, spent and weary, too weary even to fear, dared for the first time to follow the beckoning hand.

For a time he was lost in a mist. Then, suddenly, he came out of the mist into a blinding, indescribable radiance. He covered his eyes and bowed his head. Slowly a strain of sound like music breathed into the air — soft, almost silent, like the whispering rise of the wind. Gently it swelled, so unnatural and compelling that Hosea scarcely dared breathe in its presence. Melodies of surpassing loveliness melted phrase to phrase, a haunting blend of sadness and joy. It spoke of sorrow and anguish, of love and compassion . . . so boundless that it surpassed understanding. The sound then grew more distant, seemed to pass into the light, and then the light dimmed.

Fearfully Hosea raised his eyes. For a moment he could not see and then, suddenly, he looked into the face of God. He saw the face of God streaked with tears, and in the eyes of God a sorrow so great, so deep, it stopped Hosea's breath. Through long ages, it seemed, the puzzled words of Amos came back to him: "The LORD will seek you out. He drew me close to His mouth. You, I think, He will draw close to His heart."

Hosea cried out and fainted from the vision.

After a time he rose to his knees. His face glowed with knowledge beyond his understanding. Suddenly Hosea saw deeper into the heart of God than any man who had lived to that day. With pain and joy trembling on his tongue, he spoke again to God, words coming of themselves to his lips, speaking the strangeness of the vision he had experienced.

Are you lonely, O God,
When your people stray?
Do you *suffer* when your people play the harlot?

How little, how little
I have understood.
I have murmured my complaint,
Blind to sorrow far greater than mine.
How little I have known,
How little.

The heart of the LORD is the lodge of
Love, mercy and measureless compassion,
Forgiveness that seeks out the beloved.
His wrath and indignation
Are masks of His love.

LORD of the Heavens,
Who created this world
And all that is in it,
Who orders the flowing of the tide
And the rushing of the wind,
Who chiseled the mountains
Out of a wasteland

And painted the loveliness of a flower
With the colors of Heaven,
Who fashioned out of nothing
The creatures that pace the earth,
And made Man
To govern your creation —
Your love lightens the darkness of my ignorance.
The sin of your people
Is my sin,
And their failing
Mine.
We have run from your love
And hidden ourselves in the ignorance of our sin.

O LORD, how awesome is your love,
How past understanding your compassion
And your mercy.
Though we pursue our sins
We cannot escape you,
Though we climb the high hill of evil
You save us from destruction,
Though we hide in the dark of night
To escape your presence
Your love seeks us out,
Though we defile your creation
And blaspheme your holy name
You forgive.
You have made us, O God,
And we are yours;
Your love encompasses us
In all we do.

What words can tell your love,
O my God?

What utterance
Express your mercy?
You have loved,
Taking no thought of our worth.
And forgiven,
Taking no thought of our sin.

In you the pain is eased
And my spirit finds rest.
As you love Israel
So may I love.
As you draw your people into forgiveness
So may I.
As you have sought out your children
So may I seek out the one whom I love.
The love that was spurned
Is swallowed up in your suffering.

The evil I saw, I saw but darkly;
The pain I felt, I felt but partly.
The sorrow of my heart
Was your voice to me,
And in the flood of my tears
Was the Spirit of the Living God.

Hosea remained kneeling. The vision and presence of God slowly waned. Then, the first time since captivity, he heard the notable Voice — not words spoken in divine council that he overheard, but words spoken directly to him, awesome in authority: *Go again, love a woman beloved of a paramour and an adulteress; even as the* LORD *loves the people of Israel, though they turned to other gods and loved cakes of raisins.*

Chapter 43

The Search for Gomer

1

Four weeks later Hosea walked home from the food market laden with two sacks of food. The harvest had been good; food was again plentiful. He turned into his street and almost ran into a short man coming away from the door of his house.

Hosea reared back, suddenly recognizing his childhood friend and brother-in-law: "Obed! It is you! Where have you come from?"

"Yes, it is me. Who else? And from Dothan, where else!" Obed's bright, careless way of speaking never changed.

"Come in, come in," Hosea said, putting his hand on Obed's shoulder and turning him back to the house.

After they had found Gomer going into captivity in the caravan of Judas ben Ishbaal, Obed and Shania traveled to Samaria. A shoemaker from Tirzah had taken Hosea's house. He found the house empty and moved in with his family. Next door, they learned from Deborah and Ebarth that Hosea and the children had been in one of the caravans taken to Assyria.

"He had a terrible fight with four soldiers, drove them all away," Deborah said. "He left with the children, said they could not remain. They were going to the house of Diblaim. At Diblaim's house soldiers had looted everything. An old servant last saw Diblaim departing for Hosea's house to be with Hosea and the grandchildren."

"The wealthy and priests were among those deported to Assyria," Ebarth said. "We saw all of them — Hosea, the

505

children, and Diblaim — in the caravan before it left Samaria."

Private travel to Assyria was fraught with danger: a lone Israelite would be clustered with those deported, never more than a step away from slavery. Obed waited until he could attach himself to a trade caravan as a hand laborer, going from Israel and returning.

In Assyria Obed found Hosea in the East Gozan community on first inquiry. *The prophet Hosea* was a recognized name in the captive community, or even *the prophet.*

"What brings you here?" Hosea asked when they had entered the house and sat together at the eating table. "Were you in one of the caravans deported from Israel?"

"We were not among the captives," Obed returned. "I come from Israel with a message, only that, and then I return."

He told Hosea how they had met Gomer when they brought food to the caravans. "After that, Shania left me no rest. When we learned that both Gomer and you had likely been deported, she said we must get the message to you that Gomer was among the captives. So you could find her. She sees nothing but you together."

"You came from Israel only to tell me?"

"Here I am!" Obed said, his childhood laugh trailing after the words. "It may be to no purpose, but you know your own sister when she gets her teeth into something."

"Tell me how it goes with Shania. And Jeshurun."

"And Jarmel," Obed threw in. "Seven months old, and growing."

"A second boy! And Shania? It is well with her?"

Obed answered somewhat haltingly, "It is well."

Hosea set bread and cheese on the table before Obed. They fell to talking as in days past, suddenly happy, almost as though the old life was still with them. The children were with Diblaim, two streets away, Hosea explained. They would be back shortly and overjoyed to see Obed.

When their talk turned again to Shania, Obed grew solemn. He told how Shania had found Gomer in the caravan of captives and that she was in the company of Judas ben Ishbaal under the name of Miriam. Shania pushed every thought aside except searching Hosea out in Assyria to let him know that Gomer was among the captives.

"You had word that both of us were among the captives?"

"Only that Ebarth saw you in a caravan in Samaria, and we saw Gomer in another caravan at Dothan. Two caravans, separated by days, and headed we knew not where. That was the distress between us — not only between Shania and me, but between Shania and our closest friends in Dothan."

Hosea nodded slowly, sensing how grave indeed was Obed's coming. "It is a dangerous undertaking."

"Seven wives came in a body and reproached Shania that she was sending her husband to his death, or to slavery. But Shania said the LORD had shown her that you were among the deported, and if you knew Gomer was also deported, He would bring you together."

Hosea could imagine Obed's distress. Shania could be dreadfully stubborn. Obed spread his arms in a gesture of helplessness, allowing it was not always easy contending with her strong will. She could turn peevish over anything she counted bad for the family — if she thought him overlong delayed in proving his wine, or if he let others get the best of him in a bargain.

"She interferes? Speaks out?" Hosea asked, his voice barely masking disappointment.

"No, no. It is only between us, if she thinks I do not provide as richly as I could, or as she thinks I might. If she speaks harsh words, they are few and soon reined back."

"So there was disagreement between you about coming to Assyria?"

"It came to hard words between us," Obed confessed. "You are more than a brother to me, you know that. But I am also a father and a husband, and we had no certain knowledge."

"Yet you came."

"There was no changing her." Obed laughed gently. "If anything comes near family, she is a mother bear. And you are 'family' as much as I or our children."

"So you have come," Hosea said finally.

"Here I am!" Obed said, back to his old lighthearted way. "Tomorrow I must return to Dothan . . . and beg forgiveness for the dreadful words I spoke before leaving."

Hosea told Obed the word the LORD had spoken: *Go again, love a woman beloved of a paramour and an adulteress.* When Hosea heard the word, he did not know where Gomer might be, whether in Israel or Assyria, even Egypt, whether alive or dead; or whether the LORD meant someone else altogether.

"The word brought me comfort, but I did not know what to do or where to look," he said to Obed. "I had no idea where Gomer might be. Tell Shania you and she have done me more favor than you know, old friend."

Obed returned to his caravan the next morning.

2

Hosea searched for Gomer over a period of three months. He inquired of the elders in each of the Israelite communities, talked with craftsmen, vendors, and farmers, and listened for any piece of gossip at the village wells. The search was discouraging. Some thought they remembered her or Judas ben Ishbaal among those taken into captivity, but memories dim with time. Sometimes he came close to giving up. The fear haunted him that she may not have survived the journey from Israel.

The memory of his vision gave him no rest. He moved eastward, toward the villages on the Tigris River. There he came on the first word that gave him some hope. In the service of a tavern owner he discovered Donath, the innkeeper who had once been Gomer's lover in Samaria.

Donath's thick beard was matted and untrimmed. His robe hung ragged from his shoulders and his eyes reflected a dull, lifeless spirit, empty of purpose or hope. He served the crude Assyrians their wine and accepted their insults. He could not do otherwise. He was a slave of the tavern owner.

His day was ordered, from early rising through hours of drudging work and late return to his hard pallet. Once he owned an inn of his own, a finer one by far than this rat-infested hovel, on the west side of Khorsabad, close by the river. Now he did the tasks of a common servant, a slave.

His sad, lined face lit with a kind of happiness when he recognized Hosea. In faraway places, little known friends, even enemies, come as a welcome surprise from the strangeness of foreign lands and speech and peoples. He had not seen one of his own people in more than seven months. Hosea represented something familiar, despite the unhappy history between them.

"Have you any knowledge of my wife?" Hosea asked. His voice bore no anger.

"How did you find me here?" Donath's face twisted into a pitiful smile, born of the hope that Hosea, by some miracle, might rescue him from slavery.

"I have done much searching. She was said to be in the company of Judas ben Ishbaal under the name of Miriam. Can you tell me anything?"

"Him I have seen. In the marketplace, two communities eastward. He was roped to a captain in the army, seemingly his slave. I remember it well. Another man from Israel who stood next to me and said, "'The owner of a thousand slaves, now a slave himself!'"

"And Gomer? She was with him?" "No. It was only Judas ben Ishbaal."

"That is more than I have found so far," Hosea said. "At least he survived the journey from Israel. Perhaps she did also."

"Please —" Donath glanced quickly through the nearly deserted tavern. "Can you not help me?"

"How can I help you?"

"I want to be free of this place."

"They will not let you go on my word."

"But — could you not . . . buy my freedom? I would repay. I would repay a thousand fold. Only set me free. I shall die if I do not go free. You cannot know what it is to be a slave." Donath's face strained tensely as he spoke, and he clutched desperately to Hosea's robe.

"I have no money, only a few shekels."

"Please — please —"

"I — I will speak to the village elders. Ask whether they can send money for your release."

"Do! Do! I shall he grateful all my days, I shall worship at your feet."

"They may send the money. It is not right that any of our people be held slaves, if it can be helped."

"You cannot know what freedom is until you have been a slave."

"If ever you learn of my wife, send word to me."

"I shall! I shall!" Donath promised, his face lit with the first hope it had known in long months. Then suddenly he said, "Look for her in the slave market in Khorsabad. That is where I was sold."

Hosea walked into the narrow, littered streets of Khorsabad. Was it possible? Had she made it to Assyria with Judas ben Ishbaal under the name Miriam? A dim hope flickered in his breast, so faint he scarcely dared name it.

Some weeks later an elder from Hosea's community went quietly to the tavern where Donath was a slave and bargained with the owner to buy Donath's freedom for forty shekels of silver.

3

A sudden spring warmth descended on Khorsabad after weeks of cold, drizzling rain. The sun swelled triumphantly in a cloudless sky, and the city looked hopefully for an end to the season of mud that was Khorsabad in the rains.

Hosea joined the stream of merchants and tradesmen headed toward the city from the farmlands and villages. Each market day, in the two months since he talked with Donath, he had attended the slave auction in Khorsabad. He came now almost from habit, doggedly refusing to give up the one hope that remained. All other searching had proved futile.

Near the city, the flow of the crowd slowed and bubbled back from the gates. Guards and scribes inspected those entering the city, passed some through, turned others aside. Whispers raced back into the crowd that they were on the lookout for a band of thieves that looted a score of merchants the previous market day.

A rough hand grasped Hosea when he came abreast of the gate and pushed him to the scribe's table.

"What is your business?" demanded the scribe.

"I am a carpenter."

"I mean your business in the city today."

"I am going to the slave auction."

"Slave auction? An Israelite carpenter affording a slave?"

The scribe glowered suspiciously at Hosea. He was ordered to keep out of the city all suspicious persons, all but honest tradesmen and merchants, until the band of thieves was captured. A tall Israelite, with no merchandise and claiming to be a carpenter heading to the slave auction, filled completely the scribe's idea of a 'suspicious person.'

"I think not," he said decisively. "Turn him away."

"Sir, what is it? What have I done that you turn me away?"

The scribe explained tersely.

"I am not a thief," Hosea protested. "I have a different reason than you —"

511

Two more suspects crowded behind Hosea, pushing him closer to the scribe's table.

"Step aside. You are blocking the way."

"I go to the slave auction to look for my wife," Hosea pled. "She was separated from me when we left Israel and taken here to Khorsabad. I have saved money to buy her back. That is why I go to the slave auction. I am not a thief. I only want to find my wife. I have come these past two months, each week, and never have I stolen so much as a grape, I swear it."

"I do not think any of the thieves was reported as tall as this man," one of the guards interposed. A smile touched his face. He peered more closely at Hosea.

"We have no way of knowing," the scribe said curtly. "Step aside." "Sir, if you —"

"Step aside!"

The guard shrugged helplessly and motioned Hosea to leave. Hosea turned disheartened from the gate and walked unseeing against the throng of people, lonely and heartsick, the one flicker of hope that each week gave him courage to continue the search now gone.

A hundred cubits back from the gate he recognized a farmer from his own community in East Gozan, Shadrach ben Jacob. He pulled two great sacks in a small cart. Hosea thought to pass him, looking away; he was too disheartened to speak with anyone. Then a sudden idea occurred to him, and he ran to meet Shadrach.

He grasped the startled farmer by the arm and straightened him up so he could no longer pull the cart. Quickly he explained what had happened at the gate.

"Let me take one of your sacks," Hosea said. "I will carry it through the gate bent over. They will let me pass as a merchant. Inside, I will turn it back to you."

"Well, now, I do not know —" Shadrach had been a grain trader in Bethel and had a trader's instinctive caution of any circumstance that might work to his disadvantage. "If you are apprehended, the grain will be seized. I cannot risk it."

"I shall not be caught, and even if I am, they will not take the grain."

"From an Israelite they will take anything — with or without cause."

"It is a little thing. Nothing to fear. Come —" Hosea reached for one of the grain sacks.

"No, I cannot," Shadrach said with determination. "However, if you were to secure me with the price of one of my sacks of barley, then I would not be in danger of losing my livelihood if you are apprehended."

"That is good enough. What is the price?"

"Fifteen shekels. Each sack holds a homer and a half."

"Done."

Hosea counted out fifteen shekels, half the money he had in his purse. A common slave sold for thirty shekels. It was the sum he had managed to save. He swung one of the barley sacks to his shoulder and started back toward the city, alongside Shadrach.

At the gate Shadrach moved in ahead of Hosea. The guard glanced at him and waved him through. Hosea bent as low as he could and turned his face away from the guard. The guard stopped him with a hand on his shoulder. Hosea looked up. The guard recognized him and half opened his mouth to speak. Hosea pleaded frantically with his eyes; the lines around his mouth tightened.

"You have children?" the guard suddenly asked.

"I have children," Hosea answered.

"Three?"

"Yes, three." Hosea beheld the guard uneasily.

"You do not know me?" the guard asked.

"I have been coming here many weeks."

"You do not know me from Samaria?" The man spoke slowly. He knew Israelites were still uncertain in the Assyrian tongue. "We came into your house, four of us." Hosea stared down at the man in astonishment. Yes, it was the man, the soldier, the last of the four. What kind of revenge would he take?

"You knocked us off our feet with your own hands — all four of us, and you unarmed."

"It was for my children —"

The man nodded, showing no sign of anger. "You could have killed me with my own sword. You threw back my sword and waved me off." He glanced toward the scribe, then slyly nodded his head and passed Hosea through the gate.

Within the city Hosea looked about for Shadrach, but he had disappeared. He ran forward, looking eagerly through the crowd, but the farmer was nowhere to be seen.

The market thronged with people. Hosea slowly pushed toward the slave market, still looking for Shadrach. Once near the slave auction he began asking, as he always did, for any news of a woman called Miriam. Of merchants, tradesmen, slave auction scribes, and strangers standing about he asked, always the same question: "Do you know of a slave called Miriam, a fair-skinned Israelite?"

The replies were curt and rude, and always the same. A hundred women could fit the description of a 'fair-skinned Israelite.' The name of a slave meant nothing. He persisted in his search. He had grown calloused to rebuff. He knew no other way that he might find her.

He put his question to a wizened old knife grinder, adding, "Her hair is ebony black. She comes up to my shoulder."

A man wearing an Assyrian captain's leather vest overheard. "What name did you say she bears?" he asked.

"Miriam or Gomer, a fair-skinned Israelite woman," Hosea answered quickly, turning to the man. "You know of her?"

"I know nothing of Miriam. I know one who calls herself Gomer."

"That is her true name!" Hosea burst out. "Where did you see her?"

"See her? I owned her. She was caught with a pouch of stolen treasure and became my slave."

"You are selling her at auction?"

"Not I. She became ill. Wasted away. I gave her to my trooper. She may be sold today to pay off his gambling debts."

Hosea spilled out his thanks and hurried toward the slave auction block.

* * *

"Come, come!" cried the auctioneer. "Here is the auction about to begin. Slaves from every nation under heaven — Philistia, Tyre, Ethiopia, Israel, Egypt. Slaves to do your work and slaves to lighten your leisure. Tall slaves, short slaves, thin slaves, fat slaves; smooth and beautiful, rough and ugly; black slaves, white slaves, men slaves, women slaves; slaves to work with, slaves to play with!"

He patted the behind of a female slave who stood at his side and drew the bawdy laughter of the crowd. He motioned to his helper. A big black man was led to the block from the slave wagon.

"Come, come, come! Here we start. What am I bid for this giant of a man? Look at the strength of him!"

"Thirty shekels!"

"Thirty shekels? Sir, this is no common slave. He is the equal of three men. Come, my LORDS, here is your chance for a life of leisure. What am I bid?"

"Thirty-one."

"Thirty-two."

"Thirty-two shekels. My ears begin to hear. Come, who will make it thirty five? Thirty four?"

"Thirty-four."

"Thirty-five!"

"Thirty-seven!"

"'Thirty-seven,' says this man. Who will top him?"

"Thirty- eight!"

"Thirty —"

"Forty shekels!"

"Forty shekels! The man bids forty shekels. A man of judgment. Who makes it forty-five? Forty-three? Three more shekels for this king of Ethiopia? Sold! To the man with forty shekels, and a bargain at twice the price."

Hosea watched anxiously as the black man was led down and the next slave ushered from the slave cart. A slender, sloe-eyed girl, hardly more than fifteen years, followed pliantly after the auctioneer's helper. She had the dusky skin of one raised in the desert, hair that fell loosely to her shoulders, and a lithe grace that an auctioneer could tout as a sign of hidden passions. Before the auctioneer could open his mouth, a squat bulge-eyed man shouted out his bid.

"Thirty-five shekels!"

"Ah! A wise man. Look at the beauty of her. She can help your wife in the household tasks and do . . . many things to make herself useful."

"Forty shekels!"

"Forty shekels I am bid. Who makes it forty-five?"

"Forty-five!"

"Forty-eight!"

"Fifty!"

"Fifty shekels! Come, sirs, do not let me stop you. Who goes to sixty?"

"Sixty!"

"Sixty I am bid."

"Sixty-five shekels!"

"Sixty-five shekels! Will he steal her for sixty-five?"

"Seventy!"

"A man not to be outdone. Who will best him? Sirs —"

The auctioneer removed the skirt that hung low on the girl's waist, leaving her clothed only in a gossamer shift.

"Will you let him have her for seventy shekels?"

"Seventy-five!"

"Robbery at seventy-five. Who says eighty?"

"Eighty!"

"Eighty shekels! The man has an eye for a bargain. Who goes higher? Shall he have her? All the desert heat runs in these veins. Do I hear a bid? Sold for eighty shekels!"

A sudden chill gripped Hosea as the man beside him went forward to pay eighty shekels for the desert girl. He had fifteen shekels. He had been so intent on the auction, so hopeful Gomer would be among those brought up for sale, that he forgot for the moment that he could be outbid, could find her only to lose her again. The auction was more spirited this day. Never before had he seen a slave go for eighty shekels.

And then, suddenly, his fears and anxious hopes tumbled out in one stifled word.

"Gomer!"

Thin, unkempt and haggard, she shuffled to the block. She neither looked at the crowd nor away from them, but stared straight ahead, listlessly as if into a void. In the dread grip of the starvation she had chosen, she stood closer to the world of death than the world of life.

The shape of beauty was gone from her body and the flush of loveliness from her face. She had no hint of passion or attractiveness to make men desire her, nor even the hint of strength and usefulness to recommend her as a house slave. Nothing but a shrunken form that somehow breathed and sustained itself alive, though bound more closely to the death she now willed for herself.

"A slave for your kitchen. What am I bid? Come, come, Show your shrewdness. Beneath this dirt is the soul of a princess!" The crowd laughed, and shouted obscenely back at the auctioneer.

"This woman is an Israelite, and is it not known that women of Israel have the strength of oxen?"

"And look the part as well!" shouted a man from the crowd.

"Come, who bids thirty shekels? Must I return her unsold? Thirty shekels, the price of a common slave."

Hosea pushed through the crowd to the front. "I have fifteen shekels. I bid that."

"Sir, I cannot sell her for less than thirty. You know the law."

"I have no more money. Will you accept a barter?"

"Take what you can," advised a watcher nearby.

"What kind of barter?"

"I have a homer and a half of barley. Will you take that?"

"Fifteen shekels and a homer and a half of barley?"

"It is all I have."

"Keep the barley to fatten her up," shouted a young boy, laughing boisterously at his own wit.

"Take her away," the auctioneer said hurriedly, seeing that the auction was getting away from him.

Hosea flung the heavy sack of barley at the auctioneer's feet and emptied a pouch of fifteen shekels into his outstretched hand.

Gomer stared at Hosea as though struggling with a memory. He led her gently by the hand through the milling crowd, his own body trembling. She followed haltingly and, every few steps, came to a stop and had to be coaxed to continue. She spoke no word.

4

Diblaim and the children were in Hosea's house in the East Gozan community when Hosea led Gomer through the door.

They straightened up as though by command. Her appearance was so changed that for a moment no one dared move or speak.

Hosea stepped closer, gathered Ruhamah into his arm, and brought her to Gomer.

"Loruhamah," Gomer said in a faint whisper.

"My name is Ruhamah, Mama," the child said. She repeated it, and leaned to Gomer, kissing her cheek.

Gomer said nothing.

Jezreel and Ammi came closer.

"My name is Ammi," the little boy said.

"Mama, you are home," Jezreel said, hugging her about the waist, half laughing, half crying.

Last of all, Diblaim embraced her and kissed her on the brow.

"Father," she said, so softly Diblaim scarcely heard her.

* * *

Hosea sought to nurse Gomer back to health, but she continued to decline. She remained listless, distracted. She spoke only in broken phrases, or not at all. She would not eat.

On the morning of the sixth day, Diblaim came by as he did each day. Gomer sat at a low table. Hosea had set a bowl of lentils before her. She sat staring at it.

"Child, you must eat," Diblaim said, sitting beside her. Gomer turned and looked at him inquiringly.

"Eat!" Diblaim said more forcefully.

Gomer picked up the sticks that lay by the bowl and put a small bite of the lentils in her mouth. Then another.

"Good! Good!" Diblaim cried out.

Gomer continued to eat. Hosea and the children gathered about.

"Not too much at first," Diblaim cautioned. "Begin slowly." He looked up at Hosea. "When her little brother Aram died, she refused to eat until — until her mother and I sat her down. I don't remember, but I think we insisted."

* * *

In the days following, Gomer began to eat, but slowly, and with little seeming effect. She seemed not to comprehend the care that suddenly surrounded her, the chatter of children's voices, the quiet presence of Diblaim and Hosea. She lived in two worlds of her own, the world of death and the world of life, more closely to the world of death. The fear of death no longer tormented her, as it did in childhood. It beckoned with allure — a friend, escape. In her breast was stirring the last great upheaval of her spirit.

The third week after her return, Hosea woke suddenly from a sound sleep to find Gomer gone from her bed. Her clothing was laid across the dressing bench, and her night-robe lay in a heap on the floor.

Hosea called to her but no answer came. And then an awful dread flashed to him. He ran from his house toward the tent the East Gozan community had raised for their worship. He reached the entrance of the tent and stopped short. In the dim flicker of the vigil light he saw the naked figure of Gomer, the sacrificial knife poised in her upraised hand.

Hosea spoke softly to her and slowly moved toward the altar. She raised the knife over her stomach and thrust it toward herself.

"'He restores my soul!'" Hosea screamed out on sudden, unthinking impulse.

Gomer's hand jerked to a stop. She turned toward Hosea and spoke the next phrase of King David's shepherd prayer in a flat unmusical tone, her eyes closed, "'He leads me in paths of righteousness.'"

Hosea sprang to the altar and wrenched the knife from Gomer's hand. Weakened as she was, she struggled furiously in his arms, shrieking meaningless words. She bit his fingers. Then she cried out, "Harlot! Harlot! Harlot! You hate me!"

Hosea spoke quietly, holding her close, "I love you. With all my heart."

She turned her head away from him. "Let me die! I do not belong," she wailed.

"Oh LORD!" Hosea breathed.

She collapsed into Hosea's arms, mumbling meaningless words. Hosea buried his face in the shower of her hair.

"Redeem us, LORD," he murmured.

Chapter 44

You Must Dwell as Mine

In the weeks that followed, Gomer seemed to retreat into an imaginary world of her own. She wandered idly about the house, flicking imaginary dust from the furniture, playing innocently with the beads and blocks that I made for her, and washing — many times a day — her face, her hands and feet, her robes, even her sandals. In her retreat into her own world, the need for cleanliness seemed to haunt her.

She continued to eat. Slowly her speech returned but she seldom spoke with understanding. Sometimes she would mumble words from the scrolls. She was docile to my care of her but seemed hardly to notice me, or the children, or other people who came by the house. She lived on in another world. Whenever I touched her, her body tensed and her brow wrinkled with puzzlement, as though she were trying to grasp a fleeting memory.

Once, when I laid my hand on her shoulder, she took my hand in her own and pressed it to her breast.

"Who are we?" she asked.

Two days earlier I had heard the notable Voice of the LORD speak differently than ever before — as though I overheard words I myself must speak. I repeated the words quietly to Gomer as she continued holding my hand: *"You must dwell as mine for many days; you shall not play the harlot, or belong to another man; so will I also be to you."*

Gomer continued to grip my hand, holding it against her cheek. She repeated the words I had just spoken; then she spoke words from the prayer scroll. Her hollow tone softened. A note of warmth came into her voice, "'Answer me when I call, O God of my right! You have given me room when I was in distress. Be gracious to me, and hear my prayer.'"

I stood quietly by, as long as she clung to my hand. When she released me, she went back to the water bowl she had held in her lap and washed her brow and cheeks.

* * *

One evening, when Gomer had been home nearly two months, I spoke quietly to Ruhamah, "Go to your mother after she lies down. Sleep beside her."

Gomer at first stiffened and pulled back when Ruhamah came to her. Ruhamah put her arm around Gomer's neck and whispered, "Can I sleep beside you, Mama? It feels so fine."

Gomer drew Ruhamah into her embrace. Jezreel and Ammi came and crawled in on her other side.

* * *

On a morning midway through the summer Diblaim stopped by my house, as he always did when he crossed the village from his own house.

"Is she much the same?" he asked with quiet concern, stepping into my carpenter shop.

"Much of the time. Today, now, she has seemed somewhat brighter . . . more happy."

"I brought her this little bowl. She always liked small, delicate things."

Diblaim had proved adept at the potter's trade and turned out skillful work.

Gomer sat in the farthest corner from the door, crosslegged on the floor, sifting a pile of clean white shavings through her fingers.

"I brought you a little bowl," Diblaim spoke almost shyly to his daughter. Gomer looked up at him and registered the faintest smile.

"You like it?"

She took it in her slender fingers, gently traced its design.

"I made it especially for you."

She looked at him again, but neither spoke nor showed any understanding of the gift. After some moments Diblaim straightened sadly and returned to where I stood. "It is sad to see her," Diblaim said, echoing his words with heaviness in his voice.

"She was always bright-spirited."

"She is safe," I said, not much thinking what the words meant.

"Safe? Yes, of course. Yet it is sad."

"I have finished the gate for your small wagon. I grooved it on both ends, so it will slip in and out easily."

I handed the small gate to Diblaim and shuffled toward the door of the shop.

"Let me pay you for this."

"No. There is no charge between kin."

"Certainly there is. You must make a living the same as anyone else. Here —"

"Please, no. I cannot charge my own father."

Diblaim withdrew his hand, and with the other snuffed his nose.

"Well, I will give it to the family of Simeon, then. He hurt his wrist, you know, and can hardly work at the loom. They are hard put to get bread on the table."

"Simeon is not the first one you have helped. You keep an eye out for trouble — those in trouble, do you not?"

"I have no one to see to. I like to be of some use. Much of my life I was of use to no one, not even myself." He giggled self-consciously. "Strange pass that it took being led captive from my own land to teach me how poor I was, surrounded by my wealth. I have friends here, the first ones I ever had, I think."

"God must sometimes strike us poor before he can give us wealth."

"I understand. It is right."

"I am glad for you, Diblaim, for what has happened in your heart. For Israel, also, I am glad. The LORD has healed some of our sickness. He has loved us freely. He is like dew, a blossom on the lily. Israel has struck new roots. There is even beauty here. The ways of the LORD are right, even in a strange land."

For some moments neither of us spoke. We weighed our thoughts in silence.

"If you take her out for a walk, stop in to see me at my house," Diblaim said in parting. "I do not often have company, you know. I enjoy it whenever you stop."

"I shall."

"The LORD's blessing be with you."

"Go with God."

I turned back into my shop. I walked over to where Gomer sat, still fondling Diblaim's little vase.

"It is time for your rest," I said.

I took her by the hand and helped her to her feet. She seemed hesitant to follow and glanced backward at the heap of shavings that fell from her lap to the floor. I urged her toward the doorway from the carpenter shed into the house. If she did not rest at midday she became unwell.

I laid her down in the bed and pulled a light coverlet over her legs. I gazed down at her until her eyelids flickered shut. Strange, how quickly she regains her youthfulness; it was always her way. Strong in her body, seldom sick. I walked slowly toward the bench by the fire pit.

I paused in front of the small window opposite the sleeping mats. The brightness of the sun fell across my eyes. On an impulse I began to speak a prayer. A word from one of King David's psalms came to me, a favorite of my mother:

The LORD is good;
His steadfast love endures for ever,
and His faithfulness to all generations.

More words came to my lips, in a whisper at first, then more distinctly: "Never again can I declare your judgment apart from — apart from your — sorrow. Apart from your love."

A light shuffling sounded behind me. I turned back toward the sleeping mats. Gomer stood facing me, still so thin. The sound of my voice must have wakened her. She rose up, thinking she had been called.

Her face seemed caught between confusion and a glimmering of understanding she could not quite grasp. Tears rose in her eyes and spilled down her cheeks. She padded softly to my side and sank to her knees beside me.

Even with tears, her eyes were clear as they had not been since long months ago in Israel. She whispered the name she first called me the night we were wed. "My — my husband."

I took her hand and helped her to her feet.

THE MARRIAGE OF HOSEA
AND ITS MEANING

*An Interpretative Paraphrase
from the Hebrew text of the
Prophecy of Hosea, Chapters 1-3
by Larry Christenson*

SUPERSCRIPTION

I¹This is the word of the LORD that came to Hosea, the son of Beeri, during the reigns of Uzziah, Jotham, Ahaz, and Hezekiah, kings of Judah; and during the reign of Jeroboam, son of Joash, king of Israel.

HOSEA'S MARRIAGE: A PARALLEL TO GOD'S 'MARRIAGE' WITH ISRAEL

²The LORD first spoke to Hosea not in words, but in deep promptings of the heart.

Thus speaking, the LORD said to Hosea: "Go, take unto yourself a wife — a whoring wife and bastard children! For the land is a wanton whore and no longer follows the LORD!"

³So Hosea married Gomer, the daughter of Diblaim. ⁴And she conceived and bore him a son. And the LORD said to Hosea: "Name him *Jezreel* (that is, 'God sows') — for in a little while, as Jehu spilled blood in the valley of Jezreel, so will I spill the blood of Jehu's royal house, and bring to an end the kingdom of Israel! ⁵In Jezreel itself, I will scatter Israel's power!" (for Jezreel means also *scatter*.)

⁶Then Gomer conceived again, and bore a daughter. And the LORD said to Hosea: "Name her *Unbeloved* — for my love for Israel has run its course. I will forgive them no more!"

⁸When Gomer weaned *Unbeloved*, she conceived again and bore a second son.

⁹And the LORD said to Hosea: "Name him *Rejected* — for I reject Israel as my people! I am their God no longer!"

II²Then Hosea spoke the words of dismissal, sending Gomer away because of her adultery: "She is not my wife, and I am not her husband." ⁴And he said, "I will have no pity on her children. ⁵They are bastard children. Their mother played the harlot. She covered herself with shame."

THE Lord DENOUNCES ISRAEL'S UNFAITHFULNESS

²You who still know righteousness, rebuke Mother Israel — rebuke her! Tell her to ³scrub clean her painted harlot's face, and cover the wanton nakedness of her breasts lest I make her a wilderness and a parched land, and kill her with thirst.

⁵For she says, "I will chase after my 'lovers' (Israel loves her Ba'als!), who give me my food and my water, my robes and my dresses, my drink and my sweet perfumes."

⁸She doesn't know that it is I the Lord who give her the grain and the grape and the olive harvest.

⁹Therefore, I will take back my grain in its season, and my grape in the time of harvest. I will take away my wool and my flax which cover her nakedness. ¹⁰I will lay bare her folly in the sight of her 'lovers,' and no 'husband' will rescue her from my hand. ¹²I will lay waste her vines and her fig trees, which she calls her 'wages,' gifts from her 'lovers.' I will make them a tangled undergrowth, and the beasts of the field will devour them. I will put an end to all her revelry and festal dancing and new moon celebrations, her sabbaths, and all her appointed feasts. I will wreak vengeance on her for the 'Days of the Ba'als' — when she sacrifices to the Ba'als, decking herself with rings and jewels to follow after her 'lovers' . . . forgetting ME, says the Lord.

⁶Therefore, let it be known: I will hedge up her way with thorns. I will wall her in so she cannot find her well trodden paths. ⁷She will pant after her 'lovers' and not overtake them. She will search everywhere, and not find them.

Then she will say, "I will go and return to my first husband. It was better with me then than now."

THE Lord REDEEMS ISRAEL, HOSEA REDEEMS HIS WIFE

III¹Then the Lord said to me: "Go, continue to love even such a woman . . . a lover of evil, and an adulteress — for the Lord still loves the people of Israel, though they turn to other gods and love heathen ceremonies."

²So I bought her for 15 pieces of silver and a cart-load of barley. ³And I said to her: "For many days you must dwell in my house and not play the harlot, nor have relations with any man. Nor will I have relations with you."

⁴For the people of Israel will dwell many days without king or prince, without temple or altar, without priest or holy shrine. ⁵Afterward they will return and seek the LORD their God, and David their king. In that Day they will come trembling unto the LORD, seeking goodness at His hand.

THE LORD's PROMISE TO ISRAEL

II ¹⁴Therefore, let it be known: I will endear Israel to myself. I will return her to the wilderness, to the days of her purity. I will speak tenderly to her. ¹⁵I will give her her vineyards. Her valley of trouble will become her door of understanding. And she will respond to me as in the days of her youth, as in the day when she came up out of the land of Egypt.

¹⁶In that Day, says the LORD, you will call me "my husband." No longer will you call me "my Ba'al." ¹⁷For I will banish the names of the Ba'als from your lips. No longer will you mention them by their names.

¹⁹And I will betroth you to me forever. I will betroth you to me in righteousness and justice and steadfast love and mercy. ²⁰I will betroth you to me in faithfulness and you shall surely know that I am the LORD.

¹⁸And I will make for you a covenant in that day with the beasts of the field and the birds of the air and the creeping things of the ground. And I will banish bow and sword and warfare from the land. And Israel shall be a land at peace.

²¹In that day, says the LORD, I will call out — I will call out to the heavens. And the heavens will respond to my call and answer the earth. And the earth will respond to the heavens and answer the grain and the grape and the olive. ²²And the grain and the grape and the olive will call out: "It is the LORD who sows!"

[23]I will again sow children in Mother Israel, and raise up offspring in the house of Jacob. I will pour out my compassion on the *Unbeloved*. I will say to the *Rejected*: "You are my people once more! And they will answer: "Thou art our God!"

I[10]And the number of the children of Israel shall be as the sands of the sea, which can neither be measured nor counted. And where they were once called *Rejected*, in that Day they shall be called *Sons of the Living God*.

[7]And I will have compassion on the house of Judah. I will deliver them — not by bow or sword or warfare or horse or horseman — but by the power of the LORD their God. [11]And the people of Judah and the people of Israel shall be gathered together as one people. They shall appoint for themselves a single ruler. And, as in the day of Moses, they shall worship before the LORD.

II[1]For great will be the Day when the LORD sows salvation in the land. No more will you call one another *Rejected* and *Unbeloved*. But you will call your brothers *God's People*, and your sisters, *Beloved of the LORD*!